Also by Kait Ballenger

WILD
COWBOY WOLF

KAIT BALLENGER

sourcebooks
casablanca

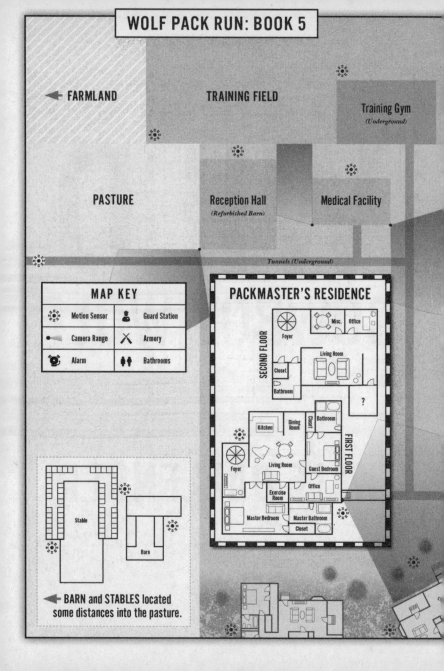

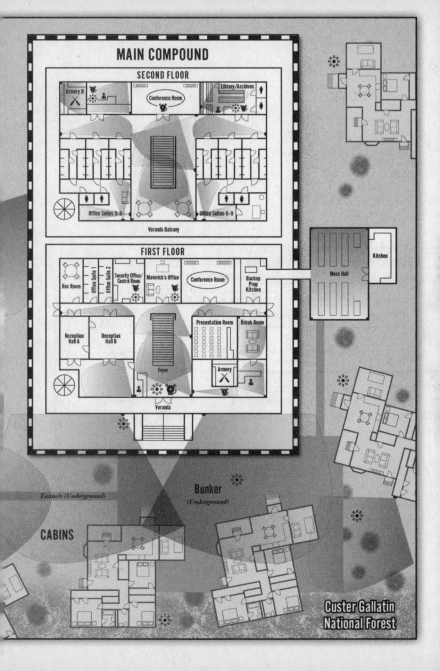

Published by Sourcebooks Casablanca, an imprint of Sourcebooks
P.O. Box 4410, Naperville, Illinois 60567-4410
(630) 961-3900
sourcebooks.com

Printed and bound in Canada.
MBP 10 9 8 7 6 5 4 3 2 1

To my two wild boys
and to Jon, the wildest of them all,
I love you

Chapter 1

READING A ROOM FULL OF SHIFTERS MADE FOR ONE HELLUVA dull evening. Blaze lingered at the bar, whiskey in hand and bored out of his goddamn mind as he scanned the crowd for potential threats. Quick thinking had earned him the job; the same made it duller than a post. Inside the decked-out old barn, the collective behavior of the pack ebbed and flowed with the pulse of the western music. Fast songs and quicker liquor meant high spirits and too-loud laughter with plenty of decisions to regret in the morning. Pack mentality at its finest.

At least the whiskey was decent.

Blaze threw back the dregs of his glass, feeling the burn slide down his throat. It'd take five times that for a wolf his size to even feel it. And he *wanted* to feel it, considering what kept catching his eye at the far side of the dance floor.

A feral growl rumbled in his throat.

"Another?" Austin's slow Texas drawl was nearly drowned by the din of the reception's noise.

With a shake of his head, Blaze slid the tumbler into Austin's outstretched hand. "Not unless it's beer." Then at least he'd have something to do with his hands.

Austin waved at the bartender.

From two seats down, Malcolm eyed Austin with a disapproving frown. "Since when did you become Blaze's personal assistant?"

Blaze fought not to roll his eyes. The Grey Wolf executioner turned warrior had two facial expressions: scowl and deeper scowl, which meant the grumbling edge in his tone was unfortunately permanent, right along with that mean-ass mug of his. More than once, Blaze had tried to remove it, but the fellow warrior was dead to humor.

Such was his luck tonight.

"Since I'm the one on detail while you two sit there looking…" Blaze scrunched his nose. "Well, no one would dare call you pretty." The teasing grin that pulled at his lips came easy.

A permanent mask he'd never be rid of.

Malcolm bared his teeth in response.

"Snarly seems a more appropriate description." Austin hopped over the bar top after several failed attempts to flag the bartender.

The hired buxom blond of a witch on loan from the relocated Midnight Coyote Saloon wore her pants a little too tight and had been calling Blaze "sugar" more than half the evening. Apparently, she thought Malcolm was a peach, because she'd said as much as she'd batted her eyes through that too-thick layer of mascara.

Yeah, a *peach*. Malcolm.

Blaze had choked on his own drink from snorting too hard.

Behind the bar, Austin cast their glasses into the dish sink and pulled three Coors from the mini fridge. "Ain't nothin' as ugly as that suit you're wearin' though."

Blaze let out a harsh bark of a laugh. "Truth."

Instinctively, he went to reach for his Stetson, then thought better of it. He'd forgone the cowboy hat this evening since it didn't match his attire—an obnoxiously bright-orange monstrosity covered in palms and pineapples. Needling the packmaster never got old. Honest to wolf, Maverick took life *way* too damn seriously, even his own wedding reception…

"At least my suit is *supposed* to be ugly." He cast Malcolm a cheesed-up grin before receiving another growl in response.

A dull evening indeed. He'd find humor where he could take it.

Austin popped open one of the beers and pushed it toward him, but Blaze ignored it.

His eyes caught on Dakota again.

She'd been stuck with Jasper for the better part of three songs, and the way she danced ever closer to the other wolf was killing him.

"Who's making the rounds this time?" Blaze asked, his voice giving away more than a hint of his frustration.

Fuck the friend zone.

"I'll do it." Austin vaulted back over the bar, grabbing his Coors off the bar top and promptly taking a quick swig.

"Ever the volunteer." Blaze made as if to tip his hat.

"*Siempre.*" The Texan raised his drink as he disappeared into the crowd.

Malcolm pushed off his barstool with a huff.

"Where you off to?"

Malcolm grunted. "Need to hit the head."

"Breaking the seal is not advised when on patrol."

Malcolm flipped him the bird and Blaze chuckled again.

Maybe not a total lost cause.

Alone, finally, in spite of the surrounding party, Blaze scanned the crowd again. No changes. Figured. Desperate for a hit of dopamine, he turned his back to the writhing bodies, mainly *Dakota's* writhing body, grabbed the still-waiting Coors, and took a swig.

As he did, the thump of deep bass through the speakers assaulted his wolf senses. Immediately, he tensed. The Montana cold nipped at the edge of the old barn's doors, but that didn't account for the chill that raced down his spine. The feeling of being watched made him far colder.

Awareness prickled through him. With a thud, he set down the Coors and slowly rounded toward the crowd. Weaving his way onto the floor, he navigated to his first target. As the heat of his palm slipped onto the bare skin of Dakota's lower back, she stilled beneath his touch.

Fuck, why had she worn *that* dress? The deep-blue one that brought out the cobalt undertones of her midnight hair and dipped so low on her spine it left little imagination of what her tight, round ass would feel like cupped in his hands. It tortured him every time. He'd tried to get her to leave it in her closet where it belonged, but she hadn't taken the bait.

Leaning down, he whispered into her ear. "Stay with Jas."

It was an order. Protective. Harsh. No humor.

Not like him.

She froze, blinking at him as if he'd startled her. He hadn't. He was attuned to her every move, and she had been casting glances toward him for the better part of the night. He'd been living for it.

Dakota nodded, trusting him enough not to question. "I was planning on it."

Unfortunately, he'd been hoping for that. She was a capable warrior in her own right, but he didn't like the idea of taking his eyes off her for long. Whoever's gaze was tracking him wouldn't take care of themselves. Inside, his wolf stirred.

"Good."

As he stepped away, Jasper raised a brow, but Blaze gave the other warrior a slight shake of his head. *Later.*

Blaze's eyes darted down to Dakota with silent communication. *Stay with her.*

Jas nodded. The Grey Wolf international relations liaison was a fierce fighter. He'd protect any of their pack with his life, but not like Blaze.

He was made for this.

Blaze disappeared into the maze of the dance floor. It didn't matter where he went, the uneasy feeling followed. After several rounds playing cat and mouse through the decked-out barn hall, he finally ducked into a darkened alcove near the exit.

A strong hand clamped onto his shoulder.

Blaze spun. He slammed the assailant against the wall, pinning him with ease. The sharp edge of his blade pushed against the attacker's throat as he let out a feral snarl.

But it was silenced by his victim's deep-throated laughter.

Blaze stilled. He knew that laugh. Had served alongside the wolf it belonged to for several years.

The colored overhead lights of the party flashed through the dark, revealing a familiar face. Amarok "Rock" Saila. Mercenary for the Yellowknife Pack, their Arctic wolf allies, and as Blaze knew him, former MAC-V-Alpha soldier. They'd served together in the shifters-only unit of the U.S. military until Blaze had finally gotten out a few years back.

Blaze let out a curse, sheathing his blade. "You're lucky I didn't kill you, you bastard."

"I wouldn't be your first. Luck has never favored either of us." Rock rubbed at his throat where Blaze's knife had been, his expression turning grim. "You act like you're still in Russia, brother."

Blaze huffed with mild amusement. He glanced toward the floor as he ran his fingers through his hair. "I don't think I ever really left."

A beat of silence passed between them before Blaze cracked a grin to ease the tension. The dark Arctic wolf returned the smile and extended his hand.

Blaze swatted it away. "What the hell are you doing here?" He pulled the other man in for a quick thump of a hug.

Rock gave him a hard clap on the shoulder in return. "The better question is, what the fuck are you wearing, soldier?"

Blaze shrugged. "It irks Maverick." He nodded toward the dance floor, where the Grey Wolf packmaster was no doubt waiting on the arrival of his bride.

Rock shook his head. "You always did cause trouble with your superiors. Me being one of them."

"My superiors were never all that *superior*." Blaze winked.

Rock let out a harsh laugh. "Only because you never wanted to play leader."

"Don't I know it." Blaze nodded. "Still don't." Rock had him pegged all right.

Once he'd come home, as the Grey Wolf security specialist, he'd worked hard to keep a low profile among his packmates, at least when it came to anything away from his computer. With more than two tours serving in MAC-V under his belt, Blaze didn't hold any illusion that he was a better fighter than most. He could have easily worked his way up the ranks of his fellow elite warriors, besting Colt, their high commander, or hell, maybe even Wes, their pack's second, but that didn't mean he wanted the responsibilities that came with it.

He knew all too well the blood that could leave on a man's hands.

Rock gave him a once-over, sizing him up. "I know what you're capable of, even if you've made certain your packmates don't."

Blaze gave a mock wince. "They have *some* idea."

"Not enough."

A cryptic response. He should have known.

Blaze's expression darkened. It'd been to protect them, all of them, but if his packmates ever learned the truth…

"You're not here to shoot the breeze," he said, cutting straight to the point. A wolf like Rock didn't do anything for shits and giggles.

"No." Rock lowered his voice despite the sounds of the reception around them. "There's been a breach."

The cold nipping at Blaze earlier was nothing compared to the ice now coursing through his veins. The snarl that ripped from his throat was more wolf than man. "That's not possible."

"Possible or not, it happened," Rock countered. "You know better than most what's *possible* for those monsters."

Everything inside Blaze coiled like a viper ready to strike. He hadn't anticipated this.

Not now. Not ever.

Not when he'd thought he'd buried the truth.

Unintimidated by his venom, Rock reached out and gripped Blaze's shoulder—hard.

Blaze growled. "I created those encryptions myself," he ground out.

They'd been near impenetrable.

Unless…

His eyes flashed to his wolf as the beast inside him reared its head. He'd need to shift soon for the sake of his own sanity.

"Exactly," Rock hissed. The golden amber of his gaze now matched Blaze's own.

With a guttural curse, Blaze pulled away from the other wolf, retreating farther into the darkness of the alcove. He needed to move, pace. Something. He snarled. "Tell me my file wasn't accessed." He didn't have an ounce of hope he was that lucky. Who the hell was he kidding? Of course it had. He'd been the shield for the whole damn unit.

"I don't know," Rock answered.

Blaze slammed his fist on the nearby wall. "Fuck."

"My words exactly." Rock crossed his thick arms over his chest, looking as deadly as Blaze felt.

The pulse in Blaze's temple quickened. "Tell me there isn't anything else."

"There *couldn't* be anything else." The gold of Rock's wolf eyes flared. "We both know this is as bad as it gets."

Blaze's mouth went dry.

No. Rock was wrong. This wasn't even close to the worst.

Something in his gaze must have given his thoughts away, because Rock reached for him again as if to lend him strength. "You've bested them before. You can do it again."

The weight of Rock's hand on his shoulder felt too heavy. Blaze tried to brush it off but failed. "The last time nearly killed me."

"This time, it won't." Another squeeze before Rock released him. "You'll know they're coming."

Blaze let out a harsh, humorless laugh. "I'm not sure that's preferable." He could still practically taste their blood in his teeth. Iron. Metallic. Nauseating.

"Anything that keeps you and your pack alive is preferable."

Blaze shook his head. "Easy for you to say. It's not you they're after."

Rock stiffened, the unspoken words between them brimming with tension.

"They'll come for me next." Rock smirked, but with the quick gleam of his wolf canines, it appeared more threat than pleasure. "That's why I came to warn you." He paused. "Watch your back, soldier."

Blaze nodded. "I always do. I never stopped."

Rock moved to step away. "I'll be in touch." He withdrew into the darkness of the party's shadows as swiftly as he'd emerged, pausing only seconds before he disappeared. "And for what it's worth, brother, I prefer the cowboy hat."

Blaze let out a bark of a laugh, now standing alone in the alcove, despite the hundreds of bodies filling the building. Feeling suddenly overheated, he stripped off his suit jacket, tossing it on a pile of coats near the door.

He inhaled a deep breath, settling his expression as much as he could before he emerged onto the dance floor and headed toward the bar. Austin. Malcolm. Detail. Responsibilities.

Then he could come apart.

At the bar, Austin was still absent, making rounds, but Malcolm had returned. Blaze beelined straight toward his scowling packmate until he was within hearing distance. "I need you to take over detail for the next half hour."

The lines of Malcolm's face deepened. "Since when do I take orders from—"

"Just do it," Blaze growled.

Malcolm fell silent. The other wolf gave a grim nod.

Blaze headed back toward the barn door, eager to shift, to run, to feel the mountains beneath his feet. He was already out in the freezing Montana cold and unbuttoning his dress shirt when a small hand caught his.

He hadn't heard her approach. Dakota was stealth incarnate. The sounds of the party inside were silenced as she gripped his hand in hers. But he couldn't turn to look at her.

"Are you okay?" Dakota's voice was soft, concerned. If she hadn't been his packmate, he would have thought she'd be freezing out here in that dress, the one he couldn't bring himself to see her wearing again.

But his sexy little she-wolf was made of far tougher stuff than that.

He gave a sharp nod, casting a fake grin over his shoulder. "Always." He forced any hint of anguish from his voice. "Go back inside. We both know Jasper will be lost without you. He'll have to resort to staring at his own reflection in the mirror again."

Dakota laughed, but the sound quickly fell short against the quiet of the falling snow.

He didn't have to look at her to know the way the bright gleam in her warm brown eyes faltered. He'd seen it before, as if she wasn't certain she believed he was all right. She was the only one who never really believed him.

She ran a gentle thumb over his hand, and he shivered beneath her touch.

"If you say so," she whispered. She released his hand.

A moment later, he heard the barn door open, then close again as Dakota returned to the party, leaving him well and truly alone. That was the rub of Rock's news, wasn't it? Even in a room full of people, standing with the one woman he wanted to have by his side, Blaze would always be alone.

Without looking back, he shifted into his wolf, not bothering to wait until he reached the cover of the forest's towering pines before he let out an echoing howl.

Chapter 2

Nine months later…

"You need to let this go, brother." Maverick's sharp command cut through him.

Blaze tipped his Stetson low on his forehead, fighting to mask the frustrated snarl that tugged at his lips. His eyes changed to his wolf's. He couldn't let it go. He'd tried. More than once.

Refusing to turn and look at the packmaster, he slowly straightened to his full height from where he'd been standing, stooped over his desk again. The muscles of his biceps ached with tension. Blaze flexed, rolling his shoulders like a predatory animal as he tried to release the stiffness there. But it was no use. The want for violence still lingered.

Inside, his wolf clawed at him.

For the past two hours, he'd been holed up here in the security office at the center of Wolf Pack Run's ranch compound, fingers pounding across his keyboard in a frenzied rage. He hadn't been able to stop himself. Since the moment he'd seen movement in the darkness near the pack's borders on his phone's security stream, he hadn't been able to think of anything else. Command. Protect. Serve.

Kill, if necessary.

De Oppresso Liber. He'd been trained for it.

Only to find himself at yet another dead end.

Blaze snarled. *Fuck.*

"It doesn't work like that and you know it," he growled over his shoulder at Maverick.

As if in answer, one of the wall monitors in front of him glared blue through the darkness, enough to sting against wolf retinas.

Maverick let out a grumbled curse, but Blaze didn't so much as blink. With a quick stroke of his finger on the keyboard, the screen went black before he turned toward the packmaster. The scent of Blaze's stale coffee in the mug on his desk hung in the air.

Closing the office door behind him, Maverick flicked on the dim overhead light and pegged Blaze with an all-too-knowing stare. From the dirt on his jeans, the Grey Wolf packmaster been out in the stables, and now standing amid all the pack's security monitors, the fellow cowboy wolf warrior looked out of place. Maverick was the fiercest the pack had to offer, but as alpha, he was also a testament to their lineage, a legend born of their true nature. Like most of the pack, that meant even in human form, he was still sensitive to blue light and not fond of human technology.

Blaze, on the other hand, had been forced to adapt, change, camouflage. Whatever it took. Years ago that was exactly what Maverick had asked him to train for—burying the truth.

He'd gotten a bit *too* good at it.

Blaze leaned against the edge of his desk.

"Where's Kieran?" Maverick asked, referring to the young wolf who was *supposed* to be in the office tonight.

Blaze shrugged, as if he didn't know.

Maverick growled.

Blaze rolled his eyes and released a short sigh. "I sent him home."

"Call him, damn it." Maverick pointed an accusatory finger at Blaze. "You're supposed to be off duty."

"We're having a pissing contest because I'm doing *extra* work?" Blaze raised a smug brow.

Maverick frowned. "Don't get cheeky with me, Blaze."

Blaze cast him a wide, intentionally cheeky grin. "I wouldn't dream of it."

Maverick swore and shook his head with a frustrated grumble. "It's been over nine months since the reception, since Amarok's warning."

"I know."

"You're not going to find anything."

Blaze nodded. "I know."

"Yet you've been poring over those damn screens every god-damn chance you get."

"And?"

Maverick didn't take the bait. Not this time. "And if they were going to attack by now, they would have."

Blaze shook his head with an unamused grin. "You don't know that."

The movement he'd seen on the forest cams tonight had turned out to be little more than a deer. But the thought of what *could* have been had still sent him prowling through the more unsavory corners of the dark web in search of information again.

For something. Anything. A lead.

Whatever it took to keep them all safe.

To keep his secrets hidden.

Maverick let out a disapproving grunt. "I understand your drive to protect the pack, but you can't run yourself into the ground while doing it."

"*You're* lecturing *me* about work-life balance?" Blaze snorted. "That's rich."

Maverick growled again. "Cut the jokes, warrior. I say this as your alpha, not as your friend." The packmaster purposefully held his gaze for a long beat. "Let it go."

Blaze refused to look away. "I can't."

"You will." Maverick placed his hand on the door handle.

To Blaze's surprise, Maverick was the first to look away.

Blaze smiled an unamused grin as he shook his head. "You asked me to go to Russia, Mav, and I did. You don't get to choose how I behave now that I'm back. Not as long as I'm doing my job."

Maverick hadn't been there. For all the experience, bloodshed, and battle the Grey Wolf packmaster had seen, Russia would always be worse.

Blaze knew because he'd relived it every goddamn night for the past four years.

"I know what you saw there was—"

"Don't," Blaze warned. The feral snarl in his voice was barely contained.

Maverick didn't know the half of it.

Turning away, Blaze cleared his throat and sat down in his desk chair. The dozen monitors covering the wall offered multiple views of Wolf Pack Run, the Grey Wolves' sprawling ranchlands, and the bordering Custer-Gallatin National Forest. This time of night, with most of the pack shifted and in true form, the woods were alive with their howling. The compound, on the other hand, proved quiet.

"If you start being too mushy instead of grunting all the time, hell might freeze over. Montana doesn't need any more snow." Blaze grinned over his shoulder.

Maverick didn't so much as laugh.

Typical.

"There're more important things on the table at the moment." Maverick's voice held more than a hint of concern.

Blaze rotated his chair back toward the packmaster.

"Josiah called today. One of the subpack members out in Bozeman hasn't come home."

Blaze shook his head and turned back toward the security monitors. "Big surprise. They shift, then disappear on a long hunt and lose all sense of time out there. Must be nice to have so few responsibilities. They always turn back up."

"This one *hasn't*. Not in over seventy-two hours."

Blaze hesitated from where he'd been about to start typing again. A chill ran through him. That long with no sign of a pack-mate *was* unusual, even in the subpacks.

His mind quickly scanned over the list of possible foul play. Their treaty with the human hunters of the Execution Underground had been recently restored, providing the Grey Wolves immunity while still keeping their agreement with the rogue wolves in place. The last of the Wild Eight had also recently been wiped out, the only remaining members having been incorporated into the Grey Wolf Pack. That left the bloodsuckers.

But the vampires hadn't attacked the outer subpacks since the Missoula massacre nearly two years earlier, and it was only recently that they'd seen a resurgence of movement among them closer to Billings and here at Wolf Pack Run.

Could it be…?

"Don't let paranoia rule your instincts, brother," Maverick said, cutting the thought short. "I need you to look into it."

Blaze nodded. "I'm smart enough to do both." He powered up the monitor again and placed his hands on the keyboard.

Maverick crossed the room in two quick strides and clicked the monitor back off with a sharp grumble. "You're *smart enough* to listen to your alpha. You *won't* do both. That's an order."

Blaze lifted a brow in surprise and laughed. "Look at you. Since when have you learned to power off a computer?"

The Grey Wolf packmaster could kill a man as soon as look at him and never struggled to operate any of the ranch machinery, but when it came to computer technology, he was nearly illiterate.

Maverick crossed his large arms over his chest with a frown, the black-banded tattoos of his packmaster's markings writhing along with the movement. Despite his usual grumpy demeanor, for a brief moment, he looked sheepish, if a bit embarrassed. "Sierra taught me." Maverick cast Blaze a smirk.

His new mate.

Blaze smiled. "So you really *are* going soft?"

"I mean it, Blaze." Maverick's grin fell and his lip curled in warning again.

Blaze expected the frustration. It was the concern underneath that he couldn't handle.

"Yeah, I know." Blaze waved a hand, brushing him off. "I'll take care of it. You have my word. But you're late for a meeting."

"There's no keeping secrets from you." Maverick shook his head. "Especially not when it has to do with Dakota." Maverick cast him a pointed look.

Blaze grunted in acknowledgment. He didn't want to have this conversation, even with Mav.

The packmaster's brow only inched higher, waiting.

Blaze ran a hand through his hair and released a long sigh. "That obvious, huh?" He slumped lower in his desk chair, tilting his head back as he scrubbed a hand over his face.

"No one ever called you subtle, Blaze. The only one who doesn't realize is her."

"Good." Blaze ran his tongue over his teeth.

"You could tell her, you know," Maverick said.

Blaze shook his head. "It's better this way."

Maverick scoffed. "I don't think even *you* believe that."

"Would you have told Sierra on your own?" Blaze's eyes flashed to his wolf, and he gave the packmaster a warning stare. "I don't have anything to offer her."

"You offer her yourself. That's all you need, warrior."

"I lost all sense of myself back in Russia." Blaze twisted back toward the computer.

"Then rebuild, damn it." Maverick fist's thumped hard against the doorframe. "You can't let your enemies win, Blaze."

Blaze released a long breath. He hesitated for a long moment, choosing his words carefully. "You weren't there, Mav… They go for families first, loved ones. There're no survivors. *Ever.* I can't put her in harm's way like that. If they decided to target her because of me, I wouldn't be able to protect her. If something happened to her…" He swallowed. "I wouldn't—"

"Perhaps *she* should be the one to make that decision," Maverick said, sparing him from the more gruesome details. "She's a fierce warrior. You're making excuses. She doesn't need you to protect her and you know it."

Blaze shook his head and let out a low whistle. "Sierra really *is* softening you."

At that, Maverick smiled. "Consider it." He turned to leave. "There's been no movement since Amarok warned you. Let it go."

The packmaster was already halfway out the door before Blaze managed to speak again. "Maverick."

Maverick grunted in acknowledgment.

"Just…promise you'll keep the extra patrols and drills in place like we talked about."

For a long moment, Mav didn't respond, until finally, he nodded. "If it'll help you sleep at night, warrior, you have my word."

Blaze cleared his throat again. "Nothing helps me sleep, Packmaster."

"I know." Maverick's voice was grim as he started to close the door. "That's what concerns me."

———

Luck had always been on Dakota Nguyen's side—or at least her mother had always said so. Dakota struggled to still her shuffling feet as she waited for the packmaster's arrival. She'd been in his office countless times before. The high bookshelves, thick with bulging tomes detailing the Grey Wolves' centuries-long history, and the coffered ceiling that spoke of generations of the pack's wealth had never intimidated her. Yet still, she wrung her hands.

Glancing toward an available chair, she considered sitting, then thought better of it.

No. Luck had little to do with it. What Mẹ called luck was equal parts hard work and focus, mixed with a hint of preparation. In truth, Dakota didn't have much luck.

But she had grit.

Behind her, the office door swung open with the *thunk* of heavy wood against frame. A moment later, the Grey Wolf packmaster rounded the far side of his desk.

Maverick Grey was a formidable beast of a man who never failed to intimidate. With a puckered knife scar over his left eye and canine teeth a little too sharp, he looked handsomely brutal on a good day and downright feral on a bad one. Until he grinned. These days, those grins came easier, considering he was now happily mated with a pup on the way.

Maverick nodded toward the chair, his deep voice filling the space with the commanding tone that marked him as alpha. "You could have taken a seat."

Dakota shrugged. "I didn't want to assume."

With an acknowledging grunt, Maverick dropped into his desk chair before Dakota followed suit.

The packmaster eyed her for a moment, sizing her up and then clearing his throat. "About Sierra's maternity leave…"

The subject dangled between them.

Dakota leaned forward, accepting the prompt to lead the conversation. "There's no rush on her returning. When I said I'd fill in for her as long as she needed, I meant it."

And she had, for the past seven months and two weeks to be exact.

When Sierra, one of her closest friends and the packmaster's new mate, had announced she was expecting, following her appointment as the first female among the pack's elite warriors, to say that Dakota had been thrilled would've been a misrepresentation.

Sure, she'd been happy for Sierra. Any good friend would be. Not to mention she was proud of her friend's accomplishment. Sierra had more than earned the position and deserved her happiness. But in truth, Dakota had also been disappointed.

She and the other elite warriors had worked equally as hard at supporting Sierra's candidacy. Sierra's accomplishment had been the work of them all, yet the pregnancy had meant another nine long months before they could all fully experience the fruits of their hard labor. Pups were a dime a dozen with the pack now in a breeding boom, but female elite warriors were few and far between. Now that Sierra held the position, they still had to win the hearts and minds of the few who had doubted them to ensure more females could follow in Sierra's footsteps. And that long worked-for goal had been within their reach, only for Sierra to get pregnant.

Yes, *thrilled* was a misrepresentation.

"Do you think it will be much longer?" Maverick raised his scarred brow, suddenly looking far less intimidating. He had that stricken look every male of the pack held anytime the discussion of birth and labor was within spitting distance.

"Belle and the other midwives said they'd induce labor if she went more than two weeks over, so I think not."

Maverick nodded, settling deeper into his chair. "I'm not certain I'll be any good at it. Being a father."

"You'll be excellent at it, Alpha." Dakota didn't hesitate. Maverick may have been intimidating, but he led the pack with a fierce love and protectiveness that would make him a wonderful father.

The packmaster held her gaze for a beat as if searching her intent. What he found there must have satisfied him because he nodded his approval. "The strength of a wolf is his pack. My success is dependent on the wolves that stand by my side, which is why I need you, warrior."

"To continue to fill in for Sierra?" she offered.

"To take the position permanently."

The breath she'd been about to take seeped from her lungs. She couldn't have heard him correctly. "Sierra doesn't plan to return?"

Maverick pulled open his desk drawer. Retrieving a small pair of gold-rimmed glasses, he placed them on his nose. "Sierra will return once our pup is up and running on all four legs. But with so many others on the way, pack law requires the proper ratio of elite warriors for protection." He stared at her through the spectacles.

"I'm offering you your own position, serving beside *her*, beside *me*, because you've more than earned it over the past few months and longer. Sierra's win was as much yours and the other females' as it was her own. She knows it and so do I and the rest of the pack."

A long beat of silence passed between them as Dakota struggled to speak.

"You need time to consider it," he said.

"No," she said sharply. "No, there's nothing to consider. I accept."

Maverick smiled. "It's settled then." The packmaster grabbed his ballpoint pen from its holder, clicking it before he pegged her with his hardened stare. Even with the glasses to soften him, he was... unnerving in his power. "You're a fierce fighter, Dakota. We're all honored to have you on the team."

After a few exchanged details about the official announcement, Dakota left the packmaster's office, more surprised than elated. Immediately, she sank against the adjoining wall, supporting her weight against the doorframe. She could barely keep her own feet beneath her.

Her. An elite warrior. The second in the pack's entire history.

The first alpha female of color.

She should have been happy, overjoyed, thrilled even. She'd worked her butt off for this. It was everything she had spent years fighting for, and yet...

Now she would have to prove she deserved it.

By the time Dakota had stumbled back to her cabin, she felt oddly...numb, and to make matters worse, she didn't know *why*.

This wasn't like her. She prided herself on being calm, level-headed, if a bit fierce when challenged. But *never* numb, never unaffected. If Mẹ saw her like this, she would scold her for her self-pity and not being grateful.

But she *was* grateful. She knew in the deepest marrow of her bones how fortunate she was. She'd worked hard for this, yet...

The work still wasn't done.

It never was.

She fumbled with her door latch, then switched on her cabin lights and tossed her keys into an empty bowl near the doorway. Inside her cabin, the normally spacious open floor plan suddenly felt too large, too vacant despite the warm-colored decor, wooden furniture, the plethora of pictures of her family, and the stone fireplace.

Maybe she needed time to process?

A shower to calm her nerves?

Half an hour and a hot shower later, she felt no difference.

Stricken, Dakota collapsed into the cushions of her couch, finally allowing a few tears to fall down her face from frustration. Her head hurt and throat ached. She ran her fingers through her hair. Post-shower with no makeup and with her dark locks a damp, tangled mop, she was more of a hot mess than she'd been in years.

Years. She closed her eyes, exhaling as she admitted the worst of it to herself. She was brave enough to face the truth.

She'd been here time and time before.

A frustrated growl tore from her lips.

When she'd come of age, she'd set the goal of becoming the pack's veterinarian, a position that—she'd felt—they'd been con-tracting out to humans off Wolf Pack Run's ranchlands for too long. She loved caring for animals and all things science. It'd been a natural fit, a position she hoped would make her family, make Me, proud. She'd spent years making that dream a reality. Yet when she'd returned to Wolf Pack Run, qualifications in hand, the joy of accomplishment had only lasted for so long...

Committing to something greater than herself had been her first solution. She had thought that perhaps she could fill the void, create meaning in her life by serving the pack as a warrior. Every member of the Grey Wolf Pack held two roles, one that served the pack and one that served the ranch they called home. Defending her pack, her family, had seemed like as noble and worthwhile a goal as any. Her father had done so; why couldn't she? She appreciated a good challenge. Why not push herself? Being a warrior had been all she'd imagined it to be and more, but again the taste of success only lasted so long, so being one of the first females among the select elite warriors had proved to be the next challenge.

For the past several years, she'd worked with a singular focus, tending the pack's ranch animals during the day and running vampire patrols at night. The work had been hard and grueling, often thankless. She'd thought this time, when she finally reached her achievement, maybe she'd find what she was looking for. But that was the problem, wasn't it? There was always a next challenge, a next goal, a next accomplishment, because whenever she looked in the mirror at the end of the day, despite her pride in herself, she still felt like she was in this alone...

She pressed the heels of her palms to her eyes, willing the tears to stop. This was ridiculous. Badass she-wolf warriors were *not* supposed to cry. Were they?

Maybe sleep? A glass of wine?

Anything to make this feeling go away.

Chapter 3

A KNOCK SOUNDED AT HER FRONT DOOR, DRAWING DAKOTA'S attention.

She glanced out the front window of her cabin. The orange and blue sunset had long since faded over the mountain peaks, plunging the ranch into darkness, which meant at this time of night when she was off duty, it could only be...

Seconds later, Blaze stood over her, tipping off his Stetson to run his fingers through his brown-blond hair. Dakota jumped, startled by his swift appearance. She'd given him a key a few months back, but knowing her best friend, she'd thought he'd probably lost it in his sock drawer or somewhere equally disorganized. Clearly, he hadn't.

"Crap. You scared me," she mumbled, sinking back into the couch cushions.

His approach had been so stealthy, she hadn't even heard the door open or his footfalls for that matter. But these days, it was easy to forget that Blaze Carter, the Grey Wolves' security specialist, was one of the most lethal wolves on the North American continent. Despite his wry grin, easygoing humor, and wild fashion sense, the former MAC-V-Alpha soldier had more than a handful of enemy kills beneath his belt and his fair share of battle scars to prove it.

But for tonight, Blaze's past seemed to be forgotten and that playful expression of his was in full bloom. This evening, his outrageous style of choice was a graphic all-black T-shirt that in a large, white font read: "Hide Your Girlfriend."

Dakota chuckled at the handsome, joking grin that followed in response to her smile. Hide your girlfriend indeed.

Blaze leaned against the back edge of her couch. "Scared is not usually the response I get when I show up at a woman's door late at night."

Dakota shook her head in amusement as her gaze trailed down the bulk of his toned arm in teasing appreciation. No, it likely wasn't.

The cowboy was carrying a bottle of wine by the neck in one hand and a flash drive in the other, and from that sheepish expression on his face, it could only be a peace offering.

All her favorites, of course. Blaze knew better than to skimp on the details. Whoever *actually* caught his attention someday would be a lucky woman.

She smiled, tears, headache, and doubts from the earlier part of the evening forgotten. "What did you do?"

Blaze gave an overexaggerated shrug like he couldn't help being...well, Blaze. "I forgot Peaches's insulin shot and now I can't find her."

Dakota sighed in mock frustration. What else was new?

"I thought you set an alarm?" They'd had this conversation more than once.

Blaze's old barn cat, Peaches, was a decrepit monster of an animal who, like all cats, thought she was queen of the universe. Shortly after Blaze had returned from his last tour in Russia, he'd found the wild adult feline in the barn and claimed her as his own. Neither of them were sure how old the ancient tortoiseshell cat was, but they liked to joke that with her meow that could wake the dead and a body that was equal parts plump, diabetic, and oddly skeletal beneath all the chub, Peaches's age didn't matter.

The kitty queen was clearly immortal.

"I *should* have set an alarm." Blaze feigned a guilty cringe. "Help me? Please?" He cast her another smirk.

With his gaze turned full force on her, a sharp breath tore from her lips. Good God, that grin. No man should be that handsome.

Nature wasn't fair, really.

He lifted the wine and flash drive again, giving them a little shake for emphasis. "Cabernet and newly streamed K-dramas wait in exchange."

She shook her head even as she smiled. How could she say no?

Sitting up, she snatched the bottle from his hand with a playful smile of her own. "You're lucky I tolerate you," she teased.

Blaze let out a short bark of a laugh. "I'm lucky anyone tolerates me, but *you* not only tolerate me; you *enjoy* my company, which puts you at a whole different level of committable insanity."

"Tonight, that feels about right." Swiping at her eyes one last time, she removed a hair tie from around her wrist and quickly threw her hair into a messy bun. She knew Blaze had to realize she'd been crying by now, but thankfully, he didn't prod.

That would have started the tears all over again.

"Where'd you last see her?" Dakota asked.

Minutes later, they both stood in the orange glow of the barn's lamplight, flashlights in hand, searching for Peaches per their usual routine.

"You should have set the alarm," Dakota said again after they'd searched for nearly twenty minutes and still found no sign of the old feline. But considering Blaze had been intermittently making her laugh with well-timed jokes about Peaches's less-than-queenlike qualities, she couldn't exactly be annoyed with him.

Finally, a decrepit yowl from the hayloft raised gooseflesh on Dakota's neck. She and Blaze exchanged a knowing glance.

The queen had made herself known.

"How the hell the old monster managed to climb that high is anyone's guess," Blaze muttered. He was up the ladder within seconds. Dakota quickly followed suit.

Once in the loft, they shined their flashlights through the dark again until a pair of greenish-yellow eyes glared back.

"Found her," Dakota called out.

She clicked off her flashlight, reaching over the hay bale and into the darkness where Peaches lay in wait. She scooped the feline into her arms. Save for Blaze, Dakota was the only one the beast actually allowed to hold her. Queen Peaches was *not* to be coddled by any unfamiliar subjects, lest they receive a yowling hiss that rivaled a banshee and a fierce bite on the nose. Austin, the pack's medic, had given more than one packmember a facial stitch or two.

Hoisting the hefty feline over the hay bale, Dakota turned back toward Blaze. "Do you have the insulin?"

Blaze glanced toward the hayloft floor and scratched at the nape of his neck like he was the cat who'd caught the canary instead of a lethal wolf. The dark inside the barn cast a shadow across his handsome face so that only his white-toothed smile was visible. Like many among their pack, in human form, his canine teeth made him look more than a little wolfish, like he might devour every inch of her and enjoy it.

She blushed at the thought.

"Blaze," she chastised. "You forgot the insulin?"

That wry grin beneath the rim of his Stetson only widened, instantly making her heart beat faster.

She let out a short huff as realization dawned on her. "You saw I was upset on the pack security cams, didn't you?"

Blaze pawed at the back of his neck again. "Maybe." He gave her that sheepish grin.

"You didn't actually forget Peaches's shot, did you?"

"No." Blaze shrugged as if the harmless deceit came all too easily. "I figured we wouldn't actually find her."

At that moment, Peaches chose to bristle against Dakota's touch, twisting herself so her large puff of a tail turned toward Blaze.

Clearly, the queen didn't appreciate being used as a decoy.

"I figured you needed a distraction," Blaze said.

Dakota smiled as she shook her head. "You're awful."

"But you like it."

"Only from you," she admitted.

A brief silence settled between them.

Blaze tipped his Stetson low, his rough voice humming through her. "I hear congratulations are in order."

Dakota stroked a hand over Peaches's fur, ignoring the effect his low voice had on her. "I don't feel much like celebrating."

Blaze quirked a brow in confusion. "If you wanted someone to rain on your parade, all you had to do was ask. I could've burst into Maverick's office and spoiled the whole thing for you. No need to do it yourself."

A smile tugged at her lips.

Blaze was always good at that, making her smile. She could be her full self in front of him in a way she could with no one else. She didn't have to worry about her messy hair or her puffy, post-crying face or aiming to impress. With his own plethora of quirks, he never judged or held anyone to unreasonable expectations. Certainly not the perfectionist standards she held for herself. He simply saw everyone in the pack as they were, her included, for better or worse, and fiercely loved them all anyway.

Enough to risk his life for them.

When she didn't respond, Blaze drew closer, his gaze raking over her in slow, deliberate assessment. He was looking for the source of tension in her muscles and she knew that, but the way he circled her was like a predator would its prey—slow, deliberate, observant. Heat filled her cheeks as she tried not to stare, choosing instead to glance down at Peaches.

From the corner of her eye, she watched him, unable to see his face. The quiet sound of his boots against the wood of the loft was so measured that she stiffened in anticipation. In the orange glow of the heat lamps below, the scars on his tanned forearms became a pale, near-transparent silver as he prowled toward her. The dark grays of the inked artwork on his bicep writhed, making it appear as if his army patches were as present beneath the tattooed tear in his skin as his wolf was.

Finally, he came to a stop behind her. She could feel the heat of him, lingering. At his touch, a shiver ran through her. Gripping both her shoulders, he massaged away the tension there, with Peaches still coddled to her chest. His large hands felt warm and welcome against the tight muscles of her neck. She moaned a little and melted into his touch, enjoying the mixture of pleasure, warmth, and safety she found there.

"What's wrong, Kotes?" he whispered.

Kotes, like "coats." The nickname instantly softened her.

She let out a contented sigh, continuing to stroke Peaches's matted, motley fur. "I thought being an elite warrior was what I wanted it, and I'm happy. I really am. When Maverick delivered the news, I was excited, even though there's still the challenge of proving myself, but..."

Blaze remained silent for a moment, clearly waiting for her to continue. His deft fingers penetrated the sore muscles of her neck, making her groan again. "But?"

"But then I thought about racing back to my cabin and I realized..." Her voice trailed off as a fresh round of tears welled. "Who do I have to share it with?"

Peaches chose that moment to leap from her chest, and Dakota turned toward her friend.

Blaze stopped massaging her shoulders though his hands remained there. "Me, your siblings, your mom, Sierra, *me*," he emphasized again.

A small smile curved her lips. "Yes, I know, *you*. But you know what I mean. No matter how big the accomplishment, Mę won't be satisfied until I'm married, and you're not..." Her voice stopped short again. What *wasn't* he exactly?

A friend. A partner. A confidante. He was all those things, except...

She swallowed, hard.

A lover.

Her pulse thumped in her temple. She had so much to be grateful for and yet no one to share her life with. She was happy. She didn't need a man to take care of her. She'd proved that for years. She did just fine on her own. Though admittedly, she was even happier when she was with Blaze. Relationships weren't for everyone of course, but...

Lord, if she wasn't tired of being alone.

Dakota turned the rest of the way to face him. Her gaze fell to her best friend, lingering there long enough that she was obviously staring at him. Blaze released her shoulders, giving a rough clear of his throat before he stepped back. The sound sent a shiver down Dakota's spine, causing the small hairs on the back of her neck to prickle. Her nipples tightened and her breasts felt heavy, full like she wanted him to...

Her eyes widened.

She'd always figured the flirtatious banter between them was a joke. Harmless fun. Blaze was like that with everyone, wasn't he?

Her eyes lingered on him, on the lack of humor in his face, however brief.

Suddenly, she wasn't so sure.

Blaze glanced toward the floor, refusing to look at her as another rough grumble broke the silence between them. "We headed back to your cabin or not?" That familiar wolfish grin crossed his lips again.

A shiver of awareness shuddered through her.

Did he mean...?

She blinked, stunned momentarily, before a flush of warmth flooded her cheeks. No, of course not. He meant for their movie night. He always came by when they were both off duty for a marathon of lovably overdramatic anime, K-dramas, and cheesy human horror films. Nothing had changed about that. Absolutely nothing.

But did she want it to?

She already knew the answer to that. She had for a long time.

"Yeah, yeah, of course," she said, finally answering him. Her voice was breathier than she intended. Why did she sound like she'd run a marathon, only…sexier?

She shook her head. She and Blaze were just friends. This was insane. At this rate, she'd need professional help before the night's end.

———————

Two hours and a bad horror film later, Dakota's problem had only worsened. As if her emotions tonight hadn't been in enough of an upheaval already, all her normal interactions with Blaze had taken on a whole new meaning. When she'd struggled with the wine cork and he'd come up behind her to help pry it out, the quick brush of his breath against her ear had sent a rush of heat to her core. When he'd offered to make a quick dinner for them like he always did, she'd almost salivated and *not* at the thought of food, and when he'd patted the spot next to him on the couch and then wrapped his arm around her, pulling her close, she'd nearly moaned. Literally *moaned* at the thought of crawling the rest of the way on top of him.

She was a mess. A crazy hot mess.

The knowledge that maybe he really *was* interested in her, that all the tension between them wasn't some fun game changed everything.

Uncertain what to do, she snuggled into Blaze's chest again with all the purring contentment of satisfied, sleeping Peaches who was currently in her lap. Heat built in her chest. Like always, she and Peaches had been cuddling against Blaze most of the movie, but to say the closeness was getting to Dakota in a newfound way was an understatement. She'd always thought he was sexy, that any woman would be lucky to have him, but she'd never allowed herself to consider that woman could be her.

But now that she'd considered it…

Was wanting to ride your best friend harder than one of the ranch horses a bad thing?

Twisting from where her head lay on his shoulder, she blinked up at him. His warm, blue irises were fixated on the screen again, seemingly unaware of her turmoil. Her gaze traced over the five-o'clock scruff on his face, the strong curve of his jaw, his straight blade of a nose.

It felt...*good* to be tucked against him like this. Too good. Like so good she never wanted it to stop, and how hadn't she noticed it before? And had he always been this...large? This handsome? This...mouthwatering and sexy? She nearly giggled.

Good Lord, there was no other phrase for it.

Sensing her gaze on him, Blaze glanced toward her, his forehead drawn low in concern. "You all right, Kotes?"

Kotes.

The intimacy of the nickname while she lay wrapped in his arms brought another rush of heat to her core. He was the only one who called her that. For the first time, it felt like a secret promise between them, something only they shared.

"Yeah," she squeaked, sounding strangely like a caricature version of herself. "Yeah, I'm fine. P-peaches was just, you know..." She scrambled for an explanation before she made some awful, pawing motion with her hands. "Mushing her claws into me. That's all."

Blaze quirked a brow before he glanced toward the cat.

Peaches had been asleep on top of her for the better part of an hour, and the kitty queen was so soundly unconscious that she looked as if she were dead. She wasn't.

Blaze shrugged. "If you say so." Wrapping a large arm around her, he tucked Dakota closer into his side as he reached toward the feline. He stroked a hand over the cat's back before giving Peaches's motley fur a quick ruffle. Giving the barn cat a bath was about as pleasant as gouging one's own eyes out with a dull spoon.

Gently jostled awake, Peaches opened a single yellow eye, casting an annoyed glare at Blaze before she hissed and jumped down from Dakota's lap.

"Problem solved." Blaze flicked his tongue across his too-sharp canines before he cast Dakota that wolfish smirk. "I've petted a lot of pussies before, but *leaping* isn't the usual response." He winked.

For a brief moment, Dakota only seemed capable of gaping at him until finally she let out a cross between a turned-on mewl, a pathetic whimper, and a snort.

Blaze chuckled, his wide grin lighting up the room. Clearly he thought she was mimicking the cat like the infatuated fool she currently was. Normally she would have thought he only meant the comment to be funny and yet...

She glanced up at Blaze, then to her still-full wineglass and back again. Internally, she tried to dissuade herself, to see reason, but she couldn't. Like it or not, this was happening. Anxiety and fear nagged at her. Facing the pack's enemies was nothing compared to this...

Because God help her, she was going to seduce her best friend.

Chapter 4

"BLAZE, WHY HAVE WE NEVER...?" DAKOTA'S VOICE TRAILED OFF.

The movie credits had started rolling, and Blaze's brow furrowed as he tried to discern his best friend's meaning. If he didn't know better, he would have thought she'd drunk too much. Over the years he'd seen Dakota tipsy enough to know that despite the small bit of wine she'd been nursing since dinner, she was clearly sober.

Personally, he didn't drink in excess these days, considering too much alcohol tended to make him a barrel of fucking laughs who overshared war stories, but he wasn't about to spoil anyone else's fun, and Dakota had deserved to relax. She had more than her share to celebrate tonight, even if she hadn't initially been in the spirit.

Blaze craned his neck down to where Dakota watched him. She'd been snuggled comfortably into his side throughout the whole film, the jasmine scent of her hair making his wolf stir in awareness for the better part of two hours, even as the smell soothed him. Having her near was like a balm to his soul. But now she was staring at him with those warm, gorgeous brown eyes and with her chin perched atop his shoulder. Her small chest pressed flat against his abdomen. She was too close for comfort.

His throat went dry, even as he felt himself salivating like the damn wolf that he was. His eyes flashed to their true gold and he swallowed, hard. With her flush against him like this, he could feel the taut mounds of Dakota's breasts, her hardened nipples. Breasts he wanted to lick, suck, tease. She placed a hand on his chest, inching closer.

She wasn't...? Was she...?

No, she had never. Mav had even confirmed that she didn't realize.

Her small hand trailed across one of his pectorals.

Blaze growled, low and warning as he looked away. Internally, he scolded himself. He was imagining things he shouldn't, things he'd wanted for far too long and had never allowed himself to have, and with good reason. Clearly reality and fantasy were blurring again.

In spite of his sobriety, he'd been zoned out for the better part of the movie. He'd been too lost in the past, in Russia and the darkness of his own thoughts, repeatedly checking the security cams on his phone until Dakota had pushed against him. As Maverick had less than subtly reminded him, he was off duty tonight, but ever since Rock had dropped that proverbial bomb on him and his life months ago, he'd monitored the cams like a hawk. One grumbling yet well-meaning packmaster wasn't about to change him. Blaze lived by his own rules and always had. Maverick knew that.

As far as Blaze was concerned, it didn't matter that there hadn't been any movement yet.

They *were* coming.

It was only a matter of when…

The thought instantly chilled him, temporarily dousing whatever tension Dakota had created between them. He gave a rough clear of his throat. "Why have we never…what?" He dared glance toward her again, and instantly, he regretted it.

Staring up at him, Dakota's warm brown eyes were filled with a sultry promise and she bit her lower lip, teeth tugging at the soft, tender flesh. How many times had he wished he could nip at the subtle pink curve of her mouth, tongue parting her lips to explore the possibilities between them?

Shit.

He wasn't imagining the tension between them, and fuck if that didn't make it a thousand times worse. Based on the way she was looking at him, he knew *exactly* what she meant, but he had to play this as if he didn't.

As if he hadn't imagined all the ways he'd wanted to lay her bare and enjoy her.

To bury his tongue inside her wet, hot cunt.

Over and over again until she screamed his name.

Fuck.

This was worse than torture, and he knew because he'd lived *through* torture.

He blew out a long, steadying breath, internally letting out a string of colorful curses that would've made even his fellow soldiers blush. He and Dakota were friends and nothing more.

They couldn't be anything more than that.

No matter how much he craved it.

"You know what I mean," Dakota answered sweetly, drawing his attention back toward her, as if the vague answer were supposed to be meaningful.

It *did* mean something to him, more than he wanted to admit, and he hated himself for it.

"No, I don't, Kotes." His tone was gruff, harsher than usual.

What was going on in her head tonight? He still hadn't quite figured out what she'd been crying about, and now this?

For the better part of the evening, the thought of her tears had irked him. When he'd seen her crying on the pack's security cams while she'd run back to her cabin, he'd known he wouldn't be able to think of anything else until he fixed whatever had broken her heart. He didn't like seeing anyone cry, period. But *especially* Dakota. The thought made him twitchy.

Sure, she'd said she didn't have anyone to share her excitement with, but what did she even mean by that anyway? Of course she had someone to share it with.

She had him. Exactly as they'd always been.

Wasn't that enough?

At the clarity that came with that thought, his Adam's apple gave a sharp jerk.

It hadn't been enough for *him* for a long time.

And clearly, it wasn't for her anymore either.

He shook his head. It didn't matter. Her new feelings didn't change anything. He'd soldier through like he always did. Avoid the situation and do what was best. He'd take what life allowed him and place distance between himself and anything else that it didn't.

Even when it wasn't fucking fair.

Dakota eased even closer. Blaze's cock stiffened, straining against the fly of his jeans. He tried to ignore the feeling, the scent of her so close. He even considered pushing her away, but he couldn't bring himself to. He was already failing at avoidance. Miserably.

"I don't know what you're talking about, Kotes."

Refusing to look at her, he tried to reroute his mind from the damn near filthy direction his thoughts were taking. He could not go down that road with her, no matter how much he wanted to. And *fuck* did he want to.

A sharp growl rumbled in his throat.

She plucked his Stetson off his head, tossing his hat onto the coffee table before she cupped his cheek. Her fingers brushed against the scruff there as she guided his face back to meet her gaze. "Then let me show you," she whispered.

Before he could stop her, she leaned forward and kissed him.

Blaze had imagined kissing Dakota a thousand times.

In the bleak, tundra landscape of Siberia, each night he'd imagined her face, her laugh, even at times when he'd shifted into his wolf to stave off the freezing cold. He'd dreamed about it ad infinitum. Back then, with her letters his only sparse reminder of comfort and home, he'd dared hope that when he got out of the service, something would spark between them.

The scene in his head had been idyllic. Him in uniform valiantly sauntering up to the compound at Wolf Pack Run with his duffel bag over his shoulder like a true veteran hero with war stories to thrill and excite. She'd be there waiting. His best friend, the one woman he cared for above all others since he'd been barely older than a teen, whose words and letters had given him a small piece of her heart in paper form while he'd been abroad.

In his dreams, it had been at that moment that she'd suddenly realized he'd been in love with her from the first night he'd ever spent by her side.

And that she was in love with him, too.

But the dream had been naive. Idealistic.

That'd been before Operation Dark Force.

Before he'd learned that true war heroes didn't tell stories because of the things they carried with them for life, even when they didn't want to.

In reality, he'd returned home, duffel bag over his shoulder to little fanfare.

When he'd set foot on the ranchlands of Wolf Pack Run for the first time in years, Dakota hadn't been there. She'd been delivering her dissertation for her veterinarian degree that week, and though she had offered to reschedule, he'd known what that moment had meant to her, how nervous she was, and he hadn't wanted to interfere.

He also hadn't been certain he wanted her there.

He hadn't been sure he could handle seeing her without falling apart.

Instead of returning home feeling like a war hero, he'd felt broken, damaged, like he would never be whole again. That empty feeling had eaten away at him those first few months while he'd played his favorite music album on repeat over and over again each night in a hopeless struggle to sleep. Rest had been difficult.

It still was.

But now, as Dakota's soft lips brushed against his, the fantasy was nothing compared to reality. To the scent of her in his nose, the taste of her on his tongue, the feeling of her against him. A spark lit inside his chest. For years, he'd been certain he'd never feel hope again. And like a man starved, at the first scent of nourishment, he couldn't stop himself from devouring it.

Lacing his fingers around the nape of her neck, Blaze gripped her there, hard. His tongue parted the seam of her lips, forceful and claiming with a rough need. Dakota's advance had been sweet, confident, tender. Tender enough to break him.

He couldn't allow that.

Not when he wanted to taste every inch of her before night's end.

Cupping her by her bottom, he dragged her into his lap. With a swipe of his hand, he gave a fast, heated caress to the inside of her thigh, prompting her to open her legs. She blossomed for him, spreading wide, and he pulled her down on top of his lap so that she straddled him. Thick and ready, his cock strained against the fly of his jeans, rubbing against where she rode him. Those thin, silky pajama shorts she was wearing had been flashing him subtle peeks of the round underside of her ass all night, taunting him, but now they gave him easy access.

Pulling her down to him, he deepened the kiss as he ground his erection against the center of her pleasure. Dakota gasped against his mouth, bucking against him as she cupped both sides of his face in her hands.

He growled. Fuck, she tasted good. Like a spicy mix of cabernet along with the citrusy sweetness of the Earl Grey tea and sugar cookies he knew she reached for whenever she was trying to relax in the evening. Indulgent. Succulent. Sweet.

Everything he wanted, but better.

Releasing his face, she gripped the hem of his shirt, tugging and pulling at the material there as she attempted to strip it off him. He nipped at her lower lip in playful warning. If either of them was getting naked first, it was going to be her. He'd make sure of it.

Cradling her spine, he flipped her onto her back within seconds, laying her across the couch cushions. Knee between her legs, he leaned over her, his mouth dropping from her lips to trail down the smooth skin of her neck, teasing, licking. His head dipped low as his tongue neared the mounds of her breasts. He knew she wasn't wearing a bra. One quick yank and he'd capture her nipple between his teeth.

Dakota let out a small groan of pleasure.

Blaze froze, the sound instantly bringing him back to himself.

To the fact that he hadn't checked the security cams in nearly a half hour, to Russia, his discharge papers, Amarok, Maverick, every dark secret he'd tried to bury since he'd come home.

Abruptly, he pulled back, staring down at Dakota as if he was truly seeing her for the first time. She was sprawled out on the couch beneath him, relaxed, sated eyes gazing up at him. Her lips were still plump and full from their kiss, and her cheekbones were pink from where the scruff of his five-o'clock shadow had brushed against them. She was breathtakingly gorgeous like this, beautiful, everything he'd ever wanted and yet...

The sight of her made his chest ache.

She reached for him, but Blaze pulled back, propping himself up on his arms so he could stand. "I can't do this, Kotes," he whispered, trying to pull away.

She let out a little disappointed whimper, catching his hand and gently drawing him back down toward her. She placed a hand over the mound of his erection as she whispered against the skin of his neck. "I think you can." She nibbled on his earlobe.

The playful taunt instantly angered him.

"That's not what I mean," he ground out, his frustration making him growl, though he hadn't intended to. Blaze pushed away from her and stood. "We shouldn't be doing this."

Dakota propped herself up on her elbows, lifting her head from the couch, her features wrought with confusion. "Shouldn't?"

"You're feeling vulnerable right now, Kotes. I don't want to take advantage of you."

Her jaw dropped. "Take advantage of me? *I* kissed *you*." Dakota pulled her legs up and stood. "If you don't want to do this, just say so." She snatched the long-abandoned, nearly full wineglass off the coffee table and downed the remainder of the contents before she pegged him with a challenging stare.

Blaze growled. Their kind had better metabolisms for alcohol than humans, making it harder for them to be intoxicated, but that didn't mean he wasn't still worried about her drowning herself. "*Want* has nothing to do with it, Kotes. I *can't* do this. Not when I can't be certain we won't regret it in the morning."

"We?" She blinked, her jaw dropping for a moment. She crossed her arms over her chest and scowled at him, now-empty wineglass still in hand. "What you mean is that you can't be certain you want to do this with *me*."

"I didn't say that." He grabbed his Stetson off the coffee table and placed it on his head.

"You didn't have to." She turned on her heel and strode toward the kitchen, the steps of her bare feet hitting the cabin's hardwood floor in quick and angry steps.

He growled again. "What does that even mean?"

She deposited the wineglass in the sink, roughly enough that he was surprised the glass didn't shatter beneath her strength. Considering his sizable height, Dakota was small compared to him, but as a warrior, she was still a force to be reckoned with. "It means that I know you've hung your hat on the bedposts of plenty of women on this ranch who are *not* me." She turned and strode down the length of her hallway.

Blaze tore after her. "That isn't fair and you know it."

She wasn't wrong. He *had* slept his way across the better part of Wolf Pack Run years ago, but those flings had been *before* her, before he'd realized he'd fallen for her so hard he hadn't known what to do with himself or if she was even interested or if he'd ever be able to move on with his life if she wasn't, before MAC-V-Alpha and Russia and coming back home like the broken excuse for a cowboy that he was.

He knew his reputation in bed still followed him, but any free time he had these days was spent with *her*. She had to realize that.

"That was different," he said, his voice a strange mixture of frustration and pleading.

Stopping in the middle of the cabin hallway, she spun to face him, throwing her hands in the air. "And what *exactly* was different about it, Blaze?" she snapped.

She was angrier than he'd seen her in years, which he knew meant that she was trying to hide that she was hurting. He cringed at the thought that he'd caused it.

He met her gaze stare for stare.

"Everything." He reached out and brushed a hand over her cheek. He tried to infuse every bit of meaning he could into that single word.

Couldn't she see?

He was fucking crazy about her.

Those flings hadn't just been before her; they hadn't meant anything to him. Not like she did. Fuck, she was the reason he got out of bed every goddamn morning.

She was his everything.

"Exactly." Swatting his hand away, she turned and stomped into her bedroom.

Releasing another snarl, he followed after her.

What the hell did she even mean by that?

In her room, he watched as she stomped her way haphazardly toward her bathroom suite. When she reached the wooden door, she threw it open and flicked on the light, pausing momentarily only to wrench the silk camisole of her pajama shirt up and over her head. She cast it onto the cabin floor, exposing the gorgeous, naked length of her back. The pants came next.

"Christ, Dakota," Blaze swore as he forced himself to look away.

"What?" she shot over her shoulder. From the corner of his eye, he could see the outline of her nude form. "We're packmates. Friends, remember? Nothing you haven't seen before."

For a moment, he dared glance up, only to watch as her perfect, naked pear of a bottom swayed into the bathroom. His mouth watered. Instantly, he was hard all over again.

"Dakota," he grumbled.

Damn, if she wasn't making this as difficult as all get-out. Couldn't she see he was trying to protect her?

She left the door wide open behind her. A moment later, he heard the shower turn on. Her hair had been wet when he'd arrived to cheer her up earlier in the evening, so it was her second shower in one night. He knew it was the place she retreated to whenever she wanted to escape from the rest of the world. The fact that she wanted to escape from *him* tore him to shreds.

Approaching the door, he leaned against the outside frame, his Stetson tipping back as he rested his head against the wall. "Dakota," he pleaded.

He didn't need to raise his voice. Their kind could easily hear over the sound of a showerhead.

"Don't 'Dakota' me," she called back.

From the quiver in her tone, he could tell she was on the verge of tears.

"First the stupid warrior goal and now...this," she said.

As if *this* had been a mistake.

As if she'd ruined a ten-year-long friendship with a single kiss.

Blaze shook his head. She couldn't get rid of him that easily. Not by a long shot.

But all the more reason he had called a stop on the evening, even when he hadn't wanted to. He let out a long sigh. He wanted to tell her that her goal of being an elite warrior hadn't been stupid. That it'd been daring, bold, brave, like she was, like her kiss had been, even if the accomplishment hadn't completed her in the way

she'd wanted it to. She was more than the sum of her accomplish-
ments. He wished she could see that.

"Kotes," he whispered, soft, soothing.

"Don't."

She was crying again. He heard it.

The sound flayed him open. He could hardly stand it.

"I don't even know why I'm crying anymore." A soft, muffled
sob followed those words.

"Can I come in?" he asked.

She didn't answer. The shower water pattered against the tile.

"Dakota," he pleaded. When she still didn't answer, he said, "I
promise to close my eyes like I'm some sort of gentleman or something even though we both know I'm not. Let me dry you off. Put
you to bed." He hesitated. "Please."

"You don't have to close your eyes," she answered back. "Not
unless you want to."

He didn't want to, but he would.

For tonight.

Stepping into the bathroom, he averted his gaze as he grabbed
her fluffy cotton robe off the back of the door hanger. He spread
it open and held it out toward her. Over the top edge of the robe,
he could see only her face. She was curled around herself at the
bottom of the shower tiles, legs pulled up to her chest and head
cradled atop her knees. When she didn't move from her perch,
he approached slowly, closing his eyes as he reached into the still-
running shower to turn the water off.

By the time he'd wrapped the robe around her shoulders, pulling
her up alongside him, they were both soaked. She was still crying,
quietly now, even as he cradled her against him. He lifted her into
his arms, and she rested her head on his shoulder as he carried her
to her bed, where he wrapped her in a cocoon of the towel robe and
several blankets.

When he finished, he sat on the edge of the mattress beside

her, fingers combing through the long, dark tangles of her wet hair.

They stayed like this for a long time, silent, comforted by the nearness of each other. The soft sounds of Montana's summer winds blew against the cracked bedroom window.

Eventually, Dakota fell asleep and Blaze took that as his cue to leave.

He closed the window, then tore out of Dakota's cabin like a bat out of hell, not bothering to search for Peaches or do anything other than lock the front door behind him. Casting his clothes, boots, and Stetson into the rocking chair on her porch, he shifted into his wolf. Whichever packmember was on laundry duty come sunrise would collect all the various discarded articles of clothing scattered across the ranch, and his would be back in his cabin by tomorrow at sundown.

When his four paws connected with the hard mountain ground, the moon overhead called to him. He ran along the edges of the forest, the smell of birch and pine flooding his nose. He paused, ears perking up as he listened to the sounds of the rabbit in the bushes nearby. The crescent moon cast a thin shadow overhead. But he'd let the rabbit live for tonight.

Returning to his run, Blaze didn't stop until he'd reached home. Even in his true form, his head was too consumed with her. With her scent, her sounds, replaying every moment of the evening and analyzing each step he'd taken. He didn't want to miss or forget a single moment, including where everything had gone wrong, but more importantly, where it'd gone heartbreakingly, painfully right.

He shifted back into human form. Retrieving his spare key from beneath the doormat, he unlocked his cabin's dead bolt and padded inside. He glanced over the small space. The layout of Dakota's was nearly identical to his own, standard issue among the single adults of the pack, but where hers was full of life, decorations she'd chosen and pictures of her loved ones making it warm, in contrast, his looked stark, bare. He had a family, of course, but his parents had long since retired out to the western subpacks, and after his last tour, he'd never been able to bring himself to decorate. He was too used to living out of a duffel bag.

Old habits died hard, he supposed.

Casting his key onto the hook beside the door, he went to his bedroom and tried to fall asleep, but hours later, he was still restless. He couldn't circumvent his routine, even when he wanted to. Resigning himself to the ritual of it, he pulled on a pair of athletic shorts and a T-shirt that read "I work out because punching people is frowned upon" that Dakota had bought for him two Christmases ago and made his way to the Grey Wolves' underground training gym.

This time of night, most of the pack was either out in the forest or sleeping, depending on who had ranch duty in the morning— like true wolves, he and his packmates didn't need to keep consistent sleep schedules—so he found himself thankfully alone among the gym equipment. He worked his way through the arm and chest machines first, followed by legs, glutes, thighs, weight benches.

By the time he was out of energy, it was several hours later. From his glance at the clock, the sun was likely starting to peek over the mountaintops, but still, the need for sleep eluded him. The image of Dakota laid out on her couch beneath him was still seared inside his skull. It'd changed things between them.

He didn't know how yet, but even he had to admit it.

Nothing would be the same.

Dripping with sweat, he made his way into the showers, stripping off his damp gym clothes. Maybe if he washed off, he'd finally feel like he could get some shut-eye. He left the water cold in hopes that it would somehow quell the heat from the evening still pulsing through his veins. It didn't.

When he finally resigned himself to the fact that he wasn't going to sleep tonight and that he wasn't as resistant to temptation as he thought, the water had been beating down on his back for some time and it hadn't washed the need away. The image of Dakota beneath him haunted him, and he felt himself stiffen. His hand gripped the thick base of his cock, slowly and deliberately pumping over the hardened length. He braced his other hand against the shower wall, his fist giving him only a fraction of the pleasure he knew the gripping warmth of a woman could provide.

Not any woman.

One woman.

Water sluiced over his hair, tamping the gold-brown locks to his forehead before traveling down the muscles of his shoulders, his chest. What would have happened if he hadn't called a halt on the evening? He worked the full, hardened length of himself, balls tightening in need each time he flexed his grip over the sensitive head.

He knew what would have happened.

It wasn't even a question.

He would have laid Dakota out naked before him, spreading her wide as he buried his tongue deep in her soft folds. He'd have made her come so many times she was begging him to be inside her, and then, and only then, would he have let her take her pleasure with him.

He wanted her on top, if she allowed it, wanted to see the way she milked his cock until they were both crying out in pleasure-pain. Feeling the fantasy grip him, he threw back his head and groaned as he spent himself into his own hand. The hot spurts of his seed coated his palm and he panted. Collecting himself, he washed it away beneath the showerhead, finally scrubbing himself thoroughly from head to toe.

When he was finished, he dressed in the fresh clothes he'd brought in his duffel bag and headed straight to the security office. Maverick had been right. Sleep wouldn't claim him, even though fantasy would. Fantasy was all he'd ever allowed it to be.

Blaze let out a determined growl.

That changed *now*.

Chapter 5

"WE NEED TO TALK."

Dakota had been dreading this moment for the better part of the day. She released a long sigh as she pulled on another arm-length glove and cast a glance over her shoulder. Blaze stood at the barn's entrance, leaning against the doorframe as he watched her.

It was past noon and the late-summer sun hung overhead, bring-ing a layer of comfortable warmth down on the pastures. She'd woken that morning only to find herself dehydrated, dissatisfied, and nursing a self-induced headache from her crying, still wrapped in the towels and blankets Blaze had left her in. After downing a few aspirins, she'd quickly dressed in spite of her discomfort and, in hopes of avoiding this exact conversation, had skipped breakfast in the pack dining hall and headed out to the barn early, where the chute and the day's duties waited.

The cattle weren't going to inseminate themselves after all.

She'd thought the avoidance plan had been going in her favor. For several hours, she'd been working without much interrup-tion, and now with the other hands on a late lunch break, she was pleasantly alone as she waited for Malcolm and Austin to deliver the rest of the tagged cows on her roster, a small subsection of the herd that no one seemed to be able to locate—a normal yet frustrating occurrence on a ranch this size. But clearly, she'd been wrong.

She'd known in her gut this was coming. Her best friend had never known how to leave well enough alone.

Blaze watched her, waiting on her answer. From the sight of his horse, Sarge, in the backdrop of the pasture, along with the muddied state of Blaze's boots, he'd finished whatever ranch duties were on his chore list today and was headed back into the security office.

Ignoring him, she reached for the AI gun and the semen tank. She had a harder stomach than most. It hadn't been until recently that they'd incorporated artificial insemination into the ranch plans. Beef cattle operations still largely allowed the bulls and the cows to mix during the breeding season, but it'd been her suggestion to Maverick that they separate out their best calving mamas for a more synchronized breeding protocol in order to maximize the ranch's profits. Even accounting for the time, cost, and labor of getting them in and out of the chute more than once, by her approximations, it'd be worth it if she could improve conception rates like she'd estimated. Another goal of hers.

She frowned.

If Austin and Malcolm ever showed up with the missing cattle, that is…

Blaze cleared his throat again, refusing to be ignored.

"Talk about what?" she said, turning away from Blaze and filling the AI gun once again.

"No, you're not avoiding me." Blaze shook his head. "Put down the bull semen and look at me, goddamn it."

Dakota let out a laugh and pulled back the AI's plunger. "You have to be joking." He always was, though only she seemed to recognize it for what it was—a means to deflect and avoid.

"I've never been more serious, Dakota."

Said the wolf, who for today's bad fashion specimen was wearing a BBQ-themed shirt that read: "I rub my meat while thinking of big racks."

She rolled her eyes. "No one would dare call you serious, Blaze."

He grumbled. "I mean it, Kotes."

She exhaled a long sigh. That damn nickname got her every time.

"Fine." She supposed the lowing cow in the chute wasn't going anywhere.

She set down the AI gun, careful to place it on a clean surface, though *any* surface was certainly no less unsanitary than the underside of a bull, but she didn't want to be personally responsible for any possible infections in the herd.

She stripped off her glove, then cast it into the nearby trash bin before she placed her hands on her hips, pegging Blaze with a hard stare. "Talk about what? Is Peaches missing again?"

"Don't play coy with me." He shook his head.

Beneath the brim of his Stetson, there was no hint of humor in his hardened features.

The intensity was unnerving, the mark of an alpha. Not the easygoing demeanor she was used to from him, though she knew he was more lethal than most. That didn't mean she had to like it.

She waved a hand in dismissal as she tried to turn away from him again. She'd already replayed every painful detail of last night. She didn't need to rehash it again. The memory was fresh. All the way down to how he had tasted of mint and lime and something that had reminded her of coriander but better? Mixed with the familiar smell of clove and campfire smoke that always seemed to linger on his skin. Her senses had been flooded with it, with him.

He'd felt *right* overtop her. Firm, alpha, pure male.

And she'd wanted more, wanted him to take her harder.

Claim her.

She blushed as she tried to turn away again, but Blaze's hand came down hard on the iron chute, blocking her between the metal bars and his body. "Don't try to avoid me, Dakota Le Hanh Nguyen." The growl was feral, every bit the hardened soldier she knew he was.

The fact that he knew her middle names and exactly when to use them as Mẹ always had shouldn't have made her angry, but it did. Her mother adored Blaze. Mẹ had always said he reminded her of a young version of Dakota's father, another MAC-V-Alpha veteran and Grey Wolf soldier. On more than one occasion, Mẹ had openly expressed her opinion that Dakota should date a "good boy" like Blaze.

He's not interested, she'd told her mother, though at the time she'd only said it to get Mẹ to stay out of her love life.

Somehow, the thought of that now only made the current situation worse. Mẹ's ideas about Dakota's dating, mixed with her own muddled emotions, had clearly taken over her brain last night, making her do and say things she normally wouldn't.

Making her stupid enough to think he felt the same.

"There's nothing to discuss. I'm fine." She tried to push past him, but Blaze blocked her path again. She growled at him, but still, he didn't budge.

He pegged her with a hard stare, eyes that saw too much and refused to let her hide. "I know when you lie, Kotes, just like every other wolf on this goddamn ranch. I watch body language. I was trained for it, so if you're going to try and pull wool over someone's eyes, take your pick of anyone on this ranch *but* me." His words were harsh, unlike him.

Emotion gathered in her throat, but she swallowed it down, refusing to show it. She held his gaze for a long beat, fighting to keep her lip from quivering before she pushed past him. No way was she allowing him to stop her.

He let her go.

Thankfully, she managed to save herself from showing too much of the embarrassment she was feeling. She never would have dared kiss him and risk their friendship if she'd thought the feeling was one-sided. She was organized, analytical. Not impulsive like she'd been last night. As if the thought that she'd thrown herself at him was mortifying enough, from the sounds of it, her kiss hadn't been merely uninteresting to him but unappealing.

Unwelcome.

She swallowed the lump that formed in her throat.

She knew a thing or two about feeling unwelcome.

She pushed the thought aside.

After he'd pushed her away, she'd already figured he hadn't been interested in a repeat. That fact hurt—a lot. But the idea that her advance hadn't just been uninteresting but he'd rather she *take her pick* of anyone else on the ranch but him?

That hurt even more.

Being permanently sidelined in the friend zone hadn't been how she'd wanted the evening to go. Naturally, she'd known this conversation would be difficult. She wasn't exactly ready to let go of the idea of *them* being a possibility, but now that she was thinking clearly, she would for the sake of their friendship. His rejection last night had given her clarity.

If they moved forward, they'd never be able to come back. Better that they pretend the whole thing never happened. She could set her sights back on her career where they belonged, to her next goal of proving herself in her new position, while they could still save their friendship, no matter how much she didn't want to forget it.

"The wool sure didn't seem to be pulled over your eyes when your hands were groping at every inch of my ass or laying me out on the couch beneath you," she muttered over her shoulder. It was a low blow. They'd both been caught up in the moment, not thinking straight, but she couldn't stop herself from saying it. Hurt fueled her.

She didn't see the change in him as much as her wolf sensed it— the awareness of an alpha male with a point to prove. She stiffened. Slowly, Blaze prowled into her line of vision, his movements predatory, lethal. She'd stupidly been trying to busy herself by gathering up the AI sheaths, and at his approach, she dropped them.

Blaze leaned on the fencing beside her. He didn't try to cage her in again, but he didn't have to. She wouldn't run from him, and she had no doubt that if she'd tried, he wouldn't let her go. The fact that after everything, she wanted him to do *exactly* that, to claim her like a true alpha of their species, only frustrated her more.

Her breath hitched. This close, she smelled the scent of cloves on his skin again, felt the nearness of his wolf, his presence as her packmate. She wanted that nearness, craved it. The idea of him, chasing her, wanting her, hunting her like she was his prey.

Inside, her wolf was howling for it.

"I thought you didn't want to talk about last night?" Blaze quirked a satisfied brow as that wry grin crossed his lips.

That playful smirk had never made her angry before, but this time it did. A delicious, familiar ache settled low in her belly.

His eyes flashed to his wolf as his gaze trailed over her, searing need and heat in the wake of every inch of skin his stare touched.

Across her neck, down her collarbone, over her breasts...

Her nipples hardened and a rush of warmth flooded her core. From the way that smirk only widened and the change in her scent, he knew she wanted him.

Damn him.

"I don't. That's all I have to say," she hissed. She tried to turn away.

He caught her wrist in his, his rough hands circling and caressing over the smoothness of her skin as he tugged her closer. Those warm blue eyes captured hers. The contact sent a sudden shock of desire through her. "We *need* to talk about it."

Her breath caught. That look was enough to melt her, but there was something almost...sad beneath the heat of his fiery blue eyes, and for a moment, it stilled her.

If she kept staring, she might lose herself to it.

Tearing her wrist away from him, she cleared her throat. She needed to put some distance between them, or they wouldn't come back from this. "Why? So you can reject me again? You want to talk about *taking picks* of packmembers on this ranch, fine. I get it. I'll pick someone else. Maybe Jasper, considering you seemed to enjoy me dancing with him so much at the wedding reception."

Blaze growled. "Jasper isn't good enough for you."

"Oh, and you are?" She raised a brow. "Too bad you made your feelings abundantly clear last night."

His hands came down on the chute again, pinning her now.

Exactly like she'd wanted.

Her breath caught. They were nearly chest to chest, nose to nose. One more inch and there'd be no more space between them. Her chest rose and fell in quick pants at the nearness of him. The scent of clove. The memory of mint and his tongue in her mouth.

She bit her lower lip.

Come closer. Please, she whispered inside her head.

Her whole body ached for it.

Blaze's eyes flashed to his wolf again, their close proximity clearly getting to him, too. "Stopping was the right thing to do."

"I didn't want you to do the right thing," she breathed.

The words fell from her lips before she could stop them.

They both stilled.

"I still don't want you to do the right thing," she whispered.

The rise and fall of Blaze's chest quickened, like he was struggling against himself. The Adam's apple of his throat moved as he swallowed. "I know," he grumbled.

A pained expression crossed his face, and he pushed away from her.

He stepped back, placing several feet of distance between them. Distance she had a feeling neither of them wanted. But they needed it. Their friendship required it.

Staring at the ground, Blaze placed his hands on the narrow, toned muscles of his hips as he shook his head. She couldn't see his face beneath the brim of his Stetson, but she knew that her words had struck a chord.

"It just…it didn't seem very difficult for you to walk away, that's all," she said. "That's why it hurt."

Blaze's head snapped up, his eyes a feral, fiery gold as he snarled. "You have no idea how difficult last night was for me."

She frowned. "Which is exactly why we can forget it ever happened and never speak of it again, before we ruin our friendship any more than we already have."

"I tried." Blaze shook his head, running a rough hand over his face. "I can't forget it happened. I won't."

"You can and you will. We both will."

He shook his head. "Don't say that," he growled. The hurt in his voice cut through her.

"It didn't mean anything."

Blaze froze.

The silent tension that followed nearly broke her, but she couldn't bring herself to stop. She had to fix things, put everything in reverse and make their friendship go back to normal. Anything was better than this...this...feeling that if things didn't work out, she'd lose him. She could pick someone else, but she *couldn't* lose him.

"It was a mistake, okay?" she whispered. "Like you said, I was drunk and upset. I wasn't thinking straight. I—"

"Stop, Dakota."

Dakota. Not Kotes.

Blaze held up a hand, refusing to look at her. He didn't growl, didn't snarl like an alpha normally would. He just sounded...hurt. "I've heard enough." He gave a rough clear of his throat, tipping his Stetson low as he made his way toward the exit. "I need to get to the security office. There's a packmember missing out in Bozeman."

Her eyes widened. "Is it serious?"

He didn't answer and the fact that he didn't worried her. Blaze always kept silent when things were too serious, either that or he made a joke to brush the inquiry off. Instead, he kept walking through the barn.

"Blaze," she called after him.

He growled again. "Don't, Kotes."

This time, the nickname cut her to the quick. She'd hurt him.

She followed after him, uncertain what to do. "I didn't mean to hurt you. I just wanted—"

He rounded on her then, the pain and frustration in his face tearing her in two. "Do you know how many times I'd imagined that *exact* moment?"

Dakota struggled to breathe. Imagined? He said it as if...

"Do you know how long I've waited for you to wake up and realize that I've wanted you for *years*?"

Dakota blinked. She tried to draw a breath into her lungs, but she couldn't. She'd misread his reluctance last night entirely.

"I've wanted you since long before I left for Russia, Kotes," he said, cutting her thoughts short. "Hell, if I'm honest, since the moment I broke my wrist showing off on that bronco back when we were twenty-one and while all the other females were trying to pity me, you lectured me about being nicer to the horses and told me I'd been acting like some reckless dipshit."

Dakota stifled a smile. "You were."

He reached out and brushed the rough pad of his thumb over her cheek.

She couldn't stop herself from closing her eyes, from leaning closer into his palm.

Before she knew it, his hand was gone.

Her eyes flickered open again.

Blaze was shaking his head before he glanced down at her, meeting her stare. "I don't know what happened last night or where the hell this is going, but it's going somewhere. Things are different now. I can't go back, whether you like it or not." The way he said it made it sound as if the thought terrified him.

It did her, too.

But they could get through this with their friendship intact, if they played their cards right. No more messy emotions or misunderstandings. They'd both clearly had enough of that already.

She forced a smile and shrugged. "Nothing has to change. We can go back to just being friends again."

Blaze raked a hand over the scruff of his chin. "I can't go back to just being your friend. Not after last night, and you can't either."

Her smile faded. "We can. We will. I'll prove it to you."

He let out a harsh laugh, like what she was saying wasn't even in the realm of possibility. He ran his tongue over his lips, wetting them briefly before he glanced down at her again. "There's something between us, and you know it."

She stepped closer to him, crossing her arms over her chest. "Then prove it."

The hurt on Blaze's face faded, replaced instead by that familiar, wry smile, like she was both foolish *and* amusing him. His voice was a low, growling purr. "I don't need to."

He stepped closer, coming only inches away from her, from her lips. She half expected him to kiss her right then, but he didn't.

"Don't kiss me," she breathed.

She wouldn't be able to resist any more if he did.

"I won't." He stepped back, adjusting the brim of his Stetson. "Not until you ask me to." His eyes flashed to his wolf. "And I won't have to wait long." His wolf eyes flicked over her in a quick, heated once-over before he started to step away again.

Dakota gulped. She was brave and cunning when she needed to be. She was one of the pack's elite warriors now after all. She knew battle. But this wasn't a war she was prepared to fight. Yet from the look of mischief in his eyes, Blaze was fully prepared to go to war over her heart. Against her, his best friend no less.

No enemy could ever know her better.

Blaze sauntered toward Sarge with that damn grin still on his lips. The thoroughbred had been grazing on a patch of pasture and let out a sharp nicker as Blaze placed his boot in the stirrup. He mounted the massive stallion's saddle.

Confirming her worse fear, Blaze cast her a devilish smirk over his shoulder as he tugged on the horse's reins. "Don't think I'll play fair just because we're friends."

Dakota released a long breath. She had little doubt about that.

Chapter 6

BLAZE RODE HARD, LEANING INTO THE PUSH AND PULL OF Sarge's smooth gallops until he reached the main compound that housed the security office. The noonday sun overhead lit the cobalt-blue sky, making it appear as if it and the clouds stretched on for an eternity. A gust of summer breeze rolled in, cooling where the warm sunrays had been beating down on his neck out in the pastures and causing a sheen of sweat to form. Blaze grinned. He'd tried to resist temptation, but he couldn't do it. Hell, he hadn't even lasted a full twenty-four hours.

He'd been a lost cause from the moment she'd kissed him.

Fresh mountain air filled his lungs as he inhaled, long and deep. It felt like the first full breath he'd taken in years. Who knew finally doing what he'd wanted to for far too long would have this effect? Consequences be damned. His past hadn't resurfaced, despite months of waiting, so maybe Maverick was right.

Maybe they wouldn't come for him after all.

He didn't know if the feeling would last or if it was the end of the darkness that'd held him under for so long, but if there was anyone who could help heal his war wounds, make him whole again, it was Dakota. He needed to let the past go. Give her himself, even though he feared if she looked too close, she'd see he didn't have much of himself to give anyway.

Slowing Sarge to a trot, Blaze smiled to himself. Despite his fear of what lay in their future, he'd do this for her, for both of them, though he'd never deserve her. She'd realize that soon enough, move on to someone who was truly worthy. Until then, he'd feel his way through, blind and uncertain, because he knew he'd find her even in the dark, and that was all that mattered. He wouldn't go back now—couldn't.

All he needed to do was convince her the risk was worth it. That *he* was worth it. However fleeting it would be.

Maybe then he'd start to believe it himself.

He reached the center building of the compound, pushing any question of exactly how he was going to do that aside and trusting it would come to him. Blaze tugged on Sarge's reins, drawing the horse to a stop. His mood darkened slightly. The safety of the pack didn't wait for anyone, him included, and he had all the time in the world to claim Dakota as his.

Even if he didn't want to wait another minute.

Situated at the heart of Wolf Pack Run, the Grey Wolf security rooms were housed in a massive log-cabin building along with the other ranch offices, a handful of conference rooms, and the rec lounge intended exclusively for the elite warriors, as well as the packmaster's private residence. Not far in the distance, the shadow of the log-cabin mess hall and community center loomed, the former of which led down into the pack's underground training gym. A generous array of cabins in the foreground formed the nearest homes and dorms of the more than 150 Grey Wolves who formed the main pack at Wolf Pack Run.

Even though he'd been born and raised here, it'd been a long time since Blaze had felt like he was truly home. But today he did, for a moment.

Handing Sarge off to a nearby hand who was riding back to the stables, Blaze headed into the security office with a spring in his step. Peaches had somehow found her way in alongside Kieran in the early hours of the morning, and the young wolf training underneath Blaze must not have had it in him to turn the aging feline away. Not that Blaze blamed him. Reportedly Peaches had threatened him with a tiny fang and claw.

Dismissing Kieran from his shift, Blaze spent his first several minutes in the office being bitten repeatedly as he attempted to shoe a half-awake Peaches off his keyboard. Eventually, the decrepit old cat became so annoyed with his attempts to pry her off that she scratched him across the cheek with a menacing yowl before promptly hefting up her generous weight and relocating to the cat bed Dakota had placed for her by the door.

Not *in* the cat bed but next to it, of course.

No cat had ever done anything they were supposed to.

Queen Peaches especially.

Finally seated at his computer, Blaze opened the files that he'd requested from the Bozeman subpack's security footage the previous evening. It was hours into reviewing the footage that the other shoe finally dropped. Shoulders aching from sitting at the desk for too long, Blaze flexed and tried to shake the edge of his frustration off. Clearly it'd been too much to ask that the missing subpack member, Flynn Porter, turn up unexpectedly after a long hunt, having lost all track of time, and they could all call it a day.

Hope shouldn't make a man complacent, Blaze reminded himself.

Hope didn't change reality.

He pushed back from the desk before he prowled across the room, knocking on Maverick's office door with two quick raps before he entered. Maverick sat at his desk, reading glasses on, poring over a stack of paperwork. At the sight of Blaze, he removed the gold wire-rimmed spectacles from his face. Young as he was, the packmaster's vision had always been more superior in his true wolf form than in skin. Not that it'd ever stopped him from besting their enemies.

"I have bad news," Blaze said.

Maverick's gaze fell to Blaze's shirt choice for the day and he frowned.

Blaze grinned. His outlandish fashion choices irked Maverick every damn time.

"Out with it, warrior," Maverick grumbled.

"Before Flynn disappeared, the Bozeman subpack had an

unexpected visitor." Blaze watched the knife scar over Maverick's left brow twitch. "Jonathan Felinae."

The packmaster snarled.

Led by the Grey Wolves, the seven shifter clans of the Seven Range Pact ruled the Montana mountains they called home, but for some time, a growing challenge had been mounting against the current cougar pride leader, Clay Felinae, by his own stepson, Jonathan, his second-in-command. If the tension continued much longer, the pride was primed for an internal coup.

Maverick swore. "What the hell was he doing out there?"

Blaze shook his head. "I'm not sure yet."

The pack's footage hadn't exactly been illuminating in that regard. "Do you think Jonathan…?" Maverick's voice trailed off.

The violence the question alluded to hung heavy between them.

Even for Blaze, the possibility of a dead packmate was no laughing matter, and each passing minute the wolf didn't reappear increased the likelihood they would find a body instead of a living packmember. Their packmates in Bozeman had been combing the woods for over seventy-two hours, but the other wolf's scent had gone cold, as if he'd vanished. The thought twisted Blaze with rage. Inside, his wolf howled. Finding whoever had done this would be his top priority.

And when he found them, he'd bleed their enemies dry himself.

"No." Blaze blew out a long breath. "I pulled his file, everything we have on him, and reviewed it all again. He's seedy, trying to do whatever he can to undermine Clay, not that either of us are fans of that bastard either. John's troublesome, but I don't think he's capable of that, not yet. But it's oddly…convenient." Blaze leaned against the doorframe, fists clenching and unclenching with his frustration. "In any case, Clay would welcome the news."

Maverick's eyes flashed to his wolf. "You think he'll use it as an excuse to claim we've been supporting Jonathan's challenge against him?"

Blaze's jaw drew tight. "He's been gunning to exit the Seven Range Pact for a long time. Clay's always resented that we lead instead of the cougars, even when it benefits him. We both know it's coming, ever since he hung us out to dry in that battle with the Wild Eight and the half-turned vamps several years back. Clay's never liked when things didn't go in his favor."

Maverick cast his glasses aside, shoving the stack of papers to the far side of the carved wooden desk. Sinking back into his chair, the packmaster massaged a hand over his temple for a brief moment. "I want more than just you working on this."

Blaze shrugged. "I can handle it alone. I have before."

"I know, but you don't have to. This could go wrong, fast. We need more than one pair of eyes on this."

A sharp knock sounded at the office door.

A moment later, Dakota stepped inside.

She was still dressed in the same worn jeans and teal tank top she'd been wearing in the barn earlier, and her long, midnight hair was pulled into a messy bun on top of her head. Several long tendrils fell down into her slender heart-shaped face. Blaze wanted to gently pull those strands down, watch that dark hair cascade over her shoulders like it had when she'd swayed into the shower last night.

He ached for her.

At the sight him, she frowned, as if she were unhappy to see him standing there, before she closed the office door behind her and turned toward Maverick. "I need to speak with you, Packmaster. If you have a minute." Her eyes darted toward Blaze, then back again.

"Dakota can partner with me," Blaze said, interjecting quickly. He cast a glance toward Maverick. "You've said before we're a dream team, after all."

A smirk crossed Blaze's face as he caught Dakota's eyes. He raked his gaze over her with slow and deliberate intent. That kiss had been all he could think about since last night, that and the sharp intake of breath that'd torn from her lips the moment she'd ground against the hardened length in his jeans. She hadn't been wearing any underwear beneath those satiny pajamas shorts and he'd smelled the wet heat of her, wanted to taste it.

He wanted *her* to think about that kiss, too, to remember how she'd moaned for him.

His eyes flashed to his wolf as that same familiar scent filled his nose. He couldn't ignore it, even if he'd tried. He was too attuned to her. Dakota wasn't unhappy to see him. Even in human form, he could smell her attraction, and it wasn't directed toward their mated packmaster.

Color flooded her cheeks, and from the quick way she tore her gaze away, she had to realize he'd smelled her arousal.

Blaze's smirk widened.

Dream team indeed.

"Partner on what?" she asked Maverick, refusing to look at Blaze a second longer.

Thankfully, the packmaster had enough of a poker face that if he scented the pheromones between Blaze and Dakota, he didn't show it.

"There's a missing subpackmate out in Bozeman," Maverick answered. "The situation is escalating—quickly. Jonathan Felinae, the cougars' second-in-command, may be involved."

Dakota's features drew into a look of concern. "That's not going to bode well with Clay."

"No," Blaze said. "It isn't."

Dakota cast him a frustrated look as if she wished he'd leave, even though he'd been there first. "And what does that have to do with me?"

Maverick nodded toward him. "I need you to partner with Blaze on this."

Dakota bristled. Maverick didn't notice it, but Blaze knew her well enough that *he* did. Her brow drew low in confusion. "Why me?"

"Why not you?" Blaze cast her another smirk. "I asked for you."

To his surprise, Dakota's upper lip twisted with a barely hidden curl as if she might growl at him. In front of the packmaster.

Blaze laughed.

Maverick glanced between them, clearly sensing the tension but choosing to ignore it. "I want more than one elite warrior on this."

"Dakota would be the perfect fit," Blaze said, throwing her under the proverbial bus. He crossed his arms over his chest as he leaned against the doorframe. She'd forgive him later, after he'd convinced her of the idea of *them*. "Knowing what we do now, if Jonathan's reaching out to unsuspecting subpack members for support, it's only a matter of time before things escalate with the pride. When Clay gets wind of Jonathan's involvement, regardless of how vulnerable that will make the cougars in the long run, he'll use it as an excuse to exit the Seven Range Pact. Not to mention we have a potentially dead packmate on our hands."

"We keep this on a need-to-know basis then." Maverick leaned forward, his fingers pressing together in a steeple overtop his desk. "What are you suggesting?"

Blaze pegged him with a hard stare. "We need to be prepared. While I search for Flynn, we need to have other allies in place to fill the vacancy, so it doesn't leave the Pact or Wolf Pack Run open to attack, especially since movement among the vampires is rising again. We've known they were likely gearing up for something big since they'd been lying low for so long, and this may be the start of it. Our best chance at an ally is the Arctic wolves."

Maverick nodded, encouraging Blaze to continue.

"We've been toying with the idea of a more formal alliance with them for a while now, and I hear they've been looking at following our lead and allowing female packmembers to join their elite warrior ranks. Dakota could serve that role on both fronts, be an ambassador. Invite them here to model our integration of females into the ranks while cementing the alliance. She's perfect for it. Brave, fierce, driven, organized, with strong attention to detail."

"I agree." Maverick nodded, then glanced toward Dakota. "Do you think you're up to it? That's a hefty first task. The Arctic wolves are just as hardheaded as our alpha males, maybe more, and culturally, they have different customs and expectations than us."

"She's more than capable," Blaze said.

"Are you an expert on my résumé now?" Dakota's gaze narrowed on him, and then she nodded to Maverick. "If you think I'm the right fit, I'll do any task you see fit, Packmaster. First assignment or not, I'd be honored."

"Good." Maverick stood. "It's settled then." He slipped his glasses into the top desk drawer. "Now I better go. I'm nearly late. I promised Sierra I would be at her next exam with Belle in fifteen minutes." He rounded the desk and headed toward the door where Dakota had entered moments earlier.

Dakota followed after him. "Packmaster, I need to use the pack's drones. There's a missing section of the herd. Austin and Malcolm haven't been able to locate them."

"That would have been avoided if you'd put the digital trackers on them like I suggested." Blaze brushed some of the mountain dirt from his nails onto his shirt before a wry smirk twisted his lips.

Dakota glared at him. "I was worried about infection. It was a reasonable concern," she shot back. Turning back toward Maverick, she stared at him. "The drones?"

"That's Blaze's area," Maverick said, opening the door. The packmaster flicked his gaze over his shoulder and down to Blaze's shirt again, scowling in disapproval. "He's all yours."

Maverick closed the door behind him, making a swift exit as he hurried off to his mate.

Blaze couldn't stop the low chuckle that vibrated in his chest. "See? I'm all yours, Kotes. Even he knows it."

Dakota stared at the wooden door the packmaster had exited through only a few moments before, trying to calm the growing frustration in her chest. She could feel the heat rising in her cheeks, and what mortified her most was that hadn't been the *only* place Blaze had made her feel hot in the span of a single conversation. And in front of the packmaster, no less.

She growled, rounding on her best friend. "I know what you're trying to do."

Blaze quirked a brow. "Do you?"

As if that were the end of their discussion, he retreated into his office through the open adjoining door.

She charged after him. "It's not going to work." She placed her hands on her hips. "Forcing me to work with you on this was smart, but we'll divide and conquer, stay out of each other's hair."

Blaze sat on the edge of his desk, crossing his long legs at the ankles, his muscled arms folded over the width of his chest. Who knew how sexy a man's forearms could be? Not to mention the position highlighted exactly how wide his shoulders were. How lean and narrow his waist was. It didn't help matters that she knew exactly how the ridged muscles of his stomach curved into a well-formed V. Her mouth nearly watered at the thought and she bit her lower lip. She wouldn't think about that now.

Not at all.

"I was trying to give you an opportunity to impress in your new role," he said. "You said last night you felt the need to prove yourself. I figured you'd want that. We both know how goal-oriented you are."

At the mention of her goals, she frowned. "I do, but I know you, and that wasn't the only reason." She gave him a deliberate once-over exactly as he'd done to her. "Who's playing coy now?"

Blaze grinned. "So I had ulterior motives." His eyes flashed to his wolf. "The opportunity to undress you being one of them."

Her jaw dropped before she scowled at him again. He was her best friend. How had she never realized he could be so…so…deliciously arrogant? She liked it more than she wanted to.

She growled. "You can't say that sort of thing to a coworker," she snapped.

"Is that what I am now? A friend? A coworker? A fellow warrior? The only man you've ever really wanted?" That wry grin crossed his lips. "I can't keep track anymore."

Her hands clenched into fists. He was the devil. "Quit being so cocky."

"I will once you ask me to kiss you again."

She tapped her foot with forced impatience, as if she were bored with this conversation. "We've been through this. I won't."

"Maybe someday…" Blaze pushed off the desk, crossing the small space of the security office toward her. He reached for the door, shutting it behind her with an audible snick as he leaned over her. "In the meantime, there are plenty of other things that can happen that don't involve kissing."

She could smell the hint of clove on his skin, feel the warmth radiating from him. "Don't count on it."

That easy grin widened, making her heart beat faster and slower at the same time. "Oh, I'm counting on it." His voice was a purring growl. "I can smell you want me, and we both know it."

"Desire's often best left unfulfilled." She looked away from him.

"At first." He circled around her, leaning close to her ear and whispering to her from behind. "But eventually, the ache gets so bad that you can't stop yourself from taking it." He nipped at her ear with his canines.

A shiver ran through her, even as she batted him away. "Taking what?"

"Everything that's been forbidden from you, everything you haven't allowed yourself to have. I know a thing or two about that, Kotes." He stood in front of her again now. Reaching out, he tucked a stray strand of her hair behind her ear. "I know the idea of us scares you. Hell, I know I've been fighting this for a long time, but I can't pretend anymore. We both want this. Why stop it from happening?"

She couldn't take this a second longer. The ache in her chest, the flutter of her heart, the growing need tugging low in her belly. "Because I can't lose you, damn it," she snapped. Hands clenched into fists again as she glared at him. "There. Is that what you wanted me to say? Are you satisfied now?"

Despite the fact that they were alone, he leaned down to her level, whispering against her ear as if his words were their secret. "The only thing that would satisfy me is finishing what we started in your cabin."

She pushed past him, heading for the door to his office that led into the hall. "Didn't you hear what I said? I can't lose you."

He snarled in frustration. "You won't."

He said it with such confidence, it made her chest ache. She wanted to believe it, wished she could believe it as much as he did, but she knew how hot and heavy affairs like this ended, and it wasn't in happily-ever-afters. Not to mention she didn't have the best track record when it came to knowing what she wanted from life, to being fulfilled by her goals.

This would be no different.

She was letting her mother's expectations for her life get too far into her head. That was all.

"You don't know that."

"No, I don't." He prowled toward her again, placing a hand on the door just above her head as he leaned in close. He captured the edge of her tank top between his fingers, toying with it. She felt her insides give a delicious twist with every movement. "But what I do know is that I know you better than anyone, know the way your breath hitches when you're excited, know when you're most relaxed, how to make you moan. I know every one of your darkest fantasies, Kotes, because you've told them all to me." His wolf eyes flashed with dark promise. "I could make you come so many times you won't worry about our friendship anymore. I want to. Right now. If you'd let me."

Dakota struggled to breathe as she gazed up at him. She was drunk with desire. Practically dizzy with it.

But she wouldn't give in.

Not yet.

Not when their nearly decade-long friendship hung in the balance. She loved him and what they already had together too much for that.

That had to be enough.

"I'm sure you could," she said hotly. "But I'm not going to let you." Reaching behind her, she twisted the door handle, fumbling backward through the open gap and away from him.

"We'll see." Blaze chuckled, his wolf eyes still burning molten gold. "I'm still invited to Mę's for dinner next Thursday, aren't I?"

"Of course." She waved a dismissive hand at him. "It doesn't matter that I'm angry with you. She'd pitch an absolute fit if you weren't there. Sometimes I swear she likes you more than she likes me."

"You know that's not true."

"I know. But sometimes she acts like it."

He stepped toward her and she closed the door an inch farther, using it like a shield between them.

"If you aren't on your best behavior in the meantime, I'll give Peaches a bath and then release her into the stables again. Maverick, and Wes for that matter, won't be pleased with you if she pisses off Black Jack and all the other studs, and Lord knows she could use a bath."

At even the mention of such a possibility, Queen Peaches looked up from where she'd been grooming herself atop Blaze's desk chair and hissed.

"I love you, too," Dakota cooed at her.

It was as close to affection as anyone would get from Peaches most days, unless they were catering to her every whim.

Dakota started to pull the door closed, but Blaze placed a hand there.

"You're not really angry with me, Kotes." His graveled voice was soft, tender. "I've seen you angry before, and as much as you're trying to make it seem that way, this isn't it. You're scared and we both know it."

A large lump formed in her throat. "It doesn't matter what I'm feeling."

Blaze nodded, his eyes flicking down the hall she was no doubt retreating to. "Where are you headed?"

"I'm on patrol tonight."

He smiled. "Great. I am, too." He pushed through the crack in the door and out into the hall with her.

"No, you're not. I looked at the schedule. You weren't on the list."

He adjusted his Stetson, that easy grin making her knees weak. "Checking to see if you'd see me again?"

"No. I was trying to *avoid* you, and I was pleased to see your name wasn't there."

"It is as of now." He headed down the hall ahead of her.

"You can't do that," she called after him.

He cast her a dark smile over his shoulder. "Of this entire pack, I'm ranked only fourth down from the packmaster. I can do whatever I damn well please."

She followed after him. "Tell Maverick that."

"I have. On more than one occasion." Blaze shoved his way through the exit door that led out into the warm Montana night. The summer sun had started to disappear beyond the horizon, painting the mountaintops of the Absarokas in a blended array of teal, pink, and blue.

Almost as handsome as the cowboy currently grinning at her.

"Who will watch the security office? Work the case?"

"I think it'll hold for one night." Blaze grinned again. "But will you?"

Dakota couldn't be certain.

Chapter 7

THIS GAME OF CAT AND MOUSE WAS ALREADY TEARING HER TO shreds. Why did he insist upon doing this? Dakota shook her head, following after Blaze as they headed out near the forest. She wanted to stomp off and tell him to leave her alone, but she couldn't spare another moment.

Each evening, several pairs of the pack's fighters led by the elite warriors patrolled the perimeter of Wolf Pack Run, the Grey Wolves' vast ranchlands, along with the streets of downtown Billings. Led by the Grey Wolves, the Seven Range Pact—an allied agreement among the seven shifter clans who ruled the Montana mountains they called home—held a treaty with the Execution Underground, a clandestine organization of human hunters whose goal was the protection of humanity from the supernatural world.

The agreement offered the Seven Range Pact immunity from persecution by the human hunters in exchange for keeping their mutual bloodsucking enemies at bay. For which the Grey Wolves had created their nightly patrol schedule.

As she and Blaze reached the edge of the forest, Dakota lifted a silent hand in greeting to the patrol group. Dean Royal, the Grey Wolf front-of-house director for the ranch's business operations, was the warrior in charge tonight, and he was already addressing the patrol with updates from the previous evening. Their long standoff with the vampires had been quiet for some time, but they were seeing a resurgence on that front. The vamps never stayed away for long.

Another shoulder nudged against her own, drawing her attention.

Aaliyah, Dean's mate.

"I hear congratulations are in order, Ms. Elite Warrior," she whispered, her dark eyes darting toward Dean to reveal her information source as a smile curved her lips.

Of course, the other elite warriors would have voted their approval on the candidacy before Maverick made the offer, and Dean would have told his wife. Nothing stayed secret around the ranch for long.

Dakota nodded, but the smile she returned felt forced. She bumped her shoulder back against Aaliyah's half-heartedly. "You're next. We both know it."

"Dakota," Dean's deep vibrato interrupted their whispering.

Blaze had whispered something in Dean's ear only a moment earlier.

"Care to dole out the assignments tonight?" Dean cast her a warm grin. It was part playful rebuke for not paying attention and for her late arrival and part acknowledgment of her newfound role.

Blaze grinned as if it were his doing.

"Of course she does," Aaliyah answered for her, giving Dakota's bicep a quick, reassuring squeeze before she moved to her mate's side. "We all know *tactics* aren't your strong suit, darlin.'" The affectionate jab elicited a few chuckles from their packmates as Aaliyah wrapped her arms around her mate, brushing his locs from his shoulder. Her wolf eyes flashed as the warrior met her mate's gaze with a heated stare.

Dakota had to glance away. Something about the intimacy made her chest ache. She could feel Blaze watching her. She cleared her throat. "Austin and Cheyenne take the north perimeter. Ace and Blaze, south. You and Aaliyah take the west. Malcolm and I can go downtown, then double back on the east on the way home." She shot a quick glare toward Blaze to emphasize that not having him partner with her like usual had been intentional.

If he wanted to pull strings to push them together, she could do the same to keep them apart and salvage their friendship. Two could play at that game.

Blaze grumbled a curse under his breath and his eyes flashed to his wolf.

Ignoring the subtle exchange between them, Dean's smile beamed. "Spoken like an elite warrior."

If the secret wasn't fully out before, it was now.

After Dakota awkwardly fumbled her way through a round of quick congratulations from her packmates, the pairs dispersed to their assignments. The other three duos headed into the forest, Blaze scowling the whole time as he headed off with Ace, while she and Malcolm trekked to one of the ranch's old trucks.

The ride into downtown Billings was a silent one. Dakota had chosen the taciturn, moody Grey Wolf executioner for her partner tonight in part because she'd known the conversation would be minimal. She didn't think she had it in her to make small talk, considering the confused feelings clouding her mind, but Malcolm didn't ask questions and she didn't offer an explanation for her silence.

Like usual over the past few months, their patrol through downtown was uneventful—the vampires favored subtlety to go undetected. It was how the pack knew something was happening in the vampires' ranks. Those bloodsucking peacocks were only subtle when they had something to hide. Dakota and Malcolm navigated their way through the streets of the small city with ease.

The neon lights from the late-night western bars seared against her wolf retinas. The twangs of country music inside were too loud and obnoxious for her tastes, but despite the overload of human stimulation, she couldn't shake the feeling of being watched. Humans had a sixth sense about their presence that, though they ignored it, outed their kind as *other*, but she couldn't shake the feeling that the gaze stalking her every move *wasn't* human.

She and Malcolm had already returned to Wolf Pack Run, parked the truck on the edge of the east border perimeter, and were patrolling the ranch on foot before she finally convinced herself she was being ridiculous. They hadn't seen a single vamp all night. She would have caught the scent by now.

A few yards away, Malcolm shifted back into human from where he'd been sniffing the ground as his wolf. She'd opted to start out on foot, which had slowed their pace, but she didn't want to have to retrieve her boots and clothes from the far edges of the ranch in the morning. The laundry patrol only went so far, and she only owned one pair of boots. She had clinic in the morning, so she'd need to get started early.

"Need to take a leak," Malcolm grumbled through the darkness.

The full moon overhead appeared as little more than a sliver through the trees, casting beams no farther than the tops of the towering pines.

"You could've lifted a leg," Dakota called after him as he retreated into the darkness.

The Grey Wolf executioner grumbled something unintelligible under his breath before he disappeared into the forest brush.

Dakota released a short huff and flopped down on a small nearby boulder. She'd thought maybe the familiar routine of the evening would be a comfort—meditative even—but instead, it'd only given her mind too much room to wander.

Back to Blaze and how he thought she was going to give in so easily. She wasn't.

That much was clear.

She picked up a small rock by her boot and chucked it into the darkness with all the force and frustration she could muster.

Nothing.

Still unsatisfied, she reached toward the mountain dirt, prepared for a repeat, but as her hand connected with the small piece of shale, the hairs on the back of her neck stood on end.

Slowly, she sat upright. "Malcolm?" she called into the darkness.

No answer.

Dropping the rock, her hand tentatively fell to the blade at her belt as she stood. She gripped the hilt, a pulse of bravery coming with it. There was movement in the trees to her right. Subtle. Barely noticeable.

But still there.

"Malcolm?" she called once more.

No answer.

Carefully, she drew her blade. The silver glinted in the pale moonlight.

Nostrils flared and senses alert, she breathed deep. Vampires smelled sickly sweet, a mirage they used to make them more appealing to their human prey and mask the true rancid scent of death beneath. It *had* to be a vampire. What else could it be?

But if it were a bloodsucker, she should have smelled it, and yet...

A large ripple of movement skittered through the underbrush so fast, she could barely track it, accompanied by an unearthly sound. One she'd never heard before. She lifted her blade, her eyes flashing to her wolf in warning as a feral growl tore from her lips. Vampires were fast. That was for certain. But all she could smell was woods and forest, earth and dirt, pine and shale rock. The scent of wolves, her kind, and something...not.

Crouching low, she prepared to shift within seconds, but as quickly as the building dread in her gut had come, the tension dissipated. It was gone.

She was alone in the dark again. Nothing but the chill of the night wind nipping at her.

Had she imagined...?

A louder, less subtle approach shuffled nearby, and a moment later, Malcolm emerged, clearly having sniffed out a sufficient spot to piss. Wolves would be wolves after all, and the males of their species still marked their territory as such. Malcolm grumbled something about a deer downwind, but Dakota paid no attention.

For a long beat, she remained silent, listening to the brush of the trees, before she shook her head. "Did you hear that?"

"Hear what?"

"I'm not sure exactly," she breathed out.

Malcolm shot her an annoyed look. "I'm not one for guessing games."

"Neither am I." She frowned.

Malcolm gave a dismissive shrug. "I scented a dead deer ten yards south and followed it. Damn leeches can't get their own food, so apparently they're resorting to killing ours now."

Dakota stared into the darkness. "Vampires don't drain animals." She specialized in the pack's livestock. She knew that without a doubt.

"Well, apparently, this one did." Malcolm brushed past her. "We'll search the perimeter, though it looks like you must have scared it off."

Tentatively, Dakota moved to sheath her blade, then hesitated.

The sound of the wind brushing through the pine needles and the surrounding leaves shivered around them. Empty. She exhaled a breath she hadn't realized she'd been holding.

"Must have," she said finally.

Several hours later, long after abandoning her hiking boots and clothing in favor of her true nature, Dakota reached their return point at the main compound. She shifted into human form, feeling the last of her fur draw back beneath her skin with a quick, vibrating shake of her shoulders. She was still reeling from that strange encounter and wondering whether it'd been her imagination getting the better of her or not.

After nearing home, Malcolm had pawed at her haunches, nipping at her in quiet communication before he'd disappeared deeper into the trees in favor of turning in for the night. Several of the other patrol pairs were just now returning.

Naked and panting, Dakota pressed a hand against the bark of an oak. In the distance, Dean and Aaliyah shifted into human form. Taking each other's hands, they walked slowly back to their cabin together, where no doubt their sleeping young lay waiting, watched over by another packmember. From the couple's grins as they conversed, for them, all thought of any of the evening's threats were erased. She wished she could say the same.

The sharp prickle of dread from the night's strange encounter lingered. She scanned the edge of the forest for Blaze, only to find him in wolf form a short way from the tree line. She'd recognize the gray-and-black thatched patterns of his fur anywhere.

Nearby, Cheyenne and several others of the pack's females who were poised to shift and take the next evening patrol stripped off their clothes as they chatted among one another. The pack was uninhibited when it came to nudity beneath the full moon where they were closer to wolf than human; their differences blurred into an animal unawareness. When that didn't happen, they averted their gazes, caring only to look in one another's eyes as true wolves did. The eyes were the window to the soul, the indicator of hierarchy, pack position, and potential challenge.

Nudity was different when they were alone or when they drew attention toward it.

Dakota watched Blaze as he prowled near the other females, the hackles of his fur raised. He paused for a brief moment, sniffing the air, before he slunk farther toward them. Cheyenne called something to him that from this distance was lost on the wind, then she smiled. The apples of her cheeks turned a pretty shade of pink. Prowling closer, Blaze snapped playfully at Cheyenne's ankles in response, eliciting a round of giggles and calls egging him on from several of the other females beside the gorgeous nude she-wolf. Dakota felt herself tense.

Cheyenne was a runner, long and lean, and her body showed it.

And Blaze was never one to disappoint when called on for a show.

Circling around the group of tittering females, the air around Blaze's wolf form seemed to move and bend as he slowly shifted back to human. Not all at once as they usually did, but piece by piece. It was difficult to do, something only a handful of the pack's most powerful alphas could manage, but Blaze could with ease. He was *that* good and always willing to show off when asked. Subtlety and humility weren't her best friend's strong suits.

Dakota had seen him do it once before years earlier when he'd been showing off after too many drinks at the tail end of one of the pack's yearly ceremony gatherings, but she hadn't seen a repeat since then. It'd been before his MAC-V-Alpha days. To a human, the process would likely have been a grotesque sight, but to their kind, it was a testament to the power he held—power he could easily control and manipulate.

Even for fun.

His arms came first, followed by legs and torso, until he walked on two legs again. None of his wolf remained, save for his canine head, a pair of furred pawed hands, and the furred male part between his legs that was quickly changing back into—

Dakota gasped, forcing herself to avert her gaze as the she-wolves watching him let out a round of pleased girlish shrieks and howling catcalls. Clearly, the last transformed *appendage* for lack of a better term had been…impressive, to say the least.

Growling, Dakota turned back toward the group. Blaze was fully in human form now, and naked in a way she could manage to ignore as he shook out his head, the last of his wolf fur transforming into locks of human hair. He cast the giggling she-wolves a showy, pleased smile.

Her smile. The one he gave her.

Dakota snarled.

Shifting back into wolf form, she sprinted the dozen or so yards to where Blaze and the other she-wolves remained. Cheyenne and the other females were still ribbing him and whistling in appreciation over their shoulders as they made their way toward the forest to shift. Dakota ran straight to Cheyenne, the instincts of her wolf clouding all human reason and judgment. Her paws connected with Cheyenne's bare chest, knocking the other female to the ground.

"Dakota?" Cheyenne shrieked. "What the hell?"

Cheyenne was Dakota's friend. All the females of the pack were.

But beneath the moon like this, they were wolf first and human second.

Friendship yielded to animal instinct, to pack dominance.

Dakota snarled, hackles raised and teeth snapping at Cheyenne's heels as the other female scrambled back from where Dakota had knocked her over. Cheyenne shifted into wolf form. Dakota drew up on her, neck to neck as she bared her teeth, growling and snapping at the less dominant female to make her message clear.

Back off. He's mine.

Cheyenne tucked her tail between her legs, retreating as Dakota snapped in warning at the fur of her throat and muzzle.

A large hand wrenched at the fur of Dakota's neck, pulling her back.

She snapped at whoever held her. Cheyenne might have been retreating, but Dakota wasn't finished putting the other female in her place yet.

"Shit, Kotes," Blaze swore from where she'd nipped him.

His hand was bleeding, but he ignored it. At the rate their kind healed, the shallow, superficial wound would be gone in only a few minutes. Blaze hauled her back several feet, his strength besting hers even in wolf form. He waved a dismissive hand at the other females who'd shifted and begun circling her and Cheyenne, eager to watch a female-to-female challenge that, depending on the outcome, could shift rank within the pack hierarchy.

"Go on," he growled. "Show's over."

When the females didn't immediately retreat, he snarled, the sound as animal as any of the wolves circling them. Knowing Blaze's place as one of the pack's top alphas, the other females shrunk back in response. They slunk off into the forest, Cheyenne included, tails tucked between their legs at the reprimand.

At least Dakota's message had been clear.

Blaze looked down at her. His own eyes flashed to his wolf. "What the hell was that?"

Pulling back from his hold on her scruff, she nipped at his hand, retreating slightly before she shook out her coat. A moment later, she was in human form again, naked, but still on her hands and knees. She stood. "What the hell was that?" she repeated. She couldn't believe him. "Really, Blaze?" She glared at him. "What's wrong with you?"

He shrugged. "ADHD, PTSD. Do you want the whole alphabetic list?" When she didn't smile at the joke, he threw up his hands in surrender as he cast her a sheepish grin. "In my defense, it was the full moon and I was left unsupervised."

She growled. "Don't try to be funny."

Blaze ran a hand through his hair, shaking his head. "I didn't think you'd go full alpha she-wolf on poor Cheyenne. She didn't do anything but look at me, same as you were."

Dakota's jaw dropped. "You *knew* I was watching?"

Blaze lifted a single shoulder before he let it drop. "I may have scented you nearby."

Dakota's eyes widened in anger as her jaw dropped even more. "You instigated that on purpose?"

"I didn't *instigate* anything," he said, putting emphasis on her word choice. He drew closer, too close for comfort considering they were both naked. His eyes trailed down her nude form, aware of her in a way he shouldn't have been, considering they were in the moonlight.

Heat flooded her cheeks.

"I was showing off for *you*," he whispered, "because I knew *you* were looking. There's only one she-wolf on this ranch whose attention I want. I was playing around, having fun in front of *our* packmates because I wanted *you* to notice. Like I always have. I'm allowed to do that."

She crossed her arms over her chest and scowled at him. "Not in front of Cheyenne you're not."

A wide grin crossed his lips in response. "That wouldn't be jealousy I detect, would it, Kotes?"

Damn him. He really *was* the devil. She'd seen him rib and provoke their packmates with that irreverent charm before, but he'd never turned it on her.

His confidence was infuriating.

"Not a chance," she snapped. She turned on her heel and marched back toward the main part of the compound, ready to be done with this awful evening. She'd apologize to Cheyenne in the morning, explain what'd gotten into her. Her friend would understand that her primal instincts had gotten the best of her.

"Of course." Blaze followed her, refusing to be ignored. "But you know, if it *was* jealousy, I'm yours, Kotes. I always have been. If you wanted me to kiss you again, claim me as your own, all you'd have to do is ask."

"I won't ask."

"Pity." He stepped in front of her, blocking her path. His eyes flashed to his wolf. "I'd rather it be you watching me and wanting to warm my bed each night."

She pushed past him. "Stop it."

"Or what?" he called after her.

She turned back toward him. "You'll ruin it," she yelled.

"Ruin it?"

She swallowed down the lump in her throat. "Our friendship."

Blaze let out a short huff of a laugh. "You should have thought of that *before* you kissed me."

She glared at him. He was right. She hadn't thought of it. She'd started this, and she hated that she had. Now more than ever. "Well, I didn't think about it, alright? But now that I have, at least one of us has to have some sense."

He closed the space between them, drawing near enough that

she was aware of how large he was, his predatory gait and the smooth way he moved. "The only sense I have is that you want this as badly as I do." He reached out, placing two fingers underneath her chin. "Given enough time, I'll make you see it. Our friendship can withstand the test."

"Don't be so confident."

"Don't make it so easy." He started to walk away.

Dakota growled again, following after him. "I sent an email to Jasper this afternoon." She placed her hands on her hips, giving him a triumphant grin. She hadn't sent Jasper anything, but she said it anyway. To irk Blaze, of course.

Jasper was handsome but not interested in her. At least, she'd felt that way when she'd last seen him at the packmaster's wedding reception. The Grey Wolf international liaison and lawyer was appealing. He had a cosmopolitan air about him that was a novelty among all the rugged cowboys of Wolf Pack Run. Not to mention the Indian Brit's sexy accent was enough to make any of the pack's females swoon, but he hadn't seemed very into her. There hadn't been much in the way of chemistry. But if she mentioned him, maybe then Blaze would get the memo that they were going to stay friends like she said—and that was final.

"You want to play hardball with jealousy, chew on that." She sped up her gait.

They'd nearly reached her cabin, and she realized too late that she'd unwillingly let him walk her home. He always did, but somehow that seemed unacceptable now, different.

Everything was different—and she had to fix it.

Blaze snarled. "If you think that'll work, you're wrong."

She mounted her porch steps. "And why's that?"

Blaze gripped the railing, staring up at her through the darkness. She tried not to notice how the muscles of his arm bunched, causing his military tattoo to flex. She wouldn't let her eyes go any lower. Even though she wanted to.

Blaze's voice was a growl as he watched her. "Because you're mine. You have been for a long time, and every other wolf shifter in this pack knows it. You're the only one who refuses to see it."

She stared down at him from the top of her porch steps. "I'm not yours unless I say so."

"You will." He gave a single nod. "Give it a week."

He turned, heading back in the direction of his own cabin, or maybe the security office, still nude post-shift. She tried not to notice the large expanse of his shoulders, the muscled, round curve of his ass. She really, really did. But dear Lord, the man was a sight.

"I expect my drone for the cattle ready first thing in the morning," she called after him. "If I don't locate the missing part of the herd soon, their calving will be off schedule by a week."

"A week won't make a difference. The cattle will hold." He waved a hand at her.

"What does that mean?"

He cast a dark smirk over his shoulder. "It means you'll get your drone as soon as you agree to talk about whatever this is between us—or when you ask for another kiss. Whichever comes first."

She gaped. Just when she was warming up to him again. "You can't do that. That's blackmail."

"Clearly you have no idea the kinds of things I did in Russia. Blackmail would be the least of it."

"I would have an idea if you'd told me." The hurt in those words was genuine.

She'd never asked him what had happened there. Her father had been a soldier, too. She knew better. But that didn't mean she wasn't highly aware of the fact that he hadn't told her either, hadn't trusted her with the darker parts of himself.

"Believe me when I say you don't want to know, Dakota." He placed his hands on the narrow ridges of his hips. "If you think a single kiss would ruin our friendship, my war stories would set your hair on fire, make our enemies look like fucking saints." He huffed a humorless laugh.

"I hate when you do that."

He was walking again, headed back home. "Do what?"

"Push me away with a sarcastic excuse or a joke."

He paused, turning back toward her. That dark fire was in his eyes again, the one that when she stared long enough looked oddly like hurt, pain. "There's only one of us pushing the other away right now, Kotes, and for once, it isn't me." He started to shift back into his wolf. "Think about that."

Dakota did think about it. Long into the night. So long that not even the book she tried to read or the hot shower meant to wash the day's worries away released it from her mind. She thought about it until she fell asleep, all the confused feelings melting away...and the anxiety of her strange encounter in the woods slipped from her mind.

Chapter 8

Sleep proved difficult yet again.

Blaze paced the length of the security office, aware that he needed rest but unable to find it in himself to settle down, to be still. He hadn't been able to relax since the earlier part of the evening when Dakota had nearly mauled Cheyenne in response to him showing off like some kind of reckless, foolish jokester. His thoughts raced. His actions had been a poor decision at best. But he was good at poor decisions, always had been, and he was still undecided on whether it was a *complete* mistake. Dakota's response had felt like an indication that he was right, that things *were* changing between them, whether she was willing to admit it or not.

That proof hummed through him.

Exhaling a long breath, he tried to push the thought from his mind. Regardless of the evening's end, it *had* been a mistake to follow her out on patrol. His decision to do so had been impulsive, driven by the desire to be near her. Very on brand for him. Yet now, he had to catch up on the several hours of work he'd missed, which only provided him with an excuse to tell himself that he didn't *need* to sleep. At least not yet.

He'd been trained to go days without it.

A knock sounded on the office door, and a moment later, Austin poked his head in.

"Yeah?" Blaze scratched at the back of his neck. Austin had caught him pacing the room again.

"Mav tasked me with turnin' out the lights for the night, lockin' up," the Texan drawled. "Wasn't sure if you or Kieran were still in here."

Blaze waved a hand. "Don't worry about it. I'll do it."

Austin nodded before he started to close the office door.

"Austin," Blaze said, stopping him short.

The Grey Wolf medic glanced toward Blaze again.

"Do you...uh...have anything in your med kit that could help me sleep?" If sleep was difficult, asking for help, showing his wounds to his packmates was even harder, even a packmate as kind and understanding as Austin.

The Texan was one of the best among them, calm and fair, levelheaded and full of heart—a loyal friend. Not a single member of the pack disliked him; even overly pissed-off Malcolm had taken a shine to him. Blaze couldn't say the same for himself. He and his humor were too much for some. He'd never been good at being anything but unapologetically himself.

Not since he'd been discharged anyway.

"No can do, amigo. Short of a horse tranquilizer, it takes more than a couple melatonin or sleeping pills to knock a wolf your size out." Austin cast him a sympathetic look. "Have you been working out before bed to burn the energy off like I told you?"

Blaze nodded, glancing to the floor to avoid his packmate's worried expression. "It worked for a while, but lately, it's been failing me."

"Meditation?" Austin offered.

Blaze grumbled. "I'm not into any of that namby-pamby bull."

"Spoken like a true soldier." Austin shook his head. "You'll sacrifice yourself for others but hardly know when to help yourself."

"That why I'm asking you." Blaze shrugged. "Because you're good at taking care of people and shit, you know?"

Austin laughed. "I'll take that as a compliment, especially from the one wolf on this ranch who keeps all of us grinning, even when it's hard. Your jokes aren't for your own benefit, they're for ours, so we don't worry as much, whether it be about our enemies or you," Austin said, seeming to know exactly what Blaze needed to hear.

Blaze snorted. "You think more highly of me than my mother."

Austin smiled an amused grin, then he eased the door farther open, leaning inside. His dark eyes flicked to the computer where the Bozeman footage was frozen on the screen. "My advice for tonight: turn off the screens for a while, call Kieran in—too much blue light is *no bueno* for you *or* your wolf—then go wherever you feel most relaxed, even if it's out in the middle of the woods. It doesn't matter if you're in human or wolf form. Rest is rest all the same."

Blaze exhaled. "There's only one place I feel relaxed."

Austin gave him a knowing look. "Then go there."

Blaze hesitated. "Okay." He nodded. He could do that.

No matter how difficult it would be.

The Texan smiled. "Promise?"

Blaze flicked his tongue across his teeth with a quick clicking noise and nodded again. "Once I'm finished with the last few minutes of this footage, yeah. I promise."

Austin tipped his Stetson in approval before he slipped out of the office, closing the door behind him.

Alone again, Blaze turned back toward his computer. Five more minutes of footage wasn't going to kill him, and he needed to finish this last review. Then he'd shut down for the night. Sitting down at the keyboard, he pressed Play, watching the several minutes in the darkened forests near Bozeman that led up to the last section of footage in which Flynn Porter had been seen. The pack's security cams were no bigger than the head of a ballpoint pen and scattered all throughout their territory. Maverick hadn't been keen on the idea at first, preferring to give the pack their privacy and only monitor near the ranch's perimeter, but Blaze had sworn not to pull the footage except for moments when they truly needed it.

Times like this.

He'd watched the video reel countless times now, in hopes that with each additional pass he'd see something to give him a lead, something he hadn't noticed before, but so far, the effort had been fruitless.

Entering in several lines of code, he slowed the video down frame by frame, watching the muted audio frequency in the corner move up and down. A moment before Flynn stepped out of view, the last anyone had seen of him, the audio frequency spiked for barely a millisecond. Blaze's brow furrowed. The frequency spike was so fast that human senses likely wouldn't have been able to detect it. He certainly hadn't the first several times he'd watched this damn thing. Whatever it was, it'd barely registered, but it was there all the same.

Typing in several commands, he isolated that second of audio track, turning the speaker volume to max and replaying it. He hadn't heard anything during those seconds the dozens of times he'd played it before, but maybe this time...

The soft whispered sound that came through the computer's speakers chilled him.

Blaze snarled.

He shoved his chair back from the desk, retreating to the far side of the room as he gripped the hair at the base of his skull with his hands. He struggled to catch his breath. Unable to calm himself, he forced himself to play the audio again. The second time sounded no better, even though he knew it was coming. As he rested his weight on the desk, adrenaline coursed through him. When he'd played it fast, at normal speed, it could've been a blip in the audio, but slowed down, it sounded like a wolf howl.

Only *not*.

He'd only heard that sound one other place before.

One other time.

Shaking out the adrenaline coursing through him, he glanced at the clock. It was late. Damn late. Maverick had said they weren't coming. That the paranoia was getting to him. Maybe that was it. Reality blurring at the edges again. It'd been months since Rock's warning, after all. Maybe he needed sleep more than he thought.

Returning to the computer, he played the slowed-down version of the sound once more. The soft eerie sound echoed through the speakers again.

"Fuck," he snarled.

No, he hadn't imagined it. There was no way he was tricking himself with his own paranoia this time. He hadn't been wrong. They *were* coming. He felt it.

He upped the risk threat on the security panel to the next level, an action that would alert the pack's warriors on patrol that evening to call in reinforcements and increase the number of paws on the ground to guard the pack's perimeters. He'd chalk it up as their monthly training op. Protocol only allowed him to raise the red alert with an imminent threat facing them. Saving and exiting the files, he locked the computer but didn't turn it off, leaving the office lights on. He sent a quick text from his phone to Kieran, instructing the young wolf to come take over for him and to listen to the audio, just to be certain. Maybe then his worst fear wouldn't be confirmed. Maybe Kieran would tell him the noise he'd heard was all in his head.

He swallowed. That many maybes didn't sit well with him.

Not when it came to this.

Tearing out of the office, he exited the main compound building and stepped out into the cool Montana night. The chilled air that filled his lungs did nothing to calm his nerves. Too wired to shift into wolf form, he swore, realizing he needed to keep his promise to Austin. He wasn't about to go back on his word, even on something little like this.

Dazed from the adrenaline and the thought of his demons catching up with him, he was knocking on the door of Dakota's cabin before he could stop himself. He paced the length of her porch. A minute or two later, she opened the door, pawing at her eyes, still groggy from sleep.

She blinked at him through half-closed lids. "Blaze?"

Peaches pranced out of her cabin, weaving about his feet like she'd known he was headed there and had anticipated his arrival, before slinking back inside.

It was the middle of the night and he knew Dakota would have clinic for the ranch's livestock and horses in the morning, but he couldn't stop himself. Apparently, his cat couldn't resist her either. "Can I crash on your couch tonight?"

Dakota's face scrunched in sleepy confusion. "What? Wh—"

"I need to be near you. Don't ask why," he said, interrupting her. "Just…can I? Please, Kotes?"

Something in the way he said it must have alerted her, stirred her further awake.

She wrapped her arms around herself, clearly still cold from having just crawled out of bed. Unlike most of their kind, she'd always slept snuggled beneath a massive mound of blankets in spite of the internal warmth her wolf provided her. "Yeah, of course. Come on in." She held the door open for him.

He stepped inside, heading toward her couch. Taking off his Stetson, he held it to his chest like a shield. "I promise I'll be quiet. I won't keep you awake."

She gently closed the door behind her and crossed the room, slowly heading toward the hall that led to her bedroom. "I know you won't."

He sat on the sofa, watching her as she went. "Dakota."

"Hmmm?" she answered, turning back toward him with still sleepy eyes.

"I'm not trying to start anything between us. Not this time. I just…"

Her features softened, like she saw right through him. "I know you're not, not tonight anyway." Padding back toward him, her bare feet were nearly silent against the hardwood of the cabin floor.

He lay back on the couch, hands over his chest as she approached, as if sleep would claim him there. It was close but not close enough. Not where he truly wanted to be.

Coming to his side, Dakota ran her fingers through his hair, soft and soothing. Slowly, surely, he relaxed into her touch, the soft gentleness of her hands. Reaching to his chest, she clasped his hand in hers, gently pulling him up from the couch and leading him down the hall toward her bedroom with her. It wasn't sexual. It simply was.

It was them being as they had always been, if only for a brief moment.

Once in her room, Dakota climbed into her bed, snuggling beneath the sheets and quilt. "Come on." She patted the empty pillow next to hers. "Before Peaches takes your spot."

Blaze didn't hesitate.

He stripped off his boots, leaving them by her door before he crawled into the bed, lying down by her side. Her back faced toward him.

Rolling over, she came face-to-face with him, smiling at him from the comfort of the pillows. "You can hold me if that's better," she whispered.

"It's better and worse," he whispered. He pulled her into his arms.

Like she was meant to be there, she snuggled against him, her face burying into his chest with a contented sigh before she soon drifted back into an easy sleep. The slowed, soft sounds of her breathing soothed him, acting as the only true lullaby he'd ever needed. But sleep still refused to claim him.

Maybe he *had* been wrong, but not in the way he'd originally thought. They *were* coming, but maybe he could get out in front of this. Like Amarok had said, he'd bested them once before. Maybe his mistake had been in thinking that he couldn't do it again.

Resolve gripped him, reality settling in. There was no maybe. He *had* to do it again, because if he didn't...

With Dakota in his arms, slowly Blaze finally allowed sleep to claim him, lying there with her against him well into the early hours of the morning.

He'd bested their enemies before, and he *would* do it again.

Chapter 9

DAKOTA HAD LASTED THREE DAYS, AND ALREADY SHE'D NEARED her limit. If she'd thought his pursuing her had been bad, this was worse.

The following morning after Blaze had slept over, he hadn't been there when she'd woken. Dakota had rolled over in her bed, still groggy and with her eyes full of sleep as the early morning sunrise streamed over the mountaintops and into her window. The smell of the pack's laundry detergent and a hint of clove had lingered. The welcome scent filled her nose, rousing her. With summer coming to an end, the early hours on the ranch had grown cooler, and instinctually, she'd reached for him, in search of the kind of warmth no blanket or quilt could ever replicate.

The divot where he'd lain in the old spring mattress had been cold and empty. She'd been worried about him before they'd both fallen asleep the previous night, about the sad, haunted look in his eye when he'd shown up at her door, and she was eager to comfort him further, so the fact that she woke up alone came as a surprise.

Peaches had been curled up at the foot of his spot on the bed, awake and staring at her. The ancient barn cat had simply looked at the empty spot, giving an uncharacteristic, affectionate slow blink as if thinking about the cowboy who'd lain there, before looking back at Dakota incredulously. Her narrowed green eyes glared, as if to say, *Isn't this what you wanted?*

"These days I don't seem to know what I want, Peaches," she'd whispered to the old feline before scratching underneath the cat's chin.

Peaches had leaped off the bed after that, the ruffled fur of her fluffed tail lifted high in the air as she pranced off, likely in search of either Blaze or a mouse in the barn she could slowly torture. She might tolerate—and *maybe* even like Dakota—but Blaze was her person. He was always willing to feed the kitty queen a far more generous portion of cat food than he should, despite Dakota's concern for the aging cat's weight.

That won Peaches's loyalty every time.

After Peaches left, Dakota had watched the sun rise as she prepared for clinic, feeling abandoned and hollow in a way she hadn't fully understood. To make matters worse, she hadn't seen Blaze since.

The first twenty-four hours had been the worst. Even on a ranch as large as Wolf Pack Run, avoiding a fellow packmate for long was difficult. When she'd asked, others had reportedly seen him in passing, yet to her, Blaze had turned into a complete ghost, like he had something to hide. She supposed she had his military career to thank for that uncanny ability.

When she'd gone to the security office to try and reargue her case for the drone usage, Kieran had been there and seemed to have no idea where Blaze was or how to find the codes and authorize the usage himself. That had been troubling enough. Then when she'd knocked on the door of his cabin and used her key to peek in, he hadn't been home. It looked as if no one had been for days. She'd even tried to look for him in the late hours of the evening in the training gym, where he could usually be found, but he was surprisingly absent.

By day two, it was obvious he was avoiding her.

By day three, she was a mess of self-pity. She hadn't wanted to push him away, only to keep things the same between them, preserve their friendship. From the looks of it, she'd failed at that thoroughly. Dakota wasn't used to failing. She worked too hard to ensure she never did.

She went about her regular duties with little enthusiasm, still searching for the missing cattle. On a ranch this size, being without a drone made that frustratingly difficult, especially as she was work-ing to secure a meeting with their Arctic wolf allies as the packmas-ter requested. She wanted to impress, prove herself in her new role. Though to her disappointment, she hadn't been able to coordinate with Blaze to make sure she was following correct protocols. She supposed it *had* been her suggestion to divide and conquer.

The thought that she'd pushed him away made her queasy.

In any case, she intended to be direct, give the Arctic wolves a tour of Wolf Pack Run, prepare a detailed presentation for them about the pack's integration models they'd used to eliminate their previous Elder Council in favor of a more diverse advisor group and incorporate female warriors into their elite ranks, and then be forthright about negotiating the alliance the Grey Wolves hoped for. From what she understood, Alexander Caron, the Yellowknife Arctic Wolf packmaster, wasn't one for political games, and she hoped her forthright statement of what the Grey Wolves were after and all the benefits that would come along with that would be enough.

The thought that the fate of the pack's safety fell squarely on her shoulders had also weighed on her more than she'd anticipated, but with Blaze gone, she didn't have anyone to confide in about the pressure she was feeling. Sierra was due to give birth any day now, and she hadn't wanted to stress her closest girlfriend, and when she'd brought it up with her mother, Mẹ had unhelpfully pointed out that "This is what you wanted, *chó con*."

The harsh truth had immediately put her in a sour mood.

It wasn't until the afternoon on the third day, when Dakota got a notice about meeting the packmaster for a status update—which she was uncharacteristically and woefully underprepared for since she couldn't coordinate with Blaze—and simultaneously received an unexpected email from Jasper, that she'd truly cracked. She'd only been needling Blaze about reaching out to Jas. She never actually had. So the out-of-the-blue message had caught her by surprise. Apparently she'd been wrong about Jasper's interest in her. The lengthy letter of an email from the handsome Grey Wolf international relations liaison had been surprisingly heartfelt and honest, and to her shock, her heart had fluttered when she'd read it, despite her willing it not to.

She'd inhaled every word because the letter reminded her of the days when Blaze had been in the service and his equally lengthy letters had captured her heart before she'd even fully been aware of how she'd felt about him. That'd been before he'd gone so far in on an operation that she hadn't known where he was, let alone received correspondence from him. She still kept every one of those letters written in his scrawling cursive script in an old, decorative hatbox on the top shelf of her closet.

That afternoon, as she stepped inside Maverick's office, eyes still puffy from when she'd gotten teary-eyed over Jasper's message, she hadn't expected to find Blaze there. Maverick hadn't arrived for the meeting yet, and she should have known he would have called them both in. But suddenly standing alone in the packmaster's office, just the two of them after several days of absence, made all the emotions she'd felt come to a head.

She inhaled a sharp breath, taking in the sight of Blaze. This afternoon's shirt specimen was an all-black tee with a rainbow across the chest and a fluffy white cloud beneath that read "Death Metal." There was a bit more scruff on his cheeks than usual, like he hadn't rested well. From the dark, distant look in his eyes, he didn't appear pleased to see her.

She'd done the same to him, of course, but it hurt all the same.

"Hey," she said quietly, lifting a hand in greeting. She closed the office door behind her. "Haven't seen you in a few days."

Blaze scratched at the five-o'clock shadow on his cheeks. Dakota didn't usually care much for men with facial hair, but the slight shadow on his chin somehow made him look more rugged, more masculine. "Had to go out to Bozeman, was gone for a day or so."

"And the other days?"

He looked at her, his gaze distant and pained, but didn't answer.

The door to the office opened again and the packmaster stepped inside. Maverick glanced back and forth between them, immediately sensing the tension like only an alpha could. Closing the door, he then rounded the far side of the desk. He placed both large hands on top of the mahogany wood, his eyes darting between them again. "Today has been a long and stressful one," the packmaster grumbled. "Tell me the two of you have good news."

Dakota placed the meticulously organized folder with the start of her detailed plans on the packmaster's desk before glancing toward Blaze, but he didn't so much as look at her.

Sensing the tension, Maverick's eyes flashed to his wolf and shot back and forth between them again. "What happened with the missing cattle?"

Dakota opened her mouth. She tried to speak, but she couldn't bring herself to tell the packmaster that they didn't have any news on that front. Yes, it'd been Blaze who'd refused to give her the drone access, but she could have talked with him like he'd asked and then the whole thing would have been solved. They'd both been too stubborn for their own good.

Maverick growled. "The missing packmate in Bozeman?"

A long moment of silence passed before Blaze shook his head. "No update."

The packmaster's next question was directed toward Dakota. "That strange sound you heard in the forest?"

"What?" Blaze snapped to attention. In an instant, the color drained from his face.

"Malcolm told you about that?" Dakota's eyes widened as she addressed the packmaster. "He didn't seem to believe me. I might have just imagined it."

The deep vibrato of the packmaster's voice was barely distinguishable from a growl. "Malcolm may not play well with others, but he's the only one among you who doesn't keep secrets." He gave them both a pointed glare.

Inside, she felt herself wither like a scolded pup. She was *never* this unprepared.

Unconcerned by Maverick, Blaze looked as if he were two seconds away from vomiting. "What sound are we talking about?" he demanded.

Ignoring his outburst and the missing color in the security specialist's face, Maverick cast a glance toward him. "And the audio blip on the Bozeman footage?"

Dakota lifted a brow. "What audio blip?"

Both she and Blaze turned to each other, frustrations flying.

"You were supposed to—"

"Why didn't you—"

Maverick's large fist slammed down on top of his desk with a menacing *thwack*.

Dakota and Blaze both froze. Dakota was surprised he hadn't left a considerable dent in the wood.

The gold of the packmaster's wolf eyes flared. "You mean to tell me that the two of you have had several days on this, and neither one of you is any further than when you started?"

Silence answered him.

Maverick snarled. The sound sent an immediate chill down her spine. Elite warrior and alpha she-wolf or not, she knew who was the true alpha of this pack, and had she been in wolf form, she might have hunkered down and cowered to yield to the Grey Wolf packmaster's dominance.

"What's wrong with you two?" Maverick growled. "You're normally a dream team, but lately, you've clearly done nothing but be at each other's throats. What happened?"

Dakota didn't answer. Instead, she glanced toward the floor, shame filling her. "I'm sorry, Packmaster. I—"

"Dakota kissed me and then tried to say it didn't mean anything,"

Blaze blurted out. Some of the color was returning to his cheeks now, but his hands were fidgety like he had no idea what to do with them. He shrugged. "I'm trying to prove to her that it did."

"Blaze!" Dakota shrieked, completely mortified.

Maverick quirked a brow.

Blaze cast her an incredulous grin. "What? He asked."

Dakota couldn't seem to manage to say anything. Instead, she gaped at him.

Maverick turned his gaze toward her. "Is this true?"

"I..." She tried to formulate a response, but instead, a flush heated her cheeks.

Abruptly the sharp sound of cat claws against wood followed by an earsplitting yowl echoed from the hall. Peaches was scratching the door into oblivion. Obviously, the kitty queen didn't appreciate being excluded. *She* was the true leader of the pack after all.

Maverick's brow crept higher at the sound. Ignoring Peaches's complaining, he glanced toward Blaze as if he'd never seen him before, anger seemingly forgotten. "You actually took my advice to heart?" He said it as if he never in all his years as packmaster held any expectation of Blaze listening to him.

Blaze shrugged again. "It wasn't intentional. In my defense, she started it."

Dakota had no idea what the two cowboys were getting on about, but she glared at Blaze anyway.

With his features twisted in confusion, Maverick sat in his desk chair, clearly having gotten the more aggressive part of his point across—or maybe he was still in shock that of all his warriors, it had been Blaze who had actually followed his advice for once. Dakota understood that was a bit of a problem among the team. No one had ever said leading a group of alpha wolves warranted compliance.

The packmaster cleared his throat. "Whatever's going on between you two, it needn't get in the way of your work."

Maverick's disappointment in them was clear, and the feeling ate at Dakota. She was a people pleaser. She prided herself on getting the job done, even in the face of adversity. That had been part of why she'd been chosen to be an elite warrior. Maverick had even said as much, and now, on her first assignment, she'd already failed him.

She cast an angry look toward Blaze. "If he'd have let me use the drones, it wouldn't have."

"If you had talked with me, like I asked, I wouldn't have had to—"

"Enough. The two of you sound like children," Maverick snarled again. "This ends now."

Dakota cast a smug smile in Blaze's direction as she crossed her arms over her chest. "See? I told you there couldn't be anything between u—"

"What I mean by that, warrior," Maverick said, cutting her off and emphasizing her title in a way that made her wither, "is that the two of you will ride out to find the missing part of the herd tonight, and whatever *this* is . . . ." He gestured between them. "It's resolved by night's end."

Dakota stammered. "But—"

"No questions," Maverick growled. He cast a side glance at Blaze. "And no drones or hacktivism or whatever the hell you call it when you use the computer to control the ranching equipment."

"I only did it once. It's just regular automotive hacking that uses Ukrainian software. We own the tractor. Why should Big Tech say we can't—"

Maverick shot Blaze a warning look, causing the other wolf to fall silent.

"Ride it out," the packmaster growled.

An hour later, both she and Blaze rode on their respective horses, galloping out to the far ends of the pasture, the least habited sections of their lands. The sun was setting over the mountain peaks, elongating the shadows of the towering pines and casting an orange glow over the rolling green pastures spattered with yellow patches

from the approach of fall. They'd saddled up in silence, only occasionally exchanging annoyed glances with each other, but neither
daring to speak.

With the drone to locate the cattle, the task might have taken
two hours at most—one surveying the vast ranchlands from a
bird's-eye view and then another riding out to the far ends of the
pasture in the truck or on one of the ATVs. Fulfilling the packmaster's punishment, they'd likely be riding all night and there was still
no guarantee they'd find the beasts by morning.

But that was exactly how the packmaster had intended it.

Clearly, Maverick figured forcing them together would end this
standoff between them.

Once they were far enough out that the main compound disappeared in the distance, Dakota slowed her horse, Pumpkin, to a
trot. The Arabian tossed his head about with a huffed nicker. Ahead
of her, Blaze pulled back on Sarge in response. Sarge came to a halt
as Dakota steered Pumpkin around to face him.

"Let's get this over with." She couldn't take another second of
the silence. Not if they were going to be out here together all night
and not even able to shift into wolf form.

Another one of Maverick's conditions—his way of forcing them
to communicate in a way that *wasn't* growling, as he'd said.

Dakota met Blaze's stare, refusing to pull any punches. "This is
all your fault."

The anger on Maverick's face had been nothing compared to
the cold look Blaze gave her then. "If I recall, it was *you* who kissed
me, Dakota." The way he said it made her feel like now even *he*
regretted it.

That made two of them.

"I was talking about the drone issue." She nudged Pumpkin forward with the heels of her boots, drawing up close to Blaze's mount
until their horses stood side by side. "If you hadn't blocked me from
using it, we wouldn't be out here."

"Blame me if you want, if that makes you feel better." Blaze gave Sarge a nudge with his boots, spurring the horse forward and away from her.

"What does that mean?" she called to him over the evening breeze.

"It means I'm tired of fighting you on this," Blaze grumbled.

She scoffed. "So much for convincing me in a week."

"You didn't want me to convince you," he shot back.

Dakota blanched. "Blaze."

He growled. "Make up your goddamn mind, Kotes."

"Blaze," she said, sharp enough to draw his attention.

Dakota pointed above the pines. Several miles in the distance beyond the hill up ahead, a murder of crows and a few turkey vultures circled not far from the line of the forest.

Dread twisted Dakota's stomach. She released a long breath, but it didn't stop the chill that raced down her spine. "I think we've found the missing cattle."

Blaze had seen worse carnage before—not animal but human death and their kind, a living, breathing mixture of the two. They'd been shifters with thoughts, feelings, loved ones, whose fragile existence had been snuffed out by callous violence in an instant. Entire packs and generations gone within days. He'd also be lying if he said he hadn't killed before, human and shifter alike, not to mention he hunted wild prey to feed his wolf's predatory needs. They all did. They were one with the forest, the mountain ecosystem, and it was a harsh, cruel reality of a wolf's existence. Their hunt was unkind and brutal but necessary. The bloodshed and culling of game caused the forest to flourish.

But those who'd lived through war, as he had, knew that the death of an animal didn't compare. Lost life, whether human or shifter, was different. Never necessary.

It was the smell that got to him.

Blaze held his nose momentarily, fighting the bile that rose in his throat. But the scent, strong and pungent to his wolf senses, singed his nose. He couldn't escape it.

He dropped his hand. Resisting wasn't helpful. It didn't chase the demons away.

Night had started to creep up on them and it'd be dark in a handful of minutes. Dakota slowed her horse to a stop beside him, quickly dismounting as they both surveyed the valley of the hillside below. The corpses of over a dozen of the pack's cattle lay scattered across the mountainside. Flies gathered. The predatory birds that had helped them find the location hopped about in a feast of carrion.

Blaze dismounted as he watched Dakota slowly approach.

She bent down beside one of the cows, her face pale as she examined the remains. "They've been drained," she breathed.

Of blood. She didn't need to say the words for Blaze to understand her meaning.

"Vampires don't drain animals," she breathed.

"Not typically." Blaze swallowed, hard. The blood loss indicated those overgrown leeches were the culprits, but the carnage suggested they weren't the only ones. Vampires didn't chew on their food. Not normal ones anyway. Their diet was a liquid one. From appearances, black bears, scavengers, and other wolves—the nonshifting kind—appeared to have visited, too, making the bite marks indistinguishable. A normal occurrence.

Unless...

He shook his head, refusing to go down that line of thinking.

"This was purposeful," Dakota said, breaking the momentary lull of silence between them. "Deliberate." Crouching down, she placed a tender hand on the cheek of the animal beneath her. Dakota was fiercely protective and invested in the well-being of every creature she cared for. "This is my fault," she breathed.

Blaze shook his head. "Don't say that. By the smell, they've been dead for several days, long before you started looking for them. I'm surprised another packmember hadn't come this far out to scent them by now. But the deer don't come down here as frequently. They forage close to the river this time of year. That's likely why no one ventured this far east."

The last thin line of the sunset dropped beneath the mountains, casting the pasture where they stood in darkness.

"What do we do?" From Dakota's voice, he could tell she was distressed, not calloused to it like he was, but from the daring flash of her wolf eyes, she was also prepared to fight.

Skills trained into instinct took over.

Command. Protect. Serve.

De Oppresso Liber.

"We scan the forest nearby," Blaze answered. "See if we can scent out the vampires that drained them. Then we bring the lift and the truck out to haul away the bodies." Drawing up beside Sarge, he held his reins as he patted the horse. Sarge gave a nervous whinny, clearly sensing the danger and death hanging in the air. Blaze clicked his tongue and hushed the beast, doing his best to calm him, then reached into his saddlebag. He pulled out a long, thin piece of lacquered wood and tossed it to Dakota.

She snatched the stake from the air with catlike reflexes and lifted a brow. "You came prepared for once?"

"When it comes to fighting our enemies, I might as well be a fucking Boy Scout. 'Prepared' is my middle name." The surprised laugh that came from Dakota in response thrilled him, even as Blaze cast her a grim look. "And if we stay in human form, I think we're going to need it."

Chapter 10

"Be vewy quiet. We're hunting wabbits," Blaze whispered, after they'd encountered their fourth hare in the forest underbrush with not so much as a single vampire in sight.

"That reference is lost on me," Dakota answered.

"It's Elmer Fudd from *Looney Tunes*. It's an American cartoon classic," Blaze answered. "We'll work on it." Crouching down in the brush, with a quick lash of his hand, he snatched the hare from beneath the patch of rocky mountain juniper by its long hind legs. The tiny animal had been unsuspectingly nibbling on the foliage, unaware that two wolves approached.

The small animal wriggled in his grip, tiny heart thumping in response to the predator now holding it as Blaze's eyes flashed to wolf. "You could at least make it difficult," he said to the creature. "Next time, I'll eat you for dinner." He released the hare back into the underbrush, watching it dart off into the darkness of the forest.

Dakota sighed. "Unless you plan to actually eat it, leave the bunnies alone."

Typical animal lover.

From the way Dakota spoke about their prey when in human form, no one outside the pack would know she was a fierce she-wolf. That love of animals coupled with her organized, analytical nature made her an excellent veterinarian.

Blaze grumbled, resting his arms on his knees. He stared into the shadows, still watching the spot where the hare had disappeared. "They make it too easy."

"Spoken like a true wolf."

Blaze's eyes burned brighter gold. He grinned in response.

It was the first true exchange they'd had since they'd left the pasture to tromp through the forest several hours earlier. They'd caught the sickly sweet scent of vampire on the breeze, the smell instantly stirring their wolf senses, but any actual encounters had proved elusive.

But they were out there. The smell of the cattle's death in the field would draw their intrigue.

"Why do you think the vampires are draining animals?" Dakota used the stake he'd given her to gesture to where the bunny had been. "Malcolm mentioned a deer being drained in the forest when we were on patrol the other night, and now this."

Considering everything going on lately, Blaze wasn't entirely certain the vampires were the sole culprits. The smell of this much death would have drawn them, and they never missed a chance to attack the pack. Old rivalries died hard, but…

He shook his head. He still couldn't bring himself to speak their name. The packmaster had warned him about being too paranoid. Perhaps he'd been so focused on his past that he wasn't seeing what was laid out directly in front of him? Even if his enemies had come for him, they'd send two, maybe three, since they'd know from his file what he was capable of.

That small number would be enough to do the necessary damage both to him and the pack. The carnage of a dozen dead cattle they'd left behind in the field was only worthy of one—and after what he'd done to them in Dark Force, they wouldn't take their chances. Not to mention they never drained animals.

They devoured, maimed.

Destroyed.

He inhaled a deep breath, trying to reassure himself further. Not to mention all the occurrences around the ranch and the disappearance of the subpack member had had little to do with him. After Dark Force, they were supposed to be extinct after all.

But his instincts said otherwise.

Blaze shrugged, still crouched near the forest floor. "There's no way to know why they're feeding on animals unless we find one and ask it."

Dakota scoffed at his sarcasm. "You know those bloodsuckers are too tight-lipped to converse with us, even under duress—sick, insatiable monsters that they are. They—"

"Dakota, behind you!" Blaze shouted in warning.

At his word, Dakota plunged the stake in a downward arc beneath her armpit, driving it into the bloodsucker's stomach. The vamp had come on so fast using that damn warp-level speed of theirs that there'd been barely a second for her to prepare for it. But Dakota had been ready. She spun, quickly wrenching the stake from the vampire's stomach only to plunge it ruthlessly into the monster's pulsing dead heart.

Blaze grinned with pride.

The vampire sputtered for a moment before bursting like the blood bag that it was, coating him and mainly Dakota in a spray of grime. That was hardly the last of it. Their kills were so much cleaner in wolf form—then he only needed to wash the blood from the fur of his neck and muzzle. But there'd be more vampires where that came from.

Blaze shot to his feet, sensing another vamp approaching to their right. The bloodsucker raced up on him, long fangs bared. The strength and teeth of a vampire could prove deadly to their kind, if the knife in the other creature's hand didn't. He'd seen it happen too many times before.

But those wolves hadn't been him.

Meeting the bloodsucker blow for blow, he blocked the incoming blade by catching the vamp's arm with his own. He leveraged the millisecond of the vamp's hesitation and wrenched his dagger from its sheath on his chaps. With a fierce snarl, Blaze sliced his blade across the bloodsucker's torso. The vampire let out a screeching hiss, stumbling back.

Without warning, Blaze shifted into wolf form, clothes falling to the forest floor beneath him as his limbs twisted and his fur burst forth. The instant his paws connected with the cool mountain ground, he charged, meeting the bloodsucker head-on. This first vamp went down easy. The second, even easier. By the third, he was getting bored.

Darting forward, he rushed the monster, sharp claws scraping and jaws snapping. The scuffle continued for several moments longer until finally he pinned the monster. The vampire had put up a fight, but not one worthy of him.

Canines bared, Blaze snarled before he ripped into the flesh of the vampire's throat. The metallic, iron taste of blood coated his furred maw. On his hind legs and neck, his hackles raised. Inside, his instincts prickled with awareness. A familiar scent caught in his nose.

Dakota.

With all the force of an alpha wolf guarding his mate, Blaze felt a protective surge race through him. He whipped around in search of her. He hadn't been able to keep his eyes on her lest they both get themselves killed. But it hadn't mattered. She was too fierce a warrior. She didn't need him to save her. The leftover remains of two vampires lay beside her cowgirl boots, and she was coated nearly head to toe in blood—the blood of their enemies that she'd shed.

The gold of her wolf eyes burned like a beacon in the darkness, and she growled as she cast him a censuring look. "You were *supposed* to stay in human form."

———————

Dakota had never been so covered in muck in her entire life—and for a living, she sometimes stuck her arm into animals' insides. There were less than two hours left until sunrise by the time they reached the main compound at Wolf Pack Run again, which meant neither of them would be getting much sleep before their chores in the morning.

Thank you, Maverick-freaking-Grey, Dakota swore internally at the packmaster.

She knew their punishment had been deserved, but that failed to matter at the moment. If he weren't her packmaster, she'd sic Sierra on him in retribution. Considering the alpha's pregnant mate was overdue by nearly a week now and prepared to give birth any day, the hormones and impatience were making her more than a bit feral—and that was before one accounted for the fact that Sierra could still manage to wield a sword.

Dakota tore her way through the training gym, each step she took leaving a trail of red footprints across the rubber rolled mats beneath her feet. Her leather cowgirl boots weren't the only things covered in it. The dripping had stopped shortly after they reached the forest in favor of a dried stickiness that made her feel slightly nauseous. There was no way she was showering this off in her cabin. She'd be cleaning the drain of the mixture of blood, dirt, horse and wolf hair, and small bits of vampire guts for weeks. Her stomach rolled at the thought, which only caused her mood to further sour.

By comparison, Blaze had gotten off lightly, considering he'd only been sprayed by the specks of the first vamp she'd taken out, and then he'd shifted into wolf form thereafter. Vampires didn't create such a splash when a wolf's jaws tore open their throat, but using a stake like a vampire slayer was a different matter. There'd been a spray of crimson coating Blaze's jaw and down the front of his naked chest when he'd shifted back into human form, but he'd been able to wash a good bit of it off with the water from his saddlebag canteen.

She hadn't been so lucky.

The heavy metal door to the training gym slammed closed, echoing with the signal that Blaze followed her. He'd paused only long enough to tie up their horses on the posts outside the mess hall before she'd sensed him.

"Dakota," he called after her.

She didn't answer.

"Dakota."

Ignoring him, she charged into the gym shower, her boots still tracking crimson footprints across the tan ceramic flooring of the spa center. Several glass shower stalls waited in the middle of the open-concept room. The dark decorative paneling of the walls was backlit by the low, warm glow of lights encased beneath glass patterns in the flooring. The sauna room was open and visible off to the left.

Dakota paused only long enough to wrench the leather footwear from her feet and cast it near the spa area doorway. She'd have to take the barn hose to them. Lifting her shirt over her head, she gagged as she felt the sticky material peel away from her skin. Thankfully, the vast majority was on her clothes instead of her skin. Her jeans came next, which required a bit of shimmying for them to get unstuck, until finally only her underwear remained. For functionality, she'd chosen comfort over style that morning, so her bra and panties weren't even close to matching. No matter, considering they'd be unsalvageable after tonight.

She padded over to one of the shower stalls. She reached in, twisting the handle to the highest heat setting. Her wolf could take it. Their internal temperatures ran higher than most.

From behind her, she heard Blaze enter. The heavy sound of his boots fell hard against the ceramic tiling. "Where the hell are you stomping off to?"

Dakota turned toward him and gestured to the stream of hot water and steam which billowed behind her. "The shower obviously," she growled. She dipped her hair into the water, starting to wash it clean before she cupped some of the water in her hands and began scrubbing at the spots of blood that remained. She wasn't stripping off her bra and panties in front of him. Not when they were alone like this. Not after all that happened between them over the past few days. Let her underwear get wet beneath the water for all she cared.

Blaze had the wherewithal to look confused by her grumbling. "Did I do something?"

She didn't have the patience for this right now. Being covered in vampire guts had pushed her well past her breaking point. Dakota's eyes flashed to her wolf, and she bared her teeth for a moment. "No, Blaze. You didn't do *anything*, anything at all. That's been the problem for the past several days, hasn't it?"

Blaze growled low and feral in his throat. "What is that supposed to mean?"

She waved a hand in his direction, gesturing to where that ridiculous T-shirt of his hugged the thick muscles of his torso. The *audacity* of the males in this pack. Didn't they realize what they were doing to all of them? It wasn't enough for every one of them to be built like the hardworking cowboys they were, but then Blaze had to go and be equal parts funny, easygoing, highly intelligent, and protective on top of it. Not to mention that the little display he'd put on in the forest had made her breath catch in her throat. He fought against their enemies with such lethal predatory grace that he made it look effortless. She knew from her own training that it wasn't.

And to make matters worse, he had to go and be her most-trusted friend.

It was beyond irritating, really.

She brandished an accusatory finger at him. "First, you tell me you're going to seduce me with all the enthusiasm of a dog in heat."

"Wolf," he corrected. "Wolf in heat."

She scowled at the joke. "Not funny."

Blaze cast her a smirk. "It was a little funny. Admit it."

She glared at him. "Then only *after* you provoke me into nearly mauling poor Cheyenne do you decide to leave me alone." She threw up her hands with an exasperated growl. "I can't believe you."

The heat of his gaze bore through her, and she felt her nipples stiffen. The aroused growl that tore from his lips made her shiver.

She averted her gaze, focusing on one of the tiles near her feet, the still-billowing steam of the shower. She couldn't bring herself to look at him.

He drew closer, prowling toward her with all the power of an alpha of their species and only stopping once he was so near that he dwarfed her in size. Too close for comfort. Everything about him was so large and feral. His towering height—an inch taller than the packmaster himself—the width of his muscled shoulders, the long length of his limbs, the size of his hands. Beneath the heat of his stare, it was enough to make her feel delicate in a way that she wasn't.

His eyes flicked over her, lingering on the puckered teal fabric of her bra. Her breasts ached with need. From the sharp hiss of his breath, she had no doubt he saw the effect he had on her there. A rush of heat warmed her core. She felt his nearness in the way her breath hitched, the way every inch of her skin seemed to hum with want—need.

Blaze's voice as he spoke was strained, forcibly measured. "From that very first night, you've been twisting up my insides, Kotes. All because you can't make up your mind about what you want when I've been very clear from the beginning about *exactly* what I want, and more importantly, *who* I want it with."

Her stare shot up to meet his. "I didn't know how you felt that first night."

"You had to be blind not to." He wrenched his gaze away from her. Lifting his Stetson from his head briefly, he ran his fingers through his hair with a muttered curse. "The only reason you hadn't seen it before is because you didn't want to. You were too scared, and hell, so was I. But I'm not anymore." He tipped the Stetson back on his head as his eyes flicked over her, standing there in her underwear. "And you still are."

Eyes still on her, he stepped back, easing away from her.

She felt his absence by her side immediately. She frowned.

Several paces away, Blaze reached down and started to strip off his boots. He cast them to the side, where her own soiled clothes lay, before he started in on the buckle of his chaps and belt.

Dakota's eyes widened. "What are you doing?"

The gold of his wolf eyes flashed. "Exactly what I should have done days ago."

Dakota inhaled a sharp breath. From the dark look in his eyes, she almost expected him to strip the belt from his jeans and use it to make the bare skin of her ass a dusky shade of pink. The thought of her bent over his knee sent an unexpected wave of heat through her core.

Her mouth went dry as adrenaline coursed through her. "Blaze?" she breathed again, prompting more from his non-answer.

His chaps and belt were cast aside now along with his Stetson. The shirt came next. "Showering," he ground out.

His tone was harsher, more hardened than usual. She didn't exactly dislike it.

"Exactly like you are," he growled. "What else?" He turned on one of the showerheads in the adjacent stall block facing her. Another cloud of steam filled the room.

"Here?" she nearly squeaked.

"What?" he snapped. "We're both warriors, coworkers as you put it, and I may not be as drenched as your clothes were, but we're both covered in blood." His shirt was on the floor now, and those large hands and lengthy fingers worked at the button and zipper of his jeans.

The blue denim hit the floor, and from the sight of pure, virile male that sprang forth, he hadn't been wearing any...

"Stop it." She tore her gaze away in favor of focusing on the tile again. She had to if she wanted there to even be a chance of saving the history and friendship between them.

"Stop what?"

Dakota's hands clenched into fists. She couldn't keep staring at the floor, not when she could see the muscled curve of his calves, the thick brawn of his tight thighs leading up to where...

"Making me want you, for fuck's sake!" she snarled, finally allowing herself to look at him. He'd been inviting it since the moment he'd started that thinly veiled strip tease.

Damn him.

She'd seen him naked a hundred times before, but never like this.

Never thick and hot with need. Even from across the room, she could see, could feel his hunger for her. The power in that filled her.

Her eyes followed a bead of the warm shower water he now stood in as it trailed the length of his chest where he scrubbed himself clean. The broad sinew of his massive shoulders was peppered with the artwork of his military tattoos, a stark reminder that Blaze wasn't solely the kind of wolf who protected his loved ones but a fierce, lethal warrior, brave enough to risk himself for the sake of all others, for the good of his fellow man.

For the first time, Dakota allowed her eyes to trail lower, over the delicious ridges of his toned stomach and the jutted curve of his hips that led down to...

She bit her lower lip. Her mouth watered.

The thick male length of him made her want to...

She pushed the thought aside. She could still save this, stop this, couldn't she? "You ignoring me these past several days has torn me to shreds," she admitted. She was nearly breathless with desire, and she knew he had to hear it. "I don't know which is worse, you ignoring me or chasing after me."

"I left you alone just like you wanted," Blaze purred.

She laughed a humorless chuckle, eyes filling with tears as she glanced toward the ceiling. "I don't know what I want."

"I do."

The confidence in those two words stilled her.

Slowly, Blaze prowled toward her, every muscle of his nude form on display as he drew close to her again. She backed into the open shower stall, the heat of the spray easing the tense muscles of her back. Within a few seconds, her bra and underwear were drenched.

"You want to be told that you're safe, that everything is okay." Blaze eased closer, backing her farther into the shower's spray. "You want to be told that you aren't making a mistake, that every decision will have a happy ending, just like every time you reach a new goal, because you're scared of any uncertainty the future will hold."

Her back pressed flushed against the glass wall of the shower now. She couldn't get away, even if she'd wanted to. Blaze's large hands pressed next to the steamed glass on both sides of her head as he leaned over her.

"You want reassurance, to be certain."

Dakota could barely breathe. Tentatively, she reached out, placing her fingers on the dark ink across his chest.

A sharp hiss tore from his lips in response. His head dipped low, mouth drawing near.

"And you can promise me that?" she whispered.

The echo of the warm shower and the cool tile beneath her feet made her voice breathy, like it could disappear in the heady mix of heat and desire that filled the room as thick as the fogged steam.

"No." Blaze's lips brushed against the sensitive skin of her ear, the line of her cheek. She shivered. "But I can make you feel that way."

She turned toward him, lids heavy and mouth aching for him. "I thought you said you wouldn't kiss me until I asked you to."

"I lied." He growled as the gold of his wolf eyes burned hot with want for her. "A wolf only waits so long for his prey."

His mouth was on hers then, claiming hers with a force every bit as wild and untamed as the desire between them. His tongue parted the seam of her lips, seeking entry. She didn't hesitate to open to him, to the delicious, heady taste of him coating her tongue. Burying her fingers in the damp locks of his hair, she pulled him closer, meeting his kiss with her own primitive need. They'd never be close enough.

Blaze pulled her into his arms, lifting her by the round underside of her ass as he pinned her between the shower wall and his body. The thick, throbbing length of his cock pressed against the flimsy wet fabric of her underwear, grinding into her sweet spot. She moaned against his lips.

Deft hands searching, he found the front clasp to her bra, popping the hook open and exposing the naked flesh of her breasts. Good Lord, he was good at this. Too good. He broke the kiss between them, his mouth dipping down onto the tender skin of his chest. He caught one of her nipples between the long canines of his teeth and nipped at her.

She came apart on a wave of pleasure, felt the heat of her core clenching in ache for him. The high-pitched cry that escaped from her lips was unlike anything she'd ever heard from herself. She never came this quickly or from foreplay alone. Not even when she thought of him when she…

The head of his cock pushed against the sensitive bead of her clit through the wet material of her underwear, making her tremble, before he drew his hips back. He cupped her in the heat of his palm. Shoving aside the pesky crotch of her panties, he buried two fingers inside her. He angled his hand, pressing up and in until the spot he hit made her moan his name.

"Blaze," she keened.

She felt herself slicken again.

How could he—?

"Yeah, Kotes," he purred. There was a hint of frustration in his voice like she'd broken his concentration on the most important thing in the world to him—her pleasure.

Wild and shocked at the speed of her own renewed lust, she gaped at him, trying to form words. "I…I already came," she panted. "It's your turn."

"My *turn* can wait." Blaze chuckled, a low devious laugh like the thought of "turns" when it came to sex amused him. He cast her a delicious, naughty smirk. "I'm not nearly finished with you yet."

Blaze wanted to taste her—every delicious inch of her. He slid Dakota down from where he'd pinned her against the glass of the shower, allowing her to stand on her own two feet. Her legs were still unsteady and limp from the strength of her orgasm. He held her against his chest, propping her up against the panel again as he dropped to his knees in front of her.

"Blaze," she gasped, suddenly realizing what he was up to.

He tore the wet scraps of her underwear from the sweet curve of her hips, exposing her sexy bare cleft to him before he let out an appreciative growl. "You didn't think I'd let this end without tasting you, did you?"

Lifting her slight frame with ease, he positioned her legs overtop his shoulders until she was back against the glass of the shower wall again. This time, riding his face. He breathed in the scent of her, his mouth instantly salivating. She buried her hands in the scalp of his hair as she writhed against him in anticipation. His mouth watered. He'd imagined this exact scenario so many times, he could hardly believe it was real.

Until the hot slit of her lower lips settled against his mouth.

He shot Dakota a devious look from between her legs. He couldn't be held responsible for all the filthy ways he'd devour her before night's end if she kept being so damn eager. He loved how she took her pleasure with him, confident and unashamed. He loved every second of it—nearly as much as he loved her.

He buried his tongue inside the heat of her cunt, parting her folds until she cried out. The hot, earthy taste of her gathered in his mouth like a sweet nectar. He was drunk with the scent, the smell, the taste of her, but this wasn't about him. This was about her, her pleasure and making her recognize that the idea of them, however temporary, was worth the risk.

Moving to the apex of her center, his tongue quickly located and circled the hard, sweet bead there. In response, Dakota bucked against him, rocking until she found a rhythm that would bring her sweet release again.

Blaze gripped her thighs where they sat perched atop his shoulders, rough enough for her to cry out in pleasure-pain. "Not yet," he growled.

She'd come when he damn well told her to.

Not a moment sooner.

He captured her between his lips again, teasing and sucking, then withdrawing from her until she was writhing against him, wild and helpless.

"Blaze, please," she pleaded as he tortured her one last time, pulling away just far enough so the prickled hair on his cheek rubbed the inside of her thighs a soft pink.

The sound of his name on her lips as she moaned thrilled him.

He licked some of her damp heat from his lips. "Only if you do one thing for me, Kotes."

Her chest was rising and falling in quick pants as she struggled to catch her breath. "Anything."

Blaze grinned from between her thighs. "Admit that you want me."

"Blaze." Dakota let out a soft laugh as if that were already obvious as she batted a hand playfully as his head.

Oh no, he wasn't letting her laugh this off. That was *his* MO.

Placing a hand on her bottom, he lifted her hips higher, her legs still draped on his shoulders and spine against the wall as he used his other hand to toy with her. She was so soft, so perfect and pink there. She cried out as he gently rolled her clit between the callused pads of his forefinger and thumb. "Admit that I'm more than your friend," he purred.

"You've *always* been more than that," she keened.

The confession felt like sweet vindication.

"Then you can come for me." He let out a low growl as he nuzzled closer to her center. "Now." He flicked his tongue over her, gently grazing her sweet bead with his teeth as he clapped a hand on her behind with a slapping squeeze.

The sudden change in sensation was enough.

She came apart, pouring her sweet heat into his mouth as he lapped at her with his tongue. He could feel each wave of pleasure as it rolled through her, felt her tense beneath him once, twice, three times and then soften. With a contented, sated moan, Dakota slumped against the shower wall, soft and pliable in her post-sex glow.

Careful to support her weight, Blaze slipped the full curve of her thighs from his shoulders before he rose to his feet and lifted her into his arms.

"You can't carry me back to your cabin naked and with me thrown over your shoulder like some kind of caveman."

Blaze scoffed. His eyes glowing gold. "We're wolves. Who's going to stop me?" He grinned.

And to his complete joy, for the first time in days, she let out a full-throated laugh.

Chapter 11

"I TASKED AUSTIN AND MALCOLM WITH DISTRIBUTING EAR plugs to all the packmembers to keep on their person—which they fulfilled without question. I increased the patrols like you requested, ordered for there to be a weekly safety drill to keep the protocols fresh in the packmembers' minds, and authorized your visit to Bozeman to interview all the subpackmates who may have encountered Flynn Porter before his unexpected disappearance all for the sake of precaution. Is there anything else?"

The packmaster stood inside the stall gate of his recently broken-in mustang, Beast, running a brush over the massive stallion's brown coat. He cast Blaze an expectant look. It was well known that the packmaster valued his Friday afternoons, the few moments of downtime he was able to claim for himself all week. But today, from the look of impatience on the alpha wolf's features, Blaze was clearly spoiling it.

In this case, Blaze couldn't say he felt sorry for it.

He'd woken the following morning after the night he'd spent with Dakota, better rested than he had been in years. As a result, he'd risen early, gotten all his ranch chores out of the way, and with lightning-fast speed had crossed everything off his security list for the day, with hours of time to spare—and he wasn't nearly out of energy yet.

His parents hadn't named him Blaze for nothing.

"I need you to approve the budget for me to build a resonant sound device."

Maverick stopped brushing Beast and looked at Blaze as if he'd grown two heads.

"The pack won't be able to hear it," Blaze quickly added, "but when turned on, it'll emit a frequency that messes with…" He hesitated for a moment.

He hadn't spoken their name aloud since Russia. Hell, he hadn't even allowed himself to *think* it. Doing so would make it all the more real, but it was necessary.

"It'll mess with the Volk's abilities," he finished. "They're faster than us, whether in human or wolf form, and on the rare occasions when those flesh-eaters *do* actually shift like we do, they're nearly the same size as our largest alphas—all of them—and twice as hungry for the blood of their enemies, literally. But the frequency of the sound device I'm going to build will help with that. If they do come for us, it'll disrupt their echolocation with one another and their ability to get in touch with whatever is left of their wolf, or what used to be their wolf anyway. They'll be slower, unable to let out that awful sound they make. In battle, it could be the difference between surviving with only a few casualties and total slaughter."

"I don't want there to be *any* casualties," Maverick snarled before he cast the grooming brush aside.

Understanding that he needed to move out of the way, Blaze stepped out of the stall gate, allowing the packmaster to lead his horse out into the stall row.

"If it *is* them, there *will* be casualties. Even with all the extra measures and training we've put in place." He lowered his head for a moment at the thought, his Stetson casting a shadow over his face. "There's no way around that."

Maverick gave a curt, grim nod as Beast trailed him onto the cobblestones and down toward the saddle room. "Anything else?"

"Yeah, one more thing."

The packmaster lifted a brow.

Blaze cleared his throat. "Don't mention my connection to any of this to the other elite warriors."

Maverick paused. He gave Beast a hearty pat before he speared Blaze with a hard stare. "You mean don't mention this to Dakota."

Blaze didn't answer.

She'd asked him to take things slow after last night. There still wasn't anything certain about them yet. No matter how many times he'd made her moan.

Maverick shook his head. "Is this about you or them?"

"Me," he admitted. "It's about me. I'm not ready for the questions. But further, knowing my experiences will only spread fear. The kind of boogeyman fear that only takes root because it's really just a fear of the unknown. Better to just train, prepare, and be on guard for anything. We can raise awareness, preparedness, without causing undue alarm."

Maverick gripped Beast's reins again. "We don't take our safety for granted."

The balance among shifters, supernaturals, and their rivals was a precarious one. Death, war, discovery…these were daily stressors.

"Exactly." Blaze followed after him. "That's why I'm requesting we keep the information surrounding this on a need-to-know basis. For everyone. Not just her. We can train them, prepare them without getting into the details of my past. My involvement makes no difference. Knowing will do nothing at best, and it'll be detrimental at worst. The knowledge I survived the Volk before will only make them *think* they're prepared, when there's no way they ever could be. Not until they've experienced it. I learned that the hard way."

Maverick grumbled a noncommittal response.

But Blaze wasn't having it.

He quickened his pace, coming up on Beast's far side and stepping directly in the packmaster's path. Maverick growled. No other wolf would have dared.

But Blaze had earned this right and he knew it.

"You owe me," he growled back, not backing down even in the face of the Grey Wolf packmaster. "You asked me to go to Russia and I agreed, even though I had no idea what I was getting myself into. But *you* did."

It was as much an accusation as it was a statement of fact. They both knew it.

"I warned you. I tried to tell you how difficult it was going to be," Maverick shot back.

"Yet still, you asked me, knowing I've always been loyal to you even when I didn't want to be." He drew up close, daring to stand nearly toe-to-toe with Maverick. "You knew what I'd see there would be enough to break a man, yet you threw me under the damn bus anyway."

"If I could have gone myself, I would have." Maverick bared his teeth. "Other than me, you were the only one I knew could handle it." Maverick stepped back, clearly having the sense that if either of them pushed further on this, alpha instincts would take over and one of them would end up in the ground. Neither of them truly wanted that. Maverick gestured a hand to indicate where Blaze stood. "And you did, warrior. You *did* handle it. You survived."

"Barely." Blaze turned away from his friend. "If you call living every day in fear that the people I love, that our pack will be targeted for what I've done, or worse, see me for what I really am and then decide they no longer..." Blaze's voice trailed off before he swallowed the lump that had formed in his throat. He exhaled a long breath. "If you call that survival, then I suppose that I did survive. I, on the other hand, wouldn't call it that."

"What would you call it then?"

"Torture." He twisted back toward Maverick, his eyes flashing to his wolf. "A life half lived. Living in fear isn't living at all."

"And what about the woman you love? Isn't *she* worth living for?"

"Of course she is," Blaze said without hesitation. He faced Maverick fully. "Why do you think I'm still here? I wouldn't be if I didn't think, hope that someday she'd be safe from all this and then, maybe..."

The unspoken words hung heavy between them.

That maybe someday, she'd love him back.

Enough to even say it.

Maverick hooked Beast's reins over one of the stall posts, gesturing wildly in the direction of the compound. "Then tell her that, damn it. Let go of your fear, warrior. Face it. Tell her, tell me, tell any goddamn member of this pack what you saw, what you did, have a fucking confessional for all I care. Just trust that they can and will love you anyway."

"I can't," Blaze shot back. "I don't know that I'll ever be able to."

Dropping his hands, Maverick shook his head, obviously resigning himself to the fact that he wasn't going to win this battle. "Then you're right. That's not survival. But damn it, Blaze." He picked up Beast's reins again. "You're the one choosing to remain in the dark."

The packmaster led the powerful stallion past.

"My request?" Blaze called out after him. "We can prepare them for the Volk, but sharing my involvement will only bring questions I'm not prepared to answer yet."

"As you've pointed out on more than one occasion, you're more experienced on this than I am," Maverick admitted. "If you think it's best…"

"I do."

The beat of silence that followed spoke volumes. "Then your history stays on a need-to-know basis."

The rest of the night Dakota and Blaze had spent together had been amazing, both of them teasing, playing, and exploring each other's bodies, but the days that had followed since had been…awkward, to say the least. Dakota sat at one of the tables in the mess hall, munching on an apple she'd snagged from the kitchen before spreading out the pile of papers and information in front of her. It was between meals, so the mess hall was mostly empty now, save for the few wolves back in the kitchens preparing for dinner who'd graciously put down some cream for Peaches. Most of the pack ate their meals here, together, even though they all technically had their own kitchens, and Blaze's cat had been following her like a hawk as of late.

Blaze had offered for her to work at a spare table in the security office, considering she still hadn't been assigned an office space, but she'd politely declined. Since that night, they'd both been fumbling to figure out the new dynamic between them, neither one of them wanting to cross any lines but also unwilling to be the first to bring up the subject.

Were they still friends? If they were something more, what were they now? Did they even have to put a label on it? She'd told him she wanted to take things slowly.

Dakota didn't have the answers.

At first, she'd gone to the pack's library in favor of working there, but along with their supplies, Naomi, the Grey Wolf second-in-command's kindhearted human wife, and Sierra with her feet propped up beneath her protruding, overdue bump of a belly, had consumed most of the available space. The packmaster's mate had been working with the second-in-command's Native human partner for some time to bring Naomi up to speed on the pack's lengthy and sordid history, while Naomi had been providing critical information about the gaps in the pack's historical relations with the Native human tribes of the area.

Most humans weren't aware of the Grey Wolf species, with interaction between the two kinds largely forbidden on their end, but the mythology and traditional stories of the local tribes told volumes about that briefly shared history. The two women had been so busy poring over several large tomes of Grey Wolf history in the midst of an intense discussion that Dakota had slipped out and come to the mess hall instead. She'd known she would have been too tempted to chat the afternoon away with the other females rather than pore over the plethora of information about the Arctic wolves.

Who knew that the northern wolf shifters, despite being the same basic species, would have such different customs and traditions than the Grey Wolves did?

It was as if their packs had formed in separate worlds—one of mountains and lush forest land and one in the icy, glittering landscapes near the Arctic tundra. What Dakota wouldn't give to someday visit and howl beneath the aurora borealis while in wolf form.

She'd considered going back to her cabin and working there instead. But that would have placed her in close proximity to her computer, which had become another form of stress while she and Blaze formulated their plan to deal with the strange occurrences on the ranch. There'd been another two long emails from Jasper. Each a more intimate and heartfelt letter than the last. It was odd, really, like he knew her better than she'd ever thought, considering their limited interactions over the years.

The Grey Wolf international liaison mostly lived abroad. But he seemed to be more invested and interested in her than she'd expected since his last visit to Wolf Pack Run for the packmaster's wedding reception. Considering how things were with Blaze, she wasn't certain how to tell Jasper that her heart was already taken, yet...wasn't, because everything between her and Blaze was strangely nebulous. And how did one explain that without giving intimate details? It wasn't as if she could write: *Sorry I replied to you. I wasn't trying to lead you on. I just wanted to be polite because we're packmates. I only like your letters because they remind me of another guy.*

Dakota groaned. It seemed no matter what she did, she was going to let someone down.

Releasing a long sigh, she turned back to the page she'd been reading. According to Jasper's records detailing the customs of the Yellowknife Arctic Wolf Pack and their history, apparently, they weren't as hostile toward vampires as the Grey Wolves were.

That was going to prove a problem in convincing the wolves to ally with them against the Seven Range Pact's common enemy.

A large hand slapped down beside her on the wood of the great hall table.

Her head shot up. She'd recognize those hands and all the filthy, naughty things they could do to her anywhere—along with his devilish tongue.

Blaze stood over her, a grim look on his face. Flopping down on the bench beside her, he leaned back against the table. Despite his flamboyant Hawaiian shirt, a throwback to his days in SoCal where he'd earned his tech degree before enlisting in the military, he looked downright furious.

"What's wrong?"

"Flynn."

He didn't have to say it for her to understand.

They'd found the body.

Their packmates out in Bozeman had been searching for well over a week with no sign of the missing packmate. They'd known it was only a matter of time. None of their kind every went missing for that long, yet still...

Dakota hung her head, thinking of the family and friends the other wolf had left behind. She hadn't known him, considering the wolves who lived out in the subpacks only interacted with the main pack at Wolf Pack Run during certain pack holidays, like their yearly Lunar Ceremony, but she was still saddened by the news.

A lost packmate was a blow to them all.

They were one with each other.

All of them. Location didn't change that.

"And?" she asked, prompting Blaze for more information.

The dark scowl on Blaze's lips didn't loosen. "Same as the cattle," he growled.

Dakota tensed. She'd feared that. They both had. "What do you think this means?"

"It means we have less time until word gets out to the cougars. Nothing stays secret among the shifter clans in the Seven Range

Pact for long, and as far as I can tell, our suspicions that Jonathan was out there to gather support for his coup were accurate. He didn't have anything to do with the disappearance. It was coincidence, but Clay will still leverage Jonathan's presence there for his foolish agenda."

Dakota shook her head. "It still confuses me. The vampires are responsible for the blood loss, but what about the carnage? That's not their style."

Blaze didn't answer.

Maverick had warned the elite warriors of the potential threat of the Volk so they could begin training the lower-ranked warriors and run safety drills with the civilian wolves of the pack. Dakota had known that Blaze must have been involved with the monsters somehow, considering their Russian origin, but she hadn't been able to bring herself to broach the topic. As the daughter of a former soldier, she knew that what happened to a man during wartime wasn't a topic of open discussion. It had to be freely shared, and the fact that Blaze still didn't trust her with that dark part of himself hurt more than she wanted it to.

Their eyes met for a moment. A subtle tension built. There was more confusion than just the pack's enemies between them at the moment.

Sitting beside her at the mess hall table like he was, it reminded her of so many meals they'd shared together over the years, not just as packmates but as friends. Both before and after his MAC-V-Alpha days. Before they'd been something...more than friends.

Yet still, he clearly felt he couldn't trust her with his past.

She turned back toward the table, grabbing her apple from where she'd set it and taking a generous bite. She extended it toward Blaze, and he took it, accepting her offer to share. The flash of his canines as he bit into the fruit sent a surprise wave of heat to her core. The handsome sight of his side profile, of him sitting there with his mouth open and hungry reminded her of how that wide tongue had been used when…

Heat flooded her cheeks.

Blaze chewed on the bite of apple he'd taken, pausing only momentarily to look at her. His nose flared as his eyes transitioned to the gold of his wolf, as if he sensed the damp rush that pooled between her legs but wasn't going to mention it. He swallowed the bite he'd taken, with a sharp jerk of his Adam's apple.

Looking away from her, he cleared his throat, passing the half-eaten McIntosh back to her. Despite his strong come-on at the beginning of all this, he was giving her the space she needed to collect and process her thoughts, waiting for her to lead them forward, and she was grateful.

Even if he didn't appear to like it.

His voice was gruff, strained as he spoke. "It's clear this is escalating quickly. With the cougars poised to exit the Pact, we need to meet with the Arctic wolves as soon as possible." He finally glanced toward her again. His eyes had gone back from the gold of his wolf to their warm, seafoam blue.

She wondered what he'd had to think about in order to get them to do that.

"Do you think you're ready?" he asked, interrupting her thoughts.

Dakota glanced down at the paperwork she'd been poring over for the past several days. It wasn't the entire history of the Arctic pack and their customs—that extended as far back as their own nearly did—but it was more than enough to offer a hand of friendship. The Arctic wolves had partnered with them once before when the threat had been an existential one to the whole of their species. With some finessing, she felt confident she could convince them that the previous arrangement was still beneficial and would continue to be for the long term.

They'd make fine members of the Seven Range Pact.

"Set up the meeting," she said. "I'm ready for it and I'll get you up to speed."

Blaze nodded. "I'll set it up." As he moved to get up, he paused momentarily, his eyes darting to her lips and holding there as if he was considering whether or not to kiss her. Dakota stiffened in anticipation.

But he didn't.

Pushing up from the bench, he stood and padded toward the mess hall entrance.

Dakota closed her eyes, stifling her disappointment. They needed to do this. To take things slow. It was the only way they could both be certain. She blew out a short breath. "Blaze," she called after him.

"Yeah, Kotes?" He paused, looking back toward her. The devious spark in his gaze, like he hoped she was going to ask him to come back and kiss her after all, gutted her.

Awkward didn't even begin to cover it.

"Don't just invite their elite warriors," she said, picking up the stack of papers that detailed the former matriarchal history of the Yellowknife Arctic Wolf Pack. This was her chance to prove herself. "Ask Rock to send some of the pack's females."

Chapter 12

AMAROK HAD SENT HIS HALF SISTER, JESSIKA TOON, AND SHE was as absolutely fierce as she was lovely. Dakota and the other she-wolf had spent the morning touring Wolf Pack Run together, chatting and getting to know each other as they shared their individual packs' customs. Having lived at Wolf Pack Run since she'd been an older teen and her father had retired from his military career, Dakota knew all the pack's females intimately, so it was a treat to connect with another alpha she-wolf who brought a perspective that was fresh and new—and *fresh* was the perfect word for Jessika.

She was a tall, willowy woman with handsome features that spoke of her Inuit heritage. Her short, black hair was cut at a fashionable angle yet still long enough that she could easily tie it back before it was time to train or fight. She carried a blade on her belt made of copper, as was custom in the Canadian North pack, and the spark of fire and righteous feminine fury in the other female's eyes when she spoke of her goal to become her pack's first second-in-command, after the Yellowknife Pack's laws of primogeniture had cheated her out of the role of packmaster that *should* have been her birthright, reminded Dakota a lot of both herself and another fierce female warrior she knew who'd become the first among the Grey Wolves elite.

She'd instantly wanted to be this Arctic she-wolf's friend and more than ever for the alliance to work out between their packs as planned. Not to mention she still wanted to prove herself worthy of her new role.

"So your pack really used to be matriarchal?" Dakota asked as they made their way from the Grey Wolves' medical wing, where she'd told Jessika about all the pack's recent medical advances courtesy of Belle, their high commander's mate and a talented orthopedic physician, who was now the mother to three of their youngest packmembers. Their birth had ushered in the Grey Wolves' latest baby boom nearly a year before.

It was rare to have a shifter like Belle trained as a human physician who could then take those same scientific concepts and principles and apply them to their own kind. Before her, Austin, the Grey Wolf medic, had been as close as they'd had to a full physician. When they were in human form, they were anatomically the same, but not all human medicines worked on them and their normal resting body temperature and heart rate were radically different. Not to mention the rate at which they healed. Their long life expectancy alone was enough for any physician to differentiate between them and humans.

Jessika, who'd said medicine had been an interest of her mother's before she'd passed, had been fascinated by the idea. And as a science lover herself, albeit veterinarian in nature, Dakota had reveled in sharing their exciting advancements. It was a benefit that would extend to the Yellowknife Pack, should they decide to join the Seven Range Pact and ally alongside them.

"A long time ago, the Yellowknife Pack was matriarchal, yes." Jessika brushed the sharp angle of her hair away from her face as they walked back toward the main compound. "The males of the pack like to think it's forgotten history, but it's built into our blood. It's a part of us. We won't be deterred by them."

Dakota nodded thoughtfully. "If you're the firstborn and pack law prevented you from claiming the title, wouldn't it have passed to your brother?" Dakota asked.

It was a sensitive question, considering she knew that Amarok "Rock" Saila had never claimed the title of packmaster among the Arctic wolves of Yellowknife, but Jessika had been surprisingly open about their history with her, and Dakota had been honest with the other female in kind.

"He was in line to be, once he came of age," Jessika answered. "But he abdicated to Alexander years ago."

Alexander Caron, the Arctic wolves' current packmaster.

"Here it's not common for a wolf in line for packmaster to abdicate. They're groomed for the role from birth. Maverick certainly was."

Jessika's smile faded as she let out a short sigh. "It's not common in our pack either."

They reached the main compound building that held the pack's conference rooms. As the heavy door slammed behind them and the two females headed down the hall, Dakota's stomach churned. The interactions between her and Jessika had felt so natural and easy throughout the early parts of the morning that Dakota hadn't expected the nerves that were now settling into her. She held open the door to the conference room, allowing Jessika to enter before her. Dakota paused and inhaled a deep breath to steady herself and the slight tremble in her hands.

She would be fine. The pack would be fine. She'd prepared for this nearly nonstop for the past several days. She'd cement the alliance and then prove exactly how much she deserved her position—uncertainty about her own goals, abilities, and the future be damned.

Dakota stepped into the room. The conference room door fell closed behind her with a soft, near-inaudible swish. The weight of more than a dozen eyes fell on her.

She was not, in fact, fine.

Five of the Arctic wolves' male elite warriors sat at the near end of the table, the imposing size of them crowding this side of the conference room. The harsh-looking alphas staring up at her weren't pleased to see her or even cordial for that matter—to her or their female packmate. Blaze sat at the far end of the table with the documents she'd asked him to prepare, waiting. Today he was wearing a T-shirt that read:

I KNOW I SWEAR A LOT.

1. I'm sorry.
2. I'll try to be good.
3. 1 and 2 are lies.
4. Fuck off.

His was the only welcoming stare in the room.

Dakota swallowed. When the Grey Wolves had made the decision to induct Sierra to the pack's ranks as the first female elite warrior, there'd only been small, if vocal, opposition from some of the elder members of the pack. Gender equality through pack law had been the overwhelmingly popular decision at Wolf Pack Run, despite some dissenting outliers from the subpacks and the nasty matter of Maverick having to overturn the entire Elder Council.

But from the hardened stares boring through her and Jessika, the other she-wolf hadn't been exaggerating when she said the alpha males of the Arctic Pack weren't fully convinced that females should be among the pack's elite warrior ranks. She'd been *downplaying* the issue.

Both she and Jessika stood there, minimized beneath the scrutiny of the Arctic Pack males.

After a prolonged, awkward pause, Dakota gestured to an available chair near Jessika's packmates. "Please, sit."

Jessika shook her head with a nearly imperceptible nod, as if she wouldn't even consider it and neither should Dakota, for that matter, before promptly moving across the room to stand in the corner—*behind* where her packmates sat, like she wasn't even equal enough to stand beside them. Let alone join them at the table.

Clearly, the Yellowknife Arctic Wolves were a pack divided. Nearly as on the brink of a civil war between the she-wolves and the males of their species as the damn cougars whose pride politics had led to this stupid mess in the first place, and she and Blaze had now fallen into the middle of it.

Dakota blinked.

This had been a mistake.

Abruptly, Blaze stood, clearing his throat in an attempt to clear the tension in the room and come to her rescue. "Gentlemen," he said, sounding uncharacteristically formal in a way that was…well, not Blaze-like at all.

But at this moment, she would welcome anything that would save her.

Blaze nodded toward her. "This is Dakota Nguyen. She's the second among the pack's females to join our elite warrior ranks, and I think you'll find she'd be an incredibly fierce opponent for any one of you."

Ignoring Blaze's glowing endorsement of her fighting capabilities, the Arctic wolves barely cast a glance toward her. "What happened to the first?" The Arctic wolf who'd spoken was a large meathead of a shifter with a close-shaved buzz cut and bulging muscles that made him look like some strange cross between a bodybuilder, a pro athlete, and a lumberjack, courtesy of his flannel shirt.

Blaze cast Dakota a pointed look, clearly volleying the question to her, both in an attempt to give her an opportunity to lead the conversation and also in clear oppositional deference to the fact that *she* was supposed to be the one calling the shots here, but the question had been specifically asked of him—and the Arctic wolves knew it.

Dakota blushed. Good Lord, he'd never been more attractive than he was in that moment, supporting her with that spark of righteous frustration in his eyes and that once-again irreverent grin of his that seemed to say, *Fuck this. Give these bastards hell.*

Blaze had clearly decided all of two seconds ago that he couldn't give two shits what these Arctic wolf bastards thought of him if they were going to be rude to her, and at the moment, she didn't care either, which meant the two of them were going to botch this—she knew it. Neither one of them did well with keeping their mouths shut when it came to defending each other or their packmates; it was one of the many reasons they were friends.

Dakota stepped forward, mentally collecting herself as she did. She could do this if she set her mind to it. She could do anything she set her mind to, including be diplomatic for the sake of the pack. Maybe she could pull this off after all, and that'd make it an even more impressive feat. Nobody said the Arctic wolves had to follow their integration models to be their allies—though clearly they needed to, unless they wanted to keep living like it was last century while the matriarchal blooded females of their pack plotted to take them out in the middle of the night when they were unsuspecting and asleep. Or at least that was how she was feeling, even if Jessika appeared reluctant to show it.

Subversive, undetected rebellion, no matter how quiet, was just as powerful, she supposed.

"Sierra's on a short leave at the moment," she said, answering the question about the other she-wolf's absence even though it hadn't been asked of *her*. She didn't hesitate over being intentionally vague.

Meathead scoffed. "Already injured?" The question was directed at Blaze again. The wolf who'd asked it had a smug of-course-she-was look on his face, because in his mind being female obviously meant being weak.

Blaze scowled as if he were imagining impaling the other wolf with the ballpoint pen clutched in his hand. Dakota knew all the ways Blaze could kill another man with a seemingly innocuous item—or even his bare hands, for that matter—but clearly, this idiot Arctic wolf didn't.

Dakota would have growled herself if she wasn't supposed to be diplomatic, and contrary to her recent behavior, Blaze was the truly impulsive one of the two of them. "No, she's not injured."

Finally, the Arctic wolf's gaze fell toward her expectantly, waiting for an answer as if she and whatever she said were no more relevant or crucial to this conversation than a pesky fly buzzing around his haunches in wolf form. And to think, shifters on other continents thought *they* were backward, because their pack was made up of cowboys who worked the land like humans. Weren't Canadians supposed to be friendly and, well, nice, eh?

Dakota's lip twitched as she held in a snarl. "Sierra's on maternity leave," she finally answered, unable to avoid the question any longer. Who cared what this idiot thought?

Meathead sat back in his chair, his too-thick arms crossing over his chest. "Figures."

Dakota blinked. Had he just…? She scowled.

Yes, he had.

"Excuse me, but that's our packmaster's mate you're talking about," Dakota snapped. She might not have been thrilled initially with Sierra's pregnancy herself, but she'd *never* allow anyone to demean or disparage her friend—and Sierra was happy. When it came down to it, that was all that really mattered. The rest of the details about the balance of the Grey Wolves' own gender-equality issues would sort themselves out in time. She and the other she-wolves would see to it.

After all, female joy, happiness, pleasure was a revolutionary act—Sierra's included.

Ignoring her, Meathead looked back toward Blaze. "She's a bit small to be a warrior, isn't she?"

Blaze openly snarled, no longer bothering to hold his aggression back. But Dakota raised a hand to stop him. She could fight her own battles.

"I'm sorry. Who are you exactly?" she asked, more than a hint of disdain in her voice.

"Whitt Lavigne."

The Arctic Wolf high commander. Of course. She'd memorized

the names of their higher-ranking warriors before they'd arrived. According to Jasper's notes, Whitt had worked his way up the Arctic Wolf ranks with less strategic battle ability and more sheer bravado, and he could always be counted on for exactly one thing: toxic masculinity.

Jessika had mentioned that he was the most obstinate and bigoted among the opposition to the female Arctic wolves. Clearly, the alpha shifter needed to be taken down a massive peg, and if Jessika and the other females of the pack felt they couldn't, Dakota had no problem being the one to do it.

"Right, and was that comment meant to be demeaning to the fact that I'm female or are you trying to be openly racist?" Dakota crossed her arms over her chest. "I honestly can't tell." Dakota knew she wasn't as tall and muscled as Sierra or even as long and willowy as Jessika, but she wasn't small or diminutive, and the comment felt like an obvious jab at the fact that she was half-Vietnamese.

She wasn't about to put up with that kind of treatment from anyone—potential pack ally or otherwise.

Whitt didn't answer, only grumbled some vague response about women knowing their place in a way that was both as infuriating and disgusting as it was insulting.

Dakota shook her head, so angry she couldn't bring herself to respond for a moment. She crossed the room and took her seat at the table directly beside Blaze, who'd moved over in order for her to sit at the table head. Irreverent, sarcastic, and horribly snarky in his fashion choices or not, when this awful meeting was over, she was going to show him all the things his unfaltering support of her made her want to do with him—to him. He'd let her take control and lead if she wanted after all.

She meant that much to him.

Dakota was still shaking her head like she had a chunk of Whitt's hide in her wolf jaws and was tearing at it as she pulled up the conference-room seat underneath her. How could this be the pack of Alexander Caron, the openly gay Arctic Wolf packmaster who'd been to Wolf Pack Run so many times to visit that he might as well have built a small residence? The packmaster himself had seemed so amiable and willing to listen to the views of those who were different.

Or Rock, for that matter? The former soldier who'd abdicated to the current packmaster and had also served as Blaze's former MAC-V-Alpha officer before becoming a mercenary for the Arctic Wolves throughout the years. He had never treated Dakota so poorly. She'd had the pleasure of meeting him more than once when he'd stopped in to see Blaze for a quick visit. He hadn't seemed to hold these regressive opinions. Nor did Jessika, who'd presented as brave and fierce until the moment she'd stepped into this room and immediately stiffened before falling silent.

Dakota's gaze fell across the table where she met Whitt's stare head-on. Jessika had said it wasn't normal for someone like Rock to abdicate his birthright as packmaster, and to a friend like Alexander Caron no less. Nor was it normal for a warrior from another pack to be so openly hostile toward the Grey Wolves. They were the most powerful wolf pack in western North America.

Clearly, there was something deeper and more nuanced going on here.

Whatever it was, it troubled her.

And she wasn't about to let her pack be dragged to the bottom of it.

She'd planned a whole presentation of facts, spreadsheets, and charts detailing the pack's integration models and the formation of their Peer Council to highlight how well things were going with having female warriors in the pack's highest ranks. She'd planned to provide them all that information out of the kindness of her heart before asking anything of them in return, because regardless of whether her pack allied with them, she'd wanted to help the females of the Yellowknife Arctic Wolf Pack shatter their own glass ceilings. Liberation for any one of them benefited them all.

Blaze had brought all her documents in a three-ring folder per her request. She gathered them and closed the folder. As if he recognized exactly what she was doing, Blaze pulled a large manila packaging envelope from her bag that she'd also asked him to bring for her and passed it over. She slipped the three-ring folder inside the envelope, ripped off the adhesive cover and sealed it before pushing back her chair and standing.

"Take this to your packmaster per our packmaster Maverick Grey's orders."

The mere mention of the Grey Wolf packmaster's name caused the tension in the room to thicken. They didn't call the Grey Wolf packmaster the Monster of Montana for nothing, although she and Blaze knew the truth. Maverick was about as monstrous as a kitten (or maybe Peaches, considering he *was* a bit grumbly), but he was fiercely loving toward those he cared for.

And lethal to those he didn't.

They weren't technically Maverick's orders; they were hers, but not even Maverick himself would question that once he heard about the outcome of this meeting.

Whitt scowled, lifting out of his chair as if to reach across the conference table, but Dakota stopped him in his tracks. Her eyes flashed to her wolf and she glared at him as if he were nothing but a bit of manure stuck to the bottom of one of her cowgirl boots.

"Not you," she said. Her eyes fell to the far corner of the room. "Her."

Jessika stood in the corner, looking quietly furious as if she were resigned to her position but not pleased about it. The moment Dakota's gaze fell to her, the other female immediately unstiffened, as if Dakota's acknowledgment of her had somehow lent her strength.

"Me?" Jessika asked, eyes wide.

"Yes," Dakota answered. "Maverick's specific orders were for a female alpha wolf to hand-deliver this to Alexander."

At the mention of Alexander's name, the male Arctic wolves tensed. One of their lips curled in threatening menace. Clearly, exactly *who* the Arctic Wolf packmaster was remained a source of potent challenge, a source of contention.

Interesting.

But not her problem.

Without hesitation, Jessika stepped forward, taking the proffered envelope from her hand. Beside her, Blaze whipped open his laptop, the back of which had an artfully placed sticker that aptly read "Not today, Satan"—perhaps a little too on the nose at this moment—before his fingers flew across the keyboard.

"I just emailed Alexander directly. He'll be expecting it hand-delivered from Jessika, sealed and unopened." Blaze glanced up from his computer screen as his eyes flashed the gold of his wolf beneath the rim of his Stetson. That a wolf could look so menacing while sitting behind a computer was an impressive feat in and of itself—even for one as deadly as Blaze.

Taking that as her cue again, Dakota gave a final nod of gratitude and acknowledgment to Jessika before she turned back toward the male alpha wolves. "Now, I had a whole presentation prepared. I was going to detail to you all the benefits of joining the Seven Range Pact and our mutual species history, how ranchers in this area protecting their livestock nearly led to the eradication of our kind, and how despite that, our pack took that concept and turned it on its head, claiming this land and the humans' ranching practices as our own in order to protect and allow our species to thrive without having to hide ourselves away like you all do up near the Arctic tundra."

She straightened as she spoke, drawing to her full height. "We went from near extinction to undisputed pack dominance on the entire western half of this continent. I meant for that tale to underline the Grey Wolf Pack's ingenuity. Our willingness to adapt and bend to the will of progress while still holding true to our values. We don't live in fear of change, and neither should you. At least that's what I'd planned to say at the time—but clearly you all do live in fear—and of the power of your pack's females no less."

Dakota wasn't certain which she found more satisfying, the look of pure rage on the faces of male Arctic alpha wolves or the beaming pride coming from Jessika and Blaze.

"Now," she said, clearing her throat. "When you're ready to behave like fierce warriors rather than the cowards you really are, you can come back here, and then we can discuss you allying with the Grey Wolf Pack. Until then, you can tell your packmaster that it is *your* fault that I and the entirety of the Grey Wolf Pack are telling you to promptly and thoroughly fuck off. We don't need you as allies." She placed her hands on her hips. "Because there isn't a single cowgirl on this ranch who's willing to put up with your shit."

The room remained tense and oddly quiet for a moment, until Dakota nodded to the exit.

"You can see yourselves out."

Slowly, the Arctic alpha males stood. Whitt was the last. He lifted a meaty hand and pointed a finger toward her. "You'll—"

He didn't even have the time to get out the word *regret* or whatever other hackneyed, clichéd threat he'd been about to hurl at her before Blaze was on the other wolf. Dakota had barely seen him move. It was as if he'd vaulted the table within a millisecond. He clutched the Arctic wolf by the throat and slammed him into the adjacent wall. She'd known Blaze was fast, but before any of the other warriors could move, the copper of the Arctic wolf's own knife was in Blaze's hand and pushed against its owner's throat.

He'd obviously been quietly planning this from the start. He'd simply been waiting for the opportune moment. He wouldn't have dared to interrupt her or steal her thunder.

Blaze snarled, baring his teeth, the gold of his wolf eyes wild and feral. "If you *ever* so much as look at her again, I will gut you where you stand. You're not worthy to beg at her feet."

By the time he allowed the other wolf to breathe again, Whitt was gasping.

"Get out," Blaze growled.

This time, the Arctic wolves did as they were told. Jessika trailed after them, pausing momentarily to smile at Dakota with a muttered "thank you" before disappearing with the schematics and plans that would hopefully give her and the other females and their packmaster an idea of how to fix the deep-rooted inequities in their pack.

The door to the conference room closed behind her, leaving Dakota and Blaze alone.

Dakota slumped into the chair behind her, immediately crashing from the adrenaline of the confrontation. "Maverick's not going to be pleased." She breathed out. She hadn't realized she'd been holding her breath until now.

Dream team?

Not so much.

Cementing an alliance to protect the pack?

Not when it came to following the rules anyway.

Apparently, she was just as bad about not listening to Maverick as the rest of the elite warriors, and to think, she'd planned to be different.

"No," Blaze admitted. "He won't be pleased, but he'll understand and Sierra will be pleased, so he'll come around and we'll find different allies. We don't need them." Blaze stuck up the middle fingers on both hands and flipped the bird toward the closed door where the Arctic wolves had exited before he cast her an appreciative smirk. "What kind of wine goes with ruthlessly smashing the patriarchy? Because whatever it is, I'm going to buy it for you—in bulk. Like a lifetime supply."

Dakota laughed, shaking her head at him. "What were you thinking?"

"Well, I was thinking cabernet since I know it's your favorite, but…"

"That's not what I'm talking about, Blaze. I meant going after that jerk like you were my mate, instead of my…" Her voice trailed off. She couldn't bring herself to fight whatever *this* was between them at the moment. Instead of her what? Her everything? With renewed energy, she stood again. "Lock the conference room door."

Blaze lifted a brow. "What?"

"I said, lock the conference room door."

He didn't question it, just did as she told him.

Dakota came around the far side of the table, advancing toward him.

Blaze pawed at the golden-brown locks of his hair sheepishly as if he knew he'd done wrong and was about to get his ass handed to him but didn't care. "Look, I know throwing that fucker up against the wall and threatening him like some big, bad alpha wolf probably wasn't the best of ideas, nor was it exactly progressive for me to do or whatever, because you can fight your own battles, but—"

Dakota stopped directly in front of him, gripping the material of his shirt in both hands. "Blaze," she said, "shut up."

Gorgeous and perfect as he was, she reveled in the way his mouth fell openly slightly. Blaze was highly intelligent. Nothing much caught him off guard, so she didn't often get to see him look like that.

"Kotes, what are you—?"

"Shhh." She let her hands trail lower, over the ridges of his abdomen and down until she gripped the leather of his belt. She worked at the brass buckle there. "Don't ruin this for me."

Blaze's voice dropped an octave, sexy and low. "I thought you'd be angry that I acted like you were my ma—"

"I don't care what you want to call it. All I know is that you supporting me like that was the sexiest you've ever been in your life."

The wide, white-toothed grin that spread across his face was enough to make her heart beat twice as fast. "I mean, I can be an asshole to people you don't like more often. I don't even have to try that hard." Blaze had the wherewithal to look extremely pleased with himself. "And did you just call me sexy?"

"I did." Dakota laughed as she slid to her knees in front of him. "Now, drop your pants before I change my mind, soldier."

Blaze growled in approval.

And to her pleasure, he did.

Chapter 13

DAKOTA SHOULD HAVE RESCINDED HIS INVITATION TO DINNER. They'd have to talk about it, them, this, whatever *this* was eventually, not to mention the alliance they'd botched. Although, to their surprise, Maverick had taken the news rather well. She knew they would have to talk about all of it, but she hadn't wanted it to be *now* and she definitely hadn't wanted it to be with her mother present, and after a full day spent training for the Volk no less. She was both physically and mentally exhausted.

Mẹ flitted about the kitchen, hovering over the pho broth that'd been reheating for the better part of an hour. She typically spent over twenty-four hours letting it simmer days prior to when they had a guest over, only to chill and then reheat it the day of when the flavors were better married. There wasn't anything left to do to it until it was time to throw the rice noodles in. The assorted basil and bean sprouts and the slices of raw beef would be added at the table with the broth poured over it as it was served.

Somehow, Mẹ still always managed to make a fuss about it.

Personally, Dakota was tired of pho in all its many variations, but Blaze had once said it was his favorite, so now, Mẹ made it religiously before every Thursday night and insisted on inviting him over. Peaches let out a disapproving yowl from where she sat cradled in Dakota's arms. Mẹ had taken the lid off the pot again, and a drip of condensation from the steaming lid had fallen onto one of the burners with a sizzling hiss.

Dakota pulled Peaches closer, only for the barn cat to sink her tiny fangs into Dakota's wrist again. Dakota let out a surprised yelp. With how much Peaches had been following her lately, she was starting to feel as if the kitty queen was as much her pet as

Blaze's—though she wasn't certain Peaches would agree to that. Case in point, this last bite.

"I'm just saying, you should consider it," Mẹ said, peeking beneath the lid of the boiling stockpot again.

Dakota wasn't sure exactly what she was supposed to be considering, since she'd only half-heartedly been tuning in to the conversation. Her mother could go on for hours, in a fluid mixture of English and Vietnamese, barely allowing her daughter to get a word in edgewise, so occasionally Dakota tuned out. Today, she'd been so busy thinking about the rigorous Volk training, what had happened between her and Blaze following their less-than-desirable encounter with the Arctic wolves, and how they would secure another ally in the Yellowknife Pack's place for the Seven Range Pact. And that didn't even begin to touch upon the fact that they had a dead packmate out in Bozeman and their enemies were up to some complicated plot she wasn't sure how to deal with. The training drills Blaze had coordinated were brutal. Harder than any she'd ever experienced before.

"Consider what?" she said, stroking a hand through Peaches's fur, though from the way Queen Peaches bristled before leaping from her arms, she hadn't quite petted her *correctly*.

"You know…" Mẹ answered with a dismissive wave of her hand before she muttered something under her breath in Vietnamese.

Her mother's English was impeccable but still heavily accented.

Mẹ grabbed six bowls from the cabinet. Dakota's three younger siblings, two of whom were still young enough to live with Mẹ, would be joining them tonight.

"No, I don't know." Dakota grabbed the bowls from where her mother had placed the stacked set and started distributing them around the table's placemats.

"Don't you?" Mẹ said, placing a hand on a slender curved hip. In the other, she waved around an old wooden spoon. "Marry Blaze, of course."

Dakota nearly dropped the last soup bowl onto the floor, fumbling with it before using her wolf reflexes to catch it. Years of warrior training were good for something at least. "M-marriage?" she stammered, as if her mother hadn't already said it a thousand times before—and only about Blaze no less. Mẹ had never liked any of her other boyfriends.

Not that Blaze was her boyfriend. He was her best... Well, she wasn't entirely sure. Did they have to put a label on it?

In any case, the level of mortification she felt at Mẹ's insistence she marry her best friend was amplified a thousand times more than it'd been before.

"Happiness is marrying your best friend, the one you can laugh and dream with," Mẹ said with another sage-like wave of her spoon.

Dakota fought not to roll her eyes. This coming from the same woman who thought if she'd kept the plastic wrap on their TV screen for the past five years, that meant it was still new. What did her mother know about falling in love with a best friend?

Her mother had descended from Himalayan wolf shifters who'd long ago settled in parts of Vietnam among other locations in Southeast Asia, and she'd met Dakota's father there, a born and bred Grey Wolf cowboy, shortly after he'd enlisted in MAC-V-Alpha. To hear Mẹ tell it, the moment she'd laid eyes on the handsome Grey Wolf soldier, it'd been love at first sight, not a slow turn of friendship into romance. The result of which had been the thirty-eight years of marriage they'd enjoyed. Never mind that two of those years she'd spent on her own since her husband died. Mẹ had never stopped counting their anniversaries.

Based on the way Mẹ spoke to the portrait of Dakota's father that she kept hung on the wall in the cabin's hallway, the memory of Dakota's father was just as alive as the man had once been.

"Jasper's been emailing me lately," Dakota said, trying to distract Mẹ. It was the truth, but as lovely as the letters were, every time she received them, she thought back to all the letters she'd received from Blaze still sitting in that old, decorative hatbox in her closet—and the words just weren't the same coming from a wolf who wasn't him.

"He's not for you." Mę shot her a knowing look that said *Jasper isn't who you want and you know it.*

"Mę, we've been through this. Blaze doesn't—"

The rough sound of a cowboy grumbling to announce his presence stopped her short. "I'd have married her years ago, Mę, but that kind of requires her consent." Blaze leaned against the kitchen doorway, having quietly let himself in. From the looks of it, he'd been waiting for them to notice him for some time. His Stetson was tipped at the perfect angle to cast a slight shadow over that white-toothed grin, and the tight T-shirt he was wearing did nothing to hide the muscles beneath the V-cut of his jeans that led down to…

Dakota blushed a deeper shade of crimson than the inside of the black-and-red soup bowl she was holding. "Don't encourage her," she hissed. "And to marry me, you would have had to have asked."

Blaze smirked at her, casting her a playful look. "Don't tempt me." Producing a bouquet of flowers from behind his back—a bunch of native Montana bitterroots, Mę's favorite—he planted a chaste kiss on top of Mę's head.

His T-shirt tonight was a sapphire blue that brought out the color of his eyes and, very apropos, read: "Even Your Mother Loves Me."

Mę blushed as if she were a teen again.

Dakota groaned.

The fact that her mother adored her best friend was bad enough on a good day, but now, considering all that had happened between her and Blaze as of late, it somehow made it worse. Mę didn't know that, of course. Did she?

As if reading her thoughts, Mę cast Dakota a strangely knowing glance.

Dakota froze from where she'd been fishing utensils out a drawer. No, Mę didn't—

There was no way that she—

Mẹ gave her that a-mother-always-knows look followed by a subtle little cough as her chin lifted to the kitchen window, where in the distance, the pasture outside the showers and training gym waited, where Blaze had carried her off nak—

Dakota's soul lifted from her body, floating above her and her wolf with the sheer horror of her mother, who had excellent night vision for an older she-wolf, seeing her and Blaze when they'd been…

Dakota's cheeks flooded with heat. Was there a stronger word than mortification? Because she was pretty certain she was living it.

Mẹ muttered something in Vietnamese, which in rough translation meant "I didn't know for certain before, but I do now."

Gossip around the pack traveled like wildfire, particularly among the older ladies of her mother's age group. She'd *told* Blaze he couldn't carry her off like a caveman, wolf shifter or not. Dakota collapsed onto the countertop with a dramatic groan. According to her father, her mother had been a spirited young woman to begin with, but years spent traveling the world with him and enough age to make her not care as much about silly things like convention or tradition had made her far more comfortable with these kinds of conversations than any mother ought to be.

"I don't know what you're saying, Mẹ," Blaze said—he even called her mother *Mom*; Dakota groaned again—"but whatever it is, from the look on Dakota's face, I think I like it."

"You would," Mẹ answered, smiling sweetly as if she were behaving herself by keeping the secret between her and Dakota.

In what Dakota hoped would be many, many years from now, Mẹ could have taken the secret to the grave without ever telling Dakota that she knew and that still wouldn't have been secret enough.

"Can we please *not* talk about your opinions about my love life with Blaze here?"

Mẹ gave a disapproving click of her tongue as Blaze grinned.

"Or we could, you know, talk about it?" Blaze cast Dakota a flirtatious grin as if to say *Since, you know, I'm a major part of it now, and I've been impatiently waiting for you to chat with me about this since you first kissed me last week.*

That was encouragement enough for Mẹ apparently. "I just think you should marry a nice man who cares for you. That's all. Not like that Brett years ago."

"Brett?" Blaze raised a brow, obviously confused that in all their years as friends, Dakota hadn't mentioned him. "What kind of asshole name is that?"

Mẹ swatted at Blaze with her spoon. "Language."

Blaze motioned as if he were zipping his lips obediently.

"Mẹ," Dakota said, pleading, urging, *begging* her mother to please stop talking now.

"It was when you were in Russia," Mẹ said to Blaze as means of explanation. She portioned the raw beef into their bowls before turning back to the boiling pho pot. She left the other ingredients for them to add to their liking.

"Really?" Blaze was standing beside Mẹ now, who was still looming over the soup. He leaned against the counter and cast a glance toward Dakota.

Anyone else would have thought Blaze was only curious, but Dakota could see that dark hint of sadness in his eyes, the one that meant she'd hurt him, and it threatened to undo her.

"It wasn't important," Dakota muttered quickly, snatching a raw bean sprout off the counter in hope that it would distract Mẹ into slapping her hand to chastise her.

It didn't.

"She cried for three weeks," Mẹ said, holding up three fingers like she was counting bits of ginger root and not the emotional tumult of Dakota's past dating life. "I told her that's what happens when she tries to date a man who loves another."

Dakota had reached her limit—and the pho wasn't even done cooking yet.

"I didn't know he had a wife. It's not like I was *trying* to be the other woman!" she shouted.

The words came out before she could stop them.

Mẹ looked at Dakota as if she were hurt—and disrespected—because Dakota had shouted at her. "You don't have to yell," she scolded.

Dinner was oddly quiet after that, until Dakota was about midway through her pho and Blaze made her younger sisters, who'd only sat down a handful of minutes earlier, actually glance up from their phones and laugh. Teens were obsessed with the things, even when they were wolf shifters. Her brother was late, or a no-show, as usual, though Mẹ hadn't yet started to complain, or worse, make excuses for him. Not that Dakota was paying much mind to the conversation. She was too caught up with embarrassment at her own behavior. Not entirely in regard to how she'd spoken to her mother, though that was definitely a part of it, but mostly about the things she'd kept from Blaze.

If her mother hadn't let it slip, would she even have told him about any of that? They didn't talk much about when he'd been abroad and she'd still been here, alone and sometimes…not. Did she want to talk about it with him? What did it say about her if she didn't?

It wasn't until her mother had served up dessert, a delicious homemade pear ice cream with bits of tiny chocolate chips sprinkled on top, that she realized how self-absorbed she was being. Dakota had just shoved a bite of the frozen cream into her mouth, spoon still in hand, when she glanced across the table and noticed Blaze staring at her.

No, not staring at her. Staring *through* her. Like he didn't really see her there.

That haunted look was in his eyes again, like when he'd shown up on her doorstep the other night, as if he couldn't see her. She realized then that she'd been seeing far more of that look from him as of late and she'd been too caught up in her own troubles to notice.

"Blaze?" she said.

He didn't answer, just sat there with his spoon dangling from his hand as if he still didn't see her.

"Blaze?" she said it a little louder.

Immediately, Mẹ looked over from where she'd been scolding Dakota's sisters to put their phones away, and a worried crease pinched her brow. Gently, she reached over and nudged Blaze's hand with her own as if the hardened warrior might break.

Blaze startled as if Mẹ had shocked him, eyes darting around frantically like he didn't know where he was or what he was doing there.

"Blaze," Dakota said again.

His eyes fell to her and stayed there.

The fear there shook her. "Blaze, are you o—?"

Blaze shoved back his chair, not letting her finish the question. "I'm sorry," he muttered under his breath. "Excuse me." He tore from the room, spoon clattering to the floor behind him as he went. A moment later, Dakota heard the sound of the front door slam.

She could hardly breathe. She didn't know what had happened to trigger the episode for him, but the fear in his eyes had nearly crushed her and somehow that made her realize she had to tell him that she—

Dakota moved to stand, to go after him, but Mẹ caught her hand.

"Give him a moment," she said. She gave Dakota's hand a tight, reassuring squeeze. "But once you have, then he'll need you to pick up the pieces." Mẹ cast her a sad, knowing look.

Not mother to daughter but mate to mate, a partner of the kind of man and soldier who'd been broken and still struggled to put himself back together again.

A large lump crawled inside Dakota's throat. Maybe Mẹ did know what it was like to be in love with a best friend. Her parents hadn't been friends before they'd fallen in love, but weren't all true loves in some way friends?

Someone who you could share your life with.

"I only want the best for you. For you to let yourself be happy and have what you want. I like Blaze, because *you* love him, *chó con*. He makes you happy. I can see it in your eyes."

Dakota nodded with a sudden understanding of why Mẹ had been pushing her and Blaze together for years. Not because Mẹ adored him, and not because he reminded Mẹ of the great love of her life, Dakota's father, but because whenever Dakota had been broken over the past ten years, she'd needed Blaze to put her back together again. He made her happy, if only she'd stop chasing her other goals long enough to stop hiding from how she really felt. He was her person.

And right now, he needed her, too.

Blaze tore out of Mẹ's cabin, the taste of chocolate and the floral sweetness of Asian pear still lingering on his tongue. Adrenaline gripped him. His pulse raced. He could feel the vein that ran along the left side of his temple throbbing. It wasn't always sound that brought it on like they showed in the movies. Sometimes it was smell, feel, a certain tilt to someone's head, taste. Taste always wrenched him back the fastest, until even his wolf couldn't discern up from down, left from right, leaving him trapped again. A prisoner in his own fucking psyche.

The bitter cold had seeped into him first. He hadn't truly known cold until Russia. Cold so freezing that even his wolf shivered with it. Hands, toes, paws. It didn't matter. They were all fucking freezing along with the layer of ice that would attach itself to tender eyelashes. Eventually it got so cold you went numb, they said. But that was the problem. Blaze had never been good at numb. He'd only ever been able to fake it.

It was spring. Maybe March. He couldn't remember the goddamn date any more than he could control the memory eating away at his skull. It didn't matter. In Russia there's rarely true warmth, only different kinds of cold. This was so cold the wind would take the breath out of a man and the air felt thinner as it drew into your lungs. Snow wasn't covering every inch of the ground anymore, but you'd better believe you'd freeze to death come nightfall.

The trees of the forest loomed in the distance. He hadn't shifted in nearly three months. They'd warned him of that since basic, but every time his eyes caught on that tangle of gray and white limbs, inside his wolf would flay him open, fighting, clawing to get out. How did these fuckers live like this?

They'd just come from the warmth of dinner. The food had been better than usual, more robust and filling than the cold borscht they'd been eating every night for the past week. That should have tipped him off. The Volk celebrated food with food. The meal had been unctuous, warm and fatty in a way that was meant to stick to your ribs—a stew with tender bits of meat he'd never tasted before followed by little chocolate candies with jelly made with Russian Krazulya pear inside.

It'd been the first sweet he'd had in a year. The meal had of course been finished with vodka that was so goddamn close to water that the Volk drank it like water. Here, vodka didn't freeze. Water did. It had to have been not long before nightfall, considering they'd just eaten their last meal of the day, but it was that kind of gray that blocked out the sun enough that he could never tell what time it was. The kind of gray that made every other dull color brighter—the army green of his uniform, the dead yellow grass beneath his feet, the brick of the camp buildings in the background, and the red on his arm with the Volk emblem that looked all too reminiscent of the Soviet band. Every bit of it dead, drab, lifeless. Save for the blood color of that red. He'd sworn to himself only three weeks in that if he ever made it out alive, he'd never resign himself to living each day in these drab, soulless uniforms ever again.

The atmosphere as they padded out of the barracks, conversing in Russian, was lighter somehow, airy. It'd been moments like those when he'd almost convinced himself that the U.S. government had gotten it wrong. They loved to use shifters as their weapons of warfare without ever actually acknowledging their existence.

Maybe the Volk weren't so different from his pack. Maybe they weren't bloodthirsty monsters who'd wiped out so many of Russia's wolf populations that the few small packs that remained would be forced to join them, to become Volk or die. Maybe, maybe it'd been easier to think that, to depart from reality than to admit that he saw parts of himself in those sick fuckers, that he understood some of them, had become their friend. That'd been his assignment: become one of them while feeding information back to the U.S. base in Moscow.

That was when he'd seen them, ten of them, lined up on their knees in a depression in the ground that had probably been the remains of a trench back in World War II. That was all trenches were ever good for—spilling blood.

Time had slowed then. He remembered hearing the sound of Stanislav's deep voice beside him. The laughter, the clap of the other wolf's hand on his shoulder. Blaze froze. No, not wolf. They weren't wolves, not like him. They were Volk, different. Or were they?

Ivov had pulled them up first. The mother of a family of three. The children wriggled and cried beside her. The eldest was only a teen. Ivov didn't even ask if the she-wolf wanted to join them or die. She was screaming, staring Blaze straight in the eye, begging and pleading for him to do something. But he couldn't hear her.

All he could hear was the ringing in his own ears. All he could see was the small hand of the little boy beside her, young enough he'd likely never even shifted into his wolf yet. Blaze turned toward Ivov and yelled something in Russian. He couldn't remember the hell what, but Ivov *had only looked up at him at the exact moment Blaze felt several flecks of the she-wolf's blood spatter onto his face. He wished he didn't remember what came next. The confused look in Ivov's eye as he exchanged a concerned glance with Stanislav and asked Blaze in Moscow-accented Russian, "But didn't you enjoy the stew?"*

Blaze had thrown up every night for a week after that. Hadn't eaten for sixteen days—

A small hand clamped down on his shoulder. Blaze gripped the other hand hard, rounding on Ivov and shoving him back as he reached for his—

Dakota.

A *whoosh* of breath ripped from his lungs, the release of the memory nearly knocking him sideways. It wasn't Ivov's meaty wrist he was death-gripping, it was *Dakota.* Dakota's face twisted with pain as he...*he...*

Instantly, he released her, staring down at his best friend, at the woman he loved, in horror. He was shaking now, from head to toe. "Kotes, I'm sorry. I didn't know it was—"

"Shhh," she hushed him, pulling him into her arms. "I know. I know."

He dropped to his knees in the mountain dirt, suddenly feeling too weak to stand as she cradled his head against her shoulder.

"Shhh. Shhh." Dakota stroked her fingers through the locks of his hair, the sound of her hushing whispers reminding him of California and the sea, of days before he'd been majorly fucked up.

Eventually, Dakota sat on the ground beside him, bringing his head into her lap.

They stayed there like that for a long time, sitting on a cool patch of grass outside Mę's cabin porch. The porch lights went dark eventually, around the time when Mę and Dakota's younger sisters likely climbed into bed for the night.

Blaze stared up at the stars, the vast open sky of the Montana night, feeling the soft, smooth caresses of Dakota's fingers stroking through his hair.

"Do you want to talk about it?" Dakota finally whispered.

Blaze shook his head. He'd never want to talk about it, even though deep down, he knew he needed to. How did you talk about things you'd lived through that broke you, that even remembering nearly caused you to break all over again?

He didn't know the answer.

Taking his silence as a response of its own, Dakota nodded, choosing not to push him. She'd always been good at that, being tender with him, understanding even when he didn't want her to. She saw straight through to the core of him, beyond all the bravado and sarcastic bullshit right into the mess he was underneath.

She was quiet for a long time again until she whispered, "I'm sorry."

It'd been so long since either of them had spoken, Blaze wasn't certain he had it in him to respond. Not after he'd nearly…

He closed his eyes, fighting back the torrent of emotion and anger that caught in his throat as if he could swallow it down like it'd never been there. If he had hurt her, he would have never forgiven himself. The tremor in his voice came out gruff and tormented. "You have nothing to be sorry for, Kotes."

Dakota shook her head. "That's not true. I've been so caught up in this thing between us that I didn't notice that the past was catching up to you again. I'm your best friend. I should have realized—"

"Don't," Blaze warned. "It's not your job to fix me, Dakota. I'm a grown man. I can take care of myself."

"I know you can, but…" Dakota cupped his cheek in her hand, forcing him to turn toward her. "You don't have to. You'd do the same for me. You have before. You've dried my tears and scraped me off the floor so many times when I've messed up that I—"

He twisted away from her. Placing a hand behind him, he

pushed to his feet and brushed off the damp bits of grass that clung to his jeans. "It's not the same, Kotes."

"Isn't it?" She stared up at him, warm brown eyes like carved obsidian in the moonlight. "When you love someone, you're a team. You pick each other up if one of you falls. No man left behind, remember? You told me that the last time that you—"

Blaze shook his head, massaging the tension in his temples as he held up a hand. "Kotes, please, if you keep talking like that, I might actually start to think that you…"

"Blaze, I—"

"Please, Dakota." He dropped his hands with a god-awful pained sigh. Christ, he was mess. "You don't need to explain to me. I know you want to take this slow, one day at a time. I know you're not ready to talk about whatever *this* is yet, but…" He pressed his lips together into a thin line. One breath in. One breath out. "Please let me pretend otherwise. Just for one damn night."

"Okay," she breathed. She nodded slowly. "Okay."

Blaze hooked his thumbs on the leather of his belt, staring up at the stars again and mapping out Cassiopeia. From where he stood, the constellations and patterns stretched endlessly, the relative silence surrounding them. He heard the breeze blowing through the trees, the open wind, the summer crickets, the soft pull of Dakota's breath beside him.

But he was still alone with his demons. He always would be.

"There's something else I need to apologize for." Dakota spoke so softly, he almost didn't hear her.

Blaze glanced toward her. She was only years his junior, but she looked so young there, curled up with her legs to her chest like she'd been the other night in the bottom of her shower—unprotected, vulnerable.

Dakota released a long sigh. "About Brett. I know you have to realize that was when I was writing to you, and I–I don't know what to say."

Blaze shook his head. Fuck, he couldn't do this. Not now. "You don't need to explain anything to me, Dakota. I was in Russia. We didn't make any promises."

"I know we didn't, but…" Her voice trailed off for a moment as she glanced toward the night sky. "That's why I'm scared. That relationship, it didn't mean much to me, but when I realized I was the other woman, that I'd done that to someone else, even someone I didn't know, it…it shamed me. It made me scared of what kind of damage I could do if I really did care for someone, if I made a mistake. You know how I am when I set my mind on something… Sometimes I get so focused on it that I lose sight of what's important, and I–I don't want to hurt you."

She didn't want to hurt him? The idea that there was anything she could ever do that would get rid of him or make him not feel absolutely crazy about her didn't even make sense to him. She was a constant. His North Star. There was no redirection. For him, that was just what love was. He knew this was temporary, that she'd realize he wasn't enough for her, that she deserved better and she'd move on. But how he felt about her would never change. Of that, he was certain. Blaze let out a short huff as an amused grin tugged at his lips. "Kotes, I've already forgiven you for every wrong you could ever do me, past, present, and future."

The sad smile that crossed her lips then made his chest ache.

Blaze leaned down, extending a hand toward her. "Come on," he drawled.

"Where are we going?"

"For a run. On the far side of the forest, like we used to."

They both needed it.

She placed her hand in his, and he helped pull her to her feet.

Dakota smiled up at him. "Do you remember when you were still at Caltech and I came to visit you?"

Blaze grinned, scratching at the shadow on his jaw. "Yeah, I do."

"And do you remember that night we were out roaming the

campus at three o'clock in the morning or some other ridiculous hour and I'd talked you into having too many wine coolers with me?"

Blaze chuckled. "Lord, those things taste like cheap sugary shit."

Dakota laughed. "I was walking on the edge of the fountain outside the Beckham Institute, and my boot caught on a crack. I fell into the fountain and half pulled you in with me. My dress was soaked."

Blaze smirked. "Yeah, I remember. You said you looked like a drowned rat instead of a drowned wolf."

"I did." She chuckled. "God, my mascara was all over the place, but you were a gentleman even though I'd gotten all your clothes soaked."

He ran his fingers through his hair. "I'm hardly ever a gentleman. I just play one on TV sometimes."

Dakota laughed.

"What makes you bring it up?"

She bit her lower lip, toying with the soft pink flesh there. "I was just thinking that...when you pulled me out of the water. There was a moment when I caught you looking at my lips, and I remember thinking then I must have had way too much to drink because something about the way you were looking at me made me think you wanted to kiss me, and at the time, I thought that couldn't have been true, but now, I guess I just wondered..." She gazed up at him. "Did you?"

Blaze couldn't stifle his grin. "Dakota, I can't remember a time where I was ever that close to you and I *wasn't* thinking about kissing you."

"Even back then?"

He gave a slow nod. "Even back then."

"And now?"

Blaze's tongue darted out to wet his lips. "Yeah, and now."

"Blaze?"

"Yeah, Kotes?"

"Before you had said you wouldn't kiss me until I asked you to."

"I know. I'm kind of not good with patience." Blaze scratched at the nape of his neck. "I messed that up before, didn't I?"

"Yeah, you jumped the gun a bit last time, but…" She stopped walking and gave a gentle tug on his hand. "You haven't kissed me again since."

Blaze quirked a brow. He liked where this was going. "And?"

"And now I'm asking you to, again."

Blaze grinned. "You won't have to ask twice."

He tugged her into his arms, pressing her mouth against his as he buried his hands in her hair. He drew her close until she was pressed flat against him. They both stumbled slightly as he backed her up against a nearby tree. Fuck, if he didn't feel like a teenager with her. All hot tongues and exploring hands. No matter how close he got, it'd never be close enough.

Blaze felt himself stiffen with familiar, growing need. He wanted to take her, rough and hard, claiming her as his own. But he'd be damned if he didn't respect her wishes, because he respected *her*.

When they were both breathless and wanting and panting like young lovers, Blaze finally pulled away. He wouldn't push her further. Not since she said she wanted to take things slow—he'd take her however he could have her.

He sauntered a step or two back, nearing the edge of the forest. He gripped the hem of his shirt before he tugged it over his head. "If I beat you to the stream on the west side, can I get more than just a kiss?" The question was half-hopeful, half-playful ribbing.

Dakota shook her head with a small grin. "Is that a challenge?"

Blaze's eyes flashed to his wolf. "If you let it be, you bet your sweet little ass it is."

Dakota didn't hesitate. "I think I might let you win this one on purpose."

Blaze let out an aroused growl as they both shifted into wolf form. Fur sprang forth and limbs shifted before he felt his paws connect with the cool mountain ground. The wind ruffled through his fur, lifting the hair on his tail and neck. He let out an echoing howl before he nipped at Dakota's haunches, and then he was running, wild. As they darted beneath the shadows of the towering pines, all thoughts of the past were lost to him. All he could smell, all he could feel and taste were the familiar comfort of the darkened forest and the earthy scent of the she-wolf he loved running free by his side as he chased her into the moonlit night.

Chapter 14

"WHAT DO YOU CALL A CROSS BETWEEN A COW AND A TRAMPO-line?"

Dakota sighed and dropped her head into her hands. They'd been at this for hours, and clearly they'd reached the part of the evening where Blaze descended into a relentless string of corny jokes. "Blaze, be serious."

Blaze leaned back on the sofa in the rec lounge, flashing her a far-too-handsome grin that made her chest ache. He propped his feet up on the edge of the coffee table, leather cowboy boots giving a weighted clunk against the wood. "We've been at this all night. I *am* serious, seriously bored out of my mind, and it's a milkshake, by the way."

Dakota gave a mock groan. "That's a total dad joke."

Blaze pointed a finger at her. "Wrong, dear Dakota. That would require me to be a dad, which let's hope for your sake is not anytime soon." Blaze cast her a wry smirk.

Those eyes. That smile.

Dakota felt her cheeks flush as a rush of heat pooled between her legs. They'd both been skirting around the fact that they hadn't yet crossed that final base, and she hadn't been expecting for him to bring it up. "But we haven't..."

"We will." His eyes flashed to his wolf playfully. "And I'd be awful at it."

Dakota's eyes widened in confusion.

"The dad thing." Blaze chuckled. "Not the sex. I'm awesome at the sex thing. Not even *I* can self-deprecate my own skills there." Blaze shot her a smug look.

"I'm going to think you're *not* awesome at *the sex thing* if you keep calling it that." Dakota rolled her eyes, even as the color on her cheeks thickened. Considering everything else they'd done so far had been beyond mind-blowing, she couldn't even begin to imagine there was anything he wasn't good at in bed, but she couldn't help ribbing him a bit. "And you wouldn't be awful at being a dad. You've got the corny jokes down, obviously."

She hadn't ever thought much about wanting a family, but imagining Blaze several or more years from now holding a small baby or playing with an adorable chubby-cheeked toddler didn't exactly *not* make her ovaries give an excited shiver. Embarrassed at the thought, she glanced down at her notebook again before looking back up at him. "But what's with all the alpha males in the pack thinking that? Maverick said the same thing."

Blaze shrugged, ticking off each point on his fingers. "An inflated sense of ego? An abundance of daddy issues? A sharp tendency to think we're murderous monsters? I could keep going, but I haven't even gotten past Malcolm yet."

Malcolm, who'd strolled into the room only seconds earlier, let out an annoyed snarl. "Do you ever shut up?" he growled at Blaze.

"Umm…no?" Blaze answered dryly. "Though if you prefer reading…" He pointed down to the text of today's T-shirt, which read:

A LIST OF THINGS THAT AREN'T BEING CANCELED TODAY: ME BEING AN ASSHOLE.

Malcolm frowned. "I think I found something in my closet that belongs to you." Stepping farther into the room, he lifted his leg from behind the billiards table, where Peaches was wrapped around his calf like a vise, claws digging into him. Peaches meowed innocently at the sight of Blaze and Dakota before promptly sinking her tiny fangs into Malcolm's pant leg again.

Malcolm's eyes flashed to his wolf. "You're lucky I don't punt her across the room. She won't get off."

Blaze jumped to his feet, hurrying to Peaches's rescue. "See what I mean? Monster," he said to Dakota. His eyes narrowed on Malcolm. "What'd you do to her?"

"What did *I* do to *her*?" Malcolm growled.

"Blaze," Dakota chastised as he tried to pull Peaches off Malcolm's leg, only for the feline to dig her claws in further.

Dakota swept past him, quickly ducking down to massage Peaches's claws slightly until they released. Peaches let out a screeching yowl like Dakota had injured her and her feelings—she hadn't—and shot to the far side of the rec room like a small, furred rocket before she promptly began attacking the edge of the sofa with her claws.

Blaze gave Malcolm an easy grin. "At least it wasn't your face she attached to this time."

Malcolm snarled.

Dakota swatted at Blaze in an attempt to redirect him toward stopping Peaches from mauling the couch. They were already on thin ice with Maverick, who'd been in a foul mood the past several days and might pitch a fit if they let Peaches destroy another piece of furniture. If pack rumor proved right, the Grey Wolf packmaster had been sleeping on the rec room sofa the past several nights because Sierra, who was still fiercely in love with her husband but who was now officially two weeks overdue and feeling bonkers with hormones, had reached the point in her pregnancy where she was having intermittent contractions and threatening her mate's existence with accusations of "How did I let you do this to me?"

Blaze gingerly plucked Peaches off the sofa, and to their collective surprise, she settled onto the elite warrior's chest with a contented meow. "Go on and knead biscuits on my arm," he cooed at her.

Dakota shook her head. And to think that his name instilled fear in their enemies, though she supposed his demeanor could change, like when they'd been in the showers and he'd gone from his playful, easygoing self to full-on alpha male in all of two seconds flat.

Another grumble from Malcolm drew her attention as he turned to leave. Clearly he'd had enough of watching Blaze coo disgustingly sweet placations at Peaches about how that "big, bad wolfy-wolf" was never going to come near her again.

"Malcolm," Dakota said, turning her attention toward him again.

There were still the matters of training against the potential threat of the Volk, finding a different ally to replace the cougars in the Seven Range Pact, and figuring out what devious plans the vampires were up to that'd likely resulted in Flynn Porter's death.

If their pack's history with the vampires proved true, other deaths would soon follow unless the pack got out in front of this.

Malcolm paused in the rec room doorway. The massive Grey Wolf executioner was nearly as wide as he was tall, dwarfing the doorframe. Blaze did the same when he stood there. His wide shoulders, narrow hips, and long legs made him all lean, corded muscle, tall enough that he often had to duck beneath low-hanging entries and could move with a stealth and speed that could be frighteningly lethal.

But Malcolm, on the other hand, was the shifter equivalent of a tank truck. He'd steamroll over any enemy that got in his way sooner than look at them.

Malcolm's black eyes bored into her, so intense and obsidian that Dakota felt herself tense slightly. She wasn't certain she'd ever seen the Grey Wolf executioner smile, and likely with good reason. If there was any warrior on this ranch who'd seen nearly as much horror and blood as Blaze had, it was Malcolm, and since their previous second-in-command Bo had died years earlier, the fierce and snarly warrior that their packmates had nicknamed the Destroyer had never quite been the same.

Malcolm tugged at the leather flaps of his motorcycle jacket as he stared down at her, waiting for her to say her piece. For such a grouch with a constant *fuck-off* stare, beneath the brim of his Stetson, his lashes were considerably long and lush, and he had the kind of sultry, dark-rimmed eyes that made it look like he was wearing edgy, rock-star eyeliner, even when he wasn't—the kind that if they softened to something less hard and gruff, another kind of man or woman might want to fall into.

"Do you have any ideas about replacement allies to the Arctic wolves? Blaze is being useless." Dakota got the feeling Malcolm wasn't included among the elite warriors' little brotherhood enough, mainly because he was so, well, pissed off all the time, but she'd also considered herself to be the kind to include everyone, grumbly or not.

And at this point, she was desperate for any actual help she could get.

"I'm not being useless. I'm being lazy. There's a difference," Blaze said from where he now sat stroking Peaches on the sofa. "And that's only because you shot down all my good ideas over the past several hours until I've run out of them."

"That's because they all required complicated investments in technology that Maverick isn't going to be pleased about working into the budget and you know it," she countered. Blaze was one of the most intelligent wolves on this ranch, and his creative solutions were unstoppable, hell, visionary in a way that was intimidating, but sometimes that high intellect got the better of him and he didn't—or outright refused—to focus on pesky little things like budgetary details or rules.

In their work dynamic, it fell to her to fill in the gaps of attention to detail.

It was the important details that she excelled at.

"Austin and I need to ride out to the western pasture," Malcolm said, brushing her off. He turned to leave, the action flashing the hooded reaper with a wolf skull head insignia on the back of his leather jacket.

Dakota let out a sudden *eep* of excitement. "Malcolm, that's it."

Before she could stop herself, in her excitement, her hands shot out and gripped the back of his leather, stopping Malcolm in his tracks.

He snarled.

But what else was new?

"Malcolm's jacket is the answer to all our problems?" Blaze's tone had crossed over from sardonic territory and was bordering dangerously close to sarcastic.

Dakota couldn't say she blamed him. She had refused to let them break for dinner more than a few hours ago. Still, she shot him an annoyed look. "We've only been looking at allies in the West because of geographic convenience, but what if those allies can move?"

Blaze clearly wasn't ready to give up on the snark, and from the spark in his eyes, he was purposefully teasing her to get a rise out of her. She wouldn't rise to the bait. "Well, I'd hope they could move or they wouldn't be very good allies."

Dakota shook her head at him. "Move as in travel to us, because they don't have any one home location." She pointed to where she still gripped Malcolm's jacket. "The Detroit Rock City M/C, the pack that gifted you this jacket," she said to Malcolm. "They're one of the more dominant packs in the East right? Do they have any subpacks or chapters...or charters or whatever bikers call it out west, or any members who move around and don't ever settle down?"

"Nomads?" Malcolm offered with the quirk of his dark brow.

"Yes, that."

Malcolm grunted in affirmation.

Dakota released his jacket, clapping her hands together with glee. "Perfect. Can I reach out to them? Or would it be better coming from you?"

Rather than seeming displeased by the idea of extra work, Malcolm seemed strangely...surprised to be included in the discussion. Dakota got the feeling that though he obviously tried to put others off with his dark demeanor, it was a rare occasion that someone tried to push through it.

All the more reason they needed more females on the team.

She and Sierra could match alpha male bravado and also see right through it.

"I'll do it," Malcolm grumbled.

Dakota smiled. "Perfect!" She tilted her head to the side, eyeing Malcolm for a brief moment. It wasn't common for their kind to associate with packs that weren't their own, except in an official capacity, especially that far east. "What led you to get involved with them anyway?" she asked.

Malcolm looked almost taken aback by the personal question. But to her surprise, he actually answered. "Back when I was…" He hesitated, struggling to find the right word. "Freelancing," he finally said.

In other words, before he'd been made an elite warrior and to their enemies become the Grey Wolves' personal hit man.

"There was someone targeting the club's president, and I… well…I got to him first," Malcolm said. The dark, barely there hint of a grin that followed sent a chill down Dakota's spin.

Got to him being an obvious euphemism for… Well, considering the frightening flash of gold from Malcolm's wolf eyes and that twisted grin, she didn't need to infer what exactly that meant.

"Right," she said quickly, mentally cataloging one of the many reasons she would never in the rest of her hopefully very long life dare to actually cross Malcolm.

With another gruff reassurance that he'd take care of the nomads, whatever that meant, Malcolm left the rec room, leaving Dakota and Blaze alone again.

"If I'd known you were willing to search for allies that far east, I would have mentioned the Rock City wolves," Blaze said, his eyes trailing over her in a heated once-over with a flirtatious grin as she inched her way toward him.

She glared at him. "You couldn't have suggested that hours ago? It would have saved us loads of time."

Peaches leaped off his lap, darting from the room as Blaze gave a nonchalant shrug. "I could have, but it would have stopped me from spending time with you and calling it work."

Nervous butterflies fluttered inside her chest. Dakota smiled. "At least you're honest."

Ever since dinner at Mẹ's when she'd realized how much he'd needed her and how many times she'd asked the same of him over the years, for days now she'd been trying to figure out how to elicit that same response she'd seen from him in the showers, to heat things up so that she could finally tell him that she was ready to take things, well…faster. She wasn't certain how to broach the topic otherwise. She'd stupidly told him she wanted to take things slow. How did she tell him she'd changed her mind, admit she'd been wrong?

She'd never been very good at admitting her mistakes.

She was still worried about what all these changes would mean for their friendship, but that night at Mẹ's had brought clarity. The way her heart had stopped when she'd seen him in pain had been a more powerful reaction than she'd ever had with any platonic friend. It was like he was a part of her, an extension of her.

Blaze had been right about them from the start. From the moment she'd kissed him, they'd gone too far forward for them to ever go back. Things would never be the same. It was still uncertain what they were going to be to each other. Not to mention he still hadn't shared the darker parts of his past with her.

But she was slowly becoming okay with that.

Dakota shuffled her way toward where Blaze perched on the edge of the couch, looking every bit the relaxed, delicious, easygoing cowboy that he was. But that was the problem, wasn't it? She loved him this way, like they'd always been, but what she really wanted was another glimpse of him being that impressive, protective alpha wolf who'd taken her that night in the showers.

Why? Why had she told him she wanted to take things slowly?

Oh, yeah, because she hadn't wanted to embrace the uncertainty of the future between them, and exactly how well was that going for her?

The anticipation for when things would get too heated and the tension between them would reach combustible levels once again was killing her.

Dakota nestled onto the edge of the sofa near him. Blaze wrapped an arm around her, pulling her closer, but…not close enough. All she had to do was toss a leg over his lap and straddle him like the cowgirl she was, make like she was going to ride him like he was one of the wild broncos out in the stable that Austin kept for the rodeo circuit. If she did, Blaze would be on her within seconds. She knew it.

But she just…couldn't bring herself to do it.

That wasn't how her fantasy went.

Maybe if she started with conversation?

"Blaze, there's something I wanted to talk to you a—"

Austin poked his head into the room, interrupting her midsentence. "Hey, have either y'all seen Malcolm?"

Blaze dropped his arm from around her shoulder and rose from his seat. "Yeah, he just left, and I also needed to ask you about…"

Dakota tuned out the other wolves' conversation after that, watching as Blaze followed Austin out into the hallway for a moment, seemingly unaware of her and her inner turmoil. Releasing a long sigh, she racked her brain for something, anything she could do to gain back that hardened alpha wolf's attention and came up with…nothing.

Quickly, she grabbed her phone, which had been tucked into the pocket of her jeans, and fired off a text to several of her closest fellow she-wolves among the pack.

Ladies, we have an emergency.

How hadn't she realized that it had been *him* writing the letters to her, not that too-polished, cosmopolitan ninny Jasper? Of course, that'd been his intent, but that didn't make the fact that she hadn't any easier. Following after Austin, Blaze barreled out into the hall from the rec room, eager to place some distance between him and Dakota, who clearly didn't realize what she was doing to him, after asking him point-blank *not* to do the kind of things she was doing to him, or really, making him *want* to do.

The whole situation was making him frustrated as fuck, and he'd started masturbating three times a day like he was a horny teenage wolf again, back when he wanted to hump anything within a ten-mile radius close to female and a shifter that wasn't related to him.

As much as it killed him inside, he'd known from the start that he and Dakota were only temporary, that'd he'd never deserve her, and that his past made anything permanent between them an impossibility. In the long term, he couldn't risk her safety by having her as his mate. But Dakota deserved to be happy, and with the threat of the Volk increasing each day, the Grey Wolf international relations person? Lawyer? Liaison? Whatever the hell the rest of the pack called him, he had been the perfect candidate for Blaze to use for some well-meaning love-life hacktivism, or was it identity theft? Mistaken-identity matchmaking? He wasn't sure what trope the K-dramas she loved would call it.

Did it count as identity theft if it was only hacking the email of one of your packmates?

Jasper was hardly ever on the ranch anyway, considering he was always jet-setting off to the middle of...wherever, so for now he wouldn't be the least bit wiser to it. Besides, he looked like he'd stepped off a cover of *GQ* for fuck's sake and had already shown an interest in Dakota. He'd be good for her in a way Blaze could never be.

Dakota deserved a guy who looked like he'd been staring at

himself in the mirror for five hours detailing the perfect swoop of his dark hair. Blaze wasn't unattractive—he'd bedded enough of Wolf Pack Run years ago to know that he wasn't—but considering he liked to think he was a bit more down-to-earth young Bradley Cooper rather than dark and swarthy, Gucci-suit-wearing pretty boy like Sendhil Ramamurthy, he was still a bit bitter. Maybe some sadistic part of him had hoped she would recognize the letters were from him, even though he knew it was for the best…

He'd thought he'd send one message, just enough to urge the two of them together and see how she reacted to "Jasper's" harmless, heartfelt flirting, but then messaging her in the same way he'd written to her when he'd been in the service and poured his heart out to her, in a way he hadn't been able to do verbally in years, had been so cathartic, especially considering the Volk and the dark shit of his past were smack-dab in the middle of catching up to him and he couldn't even *tell* her what was going on without risking her life further. Now, he was ten emails in and buried way too fucking deep to just say, "Hey, by the way, those messages were from me. Surprise! Aren't I an idiot?"

It was better this way. He knew that. He'd known from the start it would come to this.

But that didn't make it any easier.

He'd always been far too excellent at self-sabotage and not in the fun Beastie Boys kind of way.

"Austin, wait up," Blaze called after his packmate.

The Texan turned back from where he'd been about to exit through the compound's main doors and head out to meet Malcolm at the stables. "Yeah?" Austin drawled.

"I need you to do me a favor."

"'Nother one?" The warm smile that accompanied the question indicated Austin really didn't mind being asked or helping a friend out, for that matter.

Blaze lowered his voice. "I have this…" He hesitated, not

wanting to say the words *resonant sound device that's built to slow down the Volk.* "Sound machine," he finally settled on, "that I need to test on one of the packmates to make sure that you all can't hear it. Maverick's a bit on edge these days, and I need someone who can keep their mouth shut and not say anything about it, so…" Blaze gestured toward him.

Austin gave a short chuckle. "Happy to help out. Sign me up."

"Tomorrow. Three o'clock?"

Austin tipped his Stetson like they were agreeing to an old-fashioned gunfight rather than testing highly specialized tech equipment. Blaze wasn't the most conventional of cowboys.

"See you then." The Texan nodded before heading out toward the pastures.

Blaze huffed out a long breath through his nose, turning back toward the rec room where he'd left Dakota. Once he tested the sound device out on Austin, he'd be readier for the Volk than he'd ever been. Blood would be spilled when they finally came for him, but it'd be theirs instead of his.

He'd make certain of it.

Chapter 15

THE DOOR TO DAKOTA'S CABIN FLEW OPEN AS HER CLOSEST female friends filtered in.

"We came as fast as we could," Belle called out from the doorway, where she was linked arm in arm with a very large, waddling Sierra, who from the looks of it and considering the amount of time that it had taken wasn't able to move very fast.

The two women slowly entered her cabin with Belle leading the way. The high commander's mate, who happened to be a talented physician and was thus monitoring the Sierra's pregnancy, was also herself the mother of three of the pack's young and to Dakota's relief looked significantly better rested than the last time she'd seen her.

Obviously it was Colt's turn on nighttime diaper duty.

It was a shame their young didn't start shifting until they were nearly five years old and able to control it. Letting them frolic about in wolf form as pups outside would've been so much easier than caring for gurgling infants.

Dakota rushed to Sierra's side in sympathy, gripping under her opposite arm to help Belle steady her.

Sierra let out a harsh, aggressive groan. "Walking makes it better," she ground out. "It's still not quite time yet."

"That's why we've been circling the ranch all night, love." Belle rubbed her friend's back supportively. "The contractions aren't close enough together yet," she whispered to Dakota.

Dakota shook her head. Leave it to Sierra to brave absolutely anything and everything for a friend, including the very early stages of labor. "You shouldn't have come, Sierra. You're clearly not up to it."

"She insisted," Belle said.

"I need the…" Sierra let out a guttural groan. "Distraction," she finished. "Or I might kill Maverick."

Dakota smiled. "You can't do that. He's packmaster and you love him." She knew that for a fact, considering she'd been the one to urge Sierra to… What had her exact words been? Oh yes, "climb that tree like a friggin' monkey."

Belle tried to hide an amused snicker. "She's banished him to the rec room couch."

Sierra's eyes flashed to her wolf. "He deserves it. He did this to me."

"I'm fairly certain you were a willing participant." Dakota gave a mock wince.

Sierra growled.

The still-cracked door flew open again, and a moment later, Cheyenne barreled in. "I came as soon as I could. Not that you deserved it."

Dakota frowned. "I already apologized, Cheyenne."

"You didn't deserve an apology. You broke womanly code, Chey," Sierra said hotly, "Blaze has always been Dakota's and you know it."

Cheyenne shrugged. "I didn't mean to. I wasn't actually interested. I just thought it was harmless fun among packmates."

"So what's the emergency?" Belle asked.

"Did Peaches finally croak?"

"Did Blaze tell you he loves you yet?"

Sierra let out a pained grunt.

"Wait." Dakota was still processing half of this. "You all knew?"

Cheyenne closed the door behind her with an exasperated sigh. "Oh, Dakota, it's been obvious even to me. Everyone knows."

Belle nodded. "You just weren't ready to see it yet."

"So did he?" Another groan from Sierra as she placed her hands on her lower back and arched slightly while she slowly circled Dakota's living room.

Dakota gathered her hair in her hands, using the spare hair tie on her wrist to quickly throw it up in an artful knot at the top of her head. "Well, actually I kissed him and sort of started the whole thing." She winced.

Cheyenne's eyes went wide in analytical confusion. "I hadn't bet on that."

"Pay up." Sierra made a give-it-here motion with her hand despite the continued circling.

Dakota's jaw dropped. "You were taking bets on my love life?"

Cheyenne pulled out her wallet and passed a few bills to Sierra. "We live on a ranch in the middle of nowhere, Montana. We have to have *some* excitement in our lives," said the woman who looked like a redheaded wannabe Marilyn Monroe bombshell and was Wolf Pack Run's resident grease-loving female mechanic. Like a she-wolf who could fix ranching equipment and anything with an engine in her sleep wasn't the least bit interesting. Not that poor Chey had the social skills to match. She was a blunt, creative genius.

"So have you all fallen in love and talked marriage yet?" Cheyenne folded her wallet and tucked it into the back of her short cutoff jeans.

"Yes…wait, uh. No. I'm not sure?" Dakota winced again.

"So what's the holdup?" Sierra grumbled.

Belle's features fell. "Why aren't you in love yet?"

Dakota flopped down on her couch. Belle followed suit, nestling down beside her as Cheyenne started raiding the pantry. Sierra continued circling.

"Well, after I kissed him, I was scared I would ruin the friendship and…" Dakota recounted the events of the past two weeks to them, leaving out the more—*ahem*—intimate details and then finally finishing with "So then I told him I wanted to take things slow, and he listened and respected that."

A bit of cracker that Cheyenne had been munching on toppled out the edge of her mouth. For a shifter, she was extremely picky about food, but that didn't stop her from raiding Dakota's pantry for snacks every time she came over. "Wait. What? Isn't that a good thing?"

Belle gripped Dakota's knee in disbelief. "He *actually* listened? Like he didn't even try to convince you otherwise?"

Dakota nodded.

Belle gaped. "That kind of control is…impressive. Wow."

"What kind of alpha *does* that?" Sierra growled, a slight tinge of awe behind it. "I can't believe he didn't crack and try to persuade you. Good on him."

Belle gave a romantic sigh. "Oh, Dakota. He's a total keeper. Don't let him go. He's already wrapped around your finger."

"I always did like Blaze," Sierra said with a nod of approval.

"So what exactly is the problem then?" Cheyenne threw another cracker into her mouth.

"*I'm* the problem," Dakota shot back. "I guess I sort of…" She placed a hand over Belle's in a plea for help. "Oh, please don't make me say it."

"She-wolves before…" Sierra paused. "Well, I guess I didn't really think that rhyme out. Apparently, my rhyming is as bad as my puns." Her face tightened as another contraction came on.

"Are we talking about sex now?" Cheyenne said through a mouthful of cracker before she gave an overdramatized sexy shake of her shoulders.

Dakota shrugged. "I guess I'm ready for things to move faster now, and I'm struggling to admit I was wrong. I want to signal to him that he can go ahead and do what he did before and…you know…take charge?"

"Ohhh, so you want him to go all alpha?" Cheyenne asked.

Sierra grinned. "Is that your kink, being submissive?"

Dakota blinked owlishly. She hadn't quite thought of it in those terms before.

Sierra chuckled. "Own it. Whatever you want, there's no shame in it."

Belle and Cheyenne nodded in unison as the two other she-wolves teased her in agreement.

"You want to be chased."

"Pursued."

"Hunted."

"Seduced."

"Claimed." Cheyenne's voice dropped to a lower octave while she wiggled her eyebrows suggestively.

Dakota scowled. "Do I need to get you all a thesaurus so you can keep going? Yes. I'm ready for him to…pursue me again? I thought I wanted to slow things down, but I was wrong from the start. I was hurt because I'd thought he was rejecting me at first, and now I don't know how to tell him. Admitting my mistakes has never been easy for me."

Sierra nodded in solidarity. "It's a perfectionist thing."

"Well, *you* could always initiate, Dakota," Belle offered.

"I did and that was"—Dakota blushed—"enjoyable but not quite what I was looking for."

"And why don't you just tell him this? Eat crow, admit you were wrong, and tell him you want to be seduced and be submissive to him. It's not like he won't do it." Cheyenne had gone for a can of cashews now. She tossed a handful into her mouth. "You're kind of putting him in an untenable position."

Dakota nodded. "I know, but every time I try to say it, it's like my throat closes up and I can't… I guess I'm embarrassed that I told him I wanted to go slow in the first place and that I didn't know what I wanted. I feel like… I don't know. I should be able to tell him, but it's awkward."

"Strong women are allowed to make mistakes and feel uncertain sometimes. There's nothing to be embarrassed about. Tell him and then enjoy being submissive," Sierra said, bending over. "Just be prepared to deal with the consequences." She groaned.

Dakota's eyes grew wide.

"Don't scare her, Sierra," Belle chastised. "Birth control is a thing for our kind now. You know that. But I think what Sierra would normally tell you is that one of the most fun parts of sex can be letting loose with a side of yourself you don't normally see."

Dakota nodded.

"But now that you changed your mind, you're struggling to figure out how give him the memo?" Cheyenne placed the cashews back in the cupboard.

"Exactly."

Belle nodded thoughtfully. "You need to get Blaze to move things beyond words then. You'll still have to articulate what you want once you get to that point, but there *is* one surefire way to get an alpha male like Blaze all fired up…and I think we've all done it." Belle made a slightly guilty expression in the vein of a sorry-not-sorry face.

"Tease him," Cheyenne said.

Sierra shot Dakota a serious look. "Challenge him."

Dakota quirked a brow. "Excuse me?"

"Make him jealous," Belle said point-blank. "That will move things beyond words enough that then you can give him the green light for consent."

"That's not really fair, but…" Dakota started to say it wasn't right or that it hardly seemed fair, but considering all she knew about alpha males… She breathed out a resigned sigh. "That… just might work."

Half an hour and several sympathetic mocktails so that Sierra could participate later, Dakota had a plan. This time, she really *was* going to seduce her best friend.

But now she knew exactly how to do it.

———————

Blaze knocked on Dakota's cabin door, waiting for her yell of approval to enter. It was well past nightfall, the late-summer crickets chirping in a warm serenade. By this time of night, he'd normally call it a day and shift for a long run in the forest or be tearing through his workout routine, but Dakota had insisted on inviting him over to her cabin to celebrate. Malcolm had contacted the nomads of the Detroit Rock City M/C, and thankfully, their charter's president was open to a one-on-one meeting with the Grey Wolf executioner at the Midnight Coyote Saloon in two weeks.

It was a step in the right direction, toward cementing alternative allies to the Arctic wolves, but Blaze couldn't find it in himself to want to celebrate. The security cams had been silent for days, and he had more than a passing feeling it was the calm before the storm.

When Dakota didn't immediately answer, Blaze knocked again before finally using his key. No one had ever said pack life was full of privacy. He shoved the door open. The inside of Dakota's cabin smelled of the cedar it'd been built with, along with a hint of incense and firewood. As Blaze eased inside, he started to pull the door closed, but the moment he turned and laid eyes on Dakota, he froze.

Blaze swallowed, hard. His mouth instantly watered even as his throat went dry, and he was fairly certain his eyes did that thing like in cartoons where they fly out of the wolf's head while his tongue wags with excitement, because holy fuck...

She was wearing the dress. That dress. The one she'd worn to Maverick's reception that he'd wanted her to keep in the back of her closet and never put on in public again, because he wanted the sight of her in it to be for his eyes only. Seeing her in it again did things to him.

Things that made both his chest ache and his cock throb.

"What are you wearing?" He muttered the words on a surprised exhale.

"Oh, this old thing?"

Blaze swore. Based on that response, he was in his own personal porn fantasy right now.

Christ, the dialogue had always sucked in his fantasies.

Blaze's cock stiffened, the thick length straining against his jeans. Considering all he could think about as he lay alone in bed each night were the things he wanted to do to her, damn near constant erections had been a problem as of late. He knew her taste, her smell, the sounds she made, but he still didn't know what it'd feel like to slide deep inside her, to claim her as his own, and that was driving him fucking crazy with need.

His wolf was practically howling for it.

And that'd been without the dress.

No, *before* the dress.

Even the words *without* and *dress* together in a sentence were getting to him. His dick gave a heady throb, reminding him of everything he was missing out on.

Down boy, he mentally scolded himself like he was an animal in heat.

Which considering his thoughts, he was fairly certain he was…

He growled in arousal at the sight of the woman before him.

Dakota stood in the middle of her living room, barefoot and fresh faced with no makeup and her hair artfully thrown into her usual messy bun on top of her head. Several dark, stray tendrils fell around her face as if she'd meant for them to stay put but they had gotten ruffled enough they'd had no choice but to escape. He had imagined himself being the reason for her adorable, messy bedhead more than a few times.

During the late hours of the night when he was alone, it was in this intimate, relaxed state that he imagined her most frequently. Each evening he envisioned the two of them like this, when the intimacy of their friendship crackled with unfulfilled tension until it boiled over, blurring the lines of friendship, sex, and need until neither of them could think straight. Until they didn't see anything but each other.

"I didn't expect you to get here so fast," Dakota said, completely

184

ignoring the elephant in the room and what had to be the very obvious erection in his jeans.

Blaze's eyes darted to that dangerously low neckline and the subtle hint of cleavage that made him want to...

He gave a rough clear of his throat. "Do you often sit around your house alone in evening wear you've only worn a handful of times before? Because I've known you for over a decade, and I guess I'm..."

She turned to round the side of her couch, giving him a flash of that open bare back that dipped so low it left little to the imagination. The cobalt-blue material clung so perfectly to her skin that he could practically see the two dimples above her too deliciously full peach of an...

"Blaze?" She finished her turn and stared up at him with a look of concern on her face.

Right. He was supposed to be talking, forming coherent sentences, but at the moment, that task seemed more difficult than usual.

"I'm...I'm just surprised that I'm learning this about you?" he finished.

Lord, he was an idiot. A horny, lovestruck idiot.

Dakota glanced down at the slinky, revealing dress as if she'd only now realized she was wearing it and gave a harmless little shrug. "I felt like celebrating?"

It was a poor excuse at best, but Blaze was going to take it.

For now.

Closing the door behind him, he started to take his Stetson off his head, but Dakota wagged a finger at him.

"No, leave it on."

Blaze's brow furrowed. "Okay," he said skeptically. He bent down to take off his boots.

"Keep those too," she said. "But lose the shirt if you want."

Okay. Now, he *knew* she was up to something.

"Kotes, what's going on?"

"I'm trying to get in the mood."

His heart gave a heady, hopeful thud against his chest, and he was fairly certain he was salivating again, but he kept his cool, damn it. A suggestive smirk crossed his face. "In the mood for…?"

She waved a hand like that was a silly question, dismissing him. "Writing a letter back to Jasper, of course."

Blaze snarled before he could stop himself, the base animal sound ripping from his throat involuntarily. His eyes flashed to his wolf. This was what he'd wanted, for her to be happy with someone whose past didn't put her at risk. He wasn't *supposed* to be jealous. He had no right to be. He was more evolved than this.

Wasn't he?

Dakota lifted an arched, perfectly sculpted brow at him like she couldn't understand what he was snarling about while she swept into her open kitchen. Staring at the wine rack for a moment, she went to the fridge instead and selected a Riesling before placing it on the counter and retrieving a bottle opener. As far as his best friend was concerned, it wasn't a true celebration if there wasn't wine involved.

Blaze cleared his throat again. "I thought you weren't into Jasper, considering the last time he was here, he had his chance with you and he didn't…" Blaze ground his teeth together a little harder than he should have as he struggled to find the right words.

Take you. Claim you. Like I would have if you'd let me…

"Man up?" he finally offered.

He sounded pissed off even to his own ears.

The thought of Dakota with anyone but him made his blood boil.

It didn't even matter that every one of "Jasper's" letters had been written by *him*.

The fact that she still hadn't realized that it was him romancing her via the written word shouldn't have bothered him, but it did, damn it. How could she not recognize it was him?

He swore under his breath again.

Dakota fiddled with the corkscrew, trying to position it on top of the bottle so that the cork didn't break when she removed it. She lifted one slender, bare shoulder with a little shrug.

Another growl nearly tore from Blaze's throat. She'd changed her mind about *Jasper* but meanwhile *he'd* been the one pleasuring her at every chance she'd allow for days, and she hadn't changed her mind about him? The message was clear. Mind-blowing orgasm-giver or not, mentally she'd stuck him in the friend zone once again.

It was better this way. He knew he had no right, no claim on her, damn it. It didn't matter that he'd spent years by her side, supporting her in everything she did. If she didn't want him in that way, that was the end of the subject. She didn't owe him anything because of their friendship. He knew it. In the first place, he'd never been beside her because he *expected* or even anticipated anything between them to be permanent, though he'd admit that he'd hoped.

The letters were one thing. Separate from what they had together. Somehow, he'd been able to emotionally distance himself from the whole ordeal, as if it weren't real and he wouldn't actually have to face losing her. But now that he knew exactly how she tasted, how her slick, wet heat melted on his tongue every time he buried his face between her legs and made her cry out in pleasure for him, being confronted head-on with losing her to someone else was pure, unadulterated torture.

It made him want to break something.

Jasper's too handsome face, mainly.

Then once he was done pummeling Jasper's perfectly sculpted nose, he'd tell Dakota in explicit detail all the filthy things he wanted to do to her until she was panting and that he was the one who'd written the letters. He'd leave her wanting with need for *him*, not that handsome, intelligent, actually-very-warm-and-nice-suit-wearing dandy he called a friend. But he couldn't do any of that.

Because he needed to protect her, and he'd promised he'd take things slow, respect her wishes. And he'd keep his promise to her.

Even if it killed him.

Dakota was still struggling to get the screw into the cork's bottle, wiggling and working it in a way that made the low neck of her dress sway. She was braless underneath, taut nipples pebbled through the thin material, and from the way her torso and neckline were shimmying, each movement gave him a near peek of her...

Blaze snarled again, charging over to her side and blocking her between his body and the counter. He snatched the godforsaken wine from her hand, taking the bottle in one large fist and breaking the neck off with a quick snap. The glass didn't stand a chance against his wolf strength.

"Blaze!" Dakota *eep*ed as he tossed the chunk of the bottle's broken neck into the nearby trash bin. "That was a perfectly good glass bottle. I could have used it to make something."

"Like what?" he growled.

He couldn't have stood another second of her wiggling like that. The way her nipple had nearly peeked out from beneath that dark material had made his cock pulse with need. Even now he could feel a slick bead of moisture gathering near the tip. He imagined her mouth there, her on her knees before him like she'd been in the conference room, when she'd wrapped her lips around him before she'd kissed him there from base to...

Christ. He swore under his breath again.

Dakota shrugged. "I could have used it for a craft or something? Who knows?"

A craft?

Blaze struggled to hold in a frustrated growl. "Since when are you into crafting?"

"I don't know, but I could be," Dakota said defensively. She placed her hands on her slender hips. For a woman who was mostly lean and narrow all over, her hips had a slight curve that led down to those perfect dimples of her too-round, too-pert, too-delicious behind...

Blaze snarled again.

"Like you *could be* into Jasper?" he finally snapped.

Dakota looked taken aback. "Yes, like I *could be* into Jasper," she shot back at him. "You said yourself we didn't make any promises."

Blaze's mind was still scrambled from building the audio machine and finalizing plans for the Volk if they attacked, that was all. That was why he was losing his shit and getting so riled with jealousy he could hardly see straight. Right?

"When I said that, I was talking about when I was in Russia, years ago," he ground out.

"Well, we didn't make any promises then either." Dakota brushed past him to grab a wineglass and a new bottle, then poured the contents of the previous one into the sink. The lingering hint of his own scent on her skin as she passed nearly did him in.

To another wolf, she would've smelled like his mate, damn it.

Dakota gestured wildly, waving her free hand as she spoke. "You want to talk about not manning up and not taking your shot in regard to Jasper? You supposedly wanted me for years and didn't do *anything*." Her words cut through him like a blow straight to his heart.

Blaze nearly roared.

He couldn't have, damn it. Didn't she see that?

Jasper didn't have anything at risk. He, on the other hand, could have lost everything. That was why he'd waited in hopes that she would come to him. He had been too terrified that drawing close to her would risk her life at the hands of his enemies, that he would lose her, or she wouldn't want him to begin with, because who the hell would want a broken man, or...

His mind raced with excuses.

But that was the problem, wasn't it?

Every reason he could give was an excuse.

The truth was he *could* have had her years ago, had he been braver.

Had he been strong enough.

But she made him brave now. She and the hope of that fucking kiss. How did she not see it?

"What's your point?" he grumbled.

"My point being that I don't understand why you're so angry when you said yourself you didn't know where this was going yet."

She was twisting his words *and* his insides. Enough to infuriate him. He snarled. "And how exactly does Jasper fit into that?"

"I don't know. You tell me."

Blaze searched for the deeper meaning in those words, some realization that she knew the letters were from him, but he could tell from the look in her eye that he hadn't been found out yet.

Blaze shook his head. No, whatever this was, it wasn't like the woman he knew. Dakota didn't play mind games like this. She was kind, caring, and straightforward when it came to her goals, her dreams, her fears. When she'd told him she wanted to take things slow, she'd said it because it was the truth, not because she was toying with him.

But now...

Now, she *was* toying with him. He felt it.

And he didn't like it one damn bit.

"Why did you wear that dress tonight?" The accusatory question tore from his lips.

The pink curve of Dakota's mouth pursed in disapproval, and she glanced down at it. "You don't like it?"

"I didn't say that." His eyes trailed the length of her, pausing to linger momentarily over the sight of smooth, bare skin. "I'd like it better if you weren't in it, if you let me take it off you."

Dakota sucked in a little involuntary breath. Barely there, but enough for him to notice. He looked at her with every bit of heat and frustration he was feeling, like he could devour every inch of her. His desire did things to her. He saw it. Jasper be damned. And why did she care if he liked her dress and how she looked in it if she didn't...

"So you do like it?" she asked, the question confusingly hopeful.

Blaze growled. He was over this silly little game. "Answer my question, goddamn it."

"I told you. I was trying to get into the right mood to write Jasper back." Dakota lifted her wineglass to her lips and took a quick swig, like she needed extra courage to say what came next. "You're my best friend. You're good with writing letters. I thought you could help me out with that."

She thought he would help her pour her heart out to another man? Blaze snarled again, baring his canine teeth.

That was it. He needed to shift, get the hell out of here. He couldn't stand another second of this without touching her, without showing her exactly how wrong she was, without proving that he was the only man for her. He stalked past her, heading toward the door.

Dakota's eyes went wide. "Where are you going?"

"Home." His voice was rough, part warning growl.

"What about celebrating?" She placed her wineglass down on the kitchen counter and hurried after him.

"I don't feel like celebrating." Blaze gripped the door handle and wrenched it open.

Peaches had been waiting outside apparently and shot inside the cabin between his feet.

"Blaze." Dakota chased after him. She caught his wrist in her hands. "Blaze, wait."

There was something scared in her voice, like she was regretful. Dakota let out a shaky, nervous breath as he glanced back toward her.

God, she was beautiful. Everything he'd ever wanted and more. He'd show her if she let him and yet...

He knew that look on her face. It was the same look she got whenever she was nervous and was trying to gather strength for what she was saying. She was about to sideline him to the permanent friend zone. He could feel it.

Dakota inhaled a quick breath, her next words catching him off guard. "Blaze, the truth is...I really don't give two flying figs about writing Jasper back. I just didn't want to take things slow anymore, but I didn't know how to tell you that I was wrong, so I thought if I got you all angry and alpha and jealous that you might...you know." She bit her lower lip in a way that nearly undid him. "Make me want you so badly I'd admit you were right all along?"

Blaze snarled. "Fuck me, Dakota." He gripped her hand in his. "Why didn't you just say that?"

Eyes flashing to his wolf, he had her in his arms and pinned against her doorframe within seconds. He hiked up the material of her skirt with a harsh yank before he ground his hips into hers, the hard length of his cock throbbing. She let out a pleasured little moan as the erection beneath his jeans found the nub of her clit through their clothing.

"I'm going to tear this dress off you." Blaze nipped at the skin of her neck with his teeth. "I want to ruin it."

"Ruin it?" Dakota panted. "Why?"

"So no wolf other than me can ever look at you in it again."

She moaned her approval, bucking her hips harder against him.

Blaze dipped his head lower, teasing his mouth along the sensitive skin of her breasts. "Do you know how hard it's been to keep my hands off you these past few days?" He yanked the neckline of her dress back, exposing the brown flesh of her nipple and circling it with his tongue. She arched into him, crying out as he blew a hot breath against the puckered skin there. "Do you know how hungry for you I've been?"

She panted. "Tell me."

"Every time I've looked at you, been near you, smelled you,

fuck, even thought of you, I've imagined all the ways I wanted to make you scream my name." He tugged at her exposed nipple with his teeth.

"Blaze," she whimpered.

"My name," he growled. "*Never* anyone else's."

"Why?" she whispered.

"Why?" Blaze let out a dark, amused chuckle. What the fuck kind of question was that? He snaked his hand beneath the hem of her dress, reveling in how she opened for him, before he shoved aside the crotch of her panties and dipped a hot finger inside her. He pressed up and inward, hitting that spot that made her buck and moan. "Because you're mine, goddamn it," he growled, "and you always have been, Kotes."

Lifting her by her behind, he carried her into the cabin, still fingering her with his other hand as he kicked her door closed behind him. She clung to him, wrapping her legs around his waist and her arms around his neck with his hand buried inside her as he carried her into the bedroom. A few moments later, still pleasuring her, he tossed her onto the bed, toppling down onto the mattress above her.

Dakota laughed quietly as they both fumbled to right themselves in a tangle of heated limbs. The sound of her joy, her pleasured amusement was the most erotic noise he'd ever heard.

He growled his approval.

Abandoning the sweet feel of her cunt in his hand, he pulled his fingers out of her, holding her gaze in his as he slipped those same two fingers, drenched in her wetness, into his mouth with a hot, satisfied lick. He wanted her to watch him savor her taste. Dakota let out a sharp hiss and reached for him.

Blaze growled in warning, wolf eyes flashing. Oh no. He wasn't done playing with her.

Not yet.

Dakota dropped her hands back down in submission as he tore

at the neckline of her dress, ripping it down the sides with a sharp tear. It fell from her shoulders, exposing her torso so she was naked and bare for him. Staring up at him with heavy, sultry eyes, she toyed with the hard tips of her breasts.

The gold of his wolf eyes flared, hot and possessive. "You're for my eyes only."

"I never liked that dress much anyway," she admitted. The spark of desire in her face thrilled him. "I only bought it because I knew you did and I wanted to see that hot spark in your eye when I wore it, that look you get when you watch me like I'm the only woman in the room."

"You *are* the only woman in the room. For me, you always have been. All I can see is you." He trailed a hand down the length of her neck, her chest, her stomach, and still lower until she arched toward him, squirming with need. "But I thought you didn't feel the same until you kissed me the other night."

"Be serious, Blaze." She said it like she did when he was joking with her, teasing. "We both know that's the world's worst lie."

The gold of her wolf eyes flared, matching his own. He wanted to throw back his head and howl as that small spark of hope she'd lit in him flamed. Inside, he was an inferno, burning for her.

And this time, he didn't have to hold himself back.

Chapter 16

IF SHE WANTED AN ALPHA, HE'D GIVE HER ALPHA.

And he'd enjoy every damn second of it.

Dakota lay naked before him, sprawled across the bed like his own personal feast. Blaze wanted to kiss every inch of her skin, trail soft, playful bites up the inside of her thighs until her bare cleft glistened with wet heat. Fuck, she was already damp for him, soaked from where he'd sunk his fingers into the depths of her, probing and massaging until she'd bucked against him. He loved to watch her that way, arching her back and riding his hand until she cried out with hunger and need.

He'd never taken much joy in being a selfish lover, but she made him greedy because he could see in her eyes that she wanted him to be.

"What's your fantasy, Kotes?" he purred in a heated whisper. He stood over her, hands trailing over the length of her thighs down to her knees. He hooked one foot over his shoulder, kissing the bone of her ankle. "What keeps you awake at night?"

She didn't answer. Instead, a coy little smile curved her lips.

Oh no, he wasn't letting her play hard to get. With one swift movement, he forced her legs wider, baring her to him. She gasped in approval and his cock throbbed. He couldn't wait to bury himself inside her, in the soft pink folds of her pussy.

"You," she breathed finally. A blush crossed her cheeks. "You're my fantasy."

His balls tightened. Each heated word she whispered nearly did him in.

She wiggled lower on the bed, legs against his chest. She tried to reach for him, but he caught her wrists in his hands, refusing to let her touch him. Not yet.

"And which side do you fancy, Kotes?" He massaged the arch of her foot as he kissed down the length of her thigh, canines nipping and tugging at the tender flesh there. "Your sweet, sarcastic best friend?" Another kiss, slow and sweet, as she sucked in a breath. "The easygoing cowboy?" He licked the sensitive skin just below her knee, hot and quick. She hissed at the sensation. "Or the hardened soldier?" This time a nip, a hard, playful bite.

Her wolf eyes flared and she bit her lower lip.

"All three?" she whimpered, like he couldn't already tell her preference.

"Nonsense," he teased.

Dakota laughed, smiling all the way to her eyes, dark, full lashes fluttering. "You can have me more than once, you know."

Fuck, how many times had he longed to hear her say those exact words?

Blaze chuckled, dark and low. "Oh, I plan to, but don't lie to me, Kotes. Your fantasy is specific. Tell me."

She let out a frustrated little whimper. "You're toying with me. You already know. I told you once. Years ago."

He did know. The memory had been driving him wild for years. Fuck, that night had been torture. He'd come so close to kissing her then, to dragging her into his bed, but he hadn't risked it. Though she had. He realized that now. She'd confessed exactly how she wanted him that night, under the guise of humor and harmless flirtation between friends, of course. Nothing more than a teasing game. Never real, even though now they both knew otherwise. It'd been years ago. Still, he remembered.

But he wanted to hear her say it. Now. Here in his moment.

To make all that platonic teasing over the years real.

As real as it'd felt then.

"I'm not going to let you off that easy." Blaze grinned. "I'll keep toying with you all night unless you tell me. I'm far more stubborn than you."

The blush in Dakota's cheeks deepened and she glanced down briefly. She hadn't had as many partners over the years as he had, and he knew that. But the fact that she was naked and bare before him but could still be embarrassed by her desire, her pleasure, was so fucking adorable he could hardly stand it. She seemed so innocent and naive when she blushed that way, but what thrilled him was he knew she wasn't. Not with him.

With him, she was comfortable enough she'd do anything, all of her heart's darkest desires, because she was his queen and his only duty was to do her bidding.

"I miss seeing you in your fatigues," she admitted. She toyed with that plump lower lip again. "Is that so bad of me?"

"Horrible. Filthy," he teased. He chuckled as a wide smile tugged across his lips.

In response, the blush in her cheeks deepened, creeping down to the tan skin of her delicious, pert little tits. She had the most perfectly pebbled nipples he'd ever fucking seen.

Hers were by far his favorite. It was like she'd been made for him. Or maybe he'd been made for her?

He growled with pleasure at the thought.

She was his and he was hers—as it should be. As it always had been.

It was all he'd ever wanted.

"Bad is exactly what I want you to be." The gold of his wolf eyes flared.

Pushing her legs back down onto the bed, he stepped away from her. After he tipped his Stetson off his head, Dakota opened her mouth to protest, but he shook his head with a reassuring grin. "Don't worry, Kotes. I'll put it back on."

Dakota smiled, soft and sweet.

He made quick work of stripping off his shirt, which with appropriately lewd humor read: "Enjoy life. Eat out more often." He licked his lips in promise that he'd do exactly that more than once before night's end, then he cast the shirt onto her bedroom floor. He left his jeans and his belt buckled, solely because he planned to enjoy watching her remove them.

Without warning, he crossed the room to her bedside drawer and wrenched it open. Dakota watched his every movement with rapt attention, but she didn't protest. There were few secrets between them, and he knew exactly what she kept in there. Whatever book she was reading, her journal, the small bottle of creamy-white lotion she liked to put on after she showered each night, an electric pink vibrator, and right next to it, his dog tags that he'd given her. He removed his dog tags from the drawer and placed them over his head.

The metal felt cold against the heat of his skin. Dakota's eyes lingered there, and she sucked in a harsh, excited breath.

Blaze prowled back toward where she lay on the bed, waiting. "Tell me what you want. You're in charge." His words were a dark, heated whisper.

Dakota couldn't seem to take her eyes off of him. The folds of her still-bared cunt glistened. "I want you to have your way with me. Your fantasy is mine."

Blaze's hand clenched into a fist and he snarled, biting down on the edge of it. "Fuck, you're trying to kill me, woman."

"That's what I want." Dakota's wolf eyes flared. "I want you hot and wild with need."

Blaze chuckled, hanging his head as he placed his hands on his hips. He scratched at the scruff of his chin before he shook his head. "You asked for it. The safe word is: Peaches." He grinned as he tipped his Stetson off his head, deliberately hanging it on the end of her bedpost. The next words that crossed his lips were a harsh command.

"Get on your knees."

Dakota had never seen Blaze so demanding, so rabid and wild with need that he was nearly feral with it, and she reveled in it. "Yes," she whispered in response to his command.

She wanted to be exactly what he desired, loved the way it felt when he looked at her like this, like she alone had the power to pleasure him, to make him wild. If *she* could make this wild cowboy wolf filled with desire, it made her feel like she could conquer anything.

"Yes, what?" he growled, wolf eyes flashing in reprimand.

A rush of heat flooded her core.

"Yes, sir," she whispered. She corrected herself with a tentative grin.

She pushed up from the bed and stood momentarily before she took two slow steps toward him. She dropped to her knees, bringing her head only an inch below the buckle of his belt. She didn't need to be told what to do next. She couldn't wait for it.

Gripping the metal of his belt buckle, she unhooked the clasp before making quick work with the button, his zipper. The low V-cut of his hips had a light dust of brown hair that led down until it disappeared beneath the worn material of his ranch jeans. She kissed along the skin there, a pleased smile crossing her lips when he let out an aroused growl when she finally pulled his clothes off him.

His erection sprang forth, jutting, hot and male.

She resisted the temptation to grip him in her hand, to kiss him there before she drew him into her mouth. Instead, she sat back on her knees, waiting.

Blaze grumbled in frustration. "Do I need to say it?" His eyes turned dark and commanding as he growled the words they both knew he'd been dying to say, "Suck me."

She did as she was told.

Wrapping her hand around him, she held the base of him firm as she drew the head of his cock into her mouth. Blaze threw back his head with a pleasured groan as he eased his hips forward. In response, she took him deeper.

A guttural moan tore from his lips. "Fuck me, Kotes…"

She drew back slightly, licking over the sensitive tip of him until a visible shiver ran through him. She felt his balls tighten in her hand as his cock twitched. "Is that a command or a prayer? I'm not sure." A devious little smile crossed her lips. She was the one truly in control here. She could call stop at any moment and she knew he'd listen.

Blaze growled. "Don't get cheeky or it'll be a command. That sweet little ass of yours will be dusky come morning."

"Promise?" She smiled. A bead of moisture gathered at his tip and she licked at it.

Blaze shuddered, even as he let out another animalistic snarl. "Now you've asked for it." A devilish smirk crossed his lips. "I won't stop until I've had my way with you."

Within seconds, he lifted her into his arms, then carried her back to the bed. He tossed her onto the mattress, positioning himself directly outside her entrance.

He thrust inside her, filling her with the thick, hot heat of him until she was crying out in delicious pleasure-pain. "Blaze," she said his name, because she couldn't *not* say it.

He gripped onto one of her hips, pumping and pushing deeper, harder into her until she was lifting her hips in need of him.

He was everywhere. Inside her, on top of her, his large, rough hands exploring her torso, tangling in her hair while the hardened, length of his cock made her moan. He pounded into her, unrelenting. A familiar, delicious pressure built inside her, the walls of her pussy tightening.

"Blaze," she keened.

Her orgasm rolled through her with a sudden rush of wet heat. Blaze continued to bury himself in her, reaching his own climax a few seconds later. She moaned again as she felt his cock pulse, filling her with a rush of warmth from his seed.

Dakota felt like she'd come completely unraveled.

She'd known she wanted him, but she'd never expected it to be like this.

Like being with him filled the void she'd felt inside her chest for so long. Like he made her whole. Like the key to unlocking her heart had been sitting beside her for over a decade and she had been too foolish to be with him like this, because she'd been scared.

She couldn't help the wave of emotion that filled her eyes and muddled her throat at the thought, because he was hers now and she knew her best friend well enough to know that from this point forward, Blaze's one true mission in life would be to bring her happiness.

He'd just been waiting for her to realize it.

Blaze eased back slightly, sensing a change in her, but still wrapped in her warm, welcoming heat. His features twisted with concern. "Hey," he whispered, cupping her cheek. "I didn't hurt you, did I?"

"No," Dakota shook her head. The gathering tears spilled over and slipped down her cheek. "No, you were perfect."

Blaze chuckled slightly before he dipped his head and kissed her. "No, Kotes," he whispered against her lips, the familiar nickname an intimate promise. "We're perfect." Blaze rested his forehead on her for a moment, both of them lying there, breathing each other in. "I always knew we would be."

He pulled out from inside her, keeping her wrapped in his arms. Drawing her against him, he lifted her farther onto the bed with him until they both rested their heads against the pillows. She nestled her head against the muscles of his chest. He tipped her face up toward him with a gentle lift of her chin and stared into her eyes for a long moment. She could get lost in the blue there, before he kissed her again, long and deep.

They lay like that for a while, tangled together and lost in each other's arms until their kisses grew more heated again, more fevered.

Without warning, Blaze flipped her onto her back, lingering in a plank position over her until she felt the hardened tip of his cock nudge against her entrance again.

Her eyes flew wide in surprise. "Again?"

Blaze cast her that wide, white-toothed grin that she loved. *Of course, again*, that smile seemed to say. "I said I wouldn't stop until I'd had my way with you." He growled and his eyes flashed to his wolf.

Lord, he was gorgeous. Everything she wanted. Yes, again.

With her nod of approval, he slipped inside her. This time, softer, gentler at first, though she knew it wouldn't be for long. Not with the heat that flared through his gaze.

He pumped a little harder, a little deeper, testing her limits.

Dakota cried out his name in pleasure. "Blaze!" If he kept that up, she'd be close all over again.

"Fuck, I can't get enough of that." He thrust into her again, causing her to let out a pleasured mewl. A devilish smirk crossed his lips. "It's going to be a long night."

Chapter 17

BLAZE LAY AWAKE, TUCKED IN THE FAMILIAR DIVOT OF THE BED with Dakota wrapped in his arms. He knew that naked and asleep like this, she was in her most vulnerable state. With her head nestled into the crook of his shoulder and arm, one delicate hand splayed over his chest, she looked so peaceful tucked against him. Like she was younger and less experienced than she'd been even years before she'd become one of the pack's fiercest warriors. A decade by her side meant he'd known more than one version of her as they'd changed and grown. Thankfully, time had always brought them closer, even when physical distance forced them apart.

Blaze leaned toward her, burying his nose in the soft tresses of her hair. Still asleep, she responded by snuggling into him. He inhaled the scent of her. Beneath the natural smell of her skin and the fresh scent of jasmine soap and shampoo, she smelled like comfort, home, and all the things he'd wanted but hadn't allowed himself to have for years, and for one insane moment, he thought maybe he could tell her—about where it all went wrong.

About why he hadn't fought for her, even though she was his everything, the reason he breathed. When he'd been discharged from MAC-V-Alpha, he'd been such a mangled version of himself he hadn't known *how* to breathe, let alone who the fuck he was anymore.

But she had.

She'd known even when he didn't. All the more reason it was far past time he told her everything. All of it. Everything he'd done. Everything he wished he hadn't. Maybe Maverick was right. Maybe he'd tell her the darkest truths of himself and she'd love him anyway, and for the first time since he'd come home, he suddenly felt brave enough to take that risk.

Blaze brushed the prickled hair of his evening beard across the top of Dakota's head, drawing in her scent like he would a mate's.

"I love you," he whispered against the dark coils of her hair. He exhaled, long and slow. "Fuck, I've never loved anything more."

She didn't hear him whisper it. She was still asleep as the soft sounds of her slowed breathing continued to soothe him. But the words still felt like a confession.

He didn't expect the relief that followed them, rushing over him, strong enough to wash his soul clean. He'd accused her of being scared, which was true, but he'd been equally afraid in his own fucked-up way. But he wasn't now. She'd made him brave. And he planned to tell her that the moment she was awake.

Blaze lay there in the dark for what felt like hours, not asleep or fully awake but more rested than he'd been in years. Eventually, he eased from beneath her, padding into the bathroom to piss. He relieved himself and washed his hands before splashing a bit of cold water on his face and heading back into the bedroom.

Lingering in the bathroom doorway, he watched Dakota as she slept, still snuggled into that same spot she always lay in, wrapped in the tangle of sheets. He hadn't thought he could ever feel this way again, like hope could hold a potentially permanent place inside his chest, and yet he did. She'd done that for him.

Careful not to wake her, Blaze shuffled over to where his pants had been cast onto the floor in their heated frenzy. Picking up his old, worn ranch jeans, he tugged them on before he dug in his pocket for his phone to check the time. It was still pitch-black outside, the kind of dark only found on a moonless Montana night. It felt like being dropped into an endless midnight void, where there was no way out but sky.

The gold of his wolf eyes reflected against the dark screen of his phone's surface before he hit the center button. Blue light seared through the darkness, singeing his retinas. Nearly 3:00 a.m. The creak of the old spring mattress drew his attention as Dakota rolled over.

"Blaze?" she rasped with a quiet, sleepy groan.

Shit. He hadn't meant to wake her.

"I'm here, Kotes," he whispered.

There was more truth in those words than there'd ever been.

He started to put his phone back in his jean pocket, but something about the quiet, the stillness of the trees and the forest off in the distance outside her window, about the long shadows of the moonless night stilled him.

"Do you feel that?" Blaze whispered, his voice low with warning.

Dakota sat up, instantly alert.

The skin on the back of his neck prickled as his wolf stirred with awareness. If he hadn't been awake, he'd never had noticed it.

They weren't alone.

Slowly Dakota stood from the bed, quickly pulling on her nightgown and following his gaze through the darkness. The gold of her wolf eyes flared. Their kind had clearer night vision than most, but he couldn't see anything. He eyed the line of the forest trees. No movement. None. The trees were so still it chilled him.

Tearing his gaze away, he quickly typed in his four-digit code on his phone, swiping right and hitting the app to bring up the pack's security cams, but a flash of green from an incoming call disrupted the interface. Kieran's name glared across the screen.

Blaze hit accept and pressed the phone to his ear. "Yeah?"

"Blaze," the other wolf breathed, "they're here."

Blaze didn't think.

Adrenaline pumped through him. His heart pounded. Years of training and experience mixed in an instant as muscle memory took control. Despite the summer Montana winds blowing in through the open bedroom window, the nip of the Russian cold bit at his back, harsh and foreign, even as his mind registered the sight of Dakota standing in her nightgown beside him.

They were here. At Wolf Pack Run.

They would have been watching all night.

Which meant...

The pain of the realization hit him. He may as well have stabbed a knife in Dakota's back himself, because he'd made her a target right along with him.

Blaze snarled his command to Kieran only seconds before the phone fell from his hand. "Hit the fucking alarm, damn it."

The ranch's drill sirens exploded in an earsplitting chorus, waking and alerting every creature within a hundred-mile radius. Blaze lunged for his gun on the bedside table. The still edge of the forest, of the pasture, burst in an explosion of movement. They'd only been seconds away from a blitz attack.

"Blaze." Dakota dove for her weapons on the far side of the bed, but Blaze gripped her wrist, hard, dragging her behind him with his full strength as he ran down her hallway.

"Leave it. We can't—"

The windows to her bedroom shattered. Glass flew in a sudden explosion only moments after they'd made it out of the room. The sound rang in his ears. An earsplitting familiar ring. Dakota screamed. They were out of time. Out of time. They always had been.

He'd been too stupid to see the truth.

He'd never been allowed to be happy in the first place.

They'd make sure of it.

Not stopping, he dragged her by the arm into her still-intact living room. The smoke from the back of the cabin where her bedroom had gone up in flames choked them, coating the air and their lungs with an acrid thickness. Dakota grabbed a yowling, hissing Peaches from the back of the sofa, hauling the terrified animal into her arms.

Blaze threw open the front door. Outside, Sarge was bucking and whinnying wildly, trying desperately to escape at the sight of the nearby flames but still tied to his hold.

"Easy, boy! Easy!" Blaze shouted.

He gripped Sarge's reins and the connector that led to his mouth bit and yanked the horse down to calm. Blaze mounted up and into Sarge's saddle within seconds. He reached a hand back down to Dakota.

"Blaze, we need to—" Her eyes darted to the trees, but a round of howls and shouts interrupted her.

"Get on the damn horse, woman," he snarled, gripping her hand and yanking her up into the saddle along with him. They needed to get to the main compound building—the fortress, the elite warriors' rendezvous point.

With Dakota in the saddle behind him, he kicked Sarge into motion. Sarge shot forward like a rocket, galloping at full speed, eager to escape the flames. In Dakota's arms, Peaches yowled even louder, joining the echoing, eerie chorus. The sounds of wolves howling, vampires hissing, and the faintly there screeching ring of the resonant sound device playing in a constant whir rattled inside his skull. He prayed to whatever deity that would listen that it'd be enough.

Time seemed to slow to a crawl, until they reached the main compound. Blaze pulled Sarge to a halt, both he and Dakota dismounting within seconds. Most of the team was already there, except...

"Where's Maverick?" Blaze searched through the group frantically.

Colt, their high commander, was the first to answer. In Maverick's absence, battle leadership fell to him. "He went down into the bunker with Sierra and Belle. He said it was best for her to deliver the baby there if something like this—"

If something like this happened, Blaze finished mentally, as the sound of several of the civilian wolves and some of their children came screaming toward them. The bunker entrance was only feet away. Dakota and Aaliyah nearly collided with them, ushering them down the ladder chute with calm, steady reassurance even in the face of the danger.

"We can't wait for him to get up here. They'll blow through whoever's on border patrol tonight before long. We need to—"

Another round of screams off to the eastern side of the pasture signaled that defense was already gone. All the elite warriors pulled their weapons.

Save for one.

"A cowboy's gun is shit for this," Blaze shouted over the din. They'd trained for this, but not long enough. They'd had mere days to prepare. Not the weeks they'd needed. He ripped the armory chest near the bunker open and reached down into it. "The Volk are fast, but an AR-15 is faster."

He felt strangely calm and in his element with the sounds of battle raging around him, in some twisted way he couldn't examine at the moment. It was clear his packmates didn't. He pulled out one of the pack's machine guns that'd likely never before been used outside training before and shoved it at the nearest warrior.

"This should do it."

At his direction, every fighter present grabbed for the weapons and started to gear up like their lives depended on it. They had no idea how much they likely did.

The pack had faced threats before, from other shifters and vampires alike, but never like this.

This was war like Wolf Pack Run had never seen it.

Blaze's pulse raced. He didn't even need the nod from Colt to understand it was up to him to start barking orders. He was more experienced. The only one who'd faced these fuckers before and managed to live through it.

"Colt and Wes go west. Dean and Malcolm, head north."

The directions fell from his lips with unthinking, practiced ease.

They were running out of time. Two more minutes and that ease would be gone as the Volk and the vampires reached the main compound, slashing through the last of the pack's outer resistance and defenses.

"Aim for the head," he yelled over the noise. "They're fast as hell. If you shift, go for the jugular. They won't drop without taking a chunk out of you and they'll fucking enjoy it."

The group started to disband as a feminine hand gripped his shoulder.

Dakota.

He'd nearly forgotten about her in the war-induced haze, all the more reason why—

"Am I with you?" Dakota yelled, interrupting his thoughts.

The sight of the AR-15 in her hands made him stiffen. Warrior or not, she looked out of place, even if she knew how to hold and fire it. Peaches was still yowling in her other arm, but the old feline leaped from her hold, scampering down into the bunker where she'd be safe.

At least one of them had some sense.

Blaze signaled with his hand for Wes and Colt to circle back and not leave yet.

"No," he shouted over the sounds of gunfire to Dakota. "Get in the bunker."

Dakota's jaw dropped and she glared at him in outrage.

One of the semiautomatics went off. The unsuppressed sound reverberated through the mountain pines, popping in quick succession. Another round. More shouts.

"Blaze—" Dakota started on him.

But he didn't have time for this. None of them did. He rounded on her, drawing nose to nose with her. "You will get in that bunker this instant or I swear on all that is fucking holy *I* will end you myself before I *ever* let one of them do it. It would be a mercy! Do you understand?" he snarled, baring his teeth.

Dakota refused to back down. "I can help," she snarled back.

"I know that."

"Then let me."

His eyes flashed to his wolf. "I've made you a target!" he shouted.

Dakota's eyes went wide. "What?" She looked at him as if he'd just told her the moon they howled at each night was made of fucking cheese, like *he* was the one being ridiculous.

This wasn't about pride or gender or any other ridiculous petty thing. This was about safety. Her: his whole fucking reason for existing, goddamn it. Didn't she see that?

"It's me they want, and they'll use you to get me," he growled.

Dakota shook her head. "I won't sit this one out. Not even for you, Blaze. I'm a warrior. I—"

"Wes," Blaze shouted over his shoulder and into the din, circumventing her and rounding on the Grey Wolf second-in-command. Several years earlier, he'd protected the other wolf's life with a favor by keeping his secrets. "You owe me, goddamn it."

Wes's eyes darted between them, weighing the decision within seconds. Angering the females of the pack or risking more lives. It wasn't even a question. He gave a silent tilt of his chin. A nod.

"Get in the bunker, Dakota," Blaze ordered.

"Wes?" Dakota growled.

Wes nodded, backing up Blaze. "Get in the bunker, warrior."

Another round of screams promised they had no time left.

In Maverick's absence, the will of the packmaster came through his second. Dakota's shoulder caught against one of the passing civilians as they climbed down the ladder and into the Grey Wolves underground bunker for safety. She glared at Blaze as if she were Julius Caesar—he was Brutus and she'd been betrayed. But she didn't back down.

"No," she said, refusing Wes's direct order. "I'm a warrior and I won't stand down until the *packmaster* tells me otherwise. You think you were trained for this? Well, so was I." She hoisted the AR-15 onto her shoulder and snarled at him. "Now, get out of my way or join me, Blaze."

Blaze growled. He'd deal with her anger later. "Stay behind me then."

"I'll fight *beside* you and that's final," she snapped, taking her position next to him.

"I won't be able to protect you, watch you."

"I don't need you to." She raised the gun to see down the line of the scope. Dakota was born ready, a true fighter.

And when she dug her feet in, there was no moving her. He had to admit, though he wanted her safe, he was filled with more than a bit of pride for his fierce, she-wolf friend.

Fuck, he loved her.

For now, she'd be safe alongside him. That was all that mattered. Which meant they had a pack of wolves that needed to be saved.

And he had a fucking hero complex to rein the hell in.

Dakota slammed the door to the bunker closed behind her as the last of the civilians hunkered down to remain safe. Maverick could use the underground tunnels that led from the bunker to emerge and fight. With Dakota by his side, the moment Blaze heard the bunker seal from the inside, something snapped inside him.

All he felt was rage. Rage that the Volk had found him. Rage that they'd come for him here at his home. Rage at himself that he hadn't stayed away in order to protect them all. They'd have been better off without him. Rage and the familiar rush of adrenaline. The messed-up excitement. This was what he was trained for.

And now he could put it to use.

Blaze hoisted the semiauto into position on his shoulder, feet tracking toward the sound of incoming battle in a quick-paced movement through the mountain grass, Dakota flanked beside him. Shelter. Target. Strike. In that order. His wolf senses and training led him. He didn't even need to think.

Nerves, fear, and excitement mixed. He could almost taste his own mortality.

Felt each thump of his pulse.

A vampire to their right was the first he spotted.

Aim. Pull the trigger. Move on. Dakota took out the next one.

For him, vamps were easy. Old hat.

The Volk were the true challenge. He knew that.

Duck down. Hide. Shelter. Emerge. Shoot. Repeat.

They'd taken down five vamps with blows to the head in a blur of several minutes, and he hadn't even blinked. The pack didn't use AR-15s normally, because the noise was too likely to draw human attention. But now, any risk was worth the pack's survival.

Somewhere in the midst of the melee, they found Austin and Malcolm, the usual team, and they joined forces into a wall of guns and ammo.

Down. Up. Fire. Once. Twice. Forward. Again. Repeat.

No restarts. They took hits. The whole beginning went down in rapid-fire, sustained fashion until the last of the vamps were down, but that was only the beginning.

Then the Volk came.

Excitement gave way to the sense of mission.

The Volk hadn't been prepared for the AR-15s, for the sound device that slowed them. But it didn't matter. They were still faster than any Grey Wolf. The first emerged from the trees in a rush of movement so quick, Blaze didn't have time to think. He pulled the trigger, missed. Pulled it again, missed again. He managed to get a shot in on the thing's friggin' arm, but then it was on him. Their movement was so fast, it was hard to think straight.

Hard to block. Let alone defend or strike.

He dropped the AR-15, abandoning the gun because it was too close range. The Volk in front of him shifted into its wolf—a mangled, monstrous mess of a thing that was nearly twice his size and looked more like it'd stepped out of one of his and Dakota's favorite shitty horror films. Hollywood was disgustingly accurate sometimes.

By his count, there were only six of them. But who was he

kidding? He couldn't really spare a second for a full head count, but instinct, awareness told him as much.

Six on ten elite warriors.

And at least twenty more Grey Wolf warriors. Some of which were already dead. He could smell it. It was hardly even odds. Piss-poor betting splits and not in their favor.

The Volk that'd changed in front of him lunged for him.

Blaze scrambled back. He hadn't had time to shift.

Involuntarily, he felt his wolf rip through his skin before he even commanded it. Danger would do that. Make them wild in self-defense. His jaws came out first, biting and snapping as his fur emerged. Wars were won and lost on the sum of small favors. Teeth sank into his skin. Not his. Not bite and release but bite and tear. He felt a chunk of his flank separate.

Pain seared through him. Enough he nearly blacked out. But he couldn't care. Not if he wanted to live. He took his own advice and went for the throat, even as he felt another piece of one of his limbs tear.

Push through. Giving up is how they bleed you. He could hear Rock's voice in his head. No, not Rock. Officer Saila. Same man, different rodeo.

The iron taste of blood filled his jaw as his pulse thudded in his ears.

Clamp down harder. Tear deeper.

The Volk's lifeblood throbbed against his tongue. Veins disconnected. One harsher tear against his leg. He wanted to howl, to scream, to die and get the pain the fuck over with.

And then it was done.

He stood in wolf form on the mountainside, teeth, jaw, and wounds dripping blood. Dakota wasn't far to his right, having taken out her own monster. She was bleeding, wounded, but alive. Blaze braced for a second wave, but the realization quickly came that the Volk didn't need it. The first had been brutal enough. The whole thing was over within a handful of minutes. Blaze stared at the carnage around him.

A plethora of injured Grey Wolves. More dead. Disfigured Volk bodies.

He glanced down at his feet.

The Volk he'd fought had shifted back into human form upon its death, an involuntary response. The sight cut him deeper than he wanted it to, until a cold kind of numb snaked its way through him.

The monster was just a man. Just another shifter like he was.

But he knew all too well how a monster could be made from man.

"Blaze!"

The sound of Dakota shouting his name froze him in place. He wished she'd stayed in the bunker, goddamn it.

He glanced up, still in a haze. He could feel himself bleeding. He'd need a medic, eventually. His wolf would keep him going for a few days until he returned to Moscow. Until…

Blaze blinked, snapping out of it. Dakota was running toward him. Near Austin, Malcolm, and the others. She and he weren't the only ones injured. From the corner of his eye, he saw the line of the forest trees move, and in an instant, he knew.

They weren't finished.

"Get down!" he shouted.

He'd never know what caused Dakota to listen to him then, whether it was the look in his eyes, the terror in his voice, or the sheer guttural power of how loud he'd shouted. She dropped to the ground, diving midrun as a final Volk raced forth from the forest. This one faster, more powerful than the last. Likely because it had fed on one of the members of their pack recently. Dakota missed the slash of its blade, the dive as its shifted into wolf form and opened its monstrous jaw to feed, by only a fraction of an instant.

But Austin, who had reached her side before him, to protect her, didn't.

There wasn't any time for Blaze to shout, to yell.

The Volk sank its jaws into the unguarded flesh of his pack-mate's neck, snuffing out Blaze's friend, his packmate and fellow wolf's lifeforce in an instant.

Blaze saw red.

The rage he felt inside. The shouting. The crimson that painted the ground black fell as Austin bled. The next thing Blaze knew, he was on the thing. Not even shifted into his wolf, but ripping, tearing, destroying with his strength all the same. He couldn't see straight. All he could do was maim, kill, destroy. He didn't stop even once he felt the monster fall limp beneath him. All he could feel, all he could think about was lifting the butt of the AR-15, blud-geoning, over and over and over again. He had to save Austin. It wasn't supposed to be his friend dead.

It was supposed to have been him, damn it.

He—

"Blaze," the sound of his packmaster's voice shouting, com-manding, cut through his head. He felt more than one pair of large, masculine hands on him, pulling him, hauling him off the thing, but couldn't bring himself to still.

He'd been trained to kill.

To protect. To serve.

De Oppresso Liber.

Until he died. He'd expected that, and yet he hadn't.

For the first time since he'd returned home from Russia, he wished he had.

For all their sakes.

Blaze wasn't certain what snapped him out of it. Maybe it was his packmaster whispering in the Old Tongue in his ear like he needed to hear it, or the sight of Malcolm, gripping his face and growling at him that "he was still here but Austin wasn't, damn it" as the two wolves hauled him backward, or maybe it was the sound of Dakota and the other females of the pack sobbing, howling their pain in the way only wolves mourned over their lost loved ones. At least fifteen or more, and then Austin lost right before their eyes.

Like his life had meant nothing. Like it hadn't even mattered.

He'd been the best among them, who'd helped him with the stupid sound device, because that was what Austin did. He helped them, helped them all and yet...

Blaze had ensured his death through his very existence.

Blaze felt his muscles seize from where he'd still been fighting against Malcolm's and Maverick's hold. He slumped against them, Malcolm catching him in his arms, holding him up and giving him strength like a packmate always would. They would lend him strength. They had it when he didn't. And what had he brought upon them?

Blaze's eyes turned toward Austin's limp body. Amid the Volk's attack and as his blood shed, he'd shifted into his wolf. The dark-gray form mixed with hints of red like a coyote, an inherited trait from Austin's coyote father. His mother had been a Grey Wolf and so had he, yet he was lying there in the mountain dirt, unmoving.

A renewed urgency shot through Blaze. "We have to save him. We have to—"

Malcolm gripped Blaze by both sides of his face, hard, forcing him to look at him. The gold eyes of his wolf stared back. Beneath, he knew the other Grey Wolves' irises were black, not a warm, hon-eyed brown like Austin's were.

Eyes that Blaze wouldn't see again, if he didn't...

"He's gone, Blaze," Malcolm growled. The tears in his packmate's eyes cut through him. "He's gone. Let him go." Malcolm looked at him as if he were the only other wolf on the entire ranch who could understand Blaze's hurt.

And the wish that it'd been him instead.

Blaze stopped fighting, placing his hands on his packmate's shoulders for support.

When he steadied on his feet again, Malcolm released him.

Blaze stumbled slightly, swaying with the lack of force in his limbs. He watched as Malcolm went to Austin's side, crouching low; he brushed the other wolf's eyes closed, throwing back his head with a mourning howl that would forever echo in Blaze's ears. Beneath it, Blaze heard Dakota's sobbing and the whir of the sound device that he wasn't supposed to be able to hear.

The realization that they'd not only lost Austin but Blaze had nearly lost her too shook him to his core. He had to run. He had to shift. He needed to get out of here, away from them to protect all of them. He—

Maverick reached for him. "Blaze."

Blaze snarled as he hit Maverick's hand away. He couldn't do this. He couldn't.

"Blaze," Maverick said again, louder this time.

The sound drew Dakota's attention. She lifted her head.

Blaze met her gaze, feeling as if he'd been the one gutted by the Volk as the realization, the weight of his mistake flooded through him.

He'd never be able to protect her.

———————————

Dakota couldn't even be angry with him, and boy, did she want to be. In wolf form, she chased after Blaze, following his scent through the forest with deft precision and tracking ability. He'd shifted and darted off into the trees after Maverick and Malcolm had torn him off that…that thing. The sight of his rage, of the unmitigated fury he'd wrought on the creature would stay with her for days. Nearly as much as the gruesome display of Austin's death would. A pang of grief gripped her heart, more painful than the wounds she'd endured, and she let out a long, mournful howl. That was what their kind did when they hurt, when they'd lost one of the pack they all loved. They howled their pain, releasing the emotion out into the open air of the mountainside as if the earth and nature would somehow heal them.

They never did.

Dakota only shifted back into her human skin once she'd located Blaze among the trees near the eastern pasture. He stood with his back to her at the edge of one of the fields. The cattle hadn't grazed there recently and the summer grass, filled with yellow and purple wildflowers and shoots of dense green weeds, had grown tall, nearly as high as her waist.

She watched him for a moment, approaching slowly. The muscles of his shoulders stiffened and tensed with each ragged breath he took, and the morning sun beat down on the tattoo on his arm— his army patch beneath his skin. The glint of his silver dog tags, still slung around his neck. She couldn't believe they'd managed to stay there through the whole melee, but both were a stark reminder that Blaze had a whole other life he'd lived overseas, without her, and in a single night, he'd been viciously forced back into it.

Even though he'd never wanted to go in the first place.

Dakota reached out to touch him, both to seek comfort and offer it for the grief they were feeling, but then dropped her hand at the last second. She should have been angry with him. She wanted to be. He'd tried to truncate her chance to prove herself in what would perhaps be one of the pack's most important battles in their recent history. He'd kept his secrets from her, that whole other life he'd lived, and most importantly, he hadn't been fully truthful about the danger they both faced.

Danger that had become hers the moment she'd kissed him.

But she knew in his own twisted, misguided way, he'd say he'd done it all to protect her.

Two days ago, she'd have called the whole thing horseshit, would have told him she didn't need his protection, that he could take his antiquated ideas and shove them where the sun didn't shine. They would have fought. He would have apologized, admitted he was wrong, and they would have made up. She would have told him the danger that being with him posed didn't make a difference, that she wanted to be together regardless and maybe after they both healed, they would have found their happily-ever-after.

But with Austin, Kieran, so many among the pack dead, none of that seemed to matter. Arguing, fighting, it wasn't worth it. Not even when it came to her pride.

Not after this.

Their pack, their family, would be burying bodies for days and there would have been more if it hadn't been for him, for the ways he'd urged Maverick to prepare them, if the defenses he'd put in place hadn't slowed the Volk down. He'd known those monsters were coming, had faced the terror on behalf of all of them, and he'd done it with imperfect grace. She'd heard Maverick say as much. That the only reason they hadn't lost any more lives was because Blaze ensured they wouldn't. He had used everything in his power to protect her, protect all of them as best he could, all while keeping his own demons at bay and a smile on her face. She'd heard the legends before, about wolves that were more than wolves, not like them. Wolves that were no longer part human, but until he had warned Maverick and, by extension, the pack, she didn't even remember what to call them.

But *he* knew, because he'd faced them before and lived.

And he'd been carrying all that alone for days…

She was hurt and angry that he hadn't shared his personal connection to it, but she couldn't even imagine what it felt like to live inside Blaze's head these past few weeks. Everything he'd sacrificed. Shouldering the fear of them all on his own to give the pack even a passing chance at remaining safe, at mitigating the panic with preparedness, even while he'd known the full, terrifying truth. He'd been carrying it for all their sakes. In that moment, the way she felt for him could have quieted all her anger for the rest of her days.

"Blaze," she whispered, moving closer. Finally, she reached out, placing a hand on his shoulder.

He winced as if she'd struck him and pulled away.

"Blaze," she whispered.

"There was a child there…when I was in Russia," he rasped. "He was barely a teen. They'd killed his mother. He and his younger siblings watched. They were going to kill him, too. If I saved him, I knew what they'd turn him into, knew what he'd become, but I…" He inhaled a ragged breath, shoulders shaking. "I couldn't do it, Kotes. I couldn't kill him, but now sometimes I think about…what happened because I didn't. What I did to him was worse."

Dakota chose her words carefully, her hand suspended in midair as she hesitated to touch him again. If she did too soon, he might break. "You made an impossible decision in an impossible situation. No one should have to make a choice like that."

How many times had she heard Mę say those same words to her father? But she repeated them now, knew Blaze needed them.

"But I did, damn it," he snarled. "I did make that choice and I should have killed him. If I did, this wouldn't—"

"Blaze, it's over now. It's—"

"It's not over, Dakota." He growled the harsh words over his shoulder at her like she couldn't possibly understand. There was conviction in his tone like he'd been defeated, like they hadn't won in spite of all their loss. "It's my fault. They'll come again. I knew they weren't extinct, knew they would come if they found me. I—"

"You knew," she said, cutting him off. She raised her voice, refusing to coddle him. "And like the brave soldier you are, you carried that weight alone for days. Hell, years, Blaze. You risked your life to protect the pack when you were abroad, and you did it again now. I'm so—"

"I know you're angry with me! I *know* I was wrong, goddammit!" he shouted. "But I–I could have lost you." He rounded on her then, turning to meet her gaze.

There were tears running down his face.

Regret. Pain. Shame.

She'd known Blaze over a decade, but she'd *never* seen him cry before, hadn't known the sight of it would make her feel like her heart had been ripped from her chest, like it was lying there beating on the ground between them, because she...

Dakota's breath caught as she watched him standing before her, eyes damp with tears and fresh wounds still bleeding.

Because she loved him.

She was *in* love with him. She always had been.

But like so many things in her life, she'd seen all the signs and she'd ignored everything that was right in front of her face, because she'd been afraid of the risk, same as he had been. But now...now, in the face of so many of their loved ones lost, gone...

She didn't have another minute to waste.

She didn't know how she hadn't seen it before.

"I love you," she said abruptly. Equal tears poured down her face in a sudden torrent.

She had to tell him. Time wasn't kind. Death didn't wait.

Blaze watched her with a look of abject terror on his face, like he wished she hadn't said it, like she'd driven a knife straight through his middle and gutted him. His chest rose and fell, his breathing still ragged as the deep-sea blue of his eyes traced over the lines of her face, searching, hoping until finally...

"Say it again," he muttered.

More tears slid down her face.

"I love you," she whispered.

He stepped closer. "Say it again."

"I love you."

Closer still. "Say it."

"I love yo—"

He pulled her into his arms, kissing her so hard, he knocked them both to the ground with the force of his embrace. They toppled down into the pasture, but he tucked her in to him and rolled until she was spread out across his chest. He kissed at every inch of her face. Anything and everything he could get his hands on.

"I could listen to you say that for days," he whispered against her lips, tears from both of them mingling as they brushed cheeks.

Gripping her hips, he rolled again so that she was on her back, surrounded by the high summer grass as the heat of his breath danced across her temple, her face. "Say it again."

"I love you."

For a moment, as they lay there together, Dakota could pretend the harsh cruelties of their world didn't exist. They were all hands as they fell into each other, two souls reaching out in an endless abyss for comfort. Dakota whispered those three words over and over again like a balm, like a mantra as Blaze made love to her there in the pasture with a desperate, fevered heat that would haunt her over the coming days along with their lost, fallen packmates.

She knew the words she said to him were true.

But from the way Blaze moved, from how he acted like the whole moment between them was a distant, beautiful dream he would never be able to experience again, she could tell that he didn't.

And that scared her more than any too-real, relived memory ever would, because the way he kissed her felt like a goodbye.

Chapter 18

"THERE ARE NO WORDS." MAVERICK HUNG HIS HEAD AS HE placed his hands on the wooden conference table. The silence that permeated the filled room felt too heavy.

It was the afternoon of the following day, and the whole of the pack had spent the morning and evening leading into the late hours of the night cleaning up the destruction the Volk had left in their wake. The sick and wounded had been tended, her included. She'd have stitches up the side of her upper arm for weeks. But more importantly, their fallen packmates were laid out and the preparations for burial had been made.

Sixteen packmembers lost at the final count.

It had shaken every remaining one of them.

Except for Blaze. After the initial incident, he'd seemed oddly... numb to the whole thing.

Dakota wasn't certain which was worse. She watched him as he sat in the far corner of the conference room, staring out the window with a blank, distant look in his eye that she'd seen far too many times in recent days. He'd helped with the cleanup, dug holes for the upcoming burial like he was supposed to, lifted and hauled bodies, but he'd still been absent. She hadn't truly seen him since they'd parted ways in the field yesterday. Physically, he was there, his wounds mending, but mentally, she knew he was elsewhere.

She couldn't blame him, but she didn't know how to bring him back to her.

She was still reeling from the battle herself. She hadn't been able to return home to her cabin last night after the explosion. Rebuilding would need to happen before that, and it would take time. Asking Blaze if she could stay with him had been an option, but Peaches had been hidden inside the security office ever since the bunker had opened, afraid and unwilling to let anyone near her. Dakota didn't know why, but the cat's behavior made her feel like maybe she needed to give him, and Peaches, space, room to breathe.

Maverick had offered to assign her to one of the guest cabins instead, but she'd taken a handful of her things to Mẹ's and her old bedroom when evening ended. Thankfully, all of her immediate family had remained safe. With the last of their pack's needs tended and cared for, she'd collapsed on the bed, unable to even make it to the small familiar shower down the hall per her usual ritual with the weight of everything they'd lost shaking through her. She knew she wouldn't be truly over the fear that'd resulted from this for years.

She should have stayed in the bunker.

She'd chastised and berated herself with that thought more than once as the hours on the clock seemed to both drag and speed by until they disappeared. Deep down, she knew it wouldn't have made a difference. It wouldn't have lessened the outcome, but if she'd been somewhere else when that last, final Volk attack came, maybe...

No. She gave a slight shake of her head. She couldn't allow herself to think like that. Someone else still would have died. The outcome could have been the same, or worse.

Living in the past had tormented Blaze for years.

She needed to be strong. Live in the moment. For both of them.

She wouldn't give in and allow herself to be ruled by regret. Not if she could help it.

"I'm calling all the pack home," Maverick continued, drawing her attention away from Blaze and back to the meeting. "Every subpack member. Every associate, even the rogue wolves can come if they choose. We need them all here."

"That'll play right into their hands."

The dark warning in Blaze's tone cut through the small conference room.

It was the first time he'd spoken since they'd left the pasture clearing.

The quiet, cold fury in his voice caused the entire room to still. All ten other elite warriors, Dakota included. They were all painfully aware that there was supposed to be eleven, but one seat remained empty. She looked to where Austin would have sat and felt her heart ache.

All eyes turned toward Blaze now that he'd spoken, but he didn't seem to notice what a leader he was among them, how they all turned to him when they were in need, for a favor, a smile, anything. He and Austin had that in common, more than she thought Blaze likely realized.

Her best friend stared out the window with a gaze that saw beyond what lay in the pasture yet somehow still didn't seem to truly see what was in front of him. The paradox was chilling.

"All of us here in one place, centralized. It's exactly what they want." Blaze didn't turn to look at any of them.

Maverick growled; his frustration and patience had reached their limit. The death of one packmate alone was enough to bring even the strongest of packmasters to their knees. A packmaster felt the loss, the severing of that connection in a way that none of them could ever understand. But to lose sixteen of their collective family all at once, while at the same time his first child had been born with him not able to be present, with him risking his life and fighting...

Sierra had told Dakota the previous evening that when the babe had been born, she'd been filled with fear, not knowing whether Maverick or any of them were alive or dead. The battle had raged overhead as her and Maverick's babe had been birthed inside the bunker, safe with Belle tending to her, but still shaken with terror and fear. That Sierra had to deliver the child without her partner in a way that had robbed the moment of its joy wore away at the already open wounds Dakota felt inside. Other than the stitches in her arm, she hadn't sustained any major physical injuries like some of them had, but invisible wounds hurt all the same.

Not a single member of the pack had been unaffected.

The trauma would echo through their generations for years.

"And what else would you have me do?" Maverick snarled at Blaze. "We can't leave the subpacks defenseless and open to attack. Hell, we can't leave ourselves vulnerable either. Not after this. Our children and young are still quivering in fear. They're…" Maverick paused, his voice strained.

The strongest of the entire Grey Wolf Pack were all present in that room, but Dakota didn't think any of them, warriors or not, would be able to hold it together if they saw their packmaster shed a single tear. He was the strength of all of them. He had to be.

Maverick swallowed whatever emotion he'd been feeling, his spine growing rigid as he fortified himself in a show of measured strength. Where he gathered it from in the face of so much loss, she'd never know. "I'm open to suggestions, anything that will keep the pack safe."

Dakota's heart thudded in her ears. Their packmaster's leadership was breathtaking even in the face of fear, representative of the heart of them all. She felt proud to call him her friend. She knew if Blaze had been more present, he would have, too. Dakota felt a renewed sense of purpose settle inside her, and from the expressions of all the other warriors in the room, they did too, Sierra included.

A sad smile crossed her lips as she glanced toward her partner. Cradled in her arms, she nursed her and Maverick's newborn babe, a baby girl named after Sierra's mother who, thanks to the recent change in the laws of primogeniture, would become the Grey Wolf packmaster someday. The sweet little one let out a happy sated coo, protected from the terror of the outside world because she was loved and cared for by all of them.

The purpose of a pack was to lend strength. They were stronger together. They would build back stronger than they'd been before. Even when they were afraid, the strength of the pack flourished in spite of it.

Blaze didn't answer Maverick's invitation for a suggestion. No one did. In dark times, the Grey Wolf packmaster led them with purpose and clarity. She couldn't think of any better options than all of them coming together as one. That was when they were strongest.

Maverick gave a grim nod. "It's settled then."

"And the Seven Range Pact, too?" Dakota asked before they adjourned.

Preparations would have to be made for so many packmembers returning home. Extra food brought in, excess lodgings replenished with sheets and other necessities. Even more if they were hosting warriors from varying kinds of shifter species.

Maverick nodded. "We'll call upon them to join the fight, too. That's what the Seven Range Pact is for, rallying and working together for our common shared good. It will cause the cougars to make their hasty exit. They'll use it as their excuse to break their word, but thanks to Malcolm, with a little help from Blaze and you"—the packmaster nodded his approval and implied thanks—"hopefully by the time we face our next battle with the Volk, we'll be all right on that front. There's nothing we can do other than brace for more to come."

In other words, he was confident the alliance with the Detroit Rock City Outlaws M/C would eventually go through and that the presence of the eastern wolves in the Seven Range Pact would help them. Biker wolves… Dakota shook her head. Who knew? She certainly hadn't anticipated a pack of wolves that rode Harleys instead of horses to be their eventual saving grace.

After a handful of assignments about who would tackle and delegate additional chores and things to do, both for the incoming packmates and tomorrow's funeral, the meeting adjourned without much fanfare. The usual jokes and fooling around of the warriors were absent, as distant and lost as Blaze seemed.

"Apparently the humor of the pack rises and fall with you," Dakota said, crossing the room toward him only after most of the other warriors had already left. "Though I suppose cracking a joke today would be a little too dark humor, even for you."

Blaze stared out the window, hesitating to respond for a moment, before he suddenly rose to his full height. He towered over her, though he didn't glance her way. It felt like he never would. As he rose, she noticed, to her concern, that today he was wearing nothing more than a plain black T-shirt. There was no sign of a slogan, icon, or image anywhere in sight. It wasn't like him. Even in the darkest hours the pack had experienced in previous seasons, it had always seemed like Blaze could help them all with his easygoing humor, in a way that somehow still honored and didn't minimize their grief. He could bring out the joy in all of them, even in the face of their darkest days.

Especially her.

All while protecting them with his life.

But what did that cost him?

Blaze pawed at the scruff of his beard. It'd grown in almost full over the past several days, though still close to his face. She hadn't found a moment to ask him what had stopped him from shaving it. Was that even the sort of thing a friend, a lover, or whatever they were was allowed to ask in the first place?

"Blaze, I—"

"I can't do this, Dakota," he whispered.

"I know. The funeral will be hard on all of us, especially when they lay Austin in the warrior tomb." Her voice cracked. She reached for his hand. "But we can get through this. We—"

"That's not what I'm talking about." Blaze shook his head, finally turning toward her. His eyes were bloodshot from lack of sleep. He'd clearly been awake for over twenty-four hours. A lot of them had.

She reached for his hand again, but he pulled it away. "I'm talking about me and you. Us. I can't do it."

Dakota blinked. She couldn't have heard him correctly. "What?"

"I can't do this," he repeated.

So she *had* heard him correctly. "Where is this coming from?" This definitely wasn't the man she knew, the one who'd been so confident and intent on winning her love over the past several days, weeks.

But wherever this was coming from, he wasn't through.

"This. Me and you." He gestured between them. "We can't do it anymore. There's no other choice to make. We—"

"Don't you dare tell me there's no other choice to make," she snapped. Hurt quickly turned to anger. "You were the one who was so confident when I told you I was scared about seeing this through because of our friendship. You told me not to be afraid, that we were perfect together, and I trusted you."

Blaze stepped away from her, out of her reach. "I was wrong."

"No, you weren't, Blaze. What's changed? What's gotten into you? This whole thing… I understand it's shaken all of us, but there's nothing we can do to change what happened. It's over. You—"

"I told you this isn't over," he growled. "It won't be over until they leave me for dead."

"I won't… *We* won't," she corrected, gesturing to the packlands around them, "let that happen. We won't let them come for you."

"Maybe you should." Blaze's Adam's apple gave a harsh jerk as he swallowed. "From where I stand right now, this whole pack would be a lot better off. Austin would be alive. Kieran too. And if I weren't standing in the way, maybe Jasper and you…"

"Don't bring him into this!" Dakota hissed. "Jasper has nothing to do with us."

"He sure seemed to when it was convenient for you, when you wanted to make me riled like I was your pup—"

"Stop it!" she shouted. She wouldn't allow him to finish that ridiculous thought. "I don't like fighting with you. I never have. Can we just take a step back?"

"Since when have you never liked fighting, Dakota?" Blaze's eyes turned harsh and cold. "Once every few months, this is what we do. We fight, or more importantly, you pick a fight and then we make up, so then you can make an excuse to be close to me without—"

"This is nothing like that!" she yelled. She could feel her chin quiver.

"Why not?" Blaze's normally warm blue eyes cut through her, challenging her.

"Because this time, I don't *want* to fight with you. I don't have anything to hide from you. We don't have to fight just so we can make up and lie in each other's arms until we fall asleep on my couch. We don't have to pretend anything about our relationship is platonic anymore. It never was. I see that now in the same way that you do, but this sudden change in how you feel… I don't believe it. It's not true."

Blaze turned to stare out the window again, refusing to look at her. "What you saw in the field, when I bludgeoned that Volk to death…did it scare you?"

Dakota froze. She didn't answer.

It had, but she didn't want to say it. She didn't know how to tell him the truth.

Her silence must have proved answer enough, because he laughed then, dark and humorless, like she'd told him some hurtful joke that he already knew. "*That* scared you, huh? A little bit of bloodshed and gore, and suddenly you can't see this through?"

She pointed a finger at him in accusation. "*You* said that. Not me. I never…"

"I can see it in your eyes, damn it. I scare you," he growled over his shoulder.

She drew closer, if only to prove her point. "No, Blaze, I'm scared *for* you. There's a difference."

He turned, staring down toward her. His upper lip twitched. "From where I stand, it doesn't feel any different, but I don't expect that to matter to you."

Dakota let out a long steadying breath, hands shaking to calm herself. Yelling wouldn't solve anything, even if it felt good to release the tension in the moment. "I know you, Blaze. I know you would never hurt me or anyone you love, especially not with intention. I could never be scared of you, because I know exactly who you are. I—"

"But you *don't* know me, Dakota. You don't," he said, cutting her off. "There's so much I haven't told you. Things that would make that little display with the Volk look like child's play." He gestured toward the pasture where the dark stains of their packmate's blood still hadn't been removed.

It'd take days for it to soak into the ground. They both knew.

She reached for his hand again. "I *would* know that part of you if you shared it with me, and I can promise I still wouldn't be afraid of you. If you trusted me enough."

"I can't!" he shouted, pulling his hand away again. "I want to, but I can't do that even for you! I can't, goddamn it. That's a risk I can't take. No matter how many times Austin or Maverick or Malcolm or anyone tells me I need you to know." His hands clenched into fists and he brought one to his forehead, resting his temple there. "It's not about trusting you at all. I trust you. I do. It's about…"

A gust of summer wind blew in the open window as she watched him hesitate. It'd be fall soon. The ground would grow cold and the leaves would die, and…

"It's about that look you all have in your eyes." Blaze cleared his throat. "Like I'm broken or I'm some kind of monster or I'm going to hurt you. Take your pick. I don't want the pity. If you knew the things I did in Russia, none of you…" He hesitated again, breathing. In. Out. "None of you would ever look at me the same. I wouldn't be me anymore. I'd be that monster."

Dakota shook her head. "That's not true. We'd love you. You have to let us show you."

"I don't need to be shown anything. It's the truth. All this is just a show. I *would* hurt you. You're right to be afraid. Being near me has been hurting all of you. Can't you see that, Kotes? If it weren't for me, if I hadn't been a part of that fucking operation, then the Volk would never have—"

She placed a hand over his lips, silencing him. "If I promised you that whatever it is, we could work through it, would that change things?" She wouldn't let him entertain that line of thinking—not now, not today, not ever if she could help it.

Tentatively, she lowered her hand from his lips and placed a hand on his chest, holding it there. He let her. The muscles of his chest moved up and down in a steady-paced rhythm as he breathed. Beneath her palm, the beat of his heart raced, faster the closer she drew to him. She could see the desire in his eyes, see how deep down he wanted to tell her, all while she watched him hesitate.

He was afraid of how he could hurt someone, of what love could, or worse *would*, cause him to do. She understood the feeling.

"I'll help you be brave," she whispered.

Blaze placed his hand on hers. "That wouldn't change how the Volk would threaten you."

She nodded in agreement. "You're right. It wouldn't, but I think I can make the choice of whether I want to take that burden on myself."

He shook his head. "You can't, because I won't let you, Kotes. I'm not worth risking your life over."

"Maybe not to you, but to *me* you are. I'd risk all of it."

He lifted her hand from his chest, bringing it to his cheek before he brushed her knuckles with a soft kiss. "I don't want you to have to risk anything."

She was over this, this silly insistence that he thought he could somehow push her away. She wasn't about that at all. "I didn't ask what you want. I don't need your permission to love you. Not in this way, and I won't stand here and listen to you abuse yourself, Blaze. You deserve better than that. I do, too."

"I know you do," he said, his voice lowered. "You deserve so much better than I can give you. That's why you should be with someone like Jasper. Someone put together who can love you like you deserve, an actual gentleman who hasn't slept around with half of Wolf Pack like an idiot, before figuring out he was in love with you. Not some impulsive, broken soldier who hides his war scars behind humor and a smile that most days he doesn't even mean. Not…" He breathed out a pained exhale. "Not me."

Inside, she felt stretched so thin, she might break. Her wolf was keening from within. "Don't say that."

He winced. "I don't want to hurt you, Kotes. Please don't make me."

"Then don't. Don't hurt me if you don't want to. Don't pull away from me. You don't have to." She reached up and placed both hands on the sides of his face, holding him there. "What if you didn't? What if for a moment you just let yourself be happy with me? If you put the past behind you and didn't allow it to come between us?"

He closed his eyes, leaning into her touch. "I tried, and look what happened. They could have killed you."

"But they didn't, Blaze."

"For me, they might as well have." He opened his eyes again. Seafoam-blue irises staring down at her. The depth she saw there felt like it was drowning her, pushing unnecessary space between them. "The only comfort I have is knowing that even though I can't have this, that I can't be with you, I hope eventually you can be happy without me."

"Without you? That's bullshit." She was shaking her head. "I won't ever be happy without you. I love you."

"I mean it, Kotes. We can't do this." His tone now was harsher, almost cruel.

She punched him in the arm. Not hard enough to hurt him but like they had played around and roughhoused when they were younger. Back when it'd been like she was just one of the boys, the two of them friends without all the complications. Days ago, she'd had given anything to go back to that again, but now she couldn't. "You don't mean that."

"I do, and the fact that you think I don't shows how little you really know me," he sneered. He stepped away from her, heading for the door. "I need a few days to think."

"Fine." Dakota filled that word with all the fury inherent in all women when faced with a man who refused to admit he was wrong. He knew the power of that word. She'd once bought Blaze a T-shirt for his birthday that read: "The only f-word out of a woman's mouth that should scare you is fine."

She still remembered how he'd laughed, because it was true and they both knew it.

Dakota watched as his shoulders tensed from how she'd verbally put him in the doghouse.

She placed her hands on her hips. "Maybe I don't know you as well as I think I do. If you want to think that, go ahead. But I don't have to know every part of you to be in love with you. People grow and change, Blaze. No one stays the same over time. The only thing that isn't going to change for me is how I feel about you, and I know it won't for you either. I love you and I'll keep saying it until you believe me. I hope that someday you'll feel that way about you, too—that you deserve to be loved. We all do, and I'll wait until you see it. However long it takes."

He nodded, resigned to what she was saying but clearly not comprehending it. "I think you'll be waiting a long time."

He knew what he was going to do now. What needed to be done. Blaze navigated the back corners of the dark web, poring over the information on his desk in the security office and searching with renewed purpose. This time, he'd find them. Use their own mistakes against them. Come hell or high water. He hadn't slept in three days, but that didn't matter. Adrenaline fueled him. No one orchestrated an attack of that magnitude on Wolf Pack Run without leaving a single trace. Daring to hurt his pack would be the means of their downfall. He'd make sure of it.

His thoughts turned to Dakota and the hurt look he'd left on her face. She'd wanted his reassurance that he loved her and he knew he did, but she didn't understand. *This* was all he could give her. It was the only way he knew how to show her that he cared while still keeping her safe, alive. Any vulnerability she wanted from him had long since been beaten out of him.

In basic. In the field. Over the past several years.

He'd tried her way, opening himself to her, and what had that gotten him?

Sixteen dead packmates.

Kieran. Austin. His friends. Both dead and soon-to-be-buried. His comrades and packmates snuffed out while he was still able to breathe, while he was still here. What was the point of him trying to avoid his fate?

He couldn't be what she needed him to be.

But he could be a sacrifice.

A protector.

For all of them, the whole of the pack.

Blaze slammed down his finger on the enter key as he watched the code he'd patched together over the last several hours flash across the screen. It snaked its way through the internet, putting out the call. He sat back in his chair with a twisted grin on his face.

At least the day was finally here. He didn't have to guess anymore when he was finally going to die or when he'd meet an enemy that he couldn't defeat, because now he knew. He'd reached it. As far as he was concerned, there was no better way to go than protecting the people he loved.

Pushing back from the computer screen, he stood, staring at the pad of his desk chair that would soon become another empty seat before he glanced back at the computer screen. His wolf eyes glared as his reflection stared back. He growled.

"Come and get me, you sick bastards."

Chapter 19

IT WAS GROOMING DAY AND WHAT WOULD NORMALLY BE ONE OF Dakota's favorite duties on the ranch left a bitter, sad taste in her mouth. She reached for the fur comb, the scissors, and the animal-safe shampoo that made their home in a bucket hung by the spigot and hose outside the stables. This was the one day a month when she got to devote all her time to caring for her packmates instead of the ranch animals, and normally it fulfilled her. But today, there were too many wolves who were missing. One in particular.

That fact hung over her and the rest of the pack like a dark cloud they couldn't escape.

Ranch life was a dirty business, and often after spending so much time in true form out in the forest, it was expected that they'd get dirt or patches of thistles, thorns, or other various forest debris stuck in their fur or paws that was hard to get out. When that happened, shifting back to human form only ended with constant itchiness or a thorn now stuck *beneath* the skin. Removing it while in wolf form was the only way without needing stitches or causing a self-inflicted wound, which was unpleasant in spite of it healing fast.

Fur care was easy for those with mates among them. When they were shifted beneath the moon, like true wolves, licking each other's coats clean in an act of reciprocal grooming was common for mates, especially during courtship, and the whole pack would intensely groom and care for those who were severely injured or sick, but for the single wolves at Wolf Pack Run who weren't in dire need, that was where she and grooming day came in—for the times jumping in the river and then shaking out their fur wasn't enough.

They all needed to look decent and presentable for the funeral later today.

Malcolm's tail brushed up against her, patched gray fur rubbing her bare leg as he circled near the spigot to find a good position. He'd never enjoyed this. If there was anything the Grey Wolf executioner didn't like, it was being the center of someone's attention, which was probably why he'd never gotten along all that well with Blaze. But Malcolm's fur had been coated in blood from the battle against the Volk two days prior, and though he would have showered in human form since and gone in the river for a dip, some of his fur was still matted and knotted together.

"The hose is cold, but you know that. Fair warning," she said, twisting on the spigot.

The cool water rushed forth and she turned the hose toward him, spraying it down the ridge of his back. Malcolm's fur bristled. She turned it off again after a minute or so and then worked with the brush. She caught one of the tangles in his fur, and with a fast turn of his head, he nipped at her. Sharp canines bared. Had she been human, she might have been scared.

Her own wolf eyes flashed. "Don't nip at me. I'm helping you, you big bully." She swatted at his muzzle.

Malcolm growled in response but tucked his tail down like he understood, and maybe deserved, the reprimand. All of them had been on edge as of late.

Dakota watched him for a long moment. As the pack's veterinarian, she knew both true wolves and their kind had a special layer of reflective cells behind their retinas called the tapetum lucidum, which improved their night vision and also created the eye shine caused at night. But here in the sun, the goldish yellow of Malcolm's eyes was surprisingly flat, distant.

Much like Blaze's had been when she'd last seen him in the conference room.

Dakota pushed the brush through Malcolm's fur again. "Of all the packmates, losing Austin was particularly difficult for you and Blaze."

Malcolm grumbled, shaking out his fur slightly. He couldn't speak to her of course, but even in wolf form, she recognized that as a non-answer.

"I know you and Austin had grown close, become good friends after Bo died, and having to lose Bo, and now Austin, too…" Her thoughts turned to the Grey Wolves' previous second-in-command. It'd been several years since they lost him, but while time made things easier, the adage that it healed all wounds was a lie. It didn't heal the wounds, just lessened the sharper pain of them. Loss was never really something the pack got over. Not completely.

Malcolm's ears tucked down and under as if her words had hit him harder than she anticipated. She continued to brush the comb through his fur, working out the tangles.

"I…just…I wanted you to know that I understand how hard this is on you…and on Blaze." She said the last part more to herself than to Malcolm. "You two were closest to him."

The comb snagged on his fur again, but this time, he didn't nip at her.

"He says he needs a few days to think," she said, talking to herself out loud. "But I can't help but worry he's going to do something drastic, something stupid in the interim, and now I can't stop myself from questioning whether I *do* really know him or not, and what does it mean to really know someone anyway when we're always changing, and then he wouldn't say that he loved me and then…"

Without warning, Malcolm's fur retracted, and he shifted into human form, obviously having decided he was over this whole charade. As he settled into human form, the midnight-black hair on his head was damp, along with the rest of him. He shook slightly with a canine-like shiver. "I signed up for grooming, not a therapy session."

Dakota frowned at him.

Gruff was Malcolm's usual, but it was his next words that left her speechless.

"I may not care for that overly flashy peacock we call a pack-mate," he grumbled, "but there's one thing I *do* know about Blaze, and it's that he loves you. I can see why." He turned, dark eyes cutting through her with an intensity that would have stolen any woman's breath away. "Don't lose sight of that over the coming days. Love isn't something you want to lose once you have it, and Blaze won't. He'll fight for you. Trust in that."

Without another word, Malcolm stalked away from the stables, grabbing his jeans from where they lay overtop the corral fence and tugging them on. She hoped Malcolm also would find another person he was willing to fight for, a partner who was willing to see through his rough exterior one day. An exterior—her eyes dipped lower for a moment—or posterior in this case, that if she was being truthful, wasn't half-bad to look at even if he wasn't *her* preferred cup of tea. She felt herself smile for the first time in days.

It was later that afternoon in the hours leading up to the funeral that Dakota decided it was time to take matters into her own hands. She found Sierra in the library, poring over her and Naomi's ongoing project on the Grey Wolves' history. The baby was asleep in a stroller parked next to Sierra's seat, so Dakota had to tiptoe in at a whisper. She'd missed these little sessions with her dearest female friend, but she hadn't wanted to stress Sierra leading up to the birth of the babe.

Dakota sat across from the other female abruptly and gave Sierra her best please-help-me stare. "I need to better understand Blaze."

Sierra nodded. "Okay. Where is he? I'd suggest looking for him first."

"No, he…" Dakota felt herself hesitate. He hadn't done or said anything particularly hurtful to her, but the distance he'd placed between them stung all the same. Confessing that felt difficult, but she would. She inhaled and then let the phrases she'd planned to say free. "He won't tell me about what happened in Russia with the Volk, but you were in MAC-V-Alpha, too. I know you didn't work

in the same unit and that you weren't on the Russian operation—
Dark Force? Or whatever the heck you all call it—but I need to
know."

Sierra placed a bookmark in the massive tome she'd been reading before pushing it closed. "Don't you think this is something you
should take up with Blaze?"

Dakota raked a hand over her face. "I tried, but he pushed me
away."

Sierra gave her a pointed look. "It sounds like he doesn't want
to talk about it then."

"But he *needs* to talk about it. We both do, or else he's going to
keep using it as an excuse to push me away."

Sierra shook her head. "That doesn't sound like Blaze. He's
crazy about you."

"I know, but…" She released a long sigh, eyes darting over to the
stroller. She kept her voice low, so as not to disturb the baby. "Just
what can you tell me about the Volk?"

Sierra quirked a blond brow. "You didn't learn enough from the
other day? They're flesh-eating monsters. Wolves but not."

"I knew that much from the training, but you know firsthand
that Maverick wanted this kept low-key. Other than acknowledging
their existence and making us train for the possibility of a threat,
everyone's been tight-lipped."

Sierra nodded in understanding. "I don't know all the details
because Blaze was into some next-level CIA-style operative stuff
when we were in MAC-V. His computer and coding skills didn't go
unnoticed. But I do know that the operation was to have someone
from our side go under and live among the Volk."

Dakota felt her chest constrict. "For how long?"

The baby stirred slightly, wiggling and stretching where she still
lay asleep. Sierra looked toward the newborn as if the tiny baby
were the most important thing in the world to her before glancing
back to Dakota. "Four months, I think. Maybe longer."

"But wouldn't they realize that he's not one of them?"

Sierra slid the book in front of her across the table to her. "You really need to brush up on your Grey Wolf history, Dakota."

Dakota rolled her eyes. "I didn't grow up at Wolf Pack Run like the rest of you, so forgive me that I'm not exactly up-to-date. Besides, you've only taken an interest in it because of that sweet girl." Dakota looked toward where the baby lay. She was beautiful. Her tiny features a perfect mixture of Maverick and Sierra. She'd grow up to make a fierce leader someday, just like her parents.

"Of course," Sierra said, waving her hand. She glanced toward the baby again and smiled while she whispered, "She's going to be packmaster someday. I want to raise her right, teach her our history, especially about the Grey Wolf women." Dakota's friend met her eyes with a sad smile. The last few days had been emotionally tumultuous on all of them, Sierra especially. But that didn't stop her from showing strength, courage. It was what Dakota admired most about her friend.

"The Grey Wolves and the Volk had a common ancestor," Sierra said. "They aren't native to Russia. A long time ago, they were Grey Wolves like us. But somewhere along the way, some of them separated off. They got obsessed with the idea of gathering more power. No one knows how or why but somehow, they figured out that they could gain that power by feeding on...well, on humans and other shifters."

Sierra wrinkled her nose in disgust. "They're like vampires in that way. Before they were called Volk, they had a history here, locally. Naomi says the Crow and other Nations called them *wendigo*. They migrated to Russia when they were driven out of their home here by previous generations of Grey Wolves. Over time, what they fed from fundamentally changed them, made them different from us, hungry with greed, so we've separated into two separate species over the centuries, but essentially the idea is that you can make a Grey Wolf a Volk just by...what you feed it."

Dakota blanched. "That's disgusting."

Sierra cast her a chastising look. Despite her child still being a newborn, her friend was perfecting her mothering skills more and more with each passing day. The look on Sierra's face said *Do you really want to make that choice?* "It is, but you might not want to react that way in front of Blaze. He lived among them."

Dakota's stomach churned. "You mean he…"

Sierra shrugged. "There's no way to say. I don't know exactly what he would have to have done to convince them he wanted to become one of them, but obviously whatever it was, it was awful. Being among any of our enemies for that long would be, but especially the Volk. That's why he doesn't want to talk about it, Dakota."

Dakota rested her head in her hands. How could she have been so blind? "To think all the other members of the pack and I thought the Volk were extinct before all this."

"Don't blame yourself. The only ones who knew otherwise were Maverick and those of us who served in MAC-V. Not even the whole of the elite warriors were aware. Until now, anyway. The information was on a need-to-know basis, so we didn't incite fear among everyone. The Volk were supposed to be eradicated after Operation Dark Force, but apparently some of their leaders had gotten the memo that they were about to be destroyed and they went underground into hiding. They've been regrouping over the past several years obviously and must have been gunning to go after Blaze for what he did to them. Their numbers are low, but not low enough, considering how deadly they are."

Dakota's mouth went dry. "So what Blaze went through was all for nothing?"

Sierra shook her head again as she drew the baby's stroller closer. "Not entirely. From my understanding, the Volk were destroying all the wolf packs in Russia. If the Volk had their way, they would have risen to power there, and it would only be a matter of time before the Russian government started using them to their advantage. Just like our government does with our kind through MAC-V-Alpha and the like. Meanwhile, they pretend we don't exist or can't even acknowledge our existence enough to deny it anyway."

"So if Blaze hadn't done what he did…?" Dakota said, prompting her friend to finish the sentence.

"More than the Grey Wolves would have been at stake. People would have died, both humans and shifters. Lots of them. It could have been another Cold War, but potentially worse. More bodies, less cold, I guess you would say." Sierra shrugged as if the way Blaze and the others on her team had saved the day wasn't catastrophically important. It was the kind of grim nonchalance about foreign wars that only a former soldier could manage.

Dakota nodded, sudden understanding filling her. "That's why I stopped getting letters from him for a few months."

"He wouldn't have been able to send anything then."

Dakota slumped back into her chair with a groan. "Letters have been another problem over the past few days."

Sierra lifted a brow.

"Letters from Jasper," she elaborated. "He's been writing me. They're lovely and heartfelt, beautiful and sad, but I don't know how to tell him I'm not interested in spite of all that, because if it wasn't for Blaze, maybe—"

"Letters from Jasper?" Sierra interrupted.

The baby started to stir awake and immediately Sierra reached for her, as if she'd been eager to hold the little girl and snuggle her again from the start. Dakota smiled. Sierra was just as fiercely loving a mother as she was a skilled and brutal warrior.

Dakota lifted a shoulder. "Yeah, well, email letters really. He's been—"

"Dakota, that's not possible." Sierra rocked the baby in her arms, drawing her up onto her shoulder. "Jas just got home today, and I spoke to him this morning because he wanted to come be introduced to this sweet little girl." She patted the baby gently on her back. "He'd been in some remote location outside of Mumbai. He hasn't had internet access for the past several weeks."

Dakota blinked, mouth falling open as she sputtered. "But...but they came from his pack email address. He—"

"Dakota." Sierra cast her an are-you-serious look. "Your boyfriend or whatever you want to call Blaze was one of the U.S. Army's most talented hackers. He wrote you letters when he was abroad, and you've been too focused on trying to cement things with the Arctic wolves and prove you deserve your new role—which you had already done from the moment you were made warrior, by the way—that you didn't once think that maybe *he'd* been sending you new letters. This time electronically..."

Dakota's mind raced. "But they were signed from Jasper... Why would he do that?"

"Alpha males do stupid things when they're in love. If I know anything about Blaze, it's that he wants you to be happy. If he thought he couldn't be with you because it would put you in danger from the Volk, maybe he thought nudging you toward Jas was the right thing to do? A way to make sure you wouldn't be alone? It was misguided for certain, but in any case, it's clear he *does* want to tell you what happened when he was overseas, and more importantly, how he really feels, because he's already been doing it. Maybe more than you initially realized."

"I..." Dakota's head was still spinning.

"Not everything can or needs to be boiled down into a succinct goal. You've already proved you're worthy. But I understand the feeling. We warrior women don't sometimes know when to turn that internal drive off and allow ourselves to just be happy." Sierra reached for Dakota's hand and squeezed it.

Dakota was shaking her head now. "I don't know how I didn't realize it was him. Why wouldn't he just tell me?" She knew she should feel angry, maybe even hurt at the deceit, but somehow, the thought that he'd been willing to give her up, to lose her, all for the sake of protecting her and placing her happiness above his own, made her heart ache for him.

Had the roles been reversed, she couldn't even imagine the pain of having to do the same...

Sierra's features softened. "I think you already know the answer to that, Dakota."

Dakota swallowed down the lump forming in her throat. Of course she did.

How could he not see that it was him she wanted? That he *was* good enough for her. He was more than enough.

"I've really messed things up, haven't I?" she whispered.

Sierra chuckled. "Oh, Dakota, you're still looking at this whole thing backward. When it comes to the Volk, Blaze is the hero of that story. You don't need to try and do that or prove yourself to those idiot Arctic wolves. But saving the day does fall to you, because it's been your role to save the man you love all along. That's equally important as any battle you'll fight in the coming days. Blaze loves you. You just need to teach him how to show it."

Sierra was right. She *had* been looking at this whole thing wrong.

An hour later, Dakota stood in the charred shambles of what had been her bedroom, hopeful that her most cherished possession hadn't been burned up in the fire. Thankfully, the roof was still mostly intact, and the flames hadn't reached her closet, which meant it would likely be safe. She opened the door, coughing at the trapped fumes of explosive and smoke that escaped from inside. Waving a hand in front of her face to combat the smell, she stepped into the small space.

Standing on tiptoe, she reached to the top of the closet, where the old decorative hatbox remained untouched. She pulled it down from its spot on the shelf. Sitting on the floor, she crisscrossed her legs, pulling the rolled-up printed emails from her back pocket. She picked out her favorite one before she opened the hatbox, comparing the old handwritten letters from Blaze to the emails.

Another hour later and she'd finished reading all of them. Tears poured down her face. He had been trying to tell her, and she'd been too blind to see it. Sure, he'd hidden behind using Jasper's name, but so much of what she'd wanted was here, so much of him that she couldn't understand how she hadn't seen it before. She leaned back against the closet wall, feeling more relieved than she had in days. He did love her. She wasn't certain how she had ever doubted that.

And she'd tell him that as soon as she was done wringing his neck for all the hurt he'd caused her over the past few days. She laughed in spite of herself as she felt a brush of fur up against her leg. She blinked through her tears to find Peaches nudging up against her.

The barn cat let out a loud and slightly threatening meow.

Dakota reached out to pet her, but Peaches wasn't having it. She swatted at Dakota's hand with an annoyed hiss before she sat beside her with an expectant stare.

"You're in a mood," Dakota said, gathering the letters up. "Even for you."

Peaches gave another angry hiss.

Dakota glanced to the mixed stack of letters and emails clutched in her hand. If Blaze were here, he would say something ludicrous to Queen Peaches that was half-ridiculous and half-charmingly funny...

Dakota feigned her best Lassie impression. "Timmy fell down the well?"

Peaches blinked at her. Her tail flicking back and forth as if she were unamused. She stared at Dakota with a look that seemed to say *I don't like you, I only tolerate you, but that wolf we both love hasn't fed me, you fool*. Dakota glanced at the clock on her phone. It was well past six, and Blaze fed Peaches religiously at the same time every night. It was a ritual he never missed. He'd gotten in the habit of always doing it at the same time, or otherwise he'd get distracted and forget. The ritual had been her suggestion, a way to keep her intelligent but scattered best friend organized.

Dakota swore under her breath at Blaze as she pushed to her feet and scooped a now-yowling Peaches into her arm. According to the sounds the old cat was making, she might die if she weren't fed soon. No one said felines weren't overdramatic.

Dakota hauled Peaches into her arms, barreling out of her charred bedroom as she muttered, "I knew you were going to do something stupid. Damn it, Blaze."

Which apparently meant she *did* know him after all.

Chapter 20

IT'D NEVER BEEN ABOUT HIM. IT'D BEEN ABOUT THEIR territory, the land that Wolf Pack Run resided on. That was what he'd learned over the past few days. When Blaze had woken that morning, he'd strapped on nearly every gun he owned, slipped his throwing knives into the hold in his boots, and stored a handful of grenades on his person. He'd slept like a friggin' baby for the first time in days. Now, strapped down with heavy artillery, he felt lighter than he had in years. The weaponry he wore was overkill for Wolf Pack Run, even these days, but not for a one-on-one fight with the Volk.

Not for raining down retribution on the creatures who'd nearly destroyed him.

He slipped through the shadows, his Stetson darkening his face. They'd been good about hiding their tracks before, but using their own hackers to patch over the pack's security cams when they'd invaded had been a huge mistake. Their IP address had led him straight to them.

The remaining Volk acted like an incel group, communicating mostly online until they gathered with little time to waste before a battle. Too large a group of them feeding in one place would draw too much attention in most states, except out here in Montana— where neighbors lived sometimes hundreds of miles away and there were scarcely enough livestock agents to regulate much of anything. A man or shifter could disappear for days, and no one would know it unless someone came looking for him.

Montana was the perfect place for the Grey Wolves.

But not for the Volk. He wouldn't allow it.

Russia apparently hadn't been good to the Volk over the years.

The few Operation Dark Force had left were nearly decimated by the harsh conditions there. Rebuilding their population would take time, feeding resources, so the flesh-eating monsters had teamed up with the vamps to kill and eradicate—take back the land they felt still belonged to them, the native territory and resources that had helped the Grey Wolves thrive. That was their plan. Wipe out the pack, the rightful stewards of the land.

Not on his watch, they wouldn't.

It failed to matter that their attack on Wolf Pack Run hadn't been about him after all. He was on their radar all the same. More importantly, he had a score to settle, and if everything went to plan, the old him, the one that had been trapped in the past for far too long, died today.

He couldn't fucking wait.

Ivov and three other leaders were holed up in a run-down shack in the middle of nowhere that looked more like it should have housed meth dealers than a flesh-eating shifter species. Blaze didn't allow the exterior to fool him. There were enough Volk inside that building to tear through half of the Grey Wolf pack in minutes. That was why he'd come alone, even though it felt a little bit insane and would likely get him killed. He needed to face them one last time, take out as many of them as he could to protect his packmates.

He wouldn't allow any more of the Grey Wolves to die.

This was his battle.

It always had been.

He'd parked the truck off in the distance, then slipped through the forest on foot. Ivov and the others had always been too cocky and proud for perimeter checks. They'd made the same mistake in Dark Force, but that was why the arc of history bent toward progress. Evil never changed. Lingering near the forest edge, hunkered down among the pines and maple, Blaze waited. The moment darkness fell over the mountainside, the bright colors of the sunset fading into night, he was on them. He moved with the stealth of his wolf, even though he was in human form.

Pipe bombs were his personal favorite, because who didn't like to feel like a badass and blow shit up while he was safe at least thirty feet or more away? Cowboy or not, no Grey Wolf that he knew felt otherwise. He'd specifically donned a T-shirt that morning that read "B.A.M.F." so he sort of needed to live up to it now. That was how that worked, right?

With a stealth that would have made Dakota proud, he laid out the first bomb on the grass in plain view, then shifted only his hands, using his claws and paws to dig several quick holes and bury the others like they were mortars. The sounds of voices inside the small trailer-like hut carried out through the tin walls. There wasn't much in the way of windows, which helped him avoid being seen, thankfully. The first bomb would draw them outside to check on what the hell the commotion had been, and then the others would finish them off, if everything went according to plan. But it rarely did.

Everything in position, Blaze retreated into the forest again. He supposed some could argue that this wasn't the most alpha and direct of tactics, but anyone who did could eat one of his fists for dinner. Why waste time when a cowboy could be useful and efficient? Strategy beat brute strength every time. He'd learned that as a soldier.

He pressed the control on the first pipe bomb. The heat and sound that reverberated from it were insane. The reverb sent a flock of birds nested in the trees scattering. A bit too much C-4 or potassium chloride? He'd been a bit short on Vaseline. In any case, it served its purpose.

The first of the Volk came racing out. From his recon, he knew there were four.

Nearly as many had attacked Wolf Pack Run.

Despite the damage they'd wrought, they hadn't lived to tell the tale, and neither would these. He'd make sure of it.

Two of four filtered out. Someone shouting for another to "get his ass out there" brought out number three. Number four was Ivov. Blaze's eye twitched. His finger hovered over his phone that served as the detonator. A nifty little trick he'd picked up in Iran, before Moscow.

Two tours were educational on that kind of shit.

In his head, he ticked off the Volk like seconds.

Alpha, bravo, charlie. No delta.

Ivov wasn't coming out, and the rest of the Volk were in position. He needed to go through with this. Blaze jammed his finger onto the detonator, running toward the explosions instead of away. Shrapnel flew, but he'd prepared for it. Was it bad that he smiled at the sight of these fuckers getting their just deserts? Maybe he and Malcolm had more in common than he thought. He guessed that was something he'd have to take up with his new human therapist, if he somehow managed to survive this. The first phone conversation had left her a bit scarred and concerned he needed to be immediately committed, by his guess, but at the next in-person session two weeks from now, he could just imagine her with her clipboard.

Sadism: check mark.

Gun at the ready, he took out the downed Volk with ease.

One. Two. Three.

A shot to the head each. He'd finish them off with his teeth once he took care of Ivov. Just to be certain. He wasn't below striking when they were down. Not if it protected his packmates. He didn't even bother to look them in the eye. He didn't need to. Not after what they'd done to Austin, to so many others of his kind. They didn't deserve pity or dignity.

With the sounds of the explosives and gunfire ringing in his ears, Blaze mentally regrouped for his next task. He'd already wiped all their social accounts and email, so if he took out Ivov, the other spread-out incel members would have no way to contact one another after that. He'd hit them all at once and made it look like an error. But the building was burning. One of the pipe bombs had been too close and caught it on fire.

And Ivov was still inside. Blaze would have to face him, but he was at a tactical disadvantage storming in.

Shit, he should have planned this better. The Volk were too fast, too strong. That was why it was best to attack when they were down. Attention to detail was Dakota's MO. Impulsive and off-the-cuff was his schtick. But he'd always known he'd likely die doing this, protecting his pack.

"Fuck it." He ran toward the burning building, up the steps and inside.

He kicked in the door, because why not keep the adrenaline flowing? Barging inside, he ran into the smoke-filled building, colliding with Ivov who was stumbling away from the flames. Too close for shooting range with an assault rifle.

The Russian snarled at the sight of him. "Why am I not surprised?"

Blaze shrugged. "Because I bested you once before and you were stupid enough to come for my pack?" Blaze gripped the other man by his shirt with one hand, using the other to lift his gun high. "I'm not fond of this specific phrasing these days, but in this case, you were asking for it." Blaze jammed the butt of his gun down and into Ivov's smug face.

Ivov's head flew back, blood spurting from his nose as he gave his head a harsh shake. Unfortunately, Ivov had always liked Blaze.

What that said about him, Blaze didn't know.

Ivov swiped his thick tongue over the blood now coating his upper lip with a twisted sneer. "That one I'll let you have," he said in Russian. "But not the next."

Blaze thrust his gun toward Ivov, catching him midlunge. He speed-shifted into his wolf. Ivov quickly followed. Jaw to jaw, claw to claw, they tore into each other. Teeth snapped. Fur ripped.

Somewhere in the melee, Blaze felt the gush of Ivov's blood coat his maw. But he didn't stop. Ivov was faster and stronger than Blaze. But Blaze had something he didn't, something Ivov never would.

No fear.

Because he had a pack that would never turn their back on him.

And the love of a woman that made him braver than any man should have been.

He could die right now, and it wouldn't matter, because the moment Dakota had told him she loved him, he'd reached his life's peak. Nothing would ever make him happier. That was why he was doing this.

For her. For Austin.

For all of them.

Ivov dove for Blaze's flank, where he'd been injured before. A low blow. But he wasn't surprised. Ivov sank his teeth into the muscle of Blaze's back leg, pulling and swallowing a bit of the flesh there. Blaze howled in pain until...

The sudden release felt like a jolt.

Ivov coughed, swaying and stumbling backward.

Without warning, Blaze shifted back into his human form, limbs popping and twisting back into place until his fur was tucked beneath this skin again. The wound Ivov created was a massive hole in the middle of his thigh. He'd likely bleed out in a few minutes. At least it wasn't the worst way to go.

"Burying that cyanide capsule in my own wound before I shifted was a major bitch." He shook a finger at Ivov as if he were lecturing him. "But I knew it'd get stuck there and then one of you nasty flesh-eaters wouldn't be able to resist. I hear it tastes like almonds." He lifted a brow. "What do you think?"

Ivov couldn't answer. He collapsed to the floor, mouth foaming as he shifted back into human form. Cyanide wouldn't kill the bastard, but it was enough to keep him down for now. Blaze knew he was losing blood, fast, but that didn't stop him from giving the Volk a harsh kick in the head with the heel of his boot. Blaze picked up his gun, turning the butt of the rifle toward Ivov. Bludgeoning was another favorite. It felt too good to take his enemies out that way.

"This is for all those families in Russia." He brought the butt of his gun down on Ivov's head with an audible hit. "This is for slipping human flesh into my food." Another. His gun connected with Ivov's temple, a blow for each wrong. "And this is for trying to kill my mate." The last one resulted in a skull-splitting crack.

But Blaze still wasn't finished. He dropped to his knees beside Ivov, pulling his blade from its sheath with a harsh *snick*. "I want you to know, she's the reason I'm going to enjoy watching you die." Blaze sank his blade into Ivov's throat.

He knew it was a bit excessive, considering the bastard would likely die soon from the blows to the head, but at the moment he didn't give a shit.

Destroying Ivov felt good. Like he'd destroyed everything that haunted him along with it. Metaphor and symbolism for the win.

Rising to stand again, Blaze felt his adrenaline quickly drop. The smoke of the building was choking him, making it difficult to breathe. He glanced down at his leg, only half-aware of what was going on. Of the bit of his skin skill in Ivov's teeth. Of the puddle of black that stained the putrid blue carpet.

Who kept a shag rug these days? Gross.

For good measure, he snatched one of the computers off the nearby table with a sway. Maybe the Grey Wolves would find it on his body. Even with him buried six feet under, the encryptions could prove useful. Clutching it to his chest, he stumbled toward the door. Once he managed to make it out into the cool Montana night, a sharp breath of clean air filled his lungs before he heard Dakota's voice shouting in the distance.

"Blaze!"

He wasn't surprised he was seeing her right before his death—hallucinating. He always figured she'd be the last face he ever saw, real or not. She was the angel leading him from the dark. His eyes flashed to his wolf, and a moment later, Dakota had him in her arms, cradling him as he dropped to his knees again. God, she felt real beside him. He was vaguely aware of other blurred forms, other warriors around her, but he didn't see them. All he could see was her.

"What were you thinking?!" she shrieked.

Blood-loss-induced hallucination or not, that was exactly what he'd expected her to say.

Blaze let out a dark chuckle even as the edges of his vision blurred.

What kind of ridiculous question was that?

He'd been thinking he was going to show her how much he loved her and that he'd never allow anyone to threaten him, her, or their shared family again.

Dakota smacked several times at the side of his face, trying to keep him awake but barely succeeding. He was about to pass out. He knew it. He could feel the blood draining from his face. But he had to…

She gripped both sides of his face. "Stay awake, you idiot!"

Idiot?

Maybe she was real? If she was, he hadn't meant for her to see him die like this. He'd meant to save her the pain. She was angry. No surprise there. He'd expected it.

He met her gaze, fighting to stay awake long enough so he could tell her. "I love you," he coughed, still in a haze of blood loss. "So I knew the rest would be okay."

Dakota let out a short bark of a laugh. "I love you, too, you fool."

Then he felt himself drop.

Chapter 21

DAKOTA LAY SLUMPED AGAINST THE SIDE OF THE HOSPITAL BED, forehead pounding and legs numb from where she'd been perched in the bedside chair for the last several hours. The slow, steady *beep-beep-beep* of the EKG machine had become a continual thrum in the back of her skull over the past four days, but now the sharp sound felt harsher, crueler somehow.

Carefully, she opened her eyes, lids still heavy from where she'd rested her head on the edge of Blaze's hospital bed. She'd been lying on top of their linked palms again, which meant his hand was still clutched in hers, a constant, heavy reminder of all that'd happened. She blinked long and slow, easing herself upright. She'd been caught in that semiconscious state between wakefulness and sleep again, that empty place that seemed to be the closest she'd get to rest these days. Being. Breathing. Existing.

Overhead, the fluorescent lights of the medical ward had dimmed hours ago, softening the stark white edges of the room. She lifted a hand and gently brushed it across the scruff of Blaze's beard, searching for any sign of wakefulness. His facial hair had grown longer than she'd ever seen it in the few days since he'd last been conscious, since the sedation.

In those first few hours, it'd felt like she'd spent years wishing for him to be awake, but when he finally had...

She hadn't been able to handle the screams, the flashbacks.

What did that say about her?

She swallowed hard as a fresh round of tears started.

The hallucinations, the agony. It was that night at Mẹ's again, only worse. She couldn't handle it. What had he been thinking? Even though he'd survived the encounter with the Volk physically. Mentally, the emotional trauma had nearly destroyed him again.

No one could blame her for walking away now. She knew that and yet...

From the open doorway behind her, someone cleared their throat.

Still gripping Blaze's hand, Dakota swiped at her tears before she glanced over her shoulder.

Rock.

The former MAC-V-Alpha soldier stood in the doorway, one large hand leaned against the frame as the other clutched a dense, thick file folder at his side.

He'd been the other conscious presence that'd woken her...

Not Blaze.

She wasn't certain whether to be thankful for that or not.

Nodding toward the Arctic wolf in silent greeting, Dakota turned back to Blaze, her gaze tracing over the still unmoving planes of her best friend's handsome, bruised face. She'd thought, before all this, that she'd long ago memorized every line, every curve and divot of his face that led to that wide smile she always ached to see. But she'd been wrong.

The smile had been little more than a mask.

"It's over now," she said into the quiet. "Now that he's faced them again."

She'd said it so many times before he'd awakened that somehow she couldn't bring herself to stop. Even now that she knew it wasn't true.

"You know it isn't." Rock's rough cadence cut through the small room.

The harsh truth of the words tore through her.

Blaze had thought as much, but the truth was he'd carry his war wounds for the rest of his days. Even though she was proud of him in a way for trying, as awful and messed up as it'd been.

Dakota tried to swallow the emotions that came in response to that thought but couldn't.

She knew and yet…

She couldn't accept it.

"If you need to walk away, you can. He would want that. Whatever's best for you."

"I won't leave him." She knew that without a doubt.

Even now that she realized it'd never been about facing his enemies. It'd been about facing himself.

And she wasn't certain he ever would.

Another fresh round of tears poured down her cheeks. These last few days, the torrent seemed as constant as the beeping machines. No matter what she did, she couldn't seem to escape it. "I don't know what to do," she whispered. "I don't know how to fix him."

"You can't," Rock said, confirming her worst fear. He stepped farther into the room, closing the door with the soft snick of the lock behind him before he joined her. She could feel him there, standing beside her now, even though she couldn't bring herself to look at him. "He needs to confront his own demons. That's what he was trying to do."

Dakota shook her head.

She understood that now.

She'd practically begged him to before and look where that'd gotten them. He'd nearly gotten himself killed. What had he been thinking? Risking himself on behalf of the rest of them? As if losing him wouldn't have destroyed her? Gutted her?

Hell, gutted them all.

Closing her eyes, she focused on her breathing like Mẹ had told her to do when she'd last brought her a fresh change of clothes and a thermos of pho. She hadn't been able to bring herself to eat it. One inhale. One exhale. Then another.

"He's trying," Rock admitted. "When too many of them won't. Not without help."

Them. Dakota knew exactly which *them* Rock referred to.

The wounded soldiers. The ones still left standing. The survivors.

Like Blaze. Her father. So many countless others.

Rock gripped the side of the bed railing, the metal seeming to buckle against his grip. "It's an illusion. The idea that we can save people from themselves, from their pasts. The real process is messy, brutal. But you can help him get there."

"How?" she rasped. Her voice was throaty, hoarse with tears. But she didn't care.

She'd do anything, say anything, *give* anything.

Anything to help him, to heal him.

Rock's answer wasn't immediate. Instead, the two of them lingered there, the sounds of the medical ward creating a terrible chorus around them until finally he said, "Don't allow him to be alone in the dark."

The sob that had threatened to tear from Dakota's throat every time she'd looked at Blaze for the past several days finally came then, followed by the heavy *thunk* of a file folder dropping onto the hospital bed beside her.

Startled, she blinked down at the army-green binder. "What's this?" she managed to choke out. She glanced toward Rock again.

"You know what it is." His expression was grim. "He asked me to give it to you. He's more willing to fight for you than even he would admit."

She glanced down at the folder, hesitating before she allowed herself to open it. She glanced at the first page. Blaze's name and military ID glared at her in stark black letters from the top.

His MAC-V-Alpha file. In its entirety.

All his secrets.

His worst fear cradled in her lap.

"It'll tell you all you need to know." Rock's gaze darted to where Blaze still lay unconscious. "Everything he *can't* tell you."

Dakota stared up at the now-silent Arctic wolf for a long beat. "Why?" she breathed. "Why give this to me?"

There was no doubt in her mind that the files were classified, confidential. It was information she shouldn't be privy to, that more importantly, Blaze didn't *want* her to know and yet...

He *needed* her to, if he was ever going to heal.

And he would never tell her himself.

"I can't speak for him." Rock turned his gaze toward Blaze again. "But I was his commanding officer. It's my duty to never leave a fellow soldier behind. He won't escape this unless you show him how, unless you show him that the thing he fears most *won't* happen. That's what he's trying to face." Rock glanced toward her, pegging her with a dark, protective stare that would have made a lesser woman wither. "Don't make him regret it."

On that final word, the dark Arctic wolf placed a large hand on Blaze's shoulder. "It's time to come home now, soldier." He gave his unconscious comrade in arms a silent salute before he cast one last hard glance at Dakota and left the room.

For a long beat, Dakota didn't move. She stared down at the open folder in her lap. The set of three-ring-bound pages was so thick she could barely close a hand around it. Finally, she glanced toward Blaze's unmoving features, then back to the folder again.

Whatever was inside these pages, he'd been willing to sacrifice his own life rather than let her in and allow her to see it. He'd said he wanted to protect her from it, but that wasn't the full truth, was it? It never had been. She knew that now.

He didn't need to say it for her to know that he wasn't only protecting her from his enemies. He was protecting her from himself.

Because the only thing worse than pushing her away would be if he'd told her and she chose to leave.

Rock's words echoed inside her head.

Don't leave him alone in the dark.

Whatever was inside these pages, Blaze had felt it would destroy her feelings for him, that if she knew, it would make him unlovable and yet...

She had to prove to him that it didn't. He'd gifted her that chance, to fight for him.

So Dakota read.

She read every page, every word until the long shadows of the night faded into the dim orange glow of the early morning sunrise, and when she'd finished, she wept for all the wounds she'd never be able to help him heal.

And still, she loved him anyway.

The therapy sessions were brutal. He might have convinced the poor human woman, a lovely older lady named Nancy, that he was certifiably insane with all his talk of shifters, Volk, and MAC-V-Alpha, but so far, she hadn't run away, so that had to count for something, didn't it?

And neither had Dakota.

They hadn't said much to each other in the days since he'd been awake, but she'd come to visit him in the hospital ward each morning and brought him so much pho from Mẹ that even *he* was starting to get tired of the delicious soup. He was still regaining movement in his leg from where the nerves had been severed, but according to Dakota, Belle had him on schedule to get up and walk around today. He was grateful for Dakota and her mother and all the care his packmates were showering on him, but most of all, that Dakota still looked at him the same.

She hadn't asked him any questions yet, though he knew she eventually would, but understanding what he did now, whenever that time came, he felt like he was finally ready to answer. It wasn't a part of himself he ever wanted to burden her with, but as his therapist said, it was necessary to heal and move forward. Sharing his pain wasn't a weakness or burden when he gave it to someone he loved and who loved him in return.

Someday, he was going to ask Dakota to marry him.

Once he'd sufficiently groveled for all he'd done wrong of course.

But today, his main challenge was managing to stand on two feet without feeling like he was almost dying all over again. Even with their kind's increased healing ability, if he didn't do physical therapy like the doc told him to, he wouldn't walk again. So he put one foot in front of the other and gritted his teeth.

He'd finished swearing like a sailor before Belle had passed him a cup of chocolate pudding that was somehow meant to convince him that he wasn't in fact regrowing a large part of a limb to the point his wolf was howling inside, when a soft knock sounded at the door.

He didn't have time to answer before it flew open and a small crowd of his packmates filtered in. Dakota led them, Peaches cradled in her arms.

Blaze lifted a brow. "Are cats allowed in here?"

Dakota ignored his question. "We need to talk."

Blaze glanced around the many faces in the room. Maverick. Sierra. Malcolm. Among others. Even Jasper was present, who he was certain he also owed an apology to.

"In front of everyone?" he asked.

"Yes, in front of everyone. They're part of this." Dakota nodded, Peaches still in her arms. From the annoyed look on Peaches's scrunched, whiskered face, she still wasn't over the fact that he'd forgotten to feed her the other day. In Queen Peaches's mind, his wounds were hardly sufficient punishment.

Dakota stepped forward, clearing her throat. "What you did was stupid."

Malcolm grumbled, "Foolish."

"Reckless." That one came from Maverick.

"Impulsive." Sierra rocked the baby in her arms.

"And a stark invasion of privacy," Jasper added in his cultured British accent.

"And most importantly," Dakota said, "we could have lost you."

Blaze inhaled a sharp breath, setting down his pudding cup on the tray beside him. "Is this like that time we all had that intervention with Colt after he was knocked out for a few days and told him to stop being an idiot?"

"Yes!" his friends all said in unison.

Blaze nodded. "Oh. Okay."

He should have seen this coming. He was more than a bit confident he deserved it.

It was Maverick's turn to speak now. The packmaster always led the way. "All of this to say, it's going to take more than the love of Dakota to heal you over the coming days."

Dakota nodded in agreement.

"Weeks."

"Months," Malcolm added.

Blaze waved his hand as if he were holding an auction ticket. "Anyone have the card for years?"

Peaches yowled in response, leaping from Dakota's arms. The cat scampered across the tiling of the hospital-room floor, up onto his bedside, and onto his chest. He thought she might bat him across the nose like her favorite jingly mouse toy or at least hiss at him, but to his surprise, she simply curled her legs underneath her and sat there.

She flicked her tail at him before she gave a prolonged slow blink.

Blaze was surprised at the bit of emotion that caught in his throat, but apparently his cat and his packmates weren't done.

"I told them all, Blaze," Dakota said. "I told them everything."

Blaze froze. Peaches remained perched on his chest. His initial reaction was to swear or to make a joke of the whole thing, but then he felt himself hesitate. He glanced from face to face at all his packmates present, realizing that like Dakota, every one of them still looked at him the same. He hadn't even noticed when they walked into the room.

They still loved him. In spite of all of it.

"It's our turn to save you," Malcolm said, like he wasn't exactly pleased about it. "Even if that little stunt did ensure that we only have the vampires left to defeat."

For a moment, Blaze couldn't breathe. "What am I supposed to do?"

Dakota crossed the room to his side, placing a hand on his arm. "Let us love you. Let us carry the weight for you, and we'll teach you how to love us back."

And for the first time in his life, Blaze didn't know what to say. He didn't have a single joke or sarcastic comment that could help him come back from that, that could shield him.

And strangely...he was okay with that.

Chapter 22

It'd taken nearly a month for him to walk again, which concerned Dakota at first, but Belle insisted that with the level of damage there'd been, it was normal. Dakota was out in the stables tending to one of the horses who'd managed to get an infected shoe when she realized something on the ranch was different. It was the third time one of her packmates had passed her, and every time, each of them had given her a little secret grin as if they knew something that she didn't.

What was going on with them?

Dakota quirked a brow.

A half hour later when even Malcolm passed her and cast her an uncharacteristic smile, his with a hint of *I told you so*, she quickly finished her work on the horse, resigning herself to the fact that she wasn't going to get much else accomplished today if she didn't figure out what was going on with everyone—and soon.

Wandering around Wolf Pack Run was even stranger. The smiles and giggles she received made her blush, though she couldn't bring herself to ask what everyone thought was so amusing. Was there something in her hair? Did she have a bit of food stuck in her teeth? Whatever it was, she hadn't seen the whole of the pack this happy and actually smiling like this since the Volk had come. Immediately, she felt a lift in her own spirits.

It wasn't until she reached her pack mailbox and saw that there were identical letters in each one, a handful of them missing, that she started to realize. She compared the one in her box to the others. Hers was the original. The rest were simply copies, but every one of them looked as if they'd been handwritten by…

She tore hers open, unfolding the paper inside and reading the words scrawled across the page.

Dakota,

You said you wanted to do this in front of the whole pack, so here it goes... We both know how our packmates enjoy a good love story. Chalk the public nature of this up to yet another thing I'm asking you to forgive me for, but I think the whole of the pack will benefit from hearing exactly how I feel about you. I won't have anything to hide behind anymore, not even Jasper's name—sorry, Jas—so forgive me, Dakota? Please?

I told you that you didn't know me, but what I neglected to say that day is that even if that were true, it wouldn't really matter, Kotes, because I know you.

I know that you're smart and fierce. Funny and kind. Brave and loyal.

That when you set your mind to a goal, it's only a matter of time until you reach it, because you know exactly how to persevere and make all your own dreams come true, even without me. You've never needed any help from me on that front, even though I'm willing to let go of the hero complex and be your support whenever you need me to. I know I want to be there by your side always.

But most importantly, I know that I want to fall asleep with you in my arms for the rest of our days, because you're my person, my safe space, my everything, and though I've spent the last decade by your side, I haven't told you nearly enough how I feel about you. I wish I had told you before...

That I love you.

That you're my best friend, and my mate, if you'll have me. And I don't want to live another moment of my life without calling you mine.

Yours always,

Blaze

P.S. Peaches is a part of the whole package, too. Just don't let that change your mind because she also loves you. She's just not great at showing it.

Dakota smiled, laughing to herself even as tears of joy ran down her face.

Good Lord, he was a fool, but she loved him.

"I'll take it that smiling is a good sign." The familiar thrum of her mate's voice warmed through her.

She turned to see Blaze with his Stetson tipped onto his head, leaning against the corral, low-hung jeans showing off those narrow, muscular hips in a way he knew drove her wild. His shirt for the day was a cobalt blue that brought out the deep-sea color of his eyes and read: "I'm kind of a f*ckup, but you put up with me."

Blaze pointed down to the graphic. "I'm kind of hoping this one is true."

Dakota shook her head, even as she laughed. "You are by no stretch of the imagination a fuckup."

Blaze cast her a smile of his own. "I'd like to believe that, only because you do."

"I do believe it. You're also brave, and kind, and funny…"

He pushed off the corral fence and stepped toward her. "Brave before funny, huh? I wouldn't have thought that."

"The order isn't specific." She grinned. "The only thing that is specific is how I feel about you."

He came to her side, wrapping his arms around her and pulling her in to him. He glanced toward the sky, pretending he was struggling to think. "Like I'm an impulsive, sarcastic moron who tells far too many lewd jokes and totally screwed things up and hurt the only person who really mattered to him?" He glanced down at her.

Dakota wrapped her arms around his neck. "No, but now that you mention it, that's part of it, too."

He winced. "I knew you wouldn't let me off scot-free."

"Oh no. You'll be hearing about all this for a long time. That's for certain."

Blaze pawed at the back of his neck with a sheepish grin. "Yeah, I didn't figure I'd make it out alive, so I hadn't counted on the PTSD flashbacks afterward, or..."

"Or scaring me half to death?"

He winced again. "Yeah, that too." He tugged her closer, backing them both up against the mess-hall wall next to the mailbox in a way that instantly seared heat through her. His eyes flashed to their wolflike gold. "As long as I have you by my side, I think I can manage to get through it." He dipped his head low, the scruff on his cheek brushing against hers as he laid a kiss on the side of her neck before he pulled back to look at her again. "So how do you feel about me?"

She batted at him playfully. "Blaze, be serious. I already told you. I love you. I still do."

The wry smile that crossed his face was full, genuine. No hint of darkness hidden beneath it. She hadn't seen him smile like that in a long time.

She bit her lower lip, and he growled his approval.

"Is this the part where I'm supposed to grovel some more, or can we just skip it so I can finally tell you I love you and make love to you while I'm *not* bleeding to death?"

She smiled. "I think we can skip the extended grovel for now. It'll take too long, considering the amount of groveling you have to do."

"I'll be sure to take it up with management." Blaze grinned, casting her that handsome, sexy grin. "I love you, Dakota. You're my best friend, but I've always been in love with you, so I won't pretend being by your side all these years wasn't a little self-serving, but I hope you'll forgive me for that, too."

"I think I can forgive you on that account because I love you, too. Happiness is marrying your best friend after all."

"Friends really do make the best lovers." Blaze grinned. "Mę told you that, too, huh?"

"She did, but she didn't have to. I'd already figured that out the first time I kissed you."

Dakota pulled him down toward her, covering his lips with her own as she kissed him like she was trying to make up for all the time they'd missed, for all the years they'd spent trying to hide how they felt for each other. His tongue parted her lips, seeking entry, and she gave it to him. Their mouths mingled until the heat that'd always been between them grew, and Dakota felt that all-too-familiar strain against his jeans. She knew what came next, and she couldn't wait for it.

Blaze hauled her into his arms, throwing her over his shoulder like a caveman again in a way that made her laugh. She banged her fists on his back playfully in mock protest before he smacked her square on the ass. She squealed. Beneath her, she felt the shake of his shoulders as he let out a true laugh of his own. The sound of his deep chuckling filled her ears, throatier and more full-hearted than she'd heard it in years. But this time, it wasn't because he was hiding behind his humor but because he wanted to make them *both* happy, together, for the rest of their long, shared life.

For human rancher Naomi Evans, a clash with
bad-boy rancher Wes Calhoun opens up a whole
new world—a supernatural world on the verge of war...

COWBOY WOLF
TROUBLE

Book 1 in the Seven Range Shifters series

Available now from Sourcebooks Casablanca

Chapter 1

It was more than a hunger for fresh steak that filled Wes Calhoun's belly. Violence brewed in the night air, and he sensed it. As he prowled through the stable, rays of moonlight lit his path, flooding in through the open doors. The scent of freshly baled hay, mucked stalls, and the oiled grooming polish he'd brushed into the foals' coats this morning hung heavy in the air.

When he reached the wrought-iron gate of Black Jack's stall, he paused. He had half a mind to turn back now. Just a pivot of his foot, and he could walk back into Wolf Pack Run and listen to the voice of reason. He could already hear the roar of Maverick's rage. When the Grey Wolf packmaster returned from the western packlands, he wouldn't take Wes defying his direct orders lightly. But as hard as Wes's logic yelled his life would be a helluva lot easier if he marched his ass back inside, he couldn't do it.

Kyle would be waiting, and Wes needed to know. For the Grey Wolves. For the safety of the Seven Range Pact. For his own twisted reasons.

Black Jack let out a frustrated huff, the heat of the horse's breath swirling in a visible dance around his face.

Shit. Wes jumped back, anticipating the blow before it came.

The horse reared up on his hind legs and kicked open the old stall gate with elegant ease. The weight of the massive beast fell back to the ground with a thud of his hooves, his long, black mane whipping about his face. The fierce mustang trotted out of his stall and pegged Wes with a look of *I haven't got all night*, as if it were normal for a horse to regularly escape his hold. Though Wes supposed for *this* animal, it was.

He was damn near untrainable.

A devilish smirk crossed Wes's face as he placed his hands on Black Jack's shining coat and mounted the horse bareback. Black Jack had never been very good at following the rules.

And neither was he.

As soon as Wes's leg was over his back, the horse bolted out the open stable door and into the night. Wes buried his hands in the mustang's mane for leverage, leaned forward, and gripped hard with his muscled thighs, trying his best to move with the galloping beast. The cool night air washed over his face. The fresh scent of the mountain evergreens, hinted with pine and cedar, filled his nose along with the earthy dampness of moss upon shale rock. The encroaching cold of the coming winter's first frost hung in the air.

Yes, this was what he needed, despite the trouble it would cause him. With each pounding leap, Wes felt all four of Jack's hooves connect with the cold mountain ground as they bounded into the trees, running with an abandon that only fueled Wes's defiance. Maverick refused to see the danger right in front of him, but Wes knew firsthand what waited in that darkness.

Black Jack bounded through the mountains with speed and agility the likes of which Wes couldn't replicate, even as his wolf. When Wes finally caught Kyle's scent on the distant breeze, he pulled back on the wild horse's mane, and they skidded to a stop among a dense band of evergreen trees. His ears pricked for the slightest hint of noise. Nothing but the sounds of the forest. It was a quiet October night. With the light of the supermoon bright in the night sky, hunger filled Wes, and the forest's cacophony of sounds echoed in his ears—birds snuggled in their nests, a far-off stream just starting to slow and ice around the edges in the mountain cold, a nearby fox hunkered in wait for an approaching hare.

Quickly, Wes dismounted, then inspected Black Jack with a firm stare. "Stay close."

The horse let out a pissed-off huff and started to rear up on his back legs. Wes's eyes flashed to his wolf's, and he leveled a don't-fuck-with-me stare at Black Jack.

Not tonight, bud.

The horse released an angered whinny before stomping off to forage on the remaining autumn short grass.

Wes rolled his eyes before he headed down the mountainside on two feet, slipping through the familiar pines in search of the clearing where he and Kyle had agreed to meet. The surrounding noises of the forest filled his wolf with keen, sharp awareness. He stepped through the opening in the tree line and into the clearing.

Kyle waited for him. "How goes it, my man?" Kyle extended his hand and his other arm for a brotherly half shake, half hug.

Wes towered over Kyle by nearly four inches. With a bandanna under his flat-brimmed hat and tattoos peeking out from underneath his heavy winter coat, Kyle looked like the city slicker he was. Judging from the abundance of clothing, he must have driven up on the nearby highway. Something about the oddity of that raised the hairs on the back of Wes's neck in warning suspicion. A lone wolf from Los Angeles who'd moved up to the mountains several years earlier, Kyle maintained close ties to the Wild Eight but had never sworn in. Wes saw Kyle for exactly what he was: a two-faced snitch who played any side to fuel his raging coke addiction.

True men, fierce werewolves and warriors who fought real battles, formed the Grey Wolf Pack versus the violent wolves who comprised the new members and associates of the Wild Eight, men who were now barely better than loosely organized street thugs. They were lost and weak in the absence of Wes's leadership. It was *his* fault. *His* decisions that had led to the demise of his once-mighty pack and the shared dream of freedom they'd fought for.

Seven mountain ranges surrounded Billings for seven shifter packs—grey wolves, black bears, bobcats, grizzly bears, coyotes, lynx, and mountain lions alike. Since as far back as their history was written, the shifters who roamed Big Sky Country and called

Montana's vast mountain ranges their own relied on the Seven Range Pact to govern their law, enforced by the Grey Wolf Pack's rule.

Wes's great-great-grandfather had formed the Wild Eight faction, the eighth and only illegitimate pack among these mountains. Residing in downtown Billings, the Wild Eight had wreaked havoc on the inner city and the humans dwelling there in opposition to the Seven Range Pact's sanctions. But with Wes's surrender as packmaster of the Wild Eight, the war within their species had become dormant. The packmaster of the Grey Wolves, Maverick Grey, interpreted this to mean the eventual dissolution of the Wild Eight in the absence of a Calhoun to lead, the end of their civil war. But Wes knew better. The Wild Eight would resurge, even in his absence. And when they did, they wouldn't stop until they'd claimed Wes's life for his betrayal.

"How's life?" Kyle asked, as if they were there to shoot the breeze.

Wes ignored the question, pulled the cash out of the pocket of his jeans, and held it up for Kyle to see. "You said you had information for me."

"Always down to business, huh, Wes?" Kyle swiped under his nose with an obnoxious sniff. He was jonesing alright. "So I was at the clubhouse the other day when I heard Donnie saying that there's a new alliance forming."

Wes's eyebrows climbed toward his hairline. "Between who?"

Donnie's name alone pissed off Wes. All too quickly, his one-time loyal friend had jumped in as the Wild Eight's packmaster in his absence. Under Donnie's leadership, the Wild Eight had become street scum.

Kyle leaned forward and whispered as if they weren't alone. A sly grin crossed his lips. "Word on the street is the vamps."

Wes saw red. *Lies.* He shoved Kyle squarely in the chest. "You call me all the way out here to tell me this bullshit? You think this is funny?"

Kyle backed up. He threw his hands up as if in surrender. "I shit you not, man. That's the truth." He laughed. "Donnie went to that side of town the very next day for a private meeting, if you catch my drift."

Wes raged. No, it couldn't be true. If it was, that meant everything he had worked for, everything he had sacrificed, was for nothing. He knew Donnie was scum. He knew every member of that pack was in some way scum, but there had been a time when he'd been one of them, when he'd thought better of them, *expected* better. He may have led the rebellion against the Grey Wolves to live by his own rules, but he *never* would have allowed the Wild Eight to betray their own kind. Not with the likes of those bloodsuckers. He'd given up everything to ensure that.

If Donnie was partnering with the vamps, that meant the peace the Grey Wolves had enjoyed after Wes's surrender would soon be over. For the Seven Range Pact, this would mean war.

Wes crossed the clearing to where a small stream ran. He crouched down, reached into the icy-cold water, and splashed some on his face. But it didn't help. The moonlight hit the water, causing his reflection to stare back at him. He was one of those monsters. He'd been their leader, the worst of them all. All before the night he'd trekked up this godforsaken mountainside and surrendered himself to Maverick. The blood of his father and an innocent woman had still been fresh on his cowboy boots. His anger and shame filled him like an empty vessel, screaming for release. Hunt. He needed to hunt. His tendency for violence, the impulsive rage he barely contained, was how he'd thrived as their packmaster for so long.

During the daylight hours, the physical labor of herding and caring for the Grey Wolves' wild horses and yearlings and working with his hands on their cow-calf operation kept Wes busy, unable to dwell on the wrongs of his past. But when night fell, hunting was his only release, and with the supermoon blazing in the night sky above him, calling out his wolf, he intended to do exactly that.

"Any more news on this, and you report to me, understood?" As the words left Wes's lips, he caught a familiar scent on the breeze. A mixture of whiskey, the gasoline of the cars in downtown Billings, and the musk of a male werewolf. The snarl that rumbled in Wes's throat was barely contained. He'd recognize that scent anywhere.

Wes honed in on the sounds flanking the clearing. The occasional rustle told him the Wild Eight wolves were nearby, hidden in the darkness of the trees. Now that he was aware of them, he felt their eyes on him. Kyle had sold him out, the ignorant little shit.

Slowly, Wes stood, his anger simmering. He would battle them, spill their blood for ever daring to attack him, which they clearly planned to do. But one sharp move would alert them, and he needed to gain the upper hand. First, he'd take out the weakest link in a show of ruthless dominance, a reminder that *he* was still alpha, their leader or not.

Prowling toward Kyle, he extended to his full height. He placed his hands squarely on either side of Kyle's neck, as if he were about to pull him into a brotherly hug. His eyes trained on the area of the tree line above Kyle's head where he now sensed movement. His wolf threatened to burst from beneath his skin as he felt an approaching presence from behind.

They would attack when his back was turned. It was typical of Donnie's tactics and of what the Wild Eight had now become. When *he'd* been packmaster, Wes had never been so cowardly. Ruthless, brutal, wild, and unpredictable, but never a coward. He smiled. Their cowardice meant they still feared him. That was why they needed to attack when they thought his defenses were down. Though they had waited three years, he'd always known they wouldn't stop until they saw him dead.

But clearly, though time hadn't lessened their fear, it had made them forget that Wes never let his guard down. Kyle reached for his knife, but Wes easily blocked it. With one swift move, he twisted Kyle's neck until it snapped. Kyle crumpled to the ground.

Wes didn't think. His wolf tore from his skin in a painfully satisfying release, shifting bones and sinew. Another wolf darted from the trees behind where Kyle had stood. Wes didn't recognize the newbie's scent. But it was no matter. In a bounding leap, Wes collided with the other wolf midair. They landed in a mix of snarling teeth and tangled limbs. The other wolf lunged for Wes's throat. It took all of two seconds for Wes to overpower the lesser beast, pinning him to the ground with his paws. *He* was the alpha. *He* had been their leader. But they had attacked when his back was turned, a weak strategy unbecoming of his legacy. And for that, he would spill their blood without remorse.

He ripped into the other wolf's throat. Blood dripped from his sharp fangs in a salty, iron-filled heat. Wes didn't stop to think. He had only one true target. He rounded in search of Donnie, who crouched in wolf form at the other side of the clearing. Both wolves snarled.

Slowly, they circled each other. Wes charged. The two wolves collided in a clash of claws and teeth. Wes sank his fangs in first, ripping into the fur of Donnie's shoulder. Donnie yelped in pain. In retaliation, Donnie caught Wes's front leg in the weight of his powerful jaw. Pain seared through the limb. The bite knocked Wes off-balance. Donnie used his front paws, along with Wes's momentum, to slam Wes onto his back, sending the two rolling in a fit of limbs and snarls. Paws to chests, they rolled until Wes emerged on top.

Donnie lunged forward, teeth snapping, but Wes knew how to end this. Donnie would hide behind his wolf as long as Wes let him, because he was a coward, because he feared the increased pain of his human form. But Wes knew pain. As Nolan Calhoun's son, he'd known pain his whole life, and he didn't fear it. He embraced it.

Without warning, Wes shifted, his paws changing to hands that were against the fur of Donnie's chest. He gripped the snarling beast, digging and crushing Donnie's throat with his large hands. Steadying his feet on the ground, Wes lifted the snarling wolf by the front scruff of his neck, his hand threatening to crush Donnie's windpipe with one sharp squeeze.

Donnie shifted beneath his hands, clutching at Wes's grip against his throat. Bloodlust coursed through Wes's veins. He had killed so many times in his life and never thought twice. But the fear, the hurt, the betrayal reflected back in Donnie's eyes stopped Wes short. He couldn't bring himself to crush the other wolf's trachea. Wes hated what Donnie had become, loathed it with every fiber of his being, but his enemy had once been his friend, his brother.

Wes's betrayal of their pack, then Donnie's attempt on Wes's life. Wounds deeper than knives had cut both of them to the quick. Now, they would be even.

"This is your one and only chance," Wes growled. "Next time, I'll kill you." Wes released him.

Donnie crumpled to the ground, gasping for air.

From the enraged look in Donnie's dark eyes, Wes half expected the bastard to attack him again right then and there. Donnie shifted back into wolf form, and Wes followed suit.

A loud howl suddenly echoed through the forest. Wes and Donnie froze. The scent of the Grey Wolf packmembers who were on tonight's patrol drifted on the night air. Immediately, Donnie and his men sprinted from the clearing, scattering into the darkness behind Wes in several directions.

Cowards.

Lips curled into a snarl, Wes bolted toward the trees. He may have spared Donnie, but he held no loyalty to the new members. His opponents made no attempt to hide now. He heard them, smelled them, tasted their filthy blood in his jaws. He hunted them anew, because if Maverick ever found out Wes had spared the life of a former friend on Grey Wolf packlands, the Grey Wolf packmaster would kill Wes himself.

Wes barreled behind the Wild Eight wolves at full speed, darting around trees, over rocks, under low branches. He acted on pure instinct. He and his wolf fused into one tonight. He felt it in the marrow of his bones, and his wolf was hungry.

The gamy scent of livestock drifted overhead. The Wild Eight wolves were headed toward a ranch at the bottom of the mountain. Wes saw them now, two of them up ahead. An old wooden ranch fence lay beyond.

They leaped over the fence, Wes close on their heels. Clearing the fence, he ran forward without hesitation until, with a loud metallic snap, pain shot through his front leg and paw. A yelp tore from his jaws. Uselessly, he tried to pull his paw back, only to find metal digging farther into his fur and flesh. The pain was hardly worse than the realization that the Wild Eight wolves' scent now trailed in front of him, retreating, and he couldn't follow.

A trap. The rancher had set a fucking trap. *Damn it all to hell.*

Blood poured from the wound. But it would heal. Wes could deal with the pain. It was how he was going to get the hell out of this trap that concerned him. His fellow Grey Wolves likely wouldn't find him for hours. Their focus would be on the Wild Eight wolves, not keeping tabs on him, and it would take Black Jack at least an hour to track his scent. He snarled. The night was quickly taking a turn for the worst.

About thirty yards away, a porch light flicked on, blazing and searing his nocturnal retinas. As the sound of the Wild Eight's paws against the ground faded away, the noise of a different challenge thudded in his ears. Approaching footsteps followed by the quiet click of shotgun shells being loaded into the barrel. *Shit.*

Adrenaline pulsed through him. Pack law forbade human knowledge of their kind. His choices were limited. Kill to save himself and preserve his kind as pack law allowed, or shift and risk them all for the sake of one human life. The hair on his haunches raised as his wolf prepared to fight.

Shame and regret immediately filled him. No, he couldn't. Not again. He had already taken one innocent human life too many. Three years, and he still felt as if the blood were fresh on his hands...

As the footsteps drew closer, an internal war raged inside Wes. Teeth bared, he ignored the pain coursing through his paw and focused on the only real decision he had.

The only choice that ensured his survival.

Damn that idiot brother of hers.

Naomi Evans's breath swirled in the cold autumn air as she fumed at her brother's stupidity. The bulky weight of her father's old breechloader pulled against the already-stressed tension in her shoulders. She loaded two buckshot shells. As soon as she'd heard that trap snap closed, she'd known Jacob hadn't listened to her. She'd warned him that animal traps were *not* welcome on her ranch. That hadn't sat well. Jacob was still sensitive that their father had left the ranch to her, the biologist, instead of him, the born-and-bred cowboy. She shook her head. Since the day their mother birthed him, Jacob had been determined to be a thorn in her side, but she hadn't expected him to step over the line. She'd made her message clear: her ranch, her rules.

So much for that.

The sound of her shotgun's barrel clicking into place resonated in the almost dead silence of the Montana mountainside as she walked out into the night. The summer crickets had long since left, leaving nothing but the occasional owl's hoot or the rustle of the wind.

A deep sigh shook her. She didn't want to do this. But there was no other choice now. She'd either have to call the Defenders of Wildlife to come collect it, or put that pesky beast out of its misery, depending on how bad its wounds were. Though now a rancher like her father before her, she had respect for the surrounding wild-life, something that the worldview of her Apsáalooke heritage and her interests as a former biologist had cultivated in her.

She'd tried everything. Extra fencing, chicken wire, a blow horn, warning shots, you name it. Everything the local environmental and animal protection groups suggested. But nothing had worked. She couldn't afford to lose any more livestock, and the carnage left behind had been unlike any she'd ever seen. The thought made her shudder. From the dismembered carcasses, this one was some sort of alpha brute, or worse, a whole pack.

She stared out into the abyss of her ranch's land with nothing but the swirls and bursts of twinkling stars and the stark white moonlight overhead to light her path, but the cold seeped into her skin at the thought of the wounded animal on her property.

A small rustling noise sounded. Immediately, she hoisted the gun to her shoulder. Adrenaline pumped through her. She should turn back now. Something inside her screamed this with pure certainty. There was little she could do for the animal at this point. Unless she wanted to get herself mauled, she couldn't free it from the trap, and she didn't need to see the extent of its injuries to report it to the Defenders of Wildlife. But she wanted to look this beast in the eye. As gruesome as the remains it left behind had been, the biologist in her marveled at a predatory animal that could hold such power, and the size of its tracks indicated this wolf to be some sort of anomaly—way larger than typical for the kinds that roamed this mountain range.

"You couldn't stay away, could you?" she whispered into the darkness, the question as much for herself as for the animal.

A snarl answered back. She crept toward the noise, eyes glued to the rustling animal just out of reach of the porch light. Only movement and a vague outline to her eyes, but she knew it was him.

As she reached the edge of the darkness, her eyes adjusted to the lack of light. The grey wolf lay hunkered down in the dirt. *Canis lupus irremotus*, her mind instantly cataloged. A Northern Rocky Mountain grey wolf. Yet much larger than what would be typical for the species, especially since their reintroduction to the wild. They'd been almost extinct barely twenty years earlier. The trap anchored the wolf's front paw. Around the wound, blood pooled black in the moonlit mountain dirt. From the looks of him, the Defenders of Wildlife would be able to patch this beast up and then hopefully release him back into the wild. Maybe by then, he wouldn't be as fierce and brazen about slipping fences to eat livestock.

She stepped forward. At the sight of her gun, the wolf snarled again.

But she held the gun steady for her protection. She may not want to kill the creature, but if it came down to his life or hers, she'd pull the trigger, no matter how it would break her heart. As she examined the large, majestic beast before her, a heavy weight pulled on her conscience. Animals like this withered in captivity if not treated right. "Sorry, bud. I didn't want to do this," she mumbled.

The wolf's golden eyes held her gaze for a prolonged moment. It examined her with equal curiosity. When it finally broke eye contact, the air surrounding the wolf suddenly shifted and bent. Fur retracted and limbs shifted.

Naomi's breath caught in her throat. Two seconds ago, she'd been face-to-face with a large, angry grey wolf. Now, a man crouched before her. Before she questioned her own sanity and whether she'd accidentally mixed the glass of cabernet she'd drunk at dinner with medication she'd somehow forgotten she'd taken, she lifted her gun again, clinging to her only means of protection.

His deep, gravelly voice rumbled through her chest. "Don't shoot." He lifted a hand in surrender.

Gun at the ready, she stepped backward. "Get up." She said it because she wasn't entirely sure what else to say.

He remained on the ground.

She brandished the gun. "I said, get up." She fought to keep the terror and shock from her voice, though her heart pounded against her chest.

Slowly, he extended to his full height. Instantly, she regretted her demand. Now, at the end of her gun's barrel stood a man—a very large, very naked man.

"I'm not going to harm you." His gaze followed hers to his bloodied arm. "We're at an impasse."

Funny, considering he was the one in her animal trap. "I'm the one holding the gun, asshole," she retorted.

Slowly, he nodded. "Fair enough."

She stood there, gun poised on him, unmoving. Her breath swirled around her face in the cold night air. She'd barely been prepared to kill a wolf, let alone a man. As she calculated her next move, he stood naked before her, both hands lifted in surrender. The trap clamped onto his forearm failed to faze him, despite the blood running down his arm. The expression on his face remained unaffected, distant, rather than panicked or aggressive.

She needed to subdue him. Right?

Briefly, she considered calling the police, but she quickly reconsidered. Predominantly white law enforcement had never been kind to her people. And a young Apsáalooke woman reporting a naked, unarmed Caucasian man caught in a wolf trap seemed like a recipe for harassment. Her idiot brother was out of town for the week—so there'd be no help there. She could call someone from the Nation, she supposed, but the nearest tribal police on the res were an hour away, and they didn't hold sovereign authority outside their lands. Not to mention she'd be damned if she needed a man to save her. This far into the mountains, it was just her and her father's shotgun on this one.

"Where did the wolf go?" she asked.

The slightest lift of his eyebrow questioned her sanity. But not in the way she'd been hoping.

"That's not humanly possible," she breathed.

He smirked as if she amused him. "Good thing I'm not human."

Suddenly, the eyes of a wolf stared back at her, though he was still a man. She stumbled back in fear. He lunged, and she pulled the trigger. The shot rang in her ears, echoing through her ranchland. A hard, heavy weight hit her square in the chest, and she felt herself falling. The starlight blurred before her eyes until everything faded into black.

Chapter 2

WHEN NAOMI WAS THREE YEARS OLD, SHE HAD NEARLY drowned. Her parents had taken her into the mountains to explore and see the Yellowstone River. She remembered the way the white waves of water crashed against the rocks. Her mother's voice had called out to her to stay away from the edge. She could still feel the slip beneath her small purple sneaker before she plunged into the water.

The river had engulfed her, and for a moment, all sound ceased to exist. The current had twisted and pulled her under. And then she had heard it. The sound of her mother's screams on the surface. And though she didn't know how to swim, she had kicked.

When she'd resurfaced from the water, the park rangers had said it was nothing short of a miracle. But Naomi knew the truth. She'd saved herself. In that moment, she had decided that she would be a fighter.

Even as she floated through the darkest confines of her subconscious mind, the will to break free moved through her, driving her like an invisible hand as she struggled to resurface from the darkness.

The beeping sounds of hospital machinery rang in her ears, the memory sharper and more piercing than a knife. The sun streaming through the nearby window beat down on her face, but it did nothing to warm her. Cold. She felt so incredibly cold. Cold enough that she shivered from head to toe. Staring at the empty hospital window frame, she knew what came next. She fought not to turn her eyes toward the bed, not to be reminded of the way his body had become crippled and withered.

But she lost.

Her gaze turned toward him, but not of her own accord. Her father lay in the hospital bed, half-lidded eyes staring up at her as the chorus of machines screeched their terrifying cry. The light inside those eyes began to fade. Terror gripped her. She heard it then. The sound of her voice screaming, howling like a madwoman for the nurses to come. But even then, she'd known it was too late. And that was when the weight of it had hit her.

The sounds of the hospital, of her screams, quieted, transitioning into a constant ringing in her ears as the final light faded from his eyes. Dead flat. Until they weren't…

Yellow eyes, sharp and piercing. A wolf's eyes.

Naomi came to on a jolt of energy and fear. Dreaming. She had been dreaming. Closing her eyes again, she slowed her breathing. A gentle sway moved beneath her as she lay on her stomach, her spine curved in an upside-down U. Where the hell was she? Her head throbbed, and her thoughts somehow felt fuzzy. Was she on a horse? The oily scent of coat polish permeated her nose, and from the gentle sway, it certainly felt like it. But she didn't trust her disoriented head. Hadn't she been at home just moments ago? As she attempted to push herself up, a soft tug pulled at her wrists. She shifted until her wrists were in front of her face. Loosely tied rope wrapped around her wrists. Panic flooded her. She scrambled in an attempt to sit up. Immediately, she slipped from where she'd been perched, and her back hit the cold mountain ground with a hard thud.

"Shit," a nearby male voice cursed.

The moon above bathed the normally pitch-black forest in pale moonlight. A horse's hooves leading up into thick, muscled legs stood less than a foot away from her; its coat was as dark as the night sky. *Equus ferus caballus.* A black American mustang, a typically free-roaming species. She scrambled to sitting despite the ache in her shoulders from the fall. It took her all of two seconds to ascertain she'd been riding passed out on the back of the horse. And this horse was decidedly *not* free-roaming.

She didn't think. Jumping to her feet, Naomi darted into the trees. She had to escape. Had to get back to her ranch. Her feet flew over the hard mountain terrain as she ran downhill. Ten yards in, a rock caught the toe of her boot, and she toppled into the dry autumn leaves. She started to scramble to her feet again.

And that's when she saw him, looming in front of her. Her captor.

He sat on the back of the dark horse, hands clutched in the beast's mane, those same yellow wolf eyes narrowed in her direction. Thankfully, he was clothed now. Or at least wearing pants and little more, as it were.

He rode before her as a man. But his eyes told the true story.

"Werewolf." The word fell from her lips.

"Glad we've gotten that out of the way," he said.

She jumped at the deep rumble of his voice. His voice was human, but those dangerous yellow eyes...

He dismounted the horse, and her eyes widened as she took in the full sight of him. Mangy blond hair brushed beneath his chin, wild and unkempt. He stood unnaturally still, wolf eyes ablaze through the darkness. Harsh, brutal features comprised his face. Jagged cheekbones, a bladed nose, an angry slash of a mouth, and a strong jaw lined with a thin layer of coarse blond stubble clenched tight. He watched her with relentless intent. Violent battle scars marred the skin of his chest, highlighting the bloody wound at his shoulder from where her shot had grazed him, and the deep slashes of the now-removed wolf trap in his forearm only served to make him appear all the deadlier.

Wild, fierce, virile.

Dangerous.

In her work as a biologist, she had developed a brief, flirting fascination with large apex predators. After she'd finished her degree, she'd accepted a brief summer internship at a large-cat rescue in northern Florida, where she'd worked with the rehabilitated predators up close. She'd been captivated by the languid way they moved, their ability to become so still in anticipation before they struck or lunged at prey, a trait common among predators across varying species. Being so close to such strength and power had filled her with both excitement and fear. She remembered once observing a cougar crouch in anticipation of catching a live rabbit that had been released into its cage. The intense, deadly look in its eyes had both thrilled and terrified her. Making her want to draw closer while also being thankful a cage had stood between them.

She had no such protection now.

It was the cold, ferocious intent in his golden wolf eyes that paralyzed her, that held her captive. Even in this form, he was lethal, standing well over six feet, his body unforgiving muscle and sinew that moved with predatory fluidness.

Few would have called him handsome. Terrifying seemed more accurate, yet she couldn't pull her gaze away. She didn't want to.

He wore nothing but a pair of loose jeans covered with riding chaps. The combination hung low enough on his hips to serve as a reminder there was nothing underneath. Her eyes followed the trail of blond hair on his muscled abdomen. The material covering him seemed so precariously perched there that it sent a wave of embarrassed heat straight to her cheeks.

Slowly, she shifted her legs underneath herself until she crouched over the tree roots. Though she naturally loved the outdoors, having grown up on a ranch, she'd never been a very fast runner. But she had to fight, had to try. She knew these mountains. She could find her way to her ranch, even in the dark. Right? He took one step toward her, and even that small movement was predatory, not fully human.

And she was his prey.

She didn't think.

She bolted again. She made it all of two strides before the large weight of him collided with her side. She toppled to the ground face-first, hands still bound, but she wasn't going down without a fight. She tucked her bound hands under her chest and army crawled forward. One large hand locked around her ankle and wrenched her back toward him. She screamed, thrashing and kicking against his hold. She fought with every ounce of strength she had, but he subdued her with ease. She'd known the escape attempt would be futile, but she couldn't have lived with herself if she hadn't tried.

She kicked him again.

"Oh no, you don't." He prowled up the length of her body until he pushed flush against her, his arms pinning her chest to the ground.

She was skilled in a knife fight. Despite her bound wrists, she reached with both hands for her blade, the one her brother, a decorated veteran, had trained her so well with, only to find it wasn't there.

Her opponent held one arm against her breastbone, and the other went to his belt. "Looking for this?" He held her knife up with a dark smirk.

Naomi froze. Adrenaline gripped her hard and fast. She immediately recognized the Ka-Bar her brother had given her. Jacob still held loyalty to the brand from when he'd been in the Marines. With it, she held her own, thanks to Jacob's training, but without…

Her heart thumped upward into her throat like a jackrabbit. Her captor's face hovered inches over hers, those wolf eyes staring at her with such intensity that it paralyzed her. Every inch of her burned with awareness at how close he was, that if he turned into a wolf again, he could kill her with ease with one bite of his powerful jaws.

This was one fight Naomi knew she wouldn't win.

"You killed my sheep." The sharp words bit through the night air.

Wes stared down at the human woman beneath him. Their noses

were close to touching, and his body pinned her to the ground, yet the accusation fell from her lips without so much as an ounce of fear in her voice. He had no idea what she was talking about.

Focusing on the words proved difficult. Hard as he tried, his thoughts gravitated to the feel of her. How long had it been since he'd felt a woman beneath him? Small, taut breasts pushed tight against his chest, leading to a soft, feminine stomach that tapered into full hips.

As if the curves of her against him weren't doing enough funny things to his head, he breathed in the deep scent of her as his eyes scanned the black coils of hair across her shoulders. His head clouded with the way her delicious smell tantalized his nose. Fresh-cut grass, baled hay, the open air, and the subtle smell of bitterroot flowers. They grew wild across the mountain plains in these parts.

His cock had immediately responded. He'd been ignoring the blood flowing further south in his body all evening, an unfortunate male side effect of adrenaline and battle. Or fortunate, depending on how he looked at it. But up this close and personal to her, the ache in his dick couldn't be ignored.

What was wrong with him? She'd pointed a gun at his head. Had that shotgun not been nearly as big as she was, she'd have blown his arm off. And now his body responded to her like this?

He knew he was one sick bastard, but it was still jacked up.

Until her words interrupted, he'd been so focused on the plump curve of her lips that he'd almost lost himself and kissed her.

"You slaughtered my livestock." Her voice was feminine but deep in a way that stirred low in his belly. To his ears, the noise sounded incredibly human and unintimidating, yet it raised his hackles. For a woman whose life he'd spared, then saved from the hands of the Wild Eight soon to be prowling her lands, her thanks had been shooting at him and now blaming him for petty ranch theft.

"I didn't kill your livestock." Slowly, he pushed into a plank position above her, then stood. He'd take his chance with her running again if it meant escaping the hazy fog her scent flooded over his brain. He tried not to notice the sudden chill down his front or the way his cock ached for the return of her sweet body heat against him.

She scrambled to her feet with some difficulty, considering her hands remained bound. Her full lips pulled into a scowl. "Evidence says otherwise. After all, *you* were the one in the trap not far from the sheep's pen. Not to mention I smelled it on you just now."

"Trust me, sweetheart, if I wanted a mutton steak, I'd take a chomp out of my pack's flock." He didn't know which made him bristle more: the accusation that he'd murdered her flock, or her implication that he smelled like the inside of a damn barn. Which he likely *did* at the moment, considering he'd spent the morning herding a couple hundred of the Grey Wolf calves into the barn so his packmembers could begin preparing to take them to market soon, but that was beside the point. "If it's the blood you're referring to, that's the blood of my enemies. Not your precious lambs."

She struggled with the bindings at her wrists, attempting to remove them but with no luck. "I won't take your word for it."

"You're a feisty one, huh?" He shook his head. What the hell had he gotten himself into? She was a pistol, and he *liked* irritating her. Every time those gorgeous brown eyes blazed in challenge, his head filled with naughty thoughts. He'd always had far too much appreciation for feisty women.

"If you wanted cooperation, maybe you shouldn't have abducted me from my pasture."

"You had a gun to my head," he said.

"You ate Lambie," she countered.

When the frustration on his face made it clear that he had no clue what she was blabbering on about, she sighed. "My sheep," she elaborated. "A wolf has been killing them. I can tell from the tracks left behind. My guess is that's why I caught you in the trap my idiot brother set."

"You name your livestock?" His gaze swept over her. From her faded jeans, cowgirl boots, and worn, overlaid suede jacket, she looked as if she knew her way around the ranchlands. Her dark hair and skin suggested she was Native American. Thanks to the language she'd muttered earlier, and considering their proximity to the reservation, he guessed Crow tribe. Crow Agency was only a short drive from here.

"Just one: the sheep that you slaughtered two weeks ago. His name was Lambie, and he was a sweet, gentle ram. My father gave him to me when I was ten. The only thing worse would've been if you killed our family ranch dog, Blue. You're lucky he's with my brother right now, or he would have taken a good chunk out of one of your back legs."

Wes stared openmouthed at the woman before him. He wasn't even sure where to begin. Who the hell did she think she was, Little Bo-Peep? Call him ignorant, but as far as he knew, no rancher in their right mind named their flock like they were house pets.

When he'd been stuck in her trap in wolf form and she'd stared down at him, apologizing for holding her gun on him, he'd imagined the Wild Eight wolves turning around in search of him but instead finding her, and something inside him had snapped. In that moment, he'd been back *there* again. The memory shook him as he imagined himself in that godforsaken bedroom, blood dripping from him and an innocent woman…

He closed his eyes and released a long exhale. He hadn't been able to bear the thought.

So he'd shifted in front of her. *Pack law be damned.* He'd done it both because he had no other way to escape the trap he'd been locked in—not without opposable thumbs—and also to warn her. The Wild Eight were bound to circle back looking for him, and with their blood pulsing from the night's battles, if she managed to get in their way, an innocent human female like her would serve as nothing more than a bloody diversion to them. He knew he and the woman weren't safe. Not even now that they were hidden in the forests of the Grey Wolves' territory again.

She was a stranger to him, but he'd be damned if he'd allow those monsters to kill another innocent. Though he *should* have taken her life as pack law dictated when she'd lain passed out in front of him, he couldn't bring himself to kill an innocent. Not again.

If he'd thought he'd had his ass in a sling before this, Maverick was going to lose his shit when he brought this woman back to Wolf Pack Run with him. But he wasn't allowing her to walk free. Not by a long shot.

Finally, he managed to find his words. "What's your name?"

She watched him with wary eyes, sinking into the shadow of a towering pine as if that would shield her from him. "Naomi K. Evans."

"What's the K stand for?" He couldn't help but ask. She'd offered the initial after all.

"It stands for Kitty." She shrugged a pair of slender shoulders. "My parents were *Gunsmoke* fans."

Naomi Kitty Evans? He lifted an eyebrow.

"Well, *Miss Kitty*," he chuckled. "I didn't kill your damn sheep."

"You try having several of your livestock maimed and exsanguinated, then find some freak wolf-man in your pasture and see if you believe he's innocent."

Wes froze. He ignored the freak wolf-man remark in favor of more pressing issues. "Exsanguinated? You mean bled dry?"

"That's what exsanguinated means," she quipped.

He grumbled. He knew damn well what it meant. "I didn't kill your sheep," he repeated.

Though he had a sudden suspicion of who, or more accurately *what*, might have. Tonight was getting worse by the second. If they expected to live through the night, they needed to hunker down—and fast.

"Sure." Her voice was doubtful. "And what else were you doing on my land?"

"Chasing other wolves."

At this, she eyed the tree line as if they would spring forth from the branches at any moment. It was a very real possibility. She inched farther toward the pines. The moonlight cast shadows on her face. A faint spark of hope glimmered on her pretty features.

"If that's the case, you can give me back my blade and let me go. I need to get back to my ranch. You haven't wronged me, and I haven't wronged you..." Her eyes fell to the wound on his shoulder and arm. "At least not intentionally. We can call this a truce."

Black Jack let out a flustered huff, and Naomi jumped at the sudden noise. Wes watched her with careful eyes. Despite her outward bravado, she was more terrified than she was letting on, which meant this little human woman wasn't reckless and strange—she was brave.

He shook his head. "I can't let you do that. We need to get to the nearest shelter, and fast. If you value your life, you'll come with me." When she didn't answer, he sighed. "We'll get you back to your ranch as soon as possible, but there are other wolves prowling all over these mountains tonight. Soon enough, they'll be at your ranch, too, and believe me when I say they won't show you so much kindness."

"I wouldn't call it kind—"

"Get on the damn horse, woman!" he ordered.

She was impossible.

When she still didn't move, he allowed his eyes to flash to his wolf's. He hoped a little reminder of his true nature would force her to think about the threat the other wolves had posed to her. He meant to keep her safe from them, protected.

In response, she trudged toward Black Jack. That was more like it.

Stepping toward her, Wes unknotted the rope he'd used to tie her wrists, but touching her forced him to pause. She quivered beneath his hands. *Shit.*

When she moved to pull away, he captured her hands in his, cradling them. He rubbed his thumb in a gentle circle over her skin to soothe her, the same movement that had served him behind the ears of many a scared, skittish horse.

"For tonight, you're safe as long as you're with me." He aimed for a whisper, but it was more of a growl.

An emotion he couldn't recognize flared behind her dark-brown irises. The color was so dark, they were almost obsidian in the moonlight. She snatched her hands away as if he'd wounded her. But the pain was his. He felt the pain of her fear, her blatant rejection of his attempt at kindness, in his chest. She thought he was a monster, and the reminder of his true identity seared through him. He would never escape the truth of his past.

Wes Calhoun, nefarious supernatural outlaw and former packmaster of the Wild Eight. He'd been their leader. The worst monster of them all. For years, he'd shed blood without remorse, killed without consequence, and hadn't regretted it for a second.

He'd do well to remember that.

With one last reluctant look in his direction, she turned to climb onto Black Jack, trembling. She still put on a brave face, but there was no missing her terror.

Better terrified than dead. Even if she was somehow entangled with the Wild Eight and the vampires. He pushed the feeling aside and breathed in the deep scent of Naomi's hair. Without a doubt, she was scared of him. He licked his chapped lips as he offered her a leg up in place of the absent stirrup.

No more than he was of her.

Chapter 3

A STRONG HAND GRIPPED NAOMI AND PULLED HER BACK.

She found herself facing her captor. She'd been about to climb on the "damn horse" with his aid when suddenly, he'd yanked her back again. He signaled the horse with a hand gesture, and immediately, the beast reared up. Her shotgun fell from its perch on the horse's back and into a nearby bush. The dark horse galloped at full speed into the forest, leaving them stranded on the mountainside.

"What are you—?"

Her captor clapped a hand over her mouth. Something dangerous flared in those golden wolf eyes. She started to swat away his hand, but then she heard it.

A chilling howl echoed throughout the forest, confirming her worst fear.

Wolves. And from the warning gleam in his eye...more wolves like him.

Before she could wriggle free, he scooped both arms around her, one bracing her back and the other beneath her behind. Sweeping her into his arms with ease, within seconds, he'd carried her several feet toward an oak and pressed her back roughly against a large, hollowed-out depression in the bark. His movements were swift and gentle but belied by his firm and unyielding strength. He hoisted her leg around his waist, one large hand cupping her ass as he pressed ever closer, both stopping her from running and pinning her with the muscled weight of his body. Pushed this flat against the inside of the hollowed tree and shaded from moonlight by its tremendous shadow, they were hidden from view.

He pulled her knife from his belt. She stiffened, but immediately, he pressed the hilt of the Ka-Bar into her hand. Her fingers eagerly tightened around the grip. But he must have felt her tense, because he chose that moment to meet her gaze head-on again. She wasn't sure what she saw in the depths of his golden wolf eyes, but it spoke volumes, in the way only the eyes of an animal seemed to be able to communicate straight to the soul. He held her gaze with such a sure, steady confidence, it was as if he'd whispered: *I'll protect you. You have my word.*

Slowly, she nodded. She couldn't help but trust him. In a single look, he'd confirmed what the more pragmatic part of her mind had already suspected—if he'd wanted to hurt her, he would have by now. He'd had more than ample opportunity. Granted, he had rushed her, which had caused her to fall, consequently knocking her out before he'd dragged her up the mountainside on the back of his horse, but she had drawn a shotgun on him.

Trusting her instincts, she relaxed into him. They were so close that they were pressed flush against each other. In the silence and darkness engulfing them, as she listened for the slightest noise with a heady mixture of adrenaline and fear, her senses came alive. Every touch, every sensation heightened. She could feel every slow breath he drew as the corded muscles of his chest moved against her breasts, the steady beat of his heart, and the warmth of his hips pinning her and creating a delicious pressure between her legs.

It'd been years since a man had held her in an embrace like this. Clouds shifted until a moonbeam streamed into their hidden cove within the tree. They were so close together in the gentle moonlight that she saw the planes of his bare chest clearly. All thick, rounded muscle and sinew. The thin, silvery scars of past battles, though initially alarming, served to make him all the more rugged and manly. One particular specimen marred the skin of his right pectoral in a jagged gash. With her hands braced upon his naked chest, her fingers itched to reach out and touch the puckered flesh, to feel the warm heat beneath her palms.

His skin was so warm that she felt as if she'd been wrapped in the blissful embrace of a heated blanket on a cold winter's day, a cup of steaming cocoa in her hands. The wide breadth of his shoulders dwarfed her with their impressive size. She wasn't a rail of a woman. She sported her fair share of healthy curves. Curves his large hands seemed more than capable of handling and holding with ease. With acute awareness, she felt his palm still bracing the curve of her bottom. She fit within his hand as if she'd been made for him.

He must have been aware of it, too. As the minutes stretched on, the rock-hard length of his erection grew and strained against the fabric of his jeans, rubbing against her center. The sweet, aching pressure softened her cleft until she felt herself slicken. His nostrils flared, and briefly, she found herself wondering if he smelled the wet heat between her legs with his wolflike senses.

The feel of him pressed against her tantalized her, but it was the heat in his gaze that drew her in. Those golden wolf eyes, so animal in appearance, yet full of human knowing. They bored into her with stunning intensity as he drew closer. The tip of his nose brushed against hers. Their lips were so close, they breathed the same air between them, the heat of their breath swirling in the cold autumn air.

Slowly, he brought his palm up to cup her cheek. His fingers splayed open, and the rough pad of his thumb tugged gently at the skin of her lower lip.

Something flickered in his dark gaze, something raw, animal, hungry. It roped her in, making her forget all reservation and filling her with so much desire, it was near criminal. Instinctually, she leaned in.

And that was all the encouragement he needed.

His mouth claimed hers in a kiss that was as brazen and unforgiving, as terrifying and tantalizing as the electricity between them. She fell into the destruction before her, into him and the carnal desire between them that she knew would tear her to pieces even as the pleasure put her back together again. He parted her lips, meeting not even a hint of resistance from her. He was inside her then, his tongue, his kiss, his taste consuming her until there was nothing but him. The woodsy scent of his skin filled her nose. The heavy, muscled weight of him pressed against her breasts and center, heavy and swollen with need…and the taste of him. Man, the taste of his kiss. He tasted like hot apple cider, tangy with a hint of masculine spice that warmed her from the inside out.

And she couldn't get enough.

In an instant, something told her she couldn't have stopped the electricity between them even if she wanted to. It was as if some gravitational force pulled them together, so strong and ruthless, she was helpless to fight against it. The ache between her legs grew, his erection still pressing against her center. Without thinking, she writhed beneath him. A purring growl rumbled deep in his throat. That noise alone would leave her wanting for days.

He ground against her, the aching bead of her clit hardening with each delicious, torturous movement. She whimpered and moaned in pleasure, the sounds stifled only by his kiss. That unforgiving, relentless, unstoppable kiss. She couldn't remember a time in her life when a kiss had ever felt anything close to this.

The pressure built. Her nipples tightened and her breasts grew heavy as she continued to melt into him. Just when she felt certain she would shatter to pieces in his arms, suddenly, he froze, his lips lingering in a gentle brush against hers.

Her heart stopped. She heard it, too.

A rustling near the clearing. A jolt of fear shot through her, drowning out her arousal.

Then a voice. "The horse's scent goes that way. Let's go."

The sound of the voice, no matter how human, chilled her to the bone. Thank goodness. He'd sent the horse away to lead the others off their trail.

More rustling, followed by the sound of several sets of paws hitting the ground. Then the forest fell silent again. Yet still they waited. With the heat between them deadened by fear, the minutes dragged on at a snail's pace.

Finally, he released her. "They're gone," he whispered. "I'll get Black Jack. He'll have rounded back to throw them off his scent by now. Stay here." He shifted to wolf form, his blue jeans dropping to the ground, before she could tell him there was no way in hell he was leaving her alone in the trunk of this tree. Quickly, he slunk off into the darkness. She remained where she stood, still as a statue and feeling every bit the sitting duck.

Finally, when she felt certain he wasn't returning at any moment, she inched out of hiding. If she climbed the tree, she'd be safer than tucked away in the rotted-out part of the oak's trunk. She retrieved her father's old shotgun from the bushes where it had fallen and propped it against the tree base. Just as Naomi began to feel her way around the edge of the trunk for a place to grip onto, a menacing growl sounded at her back.

She twisted toward the sound, grabbing and lifting the shotgun to her shoulder. Her heart stopped, and she struggled to breathe. A wolf equal in size and stature to her captor emerged from the darkness. She knew immediately it wasn't him from the ferocious look on its face and the lack of the distinctive black markings around its neck. Sharp fangs dripping with saliva glinted in the moonlight.

Slowly, she inched away into the shadows, gun braced in challenge.

The wolf prowled closer, refusing to retreat. *Shit.* She had no choice.

The shotgun kicked against her shoulder as she fired a warning shot at its paws. Dust flew everywhere. The buckshot hitting the ground clouded the air with dirt. But the wolf didn't retreat as she'd anticipated.

It lunged.

A pair of heavy paws hit Naomi's shoulders. The wind flew from her lungs. She slumped backward into the base of the tree trunk.

Pain seared through her as the animal's claws ripped into her skin like tissue paper. Holding the shotgun in front of her like a shield, she struggled against the wolf. It thrashed and snarled above her, fighting to push past the gun at its throat.

Blood trickled down her shoulder. Spittle from the beast's snapping jaws dripped into her face. It was only inches away from her.

If only she could reach her knife...

She screamed, though she knew no one heard her. *Shit*. She couldn't hold on much longer. Her muscles burned with exertion as her strength wavered.

Just as her arms gave, the weight of the wolf on her chest lifted with a sudden jolt. Renewed sounds of fighting followed. Flesh tearing. Jaws snapping. Naomi scrambled over the cold ground into a sitting position, aiming her shotgun in front of her.

But she didn't need it.

Her captor had returned. Faced against the wolf that had been on her chest only moments earlier, he stood directly in front of her. He held a protective stance—tail raised and bristled with legs spread wide, teeth bared in warning—as if he were guarding a mate.

Each time the attacking wolf moved closer, her guardian advanced. Slowly, the beasts squared off in a careful killing dance. Step for step. Until finally, her guardian lunged.

The two wolves collided in an all-out brawl. Teeth tore into fur and bone. Within seconds, her guardian had the other wolf pinned. He ripped into the furry flesh of his opponent's throat, striking the final blow. His back heaved with the weight of his kill. The fog of his heated breath in the cold night air twisted in a murky cloud around his face. Blood dripped from his muzzle.

But he had won...

Naomi scrambled to her feet, gun lowered at her side. Her guardian—not her *captor* now—was a terrifying, beautiful sight to behold. Bathed in the moonlight, his grey fur reflected silver with tufts of black surrounding his face and haunches. Through the darkness, the blood on his muzzle appeared near black as well. The large beast loomed over the carcass of his opponent with a fierce, predatory grace. He was breathtaking.

And he had saved her life...

"Thank you," she whispered, her words releasing on an exhale.

The wolf's golden eyes held her gaze for a prolonged moment. He trotted into the shadows. When he returned, human, his jeans hung low on his waist, he grabbed her wrist and pulled her toward his horse.

"We need to get out of here *now*," he warned.

This time, without hesitation, she got on the damn horse.

About the Author

Kait Ballenger hated reading when she was a child, because she was horrible at it. Then by chance she picked up the Harry Potter series, magically fell in love with reading, and never looked back. When she realized shortly after that she could tell her own stories, and they could be about falling in love, her fate was sealed.

She earned her BA in English from Stetson University—like the Stetson cowboy hat—followed by an MFA in writing from Spalding University. After stints working as a real vampire a.k.a. a phlebotomist, a bingo caller, a professional belly dancer, and an adjunct English professor, Kait finally decided that her eight-year-old self knew best: she's meant to be a romance writer.

When Kait's not preoccupied with writing captivating paranormal romance, page-turning suspense plots, or love scenes that make even seasoned romance readers blush, she can usually be found spending time with her family or with her nose buried in a good book. She loves to travel, especially abroad, and experience new places. She lives in Florida with her librarian husband, two adorable sons, a lovable mangy mutt of a dog, and four conniving felines.

Also by Kait Ballenger

SEVEN RANGE SHIFTERS
Cowboy Wolf Trouble
Cowboy in Wolf's Clothing
Wicked Cowboy Wolf
Fierce Cowboy Wolf